Blood Wood

PENNY MORGAN

authorHOUSE®

AuthorHouse™ UK Ltd.
500 Avebury Boulevard
Central Milton Keynes, MK9 2BE
www.authorhouse.co.uk
Phone: 08001974150

First published by AuthorHouse 12/1/2008

ISBN: 978-1-4389-0575-4 (sc)

*Printed in the United States of America
Bloomington, Indiana*

This book is printed on acid-free paper.

One impulse from a vernal wood
May teach you more of man,
Of moral evil and of good,
Than all the ages can.

- WILLIAM WORDSWORTH, THE TABLES TURNED

Chapter
1

Mark Rees despised these academic functions where he was expected to tug a forelock to the grant-givers, smoothly courteous philanthropists looking for a tax dodge.

He maundered around the edge of the room, as he always did, clutching his wine glass like a prop, bumping into people. He was no good at this game, falling into gaucheness like some overgrown gawky adolescent. He preferred to leave the schmoozing to the academic desk jockeys. An unfair soubriquet, he admitted, because he relied, in large part, on their squeezing funding from various foundations and worthy research councils, although these were obtained more easily for the applied fields in psychology like Clinical and Occupational rather than Comparative; nevertheless some proportion of such funds, with financial sleight of hand, also trickled down to finance their research at the Centre For Advanced Behavioural Studies. CABS, focussing exclusively on animal behaviour with mostly field research, was expensive to run, and generally prospective sponsors could not see the point of studying animal behaviour unless there was a clear

1

human application. So, somewhat cynically, he had to justify their funding and appease their anthropocentrism in terms of such applications, like 'linguistic studies in primates as it related to the development of language in children', or 'cultural transmission in apes and how it might relate to early hominids'.

He preferred to people-watch from a safe corner rather than mingle, and whenever he did, he marvelled at the arrogance of humans in supposing there was nothing to be learned from animals. Look at them - how did all this differ from the politicking of the great apes - alpha males strutting their stuff, hands patting shoulders, stroking sleeves, fixed appeasing smiles hiding fear, alliances formed and broken?

There! There was another lost soul standing pressed against the wall behind him. Look at him, poor sod – he could be me.

He swerved his way towards the bewildered kindred spirit, took in the pale blue eyes, the white laughter crinkles buried in the tan, sticky-up brown hair and a suit worn as though it was lined with nettles – and the rather desperately darting glances – and thought he smelt a field-worker.

Mark went up to him, holding out his hand, as the other turned to him, and opened his mouth to introduce himself.

"Professor Rees!" said the other with evident delight and relief, before Mark could say a word.

He lowered his voice a little, looking around furtively.

"I only came along in the hopes of meeting you. A friend of mine in Botany told me you'd be here. But I hadn't spotted you."

Mark was about to ask who he was talking to, and who the friend was, when the other grabbed his still outstretched hand and pumped it vigorously.

"You don't know me. Colin Wingent. I work for Forest Watch."

"Ah, yes, I've heard of it. Pleased to meet you. I just thought I recognised another fish out of water."

The other's hand grip was firm and Mark could feel the calluses on his palm as he continued to pump enthusiastically.

"Yes, yes. Wouldn't be caught dead, normally." Another quick dart of the eyes around the room.

"But you said you wanted to see me? It's Mark, by the way."

"Shall we escape to the garden?" Colin Wingent gestured to the expansive garden of the Vice Chancellor's residence.

"Please."

With a quick guilty glance around to check that the Dean of the Faculty of Science hadn't fixed his gimlet eye on him, Mark slid swiftly out the open French windows, following Colin Wingent.

Outside, on the terrace, they both drew large breaths of air uncontaminated by the taint of commerce. A luxury, he reminded himself, that not all could afford to ignore.

"He has a small lake over there - look," Mark gestured down a flagged path. "Let's walk that way."

"Not bad going for a third rate historian," Colin added, taking in the manicured grounds. There was no trace of envy in his voice, just the plain and accurate observation.

Mark chuckled as they set off down the path.

"Wise to keep that to yourself until we're out of hearing. What did you want to see me about?"

"Ah - I heard you were off to Cameroon soon. A field study on chimps?"

"That's right. Most of our research at CABS is in the field these days." Mark was curious. What interest did Forest Watch have in his research?

"What aspect of behaviour?" Colin took a battered pack of cigarettes out of his jacket pocket and offered one to Mark.

Mark stared at it, wavering.

"Go on then. I think I've earned one, obeying the three line whip," he said as he accepted one from the packet. "I'm in a permanent state of giving up and failing," he explained.

They strolled on, silent for a spell, puffing contentedly, between aromatic lavender borders, bathed in the late September sun. The leaves had barely thought of turning in Hampshire's Indian summer, and there were fat bees droning between the late tea roses.

Presently, they came to a wooden bench overlooking the 'lake' which those less pretentious than the Vice Chancellor might call a large pond, and sat.

There was the occasional slurp as a gleaming stocky carp surfaced, taking in air, and the rustle of a light breeze gently hissing through the bulrushes.

Mark was reluctant to break the peace with conversation, happy to just sit and smoke – with just the tiniest squeak of guilt.

"What aspect of behaviour?" Mark repeated Colin Wingent's question. "Tool use. Have you read of tool use in primates?"

"Certainly. Jane Goodall's seminal work on termite fishing with sticks. Later work by Boesch on bashing panda nuts. Seen the TV programmes, too." Colin nodded vigorously.

"That's the sort of thing." Mark squinted as the sun struck splinters of light from the rippling water. A moorhen bustled busily about with random darts this way and that.

They watched for a while in thoughtful silence.

"Why did you want to know about my trip to Cameroon?" asked Mark. As the other seemed reticent to divulge his reasons, he felt a small prod might help him along.

"Oh, I'm off there in two days time. There are some forest areas I have to check." A faint frown line appeared as he stared out over the water.

"What is it you check?"

"Which trees have been felled, how many, what species, how big. And, importantly, where."

"And I take it that you pass that data on to Forest Watch."

"Oh, yes. There are always violations, I'm afraid. Always. The illegal felling problem is massive in Cameroon – seventy-six percent of all timber."

Mark whistled softly. That was genuinely shocking. He knew the forests there were being devastated which was one reason that the chimp studies were so vital – their numbers were shrinking disastrously fast - but hadn't fully comprehended the extent of the headlong destruction in Cameroon, although, of course, the ongoing global march of logging was well-known from Nepal to Brazil.

Cameroon, Colin told him is the number one tropical timber exporter in Africa so the problem was most acute there.

"When we discover timber illegally felled we try to apply pressure to the various governments involved – the government of origin, the governments involved in buying, processing and utilising the wood - too often EU governments."

5

"Does that work?" asked Mark.

Colin Wingent looked at him, narrowing his eyes through blue smoke.

"What it comes down to is wearing away the opposition to do anything at all about it – the degree of apathy is frightening. You have to be bloody stubborn and determined, nagging away at the bastards. Of course, it's all about money."

Tenacity was reflected in the set of his jaw and narrowed eyes. Mark sympathised – he experienced the same frightening selfishness when it came to arguing for more protection for the Great Apes. He'd given numerous seminars and talks, taken part in endless meetings on this topic; everyone was sympathetic, agreed something ought to be done, but somehow it never translated into sufficient action. Inertia triumphed.

Mark sighed. "Ah, filthy lucre. Isn't it always, Colin? The fragmentation of forests does, of course, profoundly affect the great ape populations, from highland gorillas to bonobos to orang utans. Another national park like Jane Goodall's Gombe in Tanzania could be established for a premiership footballer's annual salary – probably two parks, in fact. But without proper protection their estimated time left is fifteen years, maybe less, then…." He shrugged, angrily stamping on the cigarette butt. It was almost too painful to contemplate. At times like this, a despairing misanthropy threatened to swamp him.

Colin turned to him. "As we've both a vested interest in seeing illegal felling stopped, Mark, I wondered when you were going, in case we overlapped. I'll be there some time, I think – maybe four weeks."

"Right. I'm off in a week. I'll be taking my research assistant along – she's going to start her PhD there. We'll be based at the Chimp Rehabilitation Unit outside Yaounde but I'll be doing preliminary field work – a pilot study, effectively – for about eight days, while she works with the rescued bonobos at the centre. So, yes, we should overlap."

"Excellent. Perhaps we should try and meet up if you're not too busy? Compare notes and such?" Colin's forehead crinkled as though he was anxious Mark might turn him down.

"Great idea – I'd like that. Let's see – mobes don't always work there, the network's patchy I've heard, so I'll give you the CRU landline number." He dug out a notebook, tore off a page and wrote the long number down from memory.

Colin smiled with apparent relief and pocketed the scrap.

"It's always good to touch base with someone you know from home when you're…" He waved a hand around, not finishing the sentence. That worried look was back on his face again as though a dark shadow had passed over him.

Mark patted him on the shoulder thinking he probably had every right to be a little apprehensive – his was an arduous, possibly hazardous, job.

"Listen, we'll meet up, have a cold beer together in Yaounde – the three of us. That thought will keep me going when the mozzies are eating me alive." He'd warmed towards Colin Wingent's combination of earnestness and mischief.

Colin suddenly smiled, looking boyish.

"You don't know how much I appreciate this, Mark." Unexpectedly, he stood quickly, glancing at his watch and stuck out his hand which Mark shook for the second time.

"Now, I think I'm going to escape. I've got stuff to do before I leave. I don't think they missed us, do you?" He unbuttoned the uncomfortable collar and whipped his tie off with evident relief.

"I put in my token appearance and I reckon that's more than enough." Mark stood, too, and stared back at the VC's red brick would-be Edwardian mansion.

"Come on, I'm with you, Colin. Let's jump ship. There's a back gate along there somewhere." He pointed to the far side of the pond.

They made a dash for it, round the pond, Mark feeling as he used to when scrumping apples from a neighbour's garden. He grinned in delight, enjoying the childish sensation.

: ⌂ :

Mark self-consciously unfurled and flexed his white-knuckled fingers, hoping no one had spotted his discomfort. He looked left to see Sue Clarke, his research assistant, blissfully sleeping, her head tipped forward, summer-bleached light brown hair swinging down over her face. How could she just switch off like that so soon?

He decided the only way to get through an uncomfortable flight was to semi-anaesthetise himself, and ordered a second vodka and tonic.

The drink came with a tiny packet of pretzels. He struggled with the fiddly bottle top, spilling the liquid in an embarrassing spot on his trousers and, getting more frustrated, tried to open the packet.

Mini-pretzels flew through the air and some landed on Sue Clarke's breast. She didn't wake up. He reached over to gently remove them and then thought better of it. Knowing his luck, she'd wake up just as he was picking them off her shirt.

He dug around in his pocket for some 'Travelcalm' pills and, blowing all caution to the winds, swigged a couple down with the vodka. He looked at his watch — three more hours of this frigging torture. He fidgeted around to try to get comfortable in his now crumpled safari suit, swallowed more vodka — and generally felt miserable and restless, trying to push thoughts of aerodynamic failures to the back of his mind. Mark put the seat back and tried to sleep. He really hated flying, couldn't cope with a window seat gazing out at all that empty space between plane and terra firma.

Eventually, the pills and alcohol took their toll and almost in spite of himself, his head nodded as his thoughts drifted off in an eddying stream...

He was in the deep green enclosing forest, listening to the whoops and yells of some adolescent males who were hunting a smaller primate...the noise reached a crescendo as they got closer..... then there was something else there, lurking unseen, but its presence felt menacing...the chimps fell silent...the bird whistles...insects...everything...quiet, expectant. He could feel it coming, though, coming nearer, the light dimmed...went out.

He woke with a start and a yelp, knocking his knees against the plastic tray. Luckily, Sue, awake for some time now, and knowing Mark's lack of coordination all too well, had had the presence of mind to remove the dregs of his vodka.

The cabin lights had been turned off.

"Wha - wha?" It always took him some time to regain his senses.

"Belt up. We're starting descent. You've been asleep most of the time. I thought you were supposed to be scared of flying." Sue was grinning at him, nudging him gently in the ribs.

"I am, sort of. Don't like landing either." He was rubbing his face awake.

Sue tutted at him.

He risked a quick glance at her shirt and saw the pretzels had disappeared. Then saw that she was staring at him with the faintest of smiles on her face.

Mark remembered the disturbing wisps of his dream – and something else.

"Do you know what Colin Wingent said – I told you about him, didn't I?"

Sue nodded. She was scrabbling around in her make-up bag.

"Well, I phoned him the next day after we first met, and when I told him where I was going to observe the chimps, he said 'if you go down to the woods today or any other day, be very, very careful of nasty surprises.'"

"Odd comment." Unconcerned, she checked her appearance in a make-up mirror and ran a comb through her hair. "Why'd he say that?"

Just then the plane banked sharply, and Mark forgot about everything but surviving. He tensed, gritting his teeth.

The Belgian plane landed at Nsimale Airport, seeking out the potholes.

: ¤ :

The air seemed like a blast furnace after the stale air-cooled interior of the plane; the one hundred percent humidity settled around Mark like a heavy mantle, sucking his breath away.

They proceeded fairly smoothly through customs, although Mark and Sue got blank looks when answering the query about their reasons for visiting Cameroon, and so all baggage was opened and searched. A bottle of whisky and two hundred Dunhills were rather lovingly caressed and admired by two openly covetous customs officers. Mark shrank inside, dreading the acute embarrassment of offering baksheesh and wasn't at all confident of how to go about it. What if the officers were insulted by an offer of payment? That could make things worse and they'd be quite within their rights. But they eventually returned the liquor and fags to the suitcase with sotto voce mutterings. Mark couldn't read their expressions. Envy? Regret?

His shirt, wringing wet – a combination of anxiety and heat - stuck to his back, and a trickles of tell-tale sweat wandered down his temples, gluing his dark curly hair to his skull.

When they'd got through, he looked around for someone from CRU. There weren't many candidates, the hall being filled mostly with arriving jostling families heaving bulky bursting parcels onto trolleys, and noisy excited relatives waiting impatiently.

There was one still body amongst the colourful chaos.

"Ah, there's our host, I think," Mark walked towards a tall dark figure who looked a bit fed-up, holding up a tatty bit of card with 'CRU' crayoned on it.

When he turned and spotted two pale people, his face lit up with a radiant smile. He dashed over and grabbed Mark's hand in both of his.

"Ekoko Roger, Senior Warden at CRU," he introduced himself, shaking Mark's hand vigorously. Mark returned the compliment, introducing himself and Sue. He turned to Sue with his megawatt beam and kissed her hand. Sue was so surprised she stood there, hand still frozen in midair, even after he'd turned to pick up their luggage.

"Why can't blokes at home do things like that?"

"Oh, we rely on our natural charm without resorting to all that continental smarm." Mark grinned conspiratorially at Ekoko.

"Your reputation stands unchallenged, I'm sure." She put her sunglasses on and marched briskly to the exit.

Chapter
2

They came at him swiftly, the two of them, as, unsuspecting he bent to inspect the stump of the felled tree to determine its species and diameter. He had already warned them that the *sapele* had had its export ban renewed, while the *ayous* could continue to be exported. He wanted a closer look. He needed to take measurements. If it was undersized as well, then...

As he reached back into his pocket to extract a tape measure, the machete sliced expertly across his throat with the hissing tear of silk. He gurgled a little and slid slowly down to the ground with his head resting on the stump.

"We need to make this look like a ritual killing as the boss suggested." The first man stood staring down indifferently at the slumped body, hands on hips.

The other one pulled a face. "Why not leave him here? Who will find him?"

"They'll come looking for him, that's why. He had to tell the Yaounde authorities where he was going, so better they find him but think his death is linked to something – someone - else. Is that too hard for you to understand?"

His companion glared at the speaker. He had had just about enough of the bastard's slave master attitude. His ugly flat vowels felt like being whacked across the head with one of his sjamboks – it gave him a headache just listening to him. It fleetingly crossed his mind that another body might just as well join this one – but then that would be the end of his job, and perversely, in spite of the red-faced South African bossing him around, he liked his job. There was plenty of beer and plenty of women.

"Get to work. You know what you have to do." He gave orders casually, knowing he'd be obeyed, and turned away dismissively.

The one with the machete looked up at the canopy. The forest was strangely still, the air suddenly thick and dark under the trees as though Jengi, the spirit of the forest, was holding its breath. 'Should the other join this one?' he murmured into the air and waited. There was no answer.

He looked down again. The blood was soaking into the coarse open fibres of the stump; it came to him that the dead tree was drinking – drinking the life of the man. He flicked a hand over his brow, wiped the sweat away. He muttered an imprecation to Jengi, as he turned the bloody corpse over.

Did this person deserve his death more than the red-faced bastard? Fascinated and repelled, he scrutinised the face, relaxed in death, trying to read meaning into the features. The pale blue eyes, already beginning to cloud, stared up at him as though questioning what he had done, but he could see no anger there. The persistent flies were gathering.

Tightening his lips in anticipation of the butchery to come, he raised the machete...

: ◻ :

Unnoticed for the moment, the three of them stood in the shadows watching the antics of the rescued bonobos in the spacious enclosure.

"Can you see which one was in your *laboratoire?*" The charming Ekoko's English was precisely enunciated with just the odd French word thrown in.

He meant their Caro, their wonderful Caro, who had been used in linguistic studies at the Centre of Advanced Behavioural Studies near Southampton. All the others in the enclosure had been rescued from painfully cramped cages, used as pitiful playthings and generally sold on as pets, or saved from the pot. But Caro - she was famous, and not just in primate circles, thanks to a couple of stunning BBC Natural History Unit programmes. She communicated using symbols like Egyptian hieroglyphs which represented words, and she had built up a vocabulary of about a thousand comprehended spoken English words and used about a thousand words – written symbols. Eleven months ago she'd been accompanied all the way from CABS to here, a decision not taken lightly either by Caro herself or by the research team, but ethical considerations prevailed – those, and the trauma she'd been through as the result of a homicidal religious maniac who'd tried to kill her and CABS staff. But there was that groundswell of opinion promoting the rights of great apes, disapproving of any primate research at Universities involving captive primates, even behavioural research, not least among certain primatologists themselves torn between the need to learn more in order to preserve the apes and the rights of their subjects.

This, Sue supposed, was a halfway house between captivity and total freedom, but several of these damaged individuals would never be able to cope in the wild. CRU was now their life.

Sue was fascinated and eager to observe how, if at all, Caro might employ her incredible knowledge within the group. Would she try to teach others just as the tutoring of tool use occurred in the wild with chimps? How would the others react to one of their own with such alien abilities? Would they be eager to learn? Would they ignore her attempts? And then there was Caro's pregnancy. Would she try to teach her offspring? If so, the very physical closeness between mother and child might facilitate acquisition as it had with Kanzi, another world-famous bonobo, and his adopted mother, Matata. Sue Savage-Rumbaugh, Kanzi's trainer, had been surprised at how fast the son had picked up language just by looking over his mother's shoulder. Bonobos were immensely intelligent and eager to learn, so she had high hopes.

She'd put forward her PhD proposal based around this study of enculturation in non-human hominids and Mark had accepted it. She was overjoyed to be here, could scarcely credit it – and, of course, how could she not know which one Caro was?

"There," she whispered to Ekoko. "There she is." How could Ekoko think they could forget her? Their lives had revolved around her until she had left last year. Her eyes filled with tears, as they watched, as yet unseen.

Apart from her obvious bulge, there was a tranquility about her as the other bonobos, younger ones mostly, spun around like fizzing electrons circling a still nucleus. She looked well, blooming, really. There was one other adult female, very quiet, sitting next to her, grooming her with one hand. Sue could see that her other hand was mutilated.

"Exactly so. Come – let us greet her."

Sue felt a pang – a melange of sadness that Caro had had to leave them, and her own feeling of deep loss, and a nervous excitement of holding her again.

As they moved around to the indoor hut where the bonobos slept and which connected to the outdoor play area, Sue asked Ekoko if Caro still had with her the portable lexigram by which she communicated when away from her computer. Normally, at CABS, Caro had a dedicated room where she used the specialised computer terminal equipped with hieroglyphic keys with which she had been taught to communicate. In preparation for this study Sue and Mark had used an identically modified keyboard to communicate with her from their University – essentially, they sent emails back and forth. So, Caro knew she would have visitors, knew who they'd be.

"Yes, of course, she has all her equipment. I told her to expect you today, but she knew because you were writing to her."

Still, Caro's concept of time wasn't that spot on, thought Sue.

Sue suddenly felt quite shy as they stepped into the enclosure. Had these been chimps they would never have entered an enclosure like this without a gradual process of habituation. But bonobos, pygmy chimps, were different. They were smaller, slighter than their cousins and more laid back, less volatile, more inclined to diffuse social difficulties with a bout of ritualised sex.

Caro had seen them, hesitated a moment, arms upraised in uncertainty, until suddenly she squealed loudly and rushed over with her familiar wide-legged, upright gait and hugged the two of them, chattering excitedly and loudly in her high-pitched voice, one arm vice-like around each neck.

Suddenly, she broke loose to dash off inside the shelter. Mark and Sue looked at each other questioningly, catching their breath.

"Her – um – language page," Ekoko offered, by way of explanation.

In seconds Caro was back holding her lexigram, a portable sixteen by sixteen matrix, much reduced from her keyboard and displaying just the more common hieroglyphs. She walked back towards them looking oddly regal with her pregnancy well-advanced, holding the laminated plastic sheet in front of her like a prize. She stopped, hunkered down, glanced quickly at the symbols, then touched two – three signs in turn and tapped her abdomen.

Sue, crouching, peered over Caro's shoulder at the lexigram, and translated: "Caro – baby – here."

Sue was moved and felt a lump in her throat. She grinned up at Mark and he squeezed her shoulder – he understood. Mark's wife had been pregnant last year when Caro was still with them, and they'd tried to explain where the baby was – and what it was doing there; they weren't sure she'd understood. It seems she had, after all.

Now Sue hugged her again and they told her how clever she was, that they'd be with her until she had her baby. Everything would be just OK. She understood spoken English, but to emphasise what they were saying and to reinforce the symbol learning, they pointed to the symbols as well as saying the words out loud – as had been done at CABS. It was obviously more convenient to use the modified keyboard, with its accompanying vocal pronunciation of words, when possible, but the simple lexigram served its purpose outside.

Caro now picked out : 'Caro – sick.'

Sue paused, worried for an instant, then it came to her – morning sickness. She had to reply, hoping she'd be understood.

"Yes, Caro, but it will stop - soon. It happens sometimes when a baby is there." She pointed at Caro's bulge. Not well explained - she needed to work out the phrasing, syntax and exact wording more carefully. This was going to be a learning process for her, too. Sue tried to reassure her, stroking the thick black hairs on her arm and patting the round stomach.

Caro pursed her lips, looking doubtful.

Sue scrutinised her carefully – the glossy black hair lying flat on top of her head, the molasses-brown eyes reflecting an unfathomable degree of intelligence that they admitted they had only just begun to tap back at CABS. She looked in rude good health in spite of her complaints.

Sue was appreciative of Mark's taking a back seat here, letting her lead – it was to be her study and she needed to re-establish her rapport with Caro. They all missed her dearly, not only for her intellect, as a research subject, but as a person. Nonetheless, Caro had to be here, ought to be here, with others of her species, even if it was too late for her to be fully rehabilitated to survive in the wild. And, most important of all, she'd expressed the desire for a baby herself once she'd seen Mark's little Joe.

"Her language usage seems unaffected by her stay here." Mark sought to reassure Sue. As he spoke Caro reached out and took his hand, holding it lightly and turning it over to examine his palm tracing the lines like some clairvoyant.

It was something they'd discussed, the possibility that her linguistic skills might fade with disuse, having no one else to talk to. So they'd initiated a programme involving Ekoko and the other wardens, to help sustain her communication. It was only partially successful, as the staff were stretched with other great apes to look after – chimps and lowland gorillas, mostly.

Caro looked around, catching sight of someone. She gave a loud cry, and presently another bonobo came bounding over. Ah, a male. So this was the father?

Caro's eyes seemed to twinkle as she watched their reactions.

"The father of your baby, Caro?" Mark asked with a smile.

She slowly picked up the lexigram, and studied it carefully, holding it close to her eyes.

"Ah, she is joking with you," said Ekoko. "She knows what you mean. She does this with her language page." He waved at her lexigram.

This was her idea of a joke, Sue realised. Humour with language. Astonishing and wonderful. She'd so missed this.

"Come on, Caro. Stop messing about." Mark gently nudged her arm.

Eventually, 'yes'.

"He's very handsome," said Sue. Then, not able to remember if that word was in her vocabulary, added, "Beautiful."

Caro said nothing, but, lips slightly pursed again, scrutinised the male as though coolly assessing his looks for the first time. Bonobos definitely weren't monogamous.

"Look, we've brought some presents." Mark dug around in his rucksack and withdrew a yellow toy bear. "For the baby. And for you – Lucozade!"

Caro trilled with delight. Apparently her favourite drink had been difficult to get hold of in Cameroon. She grabbed it, twisted off the top, far more easily than Mark had dealt with his vodka miniature, and glugged some down. She paused, lip smacking, made a difficult decision, and handed the bottle to the interested, but puzzled male bonobo who examined the bottle and then copied her actions.

So far the toy bear remained ignored. Drink was a serious business.

While both bonobos were occupied relishing the drink, Mark and Sue walked over to Ekoko – the Senior Warden – who was consulting with one of his staff, Louis Nkemi. Introductions were made again, although Sue didn't get her hand kissed this time. Louis was more reticent than the ebullient Ekoko, saying little, and departing quickly with a brief nod.

They all walked over to where a jug of lemonade and some glasses were set out on a table in the shady veranda of the bungalow where they would be staying. Sue was feeling the fatigue of the flight and the overwhelming emotion of being here and seeing Caro again.

"I'm so glad you were able to come, Professor Rees, and you, Sue Clarke. I have not really welcomed you to CRU, but we are very happy to have you here to make studies." He raised the glass of lemonade in a salute. Ekoko's age was indeterminate, perhaps mid-thirties, he was skinny, maybe a little underweight – but that smile would power Christmas tree lights.

"Please, call me Mark. We were going to come soon anyway, as you know, but when we heard that Caro was pregnant, we wanted to time our arrival to coincide with the birth. Couldn't miss that."

"Ekoko, does the father have a name?" Sue asked, pointing her chin towards the male, now absorbed in carefully peeling the label from the bottle.

"Oh, yes. I called him Utennu after the sacred baboon of Ancient Egypt – Ute for short - but Caro calls him 'Good'. It is confusing."

Sue was trying to recall this ancient god of Egypt without success.

"An interesting name, Utennu, but I'm guessing you'll have to give in gracefully, Ekoko."

Ekoko laughed. "Yes. And the older female is really called Isis, goddess of protection, but Caro calls her Hand because of her missing fingers."

"Now Isis even I've heard of – mother of Horus, wasn't she? The Egyptian names are a wonderful idea, Ekoko, but I've a hunch a certain person will have her way, like Sue says. Ah, almost forgot – a small present. I was told you like this brand." Mark rummaged in his backpack and produced a carton of two hundred Dunhill.

Ekoko was effusive in his thanks. "You cannot get these in Cameroon. *Bon.* I will give some packets to the other wardens." He ripped the cellophane off the carton, extracted a packet, tapped out a cigarette and lit up with a large satisfied smile.

At that moment, watching Ekoko, Mark gave a wistful smile.

"What?" asked Sue.

"Oh, I was just recalling my meeting with Colin Wingent – you remember. We bunked off the VC's bash, mind-numbingly boring, and legged it down the garden. I wonder how he's getting on."

"That sounds just like you, truanting - a kid at heart. Well, you'll be able to get together soon enough in Yaounde. I'm coming along, too – he sounds an interesting guy." Sue turned to Ekoko. "Ekoko, you know that I'm going to be looking at the possible spread of language among the inhabitants, as a result of Caro being here?"

Everything depended upon the occurrence of role model learning in this little group of bonobos. Caro could be the catalyst, awakening the apes' dormant linguistic abilities. This was a superb and unique chance to see how the culture of language might have spread in early hominids. She was very keen to do this, feeling that it could complement Mark's field work on the spread of tool use in chimps. Having been Mark's research assistant, she now desperately wanted to work towards her own doctorate with him as the supervisor - he was the best in their field, in her, probably subjective, estimation - although she would continue to assist him in his research back at CABS and in the field.

"Yes, of course. And I have some notes we have made for you to help with your studies. Caro tries with the others, shows them her page of signs, pointing – then pointing to objects. Some ignore her, but one or two are interested, follow her around, take the page from her, use pointing like she does – though I do not think they always understand what they are pointing at."

Sue laughed. "Excellent. That's more than we'd hoped for, isn't it, Mark? Thank you so much, Ekoko – that's going to be a great start." Sue was excited at the prospect that an attempt was being made by Caro to share her knowledge.

Mark nodded, impressed. "No excuse for delay, Ms Clarke."

"And, I understand, Mark, that you wish to journey into the interior to assess the situation of chimps in the wild."

"Yes, I plan to go to Dja Reserve in about a week's time, taking about six to eight days, depending on the situation, what I find, and so on. I must talk it over with you, when you have some time – get your advice on just who to contact."

Ekoko looked thoughtful, luxuriously blowing blue smoke into the air, relishing his Dunhill.

"It is over two hundred kilometres, in the Congo Basin Rainforest. I think you should go with one of my wardens. It can be very hazardous."

Mark recalled Colin's warning.

"Be delighted – if you can spare him. I'm going to take a preliminary look at the chimp populations there, in particular, any cultural variations in tool use behaviour with other West African chimp populations. This is only a feasibility study, Ekoko, just to see if a full-scale project would be worthwhile. But who knows…?"

Some west coast chimp populations were well-known from the work of Boesch and others who had discovered their complex methods of dealing with the hard-as-iron panda nuts. The adults used a stone and anvil method to crack the nuts – tool-using, formerly thought to be the sole preserve of man. It took several years for youngsters to learn the skill from watching their tutors. There were so many favoured techniques as individuals, and Lonsdorf's recent work suggested that young daughters learned such techniques like termite fishing much faster than sons. Was it the same for nut-cracking? What intrigued Mark was that only a few populations seemed to have acquired this ability – he guessed necessity was the mother of invention where the tough panda nuts were concerned. Which begged the question about other chimpanzee cultural developments being adaptations to particular habitats, ecological challenges, and so, as with humans, leading to great diversity in skills and customs – and language.

If his study was fruitful, it could only benefit CRU, too, providing a source of cash as visiting academics – paying guests – used it as a base.

Ekoko had loped off to fetch the warden who would accompany Mark.

"I suppose we have to regularise all this with the proper authorities, don't we?" asked Sue. She took a long draught of the lemonade. "God, that's good. Hits the spot."

"Yup, in Yaounde. It's a pain in the proverbial, but we'll go tomorrow. Got a list here." He began to fish around the various pockets in his safari jacket, and finally retrieved a crumpled piece of paper. "Here we are. The Ministry of Finance to get the stamps for our passports and the park, British High Commission, and police. From past experience, unless you have all the requisite bits of bumf for travel into the interior, you're totally buggered."

Ekoko returned with a shorter, rather solemn looking, young man of about thirty with a raised scar on his left cheek that matched Louis Nkemi's. He remained unsmiling as Mark and Sue were introduced, a brief nod of acknowledgement towards each.

"This is Tchie Nkemi, a cousin of Louis. He says little, but he is a good driver, knows the way to Dja, and some of the guides in Somalomo."

"That's the village in the Dja region?"

"Yes, on the north side of the park."

As the taciturn Tchie didn't appear to want to add anything – a family trait, perhaps - Ekoko sent him off back to his duties. Mark sincerely hoped that it wouldn't be a silent journey. He liked to get to know the people he was travelling with – it made the tedious miles fly, plus locals invariably had priceless encyclopaedic knowledge of an area's fauna and flora, and you couldn't do better than pick their brains. Still, he thought he'd be able to crack that enigmatic exterior, given time and the right circumstances. He might be useless at formal functions but he had faith in his social skills on a one-to-one basis.

He took a long swallow of the sharp, cold lemonade.

Chapter 3

Ekoko drove the Centre's dented, dusty Land Rover back into the bustling capital of Yaounde, with its meandering, noisy streets, and its bouquet of pungent smells, not all of them fragrant. They had bureaucratic business to conduct, and the warden made mysterious references to the 'Marche', saying they must visit it.

The climate was a little cooler here, in hilly Yaounde, and after a surprisingly sound and long sleep in their CRU bungalow, Mark felt quite refreshed.

First port of call was the British High Commission in the evocatively named Avenue Churchill, Centre Ville. They were expected to notify the Commission of their arrival and intentions, where Mark planned to visit, how long, what he was going to do, blah, blah, blah. All a matter of courtesy.

In an office on the first floor, the Trade and Investment Officer, William Wilkins, favoured Mark and Sue with a long, considering look over the top of his rimless spectacles, and pursed his lips like a stern headmaster put out by incorrigible juvenile behaviour. Mark fidgeted around on the shiny leather chair, feeling himself shrink in size. Ridiculous – the guy's probably younger than me, neat dark brown hair with a ruler-straight parting, what was undoubtedly a public school tie, manicured nails, irritatingly immaculate uncrinkled khaki suit; no sweat marks under *his* arms.

No doubt the man was more used to sensible trade deals in cocoa and timber, something concrete he could get his teeth into and boost HMG's exports. For him, no doubt, this was a totally frivolous, self-indulgent adventure, couldn't see the point of it at all. Still, I should be used to that by now, Mark thought.

There were usually two reactions to explanations of his research – a blank visage, followed by 'What use is that to *humans?*', or a lighting up of the face, with 'God, how did you wangle a job like that, you jammy bastard?' He forbore to say 'hard work, and plenty of it'. The po-faced Trade Officer, wee Willie Winkie, was definitely in the first camp.

So be it.

"I really would advise a guide if you're going into the Dja region. It's notoriously perilous." Wilkins fiddled with his expensive pen, but seemed genuinely concerned, his brow furrowed.

"I'm fixed up on that front, but thank you." Mark smiled, trying to be genial but just wanting to get out and started on important things.

"Someone from the CRU?" Wilkins asked with slightly raised brows. "Experienced?"

"I believe so. Recommended, anyway."

" That's something, I suppose." He pursed his lips again and paused long enough for Mark to doubt it was genuine. "And how long do you intend to stay out in the field?"

"Well, it's difficult to be certain with field work, particularly of this nature – you first find your study chimps – and then…" Seeing a faint look of impatience on Wilkin's face, he said briskly, "…about eight days, I reckon. That's an initial pilot study to see how it goes. It's likely I'll need to go back."

Eventually and reluctantly it seemed, details were taken down, and stern instructions issued to stay in touch, and out of trouble.

"Really helpful. Like we're going to stay *out* of touch, and *in* trouble." Sue grumbled as they left the building. "Everyone seems dedicated to putting you off going to Dja."

"Bit late for that now."

Mark mopped a soaking brow and pulled his shirt away from his damp back. As the day progressed and the sun rose higher, the humidity seemed to have risen in spite of the fact that Yaounde was elevated above sea level and usually more comfortable than lower lying towns.

"It's like a sauna. Never mind, I could always shed a few pounds."

"You don't need to." She patted his flat stomach. "You just need to stay healthy. And careful. Promise." Sue was gazing steadily up at him.

"Of course. What's up with you?"

"It's just what *he* said, that trade attaché." She flicked her head back at the High Commission

They walked slowly, conserving energy, towards the vehicle where Ekoko leaned against the bonnet smoking another of the Dunhill's.

"Well, perhaps the poor sod feels stuck in a no-brainer job, exiled to a tropical Siberia. The only kicks he gets are from scaring scientists witless." He opened the car door for

Sue. "Now for the Ministry of Finance. Ekoko knows the way – that right, Ekoko?"

He did.

Ekoko had a unique swerve-at-the-last-minute style of driving, which left Sue and Mark breathless, and several pedestrians with close encounters of the heavenly kind. Thank God it wasn't too far from the High Commission, somewhere down the unimaginatively named Avenue des Ministeres.

They screeched to a dusty halt outside the Ministry of Finance, and this time all trooped inside, Ekoko insisting that with his presence proceedings would be expedited far more quickly – and cheaply, he added darkly.

As expected, they were kept waiting in a shaded, but air-conditioned anteroom, furnished with surprisingly modern furniture – dark red wood and expensive looking soft leather.

Presently, they were offered tea or coffee by a graceful, striking receptionist, with shapely elegant fingers and immaculately varnished long vermilion nails. Sue, eyeing these with a conflicting mixture of envy and disdain that such frivolities were beneath her, hid her own short and bitten nails. The receptionist's smile was a touch supercilious as she gave Sue's rumpled appearance the quick once over. Then her eyes moved on and, with sparks of interest, lingered on Mark.

She poured his coffee, bending close enough for her perfume to linger temptingly.

"Great coffee," Mark slurped his drink gratefully, and smiled ingratiatingly at the girl. Privately, he was thinking, two cups of this stuff and I'll be high-wired all day.

The girl responded with a coy, flirty look, as she sashayed out the door.

"For God's sake," muttered Sue.

"I am afraid we have to be patient with government departments — the higher the status, the longer the wait." Ekoko smiled, indifferent to the receptionist's allure, and folded his hands, buddha-like, over his stomach, preparing to settle in for the long wait.

It turned out to be an hour.

"I thought you said it would be quicker with you along. Call this quick? What's one hour's wait worth, status-wise?" Mark whispered.

"Quite high. *En garde,*" Ekoko spoke out of the side of his mouth as the receptionist reappeared, eyes only for Mark.

"Right." Mark squinted at Ekoko. Was he serious? He was learning that you couldn't be absolutely sure with Ekoko. He had a dry sense of humour, which suckered you in, and Mark knew he was often slow on the uptake.

They were shown into a spacious room by the doe-eyed receptionist. Not into the presence of the minister himself, apparently they didn't rate that honour, but his deputy, judging by the prominently displayed piece of desk furniture depicting his title.

A compact figure, slightly balding, with graying hair, stood up smartly behind his desk, dwarfed by its polished mahogany expanse, and held out his right hand rather stiffly.

"Honoured to meet you, Professor Rees." The hand was dry and firm. Mark murmured a name after a quick surreptitious glance at the nameplate, hoping he'd got the right pronunciation. He needn't have bothered.

"I am Michel Bama, Deputy Minister of Finance," the figure pronounced self-importantly. "And this is…?" A raised eyebrow, directed at Sue.

"Sue Clarke, my postgraduate student." Mark turned to indicate Ekoko, "And the Senior Warden at CRU…"

"Yes, yes, I know Ekoko Roger." This was said somewhat waspishly. Mark glanced sideways at the warden. Had the two a history, then? Ekoko's face was carved from stone, giving nothing away.

" Deputy - ah - Mr Bama," Mark began, "I'm here to request permission to visit the Dja Reserve for about eight days." That was appropriately polite, Mark judged.

" So. And these others? Why are they here?" He waved his hand imperiously around.

"Ah – well, no reason, really, except Miss Clarke and I are staying at the CRU, enjoying their hospitality, and we came into town together, went to the British High Commission, and …" He tailed off lamely. Bama's face leaked disapproval. Things seemed to be taking a turn for the worse, and he really couldn't figure out why.

"So, *you* do not need to be here." Bama, raising his chin, glared at Ekoko.

"I came with my colleagues," Ekoko said with some dignity, arms folded, evidently feeling that no further explanation was necessary, but giving Bama an unwavering stare.

"I suggest you both wait outside. This won't take long." Bama gave a dismissive wave with one hand. "First, I shall issue the young lady with the requisite *timbre*, if she will show me her passport." He held out his hand expectantly, waiting.

Sue, who clearly objected to being referred to in the third person, slapped the photocopy into his outstretched hand. Bama appeared not to notice.

Ekoko, meanwhile, evidently reluctant to leave as ordered, had been edging as slowly as possible towards the door, but was not yet out of the room.

Once she was graciously granted the 'stamp' and the photocopy was returned without comment, Sue took hold of Ekoko's arm, and flounced out.

"Come, Ekoko, let's get some fresh air." Sue sounded like an amateur actress in a piss-poor drama.

The door was closed firmly – but, with admirable restraint, was not slammed.

Mark was suddenly alone, with the prickly self-important deputy, who straightened his jacket, and slowly sat with some pomp. He adjusted a tie-pin set with a brilliant white diamond; it emitted shards of fire caught from the light coming through the long window, reflections shimmering on the ceiling.

Mark waited, mesmerised by the prismatic light display, deciding to let the official take the lead.

"What is your intention in visiting Dja, Professor Rees?" Bama was making some notes on a pad as he asked the question. Or maybe they were doodles.

Was that a slightly sarcastic emphasis on 'professor'? Surely not.

He waited until the Deputy Minister actually looked up at him before replying. "I would like to observe the behaviour of the West Coast chimpanzees. Really, I'm interested in…"

Again, he was interrupted.

"Please, Professor, if it's research on animals, it's not necessary to provide me with *all* the details of your study.

33

I just want to be sure that you will confine yourself strictly to behavioural studies, stay with your guide, and not wander into – ah – prohibited areas."

"Prohibited areas?"

"It's sufficient for you to know that some of the tribes in the area may not be that pleased to see you. The Baka, for instance, are very suspicious. I can assure you that while this isn't the Wild West, Professor, it is sensible to take precautions, so I would strongly advise you to stick to the reserve."

Not exactly welcoming, but he was getting used to being warned off the Dja region, and getting used to officials who wanted to flex their muscles, and, in truth, it was not that different to Ekoko's assessment.

Michel Bama examined Mark's passport photocopy, and, reluctantly it seemed, passed over the stamp.

"Of course, you may be assured I shall assiduously observe all the reserve's rules, Mr Bama, and I thank you for your timely advice which is, of course, greatly appreciated." Acting with excessive propriety plus a touch of submission usually left a job's worth with nowhere to go. He hoped.

Instead Bama gave him a long suspicious look, as though trying to determine whether Mark was taking the Michel, then added, as though this might put Mark off. "There are park fees, of course."

Mark nodded. "Of course."

"And guide fees."

"Certainly. As I expected." Mark dug in his rucksack for his traveller's cheques.

Bama produced park forms for Mark to sign.

"CFA 7500 per day per person for park fees, and CFA 4000 for guide fees. And, of course, CFA 500 for the *timbres*." The figures were rattled off.

Mark noticed that the park forms did not state the exact amount of CFA francs to be paid, and guessed, perhaps, why Ekoko had been so reluctant to depart when he was brusquely shown the door.

"Really, I thought..." Mark began. Then, looking up, he caught the slightest self-satisfied smirk on Bama's face. He doesn't want me to go into the bush for some reason, or if I must go, I can damn well be made to pay over the odds for it.

He quickly paid the prices, keeping to himself any cutting comments about backhanders, and got out of there before the Deputy tried to up the ante.

Outside, Ekoko asked how much Mark had paid. He tut-tutted.

"Those are not the right prices for the park, Mark. They are about fifty percent more."

"I had no choice, Ekoko. I got the distinct feeling that he'd rather no one went there anyway. He tried to tell me that the people there wouldn't be too welcoming."

"Some villagers *may* be fearful – with some reason." Ekoko added mysteriously.

"What do you mean?"

"First, I'd like to show you something. We need to drive only a short distance."

Chapter 4

They got out of the Land Rover at Rue Goker, at the edge of a chaotic, raucous scene — Marche Nkoldongo.

"Before we enter this *marche*, I warn you both to stay very close to me, and carry no jewels with you. Sue Clarke, you give me your necklace, and Mark, your watch and traveller's cheques, please. And all the very expensive papers - permits and stamps." Ekoko held out a hand, looking stern.

"I'm not sure I like the sound of this at all," Sue said, nonetheless reluctantly unfastening the clasp of her gold chain with its bright blue lapis lazuli pendant. It had been given her by her boyfriend Lee Bridges as a going-away-cum-good-luck present, and she was reluctant to take it off. This expedition had come at the wrong time for their relationship; they, she and Lee, were at that interesting, stimulating stage of mutual discovery when new likes and dislikes were being uncovered daily, and then this opportunity, unrepeatable, wonderful, presented itself. How could she refuse?

"You make it sound like a den of thieves."

Ekoko put a reassuring hand on her arm. "You are safe enough with me, but there is no need to tempt rogues, *d'accord*? Do you have any other valuables on you? No? Here, I will put all these in this place, lock the doors and set the alarm on the Land Rover. People here know this vehicle and will not touch it," he concluded confidently, patting the roof affectionately and pointing out the dusty CRU logo on the door.

"Hope you're more right about this than the waiting time back at the Ministry." Mark grumbled, handing over his watch and money for Ekoko to place in the stowage tray. But in spite of Ekoko's advice, he kept quiet about another money belt around his waist containing some traveller's cheques and CFA's, so if the Land Rover was broken into, they wouldn't be skint.

Mark looked round at the market. It had a noisome Dickensian air about it – nearby, a customer and trader quarrelled vigorously, haggling with evident enjoyment. Swirling round him were bright, if shabby, clothes on wonderfully graceful women, with smooth brown skin, swaying hips and supermodel postures. Mark watched the rhythm of their walk as they glided by. And groups of loitering young men with sullen mouths, stared, a glint of hostility in their eyes. He could smell smoked meat as a lower note among the rich aroma of fruity scents and acidic stale body smells, and was suddenly hungry, saliva flooding his mouth. They hadn't eaten since a light breakfast, and it was now well after lunch.

"Come," said Ekoko. He dove into the melee, and Sue and Mark hastily joined him, like toddlers not wanting to get lost in the maze.

Ekoko wove his way among the stalls and shouting proprietors, into the centre, hailing the occasional stallholder.

If they didn't keep him in sight, they'd never find their way out of this Minoan labyrinth.

Eventually Ekoko slowed and stopped. Mark couldn't see the edge of the market - now they were well and truly at the hub of the maze. The smell of the mouth-watering meat was close, the air filled with drifting blue smoke and rich smells. Mark's stomach rumbled in anticipation.

"Look." Ekoko pointed down with his long skinny arm. Mark followed his finger and saw a gorilla. He stepped backwards, startled, bumping into Sue.

"What the hell. . .?" But this was no living, breathing ape. This was just the severed head, eyes milky and sunken under the prominent brow ridges, neck ragged and bloody where hacked from the body, the skin clinging parchment-like to the lines of the skull.

The stall holder – is that what he was? – mistaking his gaze for interest, grabbed the horror by the hair on the slightly crested head and held it out to him, gabbling at them. Sue gave a sharp scream and held her hand over her mouth, as Mark felt the bile rise into his throat. *This* was the smell that had sent his juices flowing? This obscene, pathetic, bloody mess that was once a noble ape? He turned away, closing his eyes, afraid of being sick. Now the smell had taken on an evil fragrance like a carnivorous flower that would not leave his nostrils, cloying, surrounding him. He was going to gag; he bent over making a coarse, retching noise.

He opened his watering eyes – and was confronted by a plastic sheet on which lay smaller monkey heads, colobus – smoked like the gorilla head – delicate duiker antelopes, lizards, porcupine and pangolin. A whole variety of animals as though the forests had been greedily trawled like the sea, and everything caught in the drift net had been dumped here, and smoked.

Mark swung around, grabbed Ekoko's arm, holding it fast in an angry gesture.

"Is this what you brought us to see? Why?"

Ekoko stared at Mark, as though surprised at the force of his physical reaction. "I am sorry. I did not realise that you never had seen such things before. I wanted to warn you. This is bush-meat." He held his free hand, palm up towards the carnage.

"Well, oddly enough, I guessed that." His voice was hoarse with anguish – not directed at Ekoko, but at the sight, the smell. He let go of Ekoko's arm, looking around for Sue. She was standing behind Ekoko, frozen, staring down at the pathetic bundles of meat ripped from the forest, her face ashen. The stall-holder was still gabbling at her. She raised her eyes to the trader and just glared. Under that unwavering Medusan glower, with nothing said, even his persistent chatter gradually faded and died.

Now Sue's face was beginning to change, her pallor accentuated. Mark could see the tightening of tendons in her neck, see the nostrils whiten, see her take a deep breath. In less than one second, she would blow.

"Oh, Christ." Mark pushed Ekoko aside, reached over and tried to turn her around. Her body was rigid with fury. "Best not, not here, Sue." He spoke rapidly, quietly, close to her ear. "This isn't the place to fight the good fight."

She shook off his arm; she was almost speechless, teeth clenched and eyes glaring, but her reaction had not gone unnoticed. It had sparked a vicarious interest in the neighbouring stall-holders, sensing some sort of interesting contretemps in the offing. They began to gather around, shuffling forward, looking from Sue to the bush-meat seller, eyes bright and eager with anticipation. He seemed to have recovered his composure, and obviously not wanting to appear cowed by a mere slip of a female, was once more shouting, but now pointing at her with one hand and appealing to the crowd with the other, several of whom began nodding their heads in agreement.

"See – did you see – *that*?" Sue, heedless of the reaction she had provoked, her voice high and ringing, as Mark pulled on her arm; she had no intention of leaving. "Look -gorilla – and over there, chimp meat! For Christ's sake, Mark, it's unbelievable. Everything – here - look." Words failed her, her mouth opening and closing futilely. Tears of rage gathered at the corners of her eyes.

Ekoko interrupted, glancing in all directions, frowning "You both come with me. Now."

He grabbed their arms and pushed them ahead of him, turning his head back to shout something at the crowd; the mood seemed uncertain, but nobody began to follow them.

When they got back to the fortunately intact four-wheel after a brisk convoluted trot through the market's labrynthine aisles, they were all bathed in sweat, and breathless. Mark bent over, hands on knees getting his breath back.

As they'd fled through the market, they'd picked up pace, but it was like trying to outrun a Pamplona bull. News of the little scene was spreading like a surfer's wave, faster than they could move through the knots of crowds, and the sense of menace was palpable.

"I apologise, Mark and Sue. I had not expected that your reactions would be so – ah..." He waved his hand at a loss for the right word. "Or that the bush-meat seller would get so angry. I thought you knew about this trade." He seemed puzzled.

"Yes, of course, we did, but knowing and seeing are two different things. Look, I should apologise to you, Ekoko, we put ourselves, and you, in some danger by letting our emotions show." Mark put a conciliatory hand on Ekoko's arm.

"I don't care about that," Sue burst out. "How can we *not* be enraged by that – that food pornography?" She flung an arm in the general direction of the stall of horrors. "We *must* be angry, we must *do* something. It's our duty. How can you not see that?" Her voice was still clear and carrying, causing several heads to turn, her face twisted with anger and grief as she appealed to both of them. She hastily swiped her face clear of tears that had spilled over to run down her cheeks.

"I know, I know, Sue, but you must see that it wouldn't do any good getting ourselves attacked or worse in that situation." Mark tried to calm the situation, holding both her shoulders.

"Here take this. Your nose." Ekoko offered her a tissue.

She blew her nose loudly

"We were lucky, Sue Clarke. It could have turned violent. They threaten to kill people before, people they think interfere," said Ekoko. "Remember gorilla meat is five times the price for beef. Temptation, eh?" He looked back at the Marche, scanning the stalls. "We should go now, and not try our luck again."

"What did you say to them as we left?" Mark was curious.

"I told them you were a very rich, powerful man – if they followed, your men with guns would punish them."

Mark, now that the scare was over, burst out laughing. "Christ, it was like something out of the Keystone Cops, wasn't it?"

"I'm glad you found it so funny, but what are we going to do about it?" Sue was still angry.

"Unfortunately, there is little you can do, Sue Clarke." Ekoko started the engine. "It is illegal to sell this meat, but the police are - weak - and the Marche is not a safe place. So," he shrugged, "like Judas Escariot they hold out their hands for thirty shillings and look away."

"And the killing goes on and on until the forests are empty," Sue whispered.

Chapter
5

Over the next few days, they settled into a routine at CRU. Breakfasting on fruit, together with Ekoko, on the veranda, then going to greet Caro and the other bonobos in their extensive enclosure.

There were five other bonobos as well as Caro, including 'Good' otherwise known as Utennu, the baboon god who praised the evening sun and the father of her baby, another older female, Isis, who Caro called 'Hand' as she was missing two fingers – the result of being caught in a snare - and a juvenile female, Bast, plus two youngsters.

They kept a careful watch over Caro's health; it couldn't be too long now, and all suffered a mixture of apprehension and excitement. But Caro, indifferent to their concerns, bloomed, and queened it over the others, basking in the attention like a diva with her entourage. No different to pregnant humans – his ex-wife had been much the same, making the most of hormonal changes to issue commands.

Naturally, his thoughts turned to Joe, his fourteen month old son, who he hadn't seen for several weeks now, but it was too painful to dwell on. The split with his wife Jeannie had been sudden, bitter and accusatory; somewhat pompously, he accused her of being a demanding termagant and she accused him of being an absent father and, on that score, he had to admit she was right. The very nature of his work demanded periods away - seconded to another University, field work, seminars and conferences and now this. But she knew all that when they married and he suspected a lot of the friction was born of resentment, having to do with her giving up her own academic career.

He doubted that his absence made her heart grow fonder, more likely whither away from disuse. An atrophy of the heart. Looking over at Caro playing with the others, he knew what he was missing with his son - that closeness, that warmth, and he was afraid. It could so easily be lost forever if he continued as stupidly stubborn as he had been. He must make an effort to ameliorate her simmering frustration – and his own – and come to some agreement with his ex for better access to Joe.

He brought his mind round again to Caro's labour date.

They could not be entirely sure when she was due. The bonobo gestation period was 220 to 230 days, about 31 to 33 weeks. And clearly they had been wrong about her age when she came to them – she must be older than their estimate, since sexual maturity was normally reached at about 12 years. Sue, discussing it with Mark, was pretty certain, though, that sexual maturity was accelerated under the royal conditions under which Caro had been kept at CABS, with a full rounded diet and all her needs attended to like some imperial princess. Sue said, all things considered - teeth and facial features - she thought Caro was nearer ten years than twelve, maybe even nine.

Sue had made a preliminary start to her observations of the group, recording what interest was shown by the others when she and Caro communicated together using the keyboard. The computer terminal was sited in a small room off the enclosure to which Caro had free access, while the others, for now, would have regulated and monitored access.

In some senses the portable plastic lexigram was more useful in the enclosure itself; it was always there, available for everyone to examine at their leisure – even if only to chew, smell and play with. Mark agreed they should have six more made and sent over, and sanctioned Sue to make the order.

He was pleased with the start she'd made, wasting no time, and she and Caro got on as well together as though they'd never separated.

He made his plans for the journey to Dja Reserve, but saw little of Tchie Nkemi who was to accompany him. He'd begun to think that he'd rather travel by himself than with such an enigmatically silent companion.

He'd brought over most of the equipment he needed for a brief field study, and Ekoko supplied a decent map of the reserve, the one thing he lacked. Everything fitted quite neatly into a rucksack. He tried it on for weight, and once the straps bit into his shoulders, he experienced that old surging desire to get 'out there' once more, test his rudimentary survival skills and experience the priceless excitement and wonder of watching animals behaving naturally in the wild. It had been a long time since he'd been able to get into the field, but it always exerted an insistent siren pull, which dry administrative duties involved in running CABS could never begin to match. In anticipation of this trip, he'd even worked out at the Uni gym, increasing his stamina and fitness – or so he hoped. He knew from past field work on highland gorillas in Rwanda that the rain forest was a demanding, fickle mistress. He'd need to be on the ball.

Suppose he found he was too rusty, though, got ill, broke his leg, picked up a parasitic infection. Didn't he have an added obligation because he was a father to not take risks, to come back in one piece? For God's sake, he'd have what's-his-name alongside him. And he'd have a GPS, a satellite phone. Just think of the old timers who went into the field with bugger-all preparation or equipment, blissfully ignorant and arrogant. These days, he reassured himself, it was extremely difficult to get lost.

Ekoko said over dinner that Mark and Sue must also call in at the police station, take along their passports, visas and stamps so that their visit could be 'legalised', and Mark must inform them of his visit to Dja – the latter was a security matter as well as courtesy.

Mark groaned.

"Is there no end to piddling bureaucracy and paper pushers?"

"You should know better than to ask." Sue forked into her mouth the last of her braised fish and *riz.*

: ⎕ :

Mark surveyed the outside of the Police Headquarters, and recalled his friend Paul Draper, a DCI in the Hampshire force who had a keen interest in all things scientific, especially biological. They'd met during the 'Caro case' – the violent upshot of which was Caro coming here to live with her own kind. Both Paul and Mark recognised something similar in each other. Maybe it was a lonliness that each thought well-hidden. Paul's wife had died, committed suicide eight years ago, and he'd had a difficult relationship with his daughter

Em, although Paul claimed that as she was growing up – she was nineteen, twenty, now – it had become easier. And he – well.

When the case, with all its horrors, was finally over, they sought out each other's company as a way of healing their wounds, physical in Paul's case. It led to having weekly evening trips to a pub to sink a few jars. Occasionally, at weekends, they hiked the Test Way or the Clarendon Way seeking out interesting pubs with 'proper ale', as Paul called it – choosing different pubs each time.

Intense, intelligent, Paul rapidly became a good friend. On the surface you'd expect them to have little in common – Mark was naïve in many ways, he had to admit, while Paul seemed to have a world-weary cynicism, scarcely surprising considering what he must have had to deal with in the course of his job. But, as Paul pointed, out their jobs weren't that different: both scientific enquiry and detective work followed similar paths – an empirical approach, searching for evidence, proposing hypotheses and then testing them.

Both, too, were single now. Is that really how they came together – two solitary souls seeking, needing companionship, neither openly admitting it?

Anyway, he could do with him here now to ease him through the official hurdles. He had no idea how the cops here would view a primatologist trampling all over their pristine forests.

As Mark was mulling this over, he sauntered through the door to a large reception area – to be welcomed by the noise of a furious argument emanating through the open door of a room to one side of the reception desk. Mark just stood there feeling embarrassed, like having stumbled across the vicar and one's maiden aunt in a compromising position.

The Duty Officer behind the desk stared wide-eyed at Mark, scraped back his chair and practically ran to close the door. Unfortunately, the voices were so loud and agitated that they leaked through, somewhat muffled now. Mark and the young officer, now shrinking down in his chair, stared at the floor and ceiling, saying nothing.

Just as Mark opened his mouth to break the lengthening silence, the same door so recently shut was flung back so hard that it bounced against the wall, loosening flakes of plaster which floated gracefully down to the floor. A large imposing figure in a khaki uniform loomed in the entrance, filling the entire doorway, his back to Mark, bellowing at some poor soul out of sight in the office beyond.

"I hold you *personally* responsible for this missing person, Commissaire. See that you find him – or…" The rest was left unsaid, with the swagger stick pointing accusingly at the invisible one, redolent with threat.

The majestic figure turned around and caught sight of Mark. He seemed to freeze, exopthalmic eyes agog, for a long moment, adding to Mark's discomfort.

Mark thought he ought to break the tableau, and approached the heavily bemedalled army officer, holding out his hand. He looked for stripes or pips – ah, a colonel – there was some benefit in being raised an army brat.

"Colonel, I should introduce myself…"

Before he'd got any further, the khaki-clad figure had snorted, rudely brushed past him without a word, and exited the building, slamming this door behind him, too. A few more flakes of plaster drifted gently down in the sudden silence.

Mark turned to the police officer behind the desk. Poor guy looked cowed and embarrassed in equal measures.

"Well, I just came in to notify the police of my visit to Dja Reserve in a couple of days' time. Um - should I speak to anyone in particular?"

The officer's eyes slid over towards the open door. Mark wasn't sure what to do – his timing stunk. Sidle out and come again another day, or, now that he was here, just get on with it, pretending nothing had happened.

"Shall I. . .?" He nodded towards the door.

He got a silent nod in return.

Mark stood tentatively in the doorway, not knowing quite what to expect. He would have to tread lightly, so as not to further exacerbate an evidently taut situation.

"Come in, come in." The crisp voice belonged to a dapper figure, standing very upright behind a neat desk as though nothing untoward had happened.

Mark, paused in the doorway, somewhat surprised – he had expected at the very least, judging by the vehemence and threatening bulk of the recently departed one, that anyone on the receiving end would be as limp as his duty officer outside.

Mark held out his hand, which this time was warmly shaken.

"I have heard of your visit to our country, Professor Rees. Let me welcome you to Cameroon. My name is John Beti, Commissaire of Police in this district." The voice was crisp and light without any trace of an accent. An Anglophone, one of the minority in largely francophone Cameroon.

Mark gave a warm smile, due more to relief at the absence of any embarrassment in the other's behaviour than the greeting itself, but curiosity, the currency of scientists, still prompted him to ask, with innocent wide eyes, "I'm sorry to have intruded at a difficult time, Commissaire, but did I hear mention of a missing person?"

Beti gazed at him appraisingly for a long beat. Immediately Mark wondered if he had gone too far, probing what was evidently a sensitive area – a breach of manners. He was motioned to sit down. The Commissaire must have concluded that he was no great threat to security.

Beti sat, straightbacked in his chair.

"Yes, I'm afraid so. A compatriot of yours, as a matter of fact." He paused considering, pinching the bridge of his nose. "Perhaps you might be able to help, after all. He came in on an earlier flight than you, but –perhaps you know of him. Colin Wingent."

Mark drew in a sharp breath. "What? He's *missing*? I - I know him. We met. We met before he left England. We talked together…he can't be missing." His voice had gone tight, squeaky. He scrubbed at his hair distractedly, remembering the light blue eyes surrounded by wrinkles earned squinting into the sun, his discomfort in a suit made of nettles, their sitting companionably together on the bench gazing at the bright water.

"Very nice bloke, Colin Wingent. We talked," he added irrelevantly. He couldn't believe it. "He must have just lost his way. Be back pres…."

"Did he mention to you, during your conversation, where he might be going?" Beti interrupted Mark's irrelevant murmurings.

"Um - only vaguely. Let me see – he said he was going into the forests of the South East at first. What else?" Mark tried to recall what Wingent had said to him. "He mentioned working for Forest Watch."

There were those one or two moments when Colin seemed troubled, like a dark cloud passing over his features. Had he sensed some sort of danger looming? Silly idea. More likely he was more aware than most of the dangers in the Dja.

Beti sat up even straighter. "Did he, indeed? Did he say in what capacity?"

"No — not really. Not in detail. He was going to check logged trees — their size, species, that sort of thing."

Beti looked thoughtful, pulling at his lip, but added nothing.

Mark looked up at him. "Can we get a signal here for a mobile phone?"

"Yes, of course. If we can't get one at Police HQ, where can we?" He smiled wryly.

"Good." Mark dialled the CRU and asked for Sue. While he waited, he spoke to Beti. "It's an outside chance. Colin Wingent has CRU's land line number. My postgraduate student at CRU can check for messages...Ah, here we go... Sue? ...Yes, I'm at the Police HQ...Very amusing. No, I haven't... Listen. Colin Wingent — you remember that guy? ...Yes, him. Well, it seems he's missing, and I wondered if there'd been any phone messages...No?..Any gossip at CRU?" He waited. "No, thought not, but can you ask around the wardens? They may have heard something. The police need any information we can give them...Yes...Yes. OK. Bye."

Mark shook his head. "No luck, but she will ask the staff at CRU if they've heard anything. Although he could have planned to stay in the field for longer. Anyway, he seemed a fairly capable type to me — experienced, too. Bound to turn up shortly, wondering what all the fuss was about."

"Let us hope so." Beti paused, staring at the surface of his neat desk for a while, then he looked up at Mark. "Forgive me, Professor, but I have distracted you from your purpose in coming here." He raised his eyebrows inquiringly.

"Ah, I came to show you the stamps from the Ministry of Finance and passports plus visas – mine and my postgraduate student's, Sue Clarke. I believe you have to 'legalise' these documents?" Mark dug around in his pockets.

"Correct." Beti reached for the papers. "But why did your student not accompany you? It would have been nice to have met her too."

Somewhat of a contrast to Deputy Minister Bama's reception. Sue had opted to sit this one out after Bama's rudeness, but he could hardly tell Beti that.

"Ah - sorry. I hope this won't cause you any problems, but Sue decided to stay behind as they're expecting a happy event at CRU some time soon."

"Ah, the inestimable Caro, eh?" The Commissaire's face crinkled with a smile.

Mark was surprised – not because the Commissaire had heard of Caro; she had been welcomed to Cameroon with some ceremony – even though, subsequently, the Cameroonians had diligently respected her need for privacy - but that he knew she was pregnant.

"You've heard? Yes, well, we don't know the exact date of delivery but as it's her first, strange as this sounds, we thought it might best if one of us was on hand. Also, it will help re-establish our relationship after such a – ah – difficult separation." Mark wasn't sure if Beti had heard of the events at CABS last year, and if he hadn't, Mark didn't want to go into them right now.

Beti gave Mark his long unhurried look again, flicked through the papers, wrote down a few details on a separate form which he carefully placed in a folder, and handed Mark's papers back saying, "That is quite acceptable, and these seem to be in order."

"You know I'm going to the Dja Reserve for up to eight days. That's South East - roughly in the same direction as Colin Wingent. If I can be of any assistance…?"

Beti clicked his tongue and shook his head slightly. "Just make sure *you* keep in regular contact with someone at CRU, Professor. That's what Mister Wingent should have done with his employers or someone in authority." Beti stood again and held out his hand. "Good luck with your journey, and, please, be sure to take good care to protect Caro."

Why did he say that? Then something else occurred to Mark.

"Did Colin Wingent not have to come here with his stamps and passports, and so on?"

"Of course." Beti drew himself up, straightening his uniform.

"Then, he didn't say precisely where he was going, for how long and so on?"

Beti sighed. "Unfortunately, Professor, I was absent at the time, on leave. Had the proper procedures been followed by those I left in charge we would not now be in this situation. As it is, I do not have the requisite form." The last was added with a dark look.

Right, thought Mark, time to make myself scarce.

Chapter
6

Mark returned along the bone-crunching road back to CRU, his mind on the coming trip to Dja, going over the equipment he needed. He – they - would need to be totally self-sufficient for food and drink for several days. Mosquito net and insect repellent, especially at this time of year – they hadn't chosen the best time to come to Cameroon, September. He mentally ticked off the equipment: GPS, and night vision goggles. Camera. Binocs. Knife. He doubted his mobe would work in the field.

His mind far away, he failed to register an approaching cloud of roiling tawny dust, rapidly growing larger. Before he could react, the swirl of dust and the guttural roar of a powerful 4x4 were virtually upon him, engulfing the CRU Land Rover in a ochre storm. He only had time to make a belated swerve into the ditch at the side of the road, as the other vehicle surged past, sending a wing mirror flying over his head.

The vehicle came to a sudden stop, canted at a sharp angle, causing him to bang his head painfully on the windscreen.

He briefly blacked out, head resting on the steering wheel, arms dangling down into the well of the seat.

When he came round, he couldn't tell how long he'd been out. His mind was full of dark stormy clouds shot through with flashes of forked blue-white lightning. He felt his forehead gingerly – a little egg was growing there, a dribble of blood. Damn, it was tender. He coughed – his throat clogged with fine dust.

What was that growling noise? He looked round in sudden fear causing his head to swim as his vision failed to synchronise with his motor movements. Lions? Nothing. He stared at the steering wheel until his vision stabilised, and realised that the growling was the engine still turning over. That was a blessing, but still the Land Rover was tilted – he'd ended up in a ditch. He struggled out of the vehicle, head pounding, and carefully crouched to examine the chassis and the slope of the ditch. The chassis wasn't bent and the angle of the ditch not so sharp as he'd thought. He'd give it a try.

What the hell had happened? It was all foggy in his mind.

He tried to contact CRU on his mobile first, to warn them he'd be late, but, of course, no signal. He rummaged around on the floor for a water bottle he knew must be there, found it and suddenly, frantically thirsty, greedily poured water down his throat and over the egg on his brow. The water revived him a little and the stormy clouds receded.

He revved the engine, gently pressing down on the accelerator and aiming along the ditch for a spot where the bank dipped. After some manipulation of the handbrake, and nifty footwork with the brake and accelerator, the Land Rover was persuaded to get back on the pot-holed road.

The bumping causing Mark's head to throb in time with the engine; he fought down a rising nausea.

How had he ended up in the ditch, anyway? Had he been day dreaming as usual, instead of concentrating? Had another vehicle been involved? He recalled now the cloud of ochre dust, dark shape at its centre, headed his way. Perhaps he'd better say it was down to another vehicle anyway, or he wouldn't be trusted with the Land Rover again. Then he spotted the torn wires, leading nowhere, outside the driver's door – the wing mirror was missing. It had to have been another vehicle – one that went straight on without stopping. Bastards.

By the time he got back to CRU, he was in a foul mood, slamming the door shut, kicking the tyres for no particular reason.

"Tsk, tsk. Displaced aggression." Sue's voice.

Mark whirled around and Sue gasped.

"What the hell have you done to yourself?" Her hand lifted towards his forehead, but he flinched away.

"Run off the road by some bloody maniac." He flicked at the dangling wing mirror wires. "Even took the flaming mirror off." The details of the incident were still hazy.

"Are you OK? I should look at that bump, check you out, Mark. You're supposed to be off tomorrow, remember. You can't if you're concussed."

"I'll be fine," he snapped, but he had to acknowledge she was right. The wilderness was unmerciful if you weren't in good shape, so he reluctantly traipsed over to the veranda and submitted to Sue's examination with the first aid box to hand. He wasn't going to admit to any retrograde amnesia, though, or he'd be in for a draining session of nagging until he gave way and agreed to postpone the Dja trip. That wasn't going to happen. Anyway, the blank spaces might well fill in, given a decent night's sleep.

A couple of paracetamols and a half a bottle of beer later, he was feeling a bit more mellow, sitting on the veranda with Sue and Ekoko, watching the younger bonobos playing silly beggars, rolling around, faces showing the open-mouthed play expression.

"Sorry about biting your head off earlier."

Sue shook her head, dismissing his rare flash of anger.

In an attempt to change the topic, he pointed his bottle at the bonobos. "Classic rough and tumble play – a good sign of adjustment." Mark observed.

"You said this car came at you, in the opposite direction?" Sue asked, not about to be deflected – she was nothing if not persistent.

"Four by four, more like." Mark recollected the engine noise.

Tipping up his bottle, he didn't miss a look that passed between Sue and Ekoko.

"What?"

"I don't want to jump to conclusions, particularly if they're the wrong ones..." Sue was hesitant.

"Come on, spit it out."

Ekoko took over. "We had a visit, a few hours ago. From the army."

"You mean it could have been them who ...?" He pointed to the angry-looking egg on his forehead. "Why on earth would *they* run me off the road?"

"What do you really remember?" asked Sue, narrowing her eyes at him, warning him not to be 'economical with the verite'.

He sighed in defeat. Best be honest – she'd figured out that he was air-brushing the truth. "Not much, Sue. I think I blacked out for a while. Just this cloud of dust coming at me, fast, then waking up with my head on the steering wheel, a mouthful of dirt and no signal on my mobe. Why would the army come here anyway?"

Ekoko said, "They came to warn us that there are bandits out there."

"Not exactly news, is it?" Mark was sarcastic. "Not after what we saw at the market."

Ekoko took a deep breath. "I took you to the Marche for good reason, Mark, so that you could both see the bush meat. See what we have to fight."

Mark put two and two together. "What? You mean these bandits the army were on about are after these apes for *food? Our* apes?" He felt once more the bile rise into his throat. "Christ! I can't possibly leave CRU and swan off to the Dja now." He shot up, the canvas chair clattering back, and started pacing agitatedly back and forth along the veranda, bottle clutched hard in one tight fist.

Ekoko appeared calm. "You know, it is new for you, but at CRU we have been dealing with these threats for some time now." He leaned forward. "We have arms," he said quietly.

Mark stopped and stared at him, feeling a shiver pass along through his body. "Arms? You mean guns?"

Ekoko shrugged. "Of course guns. If we have to, we will use them. The men are trained." He sounded defensive.

"How many wardens are there, Ekoko?" asked Sue anxiously.

"Enough. If there is trouble, we will fight, have no fear."

Mark ran his fingers through curly hair and began pacing again. Trouble? What qualifies as trouble?

"Fight? Christ. If you have to fight there should be more men. Sue, don't you think there should be more?"

Sue, instead of answering, turned to the Senior Warden. "Is there that possibility, Ekoko? If you need more men, you can get them?"

"I can get them." He sounded assured and calm, and this helped to quell some of Mark's fears. "My idea taking you to the Marche was so you know what we have to face – bush meat is illegal but it is sold right there at the Marche – in sight of police. It was not to frighten you."

"Wait a minute - why is this an army matter, Ekoko? Why didn't the police warn you?" Mark was thinking back to his meeting with the Commissaire. There was something else about that meeting, apart from the flaming row he'd overheard. What was it?

Ekoko shrugged, and blew a raspberry, which eloquently expressed his disdain for the police. Most citizens regarded the police as little more than the corrupt lackeys of politicians.

"Did you find out what happened to Colin Wingent?" Sue asked Mark.

That was it! He'd been discussing Wingent's disappearance with the Commissaire. His immediate recall had been fragmented by the crash.

"No – I don't think so, but I'm pretty sure that I'll be heading in the same direction as he took, so I can keep my eyes peeled."

: ¤ :

That evening, before his departure the following morning, Mark sat on the veranda with Caro and a book. She'd always shown a definite preference for men over women - and had taken to Paul Draper, calling him 'beautiful' much to his embarrassment. Sue didn't mind this favouritism; while she needed Caro's trust, she needed also to maintain a little distance between them lest she fall into the all-too ready trap of experimenter bias; so many others had fallen at that hurdle and it compromised their findings,providing their opponents with ready ammunition. So, it fell to Mark to read with her before she settled for the night; he'd always loved these moments and he could enjoy the luxury of re-establishing the closeness they'd had before she left.

They'd bought several reading books over for her. Back at CABS, they had let her choose which one he would read to her before retiring for the night, and while Ekoko wanted to continue the nightime ritual, he couldn't always spare the time. Ekoko had told him via email that currently she was enamoured of the 'What-a-Mess' series, depicting the eponymous scruffy Afghan puppy with an identity crisis and small habitats for a variety of flora and fauna developing in his messy golden coat. At CRU they only had the one dog-eared copy and would much appreciate some other books for her. She was inspecting the detailed pictures, depicting an ant colony in the puppy's fur, and smacking her lips in satisfaction.

Mark, with Caro on his lap, gazed up at the continuous African stars cast carelessly across the night sky and thought that What-a-Mess's predicament mirrored Caro's own in terms of identity crisis. She'd been torn from her dead mother's grasp before weaning, crushed into a cruel cage for selling on to some sentimental ignoramus, who gave her unsuitable food and who would have kept her only until she became inconveniently large and then sold her on for bush meat. This pathetic bundle of bones was rescued by a courageous couple who ran a primate rescue centre in the UK. From there she ended up at CABS, being taught a hieroglyphic language, their star pupil, thirsty for communication and love.

The cost, though, may have been that Caro was never fully at ease with her identity. Mark looked down at the book – was this why she identified with 'What-a-Mess' who thought he was a deer? It was inevitable, really, that when she had the choice to stay at CABS or join others of her kind, the decision was not in doubt. She had to be, needed to be, with other bonobos. And she'd wanted a baby ever since she'd set eyes on Joe.

Caro flicked over a page, and huffed her laugh at the picture of the wildlife resident in the puppy's tangled coat. She pointed out the twigs and busy ants to Mark.

Mark knew that, with her baby, Caro's assimilation at CRU would be complete. She was accepted into this little group, and enjoyed her rather exclusive status, not to mention the occasional favoured visitors who were allowed at CRU, bathing her in admiration. A touch of the prima donnas was not an exclusively human trait.

"Right, young lady. Time for bed. I have to be up early in the morning to go on a trip."

Caro suddenly put her arms round him, and kissed his cheek.

"Too tight, Caro," he gasped. "I'll be back in a few days – eight days. I'm going to see some chimps."

Caro gave a soft derisive snort. Mark gathered from Ekoko that she acted like her chimp neighbours were inferior, too noisy, dirty. Bonobos were quieter more reflective people. Superior.

"I'll be back before you know it, Caro. Back soon. Take the book with you to bed." He took her hand and led her into the sleeping area where she had a pallet on the floor.

She placed her new golden teddy bear next to her old and battered toy white rabbit and fussily rearranged her bedding.

He said his goodbyes and promised he would leave her a note on the computer. She always checked her computer correspondence.

He sat at her console, typed out the hieroglyphs, each sign standing for a word – noun, adjective, adverb or proposition. She could comprehend about a thousand words now, more than could be fitted onto a standard keyboard, although the number she used was less than that. It was crucial to keep the vocabulary going and expand it. No one knew where her limits lay, certainly not himself, but Sue's work should add another dimension to their understanding of the spread of non-human hominid acquisition of linguistic abilities.

'Back – in – eight – days.

 Love – Mark.'

He logged off.

Chapter
7

Mark had said his goodbyes – he could still feel the imprint of Caro's arm round his neck – and he and the 'silent one' were now well on their way, bumping over the potholes. They were headed east, towards the small town of Somalomo where Mark hoped to pick up a guide familiar with the Dja Reserve.

Mark had tried to get some conversation going, but it was uphill work with terse monosyllabic answers evidently counting as expansive in Tchie Nkemi's repertoire, so Mark sat back and fell to reviewing what he had learnt of his destination.

The Dja Biosphere Reserve, to give it its full name, was the largest protected area of the Guinea-Congolian tropical rainforest with impressive flora and fauna, much of it endangered, particularly chimps and lowland gorillas. Mark had been using the internet to refresh his knowledge of the peoples of the area; there were two major ethnic groups, the Bantu and the Baka pygmies. The latter suffered most from the impact of logging as it fragmented their forest and reduced the biodiversity upon which they depended, while the Bantu seemed to adapt well to the logging camps, taking up employment in various capacities.

Logging – legal logging – was confined to concessions around the reserve, circling it. Or, it was supposed to be. Increasingly, illegal loggers were nibbling at the edges of the reserve, creeping ever closer to the boundaries. In their wake came the bush meat traders – and those employees of the logging companies not provided with food but given instead a rifle to hunt for their own suppers; cheaper by far for the logging companies. It made eminent economic sense in their short term reasoning – unless you were the Baka, or an endangered species.

"We stop here," Nkemi said, peremptorily, breaking his train of thought.

"Why?" asked Mark. Trying to converse with Tchie was like trying to read a page written in invisible ink. "I thought you wanted to press on for a while, at least until it gets dark."

"The car is hot. Look" He pointed towards the bonnet. Now that they had stopped, Mark could see steam curling back over the bonnet.

"I see what you mean. We'd better open it – let the steam disperse." Mark jumped down and reached into the back to get at the supplies. They could both do with a drink, never mind the thirsty Land Rover.

He dug out two bottles of mineral water and passed one to Nkemi.

While Nkemi opened the bonnet and fiddled around, muttering to himself, Mark swigged his drink, letting the cool nectar slide down his parched throat, quenching the fires. He drank deep, then looked around. The rutted road ran straight in this area, left and right, while the tangled forest growth pressed in close on both sides. He examined the rutted track - it didn't look as if it had been travelled recently.

A loud raucous cry nearby caused Mark to start. His training reasserted itself as he tried to identify the bird. Hornbill? He couldn't be sure. How long was it going to take him to re-adjust to the bush after all this time? He'd need to keep his wits about him, and part of that was being able to recognise sounds quickly.

"How many kilometres to Somalomo?" He was learning to keep his words to a minimum in line with Nkemi's terseness.

"Not far." The voice was muffled due to Nkemi's head being buried in the Land Rover's innards. Mark sighed - he should have expected no more.

"Well, I think, when the engine's cooled, we should press on till dusk, then make camp. Is that agreeable?"

Nkemi pulled his head out of the engine and grabbed the water bottle, taking his time to reply. Mark waited him out. Maybe the man wasn't just taciturn but borderline autistic, Asperger's maybe; he hadn't looked Mark in the eye, the whole journey. As Mark thought about this possibility, he began to feel a little guilty about his attitude to Nkemi.

Eventually, still without making eye contact, Nkemi nodded his assent.

: ꕤ :

Some four hours later, with the impending dusk beginning to gather, Mark suggested they stop and make camp.

A freshening breeze had begun with the fading light as they pulled into the side of the track. As soon as they had stopped, Mark detected the faint scent of something putrid, a heavy odour, insinuating itself into his nostrils.

"Can you smell that?" Mark asked.

Nkemi paused as though considering whether to answer or not.

"That is dead animal. You have a name…" He appeared to search for a word.

"Carrion? That's what we call dead game like antelope."

"Yes, like antelope." Nkemi seemed satisfied with this, got out and began to unload what they would need for the night.

Mark searched around for a suitable spot from which to sling his hammock – two sturdy trees about six feet apart. He was eager to try out his new hammock which resembled nothing so much as a sludge green moth cocoon. Nkemi was satisfied with a simple sleeping bag on the ground, but Mark from past experience, attracted too many voracious blood-thirsty bugs – something in his blood was apparently irresistible – and, worst of all, there were spiders. He had a particular dread of spiders, which was ridiculous considering he was a comparative psychologist – an animal behaviourist - and knew full well that he should rid himself of his irrational fear. Systematic desensitisation, a gradual step-by-step exposure to ever larger and hairier arachnids, would do it, but he always found excuses to put it off. He knew why, too - cowardice. A slight shudder ran through him.

They settled down and made a small fire to brew some tea, while the African night settled like a velvet cloak around them. Nocturnal species roused themselves and stirred in the trees above, and in the dry litter underneath other creatures rustled. The main concern on the ground was the Gabon viper, deadly poisonous, but fairly lethargic, unless roused. It paid to tread lightly and wear sturdy boots.

Nkemi stared into the orange flames, keeping his council as always, and Mark felt content to respect the silence, listening to the night sounds coming from the circle of darkness and trying to identify the species. A soft breath of air brushed past his cheek as a bat, curious about the fire, dipped in and out of the flickering light.

The water, once heated, served to hydrate their rations as well as make a brew. Mark chewed indifferently - the taste was bland but nourishing. He wasn't really that hungry – the humid heat leached away appetite – but it was crucial to maintain fuel levels. He gulped the lukewarm sweetened bush tea noisily.

Something quite large started crashing about in the bush about a hundred yards away. Mark and Nkemi looked at each other, Mark's mug halfway to his lips, and kept still. Anything that didn't care too much about making a commotion was either a predator or large enough not to have to worry about becoming another's supper. Or both.

It was impossible to see anything beyond the circle of their modest fire, and the foliage was glossy and thick. Presently the sounds died away, but Mark was reminded to try his mobile. No signal. Not surprising, this far into the Congo Basin.

After bidding Nkemi goodnight, he settled into his hammock. It was a strange confection of claustrophobia, being zipped in, and comfort, with the slight rocking motion. He knew under these conditions he would be lucky to get much sleep as mosquitoes landed with an audible click on the plastic cover, and a stocky six-legged alien shape made its slow dignified way over the plastic cover, just visible in silhouette by the light of the fire. A large beetle.

Nkemi's gentle snores blended into the background noise.

Listening to the rustles and snuffles as nocturnal creatures troughed their way through the dry leaf litter, Mark's thoughts wandered back to the disastrous break-up of his marriage. There'd been no one else involved for either of them, it was just a too-hasty hitching as both he and Jeannie had seen the prospect of parenthood receding; they'd both been, for almost too long, buried in their work, oblivious to the ticking biological clock. One day, working at the same university, their paths collided and they were married in two months. Joe's arrival made Mark's world complete, but it wasn't enough to keep him and Jeannie together. In fact, they drew apart imperceptibly, their relationship eroding bit by damaging bit... Marry in haste, repent at leisure...His head lolled back and he slipped into a shallow sleep, accompanied by the noisy singing of assorted arthropods.

Chapter 8

He was woken by a scolding call from the tree above his head. Even as he struggled towards consciousness, he tried to identify the bird. Not that bloody hornbill again. He gave up trying as twinges in his neck stabbed at him, making him gasp. He carefully straightened his neck as though it was a fragile piece of china, and tried to unstick his gummy eyes.

Judging by the faint illumination dawn had barely broken, a dim grey, filtering through the netting over his hammock. He lay awhile, savouring, masochistically, his first night in the bush for fifteen years. Back then he wouldn't have been so stiff, feeling as though he'd run a marathon on quicksand. He gently stretched muscles starting with the toes and working upwards. He was parched, his tongue sticking to the roof of his mouth, a horrible taste in his mouth. Tea. He needed a cuppa. He was developing a fondness for the red bush tea that was brewed up at CRU.

He listened for sounds. No snoring – Nkemi must be up and around. Gingerly, he unzipped the hammock. In the time he had been ruminating, the dawn was turning to day, a rosy light sieving down through the burgeoning greenery. He sat up slowly. It was going to be an acrobatic feat to get out of this damn thing without being ignominiously dumped on the ground. He managed it, resembling nothing as much as a turtle on its back, spilling the small pool of rainwater that had collected overnight in the folds of the hammock.

Stretching, he called out to Nkemi. The rainforest echoed back his voice. Looking down, he saw the dead embers of last night's fire. He called again, turning and walking towards the Land Rover parked about thirty yards away. Presently he broke cover, coming onto the track - there was no Land Rover. Stupidly, he gazed up and down the track as though he'd got the wrong place. Nothing. Nkemi must have gone on an errand. Even as he told himself this, he knew it was ridiculous. Nkemi had gone - the Land Rover had gone!

He stood there for an age, unable to think coherently, rooted and still staring at the spot where it should have been.

Finally, he turned in an aimless circle, then another one. Why? Obvious really -the vehicle was expensive and desirable. Was that it, though? It must be. Perhaps that was what Nkemi had been planning all along. Was that why he'd never looked him in the eye? Asperger's, my bum. What sort of psychologist am I?

What the hell was he supposed to do now?

He dug out his phone to try again, knowing it was useless – and it was. He was going to have to find his way to Somalomo on foot. On foot? Ridiculous. Christ, he didn't even know how far away it was. He cursed himself for not taking more notice of their progress.

What did he have left? His money belt with a credit card but not much money in it. Fat lot of good that was here. Round his neck, a red cord from which hung a Silva compass. From his belt hung a fixed-blade knife. He had his analogue wrist watch. No map – that was in the vehicle. This reminded him – make a note of the direction of the rising sun, already risen now and difficult to pinpoint in the thick green surroundings. Did he remember enough of the map to be able to navigate without it? Where should he go anyway? Back or on?

Water! He looked around. Thank god, Nkemi had kindly left him a small water bottle. How thoughtful. There was his jacket dangling from a branch. He grabbed it and scrabbled frantically in the pockets for anything of use.

A strip of anti-malarial tablets. A Maglite. A packet of mints – the incongruity of mints here, in this place, made him bark a mirthless laugh. A small notebook. He dug again – his wallet! Not credit card robbery then, or had Nkemi just missed it? Or scarpered as quickly as he could? Why?

Mark, feeling vulnerable, whipped his head around. If it wasn't robbery, perhaps Nkemi had been kidnapped? Why had they left *him*, then? Attacked, maybe? Again, why had *he* been left ?

Is this what happened to Wingent?

In sudden fear, he quickly crouched close to the ground to make himself a smaller target, and, looking down, thought to search for tracks. He wasn't the most accomplished of trackers but he could see no signs of scuffling, just flattened grass and some disturbed leaves, as one might expect in an overnight camp. It was as though Nkemi had been swallowed whole or spirited away. He'd never heard the car engine. Nothing.

The place was eerily quiet. The morning breeze washed his face. Mark shivered — there was that flavour of carrion again. Stronger this time, catching at the back of the throat.

He rose, swallowed, and moved in the direction from which he guessed it came, not sure why but uneasily propelled. It was more noticeable here off the track and ahead. He tried to move quietly. This was virtually impossible as the leaf litter was so dry in spite of last night's precipitation. The stench was growing. A few more yards and he had to pull up his shirt to cover his nose and mouth. Now he could hear a droning, like a chorus of distant tiny chainsaws.

He broke into a clearing and there was the source of the cloying smell. A putrefying lump of game, flies in thick flickering swarms swirling around it. His mind fled back to that moment in the Marche in Yaounde, when he was confronted by the slaughtered gorillas and chimps. He must have stumbled on one of the killing grounds. The poor creature had probably been poached, snared or shot, and died in dreadful agony. He didn't really want to approach, see the horror close up, and began to back away, but then a stray beam of sunlight finding its way down through the canopy, struck a splinter of light off something lying near the obscene mess.

Curious, Mark took a deep breath behind his shirt, then crept forward, eyes fixed on the shiny object rather than the bloody mess. As his angle of vision changed, he went slower and slower. An awful presentiment was growing.

He crept on, slow-legged.

Shirt clamped firmly over his lower face, Mark stared down in horror, swiping at the flies. The lump of meat gradually began to take on human proportions. He felt the blood draining away from his face. Was it Nkemi? No, that was ridiculous – he couldn't have deteriorated this fast even in this heat and humidity.

He took a pace to one side to get a better view. A piece of hide – skin – was illuminated by a beam of light through the leaves. It was white, a bloody but tanned white. And the shiny object was a wristwatch.

Two yards away, Mark crouched down, his knees suddenly watery. The flies strafed around, glittering darts of iridescent green and blue, angry at the disturbance, reaching a crescendo of buzzing round his head. Was this why Nkemi fled? Or had Nkemi killed this person? No, of course he hadn't because he recalled the faint whiff of death when they'd set up camp, and their very brief conversation about it. Carrion, they'd decided. So, had Nkemi wandered about early this morning, before Mark was awake, come across this macabre scene and fled in terror taking the vehicle? That was far more understandable. He could easily empathise with that – even though Nkemi could have woken him, and they could have fled together.

He had to find out what he could, maybe the identity of the person. He turned away to take a long gulp from his water bottle trying to rid himself of the bilious taste at the back of his throat, careless about the conservation of his supply, and crept closer.

It was worse, much worse, than he had imagined. This poor soul had been mutilated horribly. Mark swallowed the bile rising into his throat. The abdominal wall had been slit open and, dear god, the intestines removed, and – he peered a little closer, using a branch he'd picked up, to retract the edges of the skin – the liver. Raising his eyes to the ravaged face, he saw the emptied, bloodied sockets, rivulets of dried blackened blood had run down across his cheeks. Jesus – did that mean he'd been alive and blood still flowing when this mutilation took place? Please god, no.

Could some predator have done this? He scanned the area without moving from the spot. There were no signs of struggle, no trampled vegetation, no indication that the body had been dragged. Anyway, that was insane - he could think of no animal that would remove just the eyeballs, intestines and liver like this. No. Only humans could do something like this.

Another swig of water as the smell caught in his throat.

When had this happened? His eyes fell to the wristwatch again – and his eyes grew large, travelled slowly, reluctantly, from the watch down the hand and rested on the white scar between thumb and index finger – and stayed there, disbelieving. He had seen that watch and that scar before…

Colin Wingent! No, please no! God, he hadn't recognised him – how could he? He rubbed his hands over his face. Christ – what the hell had happened here? He recalled the argument overheard in the police headquarters. Recalled the Commissaire alluding to Wingent's disappearance. And the warnings he'd been given and quietly sneered at. They were right, all of them. This was a place from which he, too, might not return.

Poor sod. Poor sod. He reached out a hand but didn't touch the body. Wingent's family! He must have parents, siblings, a wife, children? He didn't know. What could they be told? How could you possibly tell them about this horror? Perhaps he was single, though. He hoped so.

His thoughts were skittering around, pointlessly. He put his hands up to his face again to try to calm himself, counting breaths in and out as evenly as he could.

"Poor kid, poor kid," he muttered. "Dear God what happened to you?"

After a minute or so, he dragged his hands down his face and rummaged in a pocket of his jacket, extracting the notebook and sliding the small pencil from the spine. He needed to make some notes here. He was no forensic scientist but he was likely the first person on the scene – apart from the murderer, and maybe some lean predators looking for an easy meal. He must record what he could, and pass the notes over to the police as soon as possible.

Feeling increasingly nauseous now he knew who the victim was, he made quick jottings and a diagram of the location, looking around for landmarks. He estimated the distance from the path. Forced himself to peer again into the abdominal cavity – it was infinitely worse when you knew the victim, however briefly. He was searching for maggots or pupae. Now that he examined the area more closely, he could see fly eggs laid in the cavity. That would provide an indication of the time of death.

He crabbed sideways to get a closer view of the upper body, trying to ignore the bloody empty eye sockets, trying to remain objective, and saw for the first time the gashed throat. How had he missed that? Reluctantly, he leaned closer. A clean cut, deep, right across the neck. Jugular severed. This would have killed him if he wasn't already dead from other injuries, but Mark guessed that this was the killing blow, though there was little blood. If so, then all that followed, all that horror, he would have been unaware of. It was post mortem, although with some blood flow. A small mercy.

He noticed some splinters of fresh wood sticking to his cheek, the dried blood holding them in place and poked gently at them with his pencil, looked around at the ground. Where could these have come from? Not here – no cut wood. Not entirely sure why he did it, he tore a page from his note book, folded it into a crude envelope and carefully transferred the fragments of wood into it, dated and labelled it. He tucked it into a zipped pocket in his shirt.

He sat back on his heels, thinking, gazing at the horror that was once an amiable, slightly shy young man in an uncomfortable nettle suit. How could it come to this? This dreadful mutilation was almost ritual. Mutilation. One word triggered a related train of thought - mutilation...*muti*. He'd read up on *muti*; there had been an atrocious case a few years back.

He closed his eyes trying to recall the case back home. His memory was virtually eidetic for reading material, but it was hard to focus here. Yes, the dismembered torso of a small child was discovered floating in the Thames near Tower Bridge, about seven years ago. Only four or five years old. The sheer horror of the case ensured headline news and the usual extended articles agonising over the parlous state of society. He was an African boy, headless and limbless, dressed, grotesquely, in a pair of orange shorts bought in Germany. The police called him Adam.

An expert called in had described it as a *muti* killing where the adherents of this cult take human body parts and grind them down to make potions which bring good fortune or special powers to those who drink them. Typically, the throat is cut and the body exsanguinated, the blood being used in some ritual. The atlas vertebra at the top of the neck is removed – as it was believed to be the centre of the body where power is concentrated.

The FBI had pronounced the Adam case 'insoluble', but by an ingenious combination of DNA analysis and analysis of mineral levels in his bones the Forensic Science Service established that the child had come from the Benin area of south-west Nigeria. Pollen in the stomach contents had shown the poor boy had been alive when he was brought to London.

Rumours of *muti* ceremonies taking place among London's African communities were rife. Eventually, as many as 21 people had been arrested, a network of people traffickers, revealing an horrific underworld of abuse and slavery.

The article claimed that about 300 people may have been murdered for their body parts in the past decade. It had seemed like a vast exaggeration at the time, designed to grab attention – but now, here in this strangely hushed clearing, just the greedy whine of the flies intruding, Mark wasn't so sure.

Feeling shaken, he opened his eyes once more to gaze on the ravaged remains of Colin Wingent. He gently touched the body's hand. To die this way, alone, terrified. It was horrendous, beyond imagining. He'd enjoyed his company, sitting there in the sunny, lavender-perfumed garden a planet away. He'd looked forward to catching up with him again, here in Cameroon.

He swallowed hard, feeling tears sting his eyes, lowered his head to his hands.

Is it possible he'd been murdered for *muti*? His throat was slashed, his organs, some at least, removed. What about the atlas vertebra? He was very reluctant to feel around behind Wingent's head. Apart from anything else he shouldn't disturb a crime scene too much. But he'd already done that, hadn't he? And the dreadful remains wouldn't remain intact for long – that smell was like a honeypot to a bear for carrion eaters. No. It was just an excuse not to have to poke around and find a slippery mess at the top of his spine. He could visualise how it would be, and the thought held its own peculiar horror.

He gritted his teeth, held his shirt to his mouth and nose and slid his hand around behind Wingent's neck behind the gaping gash, and felt around, pressing at the base of his skull. Nothing. He let his breath go and slid his hand out again.

He used some more precious water to wash his bloodied hands.

So, the atlas vertebra was still there, limbs still present. *Muti* or not *muti*? There was something else amiss... What was it? He looked around the body, stood up and looked again. The deflated remains, organs removed and...blood. Where was all the blood? The vegetation, the ground, were not stained. He toed the leaf litter aside by the torso. Nothing. There should be – there should be pints of the stuff.

There was only one conclusion – Wingent had been killed and eviscerated elsewhere. Mark scribbled again in his notebook. What was the point of making a crude record, though? He was stuck here, couldn't contact the police, couldn't contact anyone.

Looking up at the sky through the gaps in the canopy he could see the sun was almost halfway up the dome of the sky in its travels from the east. He must have been here at least two hours. His watch said eight-thirty. Suddenly curious, he bent to examine Wingent's wristwatch – it was still going. Eight-thirty. Somehow that was final straw for Mark – that the watch should still be working and showing the same time as his, whilst his body had been ravaged and desecrated, was surreal.

Enough. He had to figure out how to get help. How to get to Somalomo, how to convey all this to the police.

After one last look at Wingent's remains, he ran back towards the track, stopping at the overnight camp to pick up his jacket. He dithered over the hammock, but in the end decided to leave it. He didn't expect to have to spend another night in the jungle.

Chapter 9

To go forward or back? He gazed up and down the track. In the damper mud were tyre tracks to the east in the direction they would have continued — so the 4 by 4 had gone this way. Forward, then. He had to go forward and he reckoned he must be much nearer to Somalomo than CRU or Yaounde. Besides, the rational part of his mind told him, he still had work to do, and too much time and energy and sweat was invested in this new research direction, new for him anyway, after too many years spent doing the lab work at CABS. He wasn't going to forgo this opportunity.

When push came to shove, there was always that latent but easily aroused streak of bloody mindedness and selfish determination which kept research scientists going. Not even this was going to stop him. Colin Wingent, a good-natured and dedicated young man, was dead, and awful, terrible as it was, nothing could change it, however much he felt for him and his family. 'And Death once dead, there's no more dying then.' Shakespeare's words came to mind, though he was wont to misinterpret.

He shook the canteen of water – about half full – and set off down the rusty red track towards, he hoped, Somalomo. Then stopped. How the hell would anyone know where the body was if he didn't mark the spot in some way?

He tore a small strip off the bottom of his shirt and tied it to a branch of a large tree overhanging the track.

Once more he set off down the track.

: ♡ :

He couldn't tell how many wearying miles he had trudged, but his feet were throbbing and felt swollen, and progress through the dense rainforest was painfully slow. He had no machete to clear his way. He daren't take his walking boots off his swollen feet in case he couldn't put them back on again. The humidity, he guessed, was the standard one hundred percent; it made him gasp. Sweat trickled down his back and gathered under the sopping waistband of his trousers. Surprisingly, considering what he'd seen, and his heaving stomach, he was hungry, but no food – just those bloody mints.

He had to stop.

He slumped down besides the bowl of a rough-barked tree and loosened the laces of his boots without taking them off. A piercing bird-like scolding greeted him. He looked up – the furious little black and yellow bird, puffed up in indignation, was glaring down at him. The village weaver, *Ploceus cucullatus,* a colonial nester; there would be others around, but he couldn't remember if they were really found just near to villages or not. He thought not.

He took a small drink of stale-tasting water from the canteen, and then an unbearable fatigue swept through him. Unwisely, because he knew he was too exposed but didn't care, he slumped against the bole of the tree, and was asleep within seconds.

He dreamt of cold waterfalls falling in shimmering curtains over shining icy quartz, splashing onto gleaming crystalline rock, the droplets of water sparkling like diamonds, the vegetation rich and lush with soft mossy banks, bushes hanging with glistening ruby-like sweet berries that melted on the tongue. In the distance was a high call, coming closer and closer.

He woke up with a start, unrefreshed and groggy – he could only have been asleep for minutes. The calling, shrieking, was accompanied by vigorous shaking of the foliage. A troupe of red colobus monkeys were approaching noisily, attempting to scare off any would-be predators. He watched as they leapt gracefully from one tree to another, crossing the track at canopy-height, just a few yards away from him. They appeared not to notice him. The question was, were they being driven by a predator, or were they just following their usual feeding route? Cautiously, he stood, knees stiff, and listened for any signs of pursuit, pressing into the bole of the tree. Chimps often took colobus, conducting co-ordinated hunts with 'drivers' and 'ambushers'. Under such conditions, chimps intent upon the hunt were aggressive and best left to get on with it.

The colobus cries became more distant and no chimps followed eager for meat.

He stood still waiting, expecting something – but not knowing why. What he heard then, in the distance, surprised him – a strange distant mechanical-sounding thrumming which reached a crescendo then stopped. It seemed to come from above. He looked up, saw through gaps in the canopy, a small body climbing into the sky, reach such a height that it appeared as a small dot, then fling itself down through the air, spiralling as it plummeted. The mechanical thrumming echoed again over the forest. He flicked through his memory and soon came up with the answer; this was the display of the elusive lyre-tailed honeyguide, and he was privileged to see this rare creature's display. He stared in wonder at the extraordinary display, and wished there was some one he could share this moment with — then was surprised at himself as he felt tears well in his eyes. Colin would never see such a sight.

He swore at himself, dashed a hand across his eyes, sniffed loudly and tried to gather his thoughts into some sort of order. Where he was on the track, he could spot no signs of recent use, the bush beginning to reclaim its supremacy. But the ground was drier here. It didn't mean the Landy hadn't passed this way.

He squeezed his eyes shut to recall the map of the Dja Reserve. Concentrate, he told himself. It resolved itself in his mind's eye. The north of the reserve was bounded by the river which passed through or near to Somalomo. He reckoned that the village could not be too far to the east. Should he find the river and follow it? With luck there might be some river traffic. It should be north of this track.

If he could find it, he could at least replenish his dwindling water supply. He rattled the canteen again, and risked splashing a precious quantity over his face, and slugging some flat-tasting water down his dry throat.

In a place like this, in his situation, nothing else at all mattered except that you had enough water. It stripped you down to your bare essentials, the basic core of being. Bugger that fool Maslow's hierarchy of needs. What the fuck did he know? Was *he* ever in these dire straits?

"I think not," he spoke aloud, louder than he'd meant to, and looked round warily.

No, he thought on balance, he'd be safer following the track. There had to be a branch turning north, towards the river at some point.

Slogging along with heavy legs, moving as though wading through treacle, his mind drifted aimlessly, disjointed thoughts refused to coalesce into anything resembling rational information processing.

Miles, miles. A repetitive song started going round and round in his head. 'Dancing Queen' – ABBA. He giggled. He wasn't even that keen on ABBA.

But then it wouldn't stop... on and on it went. On and on, round and round - '*Having the time of my life*'...

Ohrwurm, the Germans called it– a telling name for it; a song that becomes stuck in a phonological loop. It didn't help knowing it was a phenomenon not so far removed from Obsessive-Compulsive Disorder.

What scant reserves of humour he initially had, withered and dried up. He wanted to scream for it to stop.

: ⌺ :

How long was it before he saw a narrow car's width track branching off on the north side? He stared at it as though it might disappear, running a tongue around dry lips, wiping his forehead on his sodden sleeve. He checked his Silva compass – definitely north-ish. North-north-east.

He decided.

Without resting, since he was certain he'd never be able to get up again, he set off from the north side of the track. Glossy thick leaves slapped his face and the leaf litter crackled underfoot. He didn't even have a machete to swipe at the foliage. It got hotter and more humid as the foliage grew denser, trapping the heat under the canopy, and soon the sweat was dripping from him; he needed to replace the lost liquid. He knew the sweat would attract flies, and he didn't fancy biting blackflies or tsetse or mosquitoes so he stopped and, without sitting down, rummaged around one of the many pockets in his trousers. He was sure he'd put some in a pocket. His damp fingers closed gratefully on a small stick of insect repellent caught in a corner of a pocket – he'd missed it in his first inventory. Something at least was going right.

Once he'd covered all the exposed areas and rolled down the sleeves of his shirt, he clomped off again, afraid now to stop too long in case he couldn't start again. He knew that if he rested now, his resolve would slip like quicksilver though his fingers, so he had to keep yomping on, even as doubts about the wisdom of his choice assailed him.

What if the river wasn't in this direction? He might have done better to have kept to the main track. Or he should have gone in the direction of Yaounde.

In the dense bush the going was tough, the distance covered painfully small. Strength was going from his legs – his knees were rubbery, not giving him sufficient leverage to move forward. He stopped yet again, leaned against a tree trunk, shook the empty canteen hopefully, and looked up through the canopy. How long had he been going? Hours. Since just after eight thirty. His watch said it was four-twelve. Almost eight hours, then. What time did it get dark? About six-fifteen. And the dusk was short at this latitude, settling into night with unseemly haste. He should have brought the hammock.

He pushed himself away from the tree and stumbled on, thankful at least that he'd tried to get himself reasonably fit before coming out here.

'*Having the time of my life...*'. Shut up, shut up, SHUT UP!

Suddenly, he stumbled into a small clear space, his feet stirring up the cold ashes of a fire, a small grey cloud. What's this? A hunter's camp, he surmised, a pygmy hunter's camp with a few narrow paths meandering off in different directions. One was in the general direction he had been travelling in. Should he follow it? Or this one? As far as he could see, all three paths were crooked; they could end up anywhere.

Eeny-meeny-miny-mo...

As he dithered, confused, unable to decide, a small jewelled creature darted past his head, and came to rest on a snag on a nearby tree, not more than two yards away. Clearly the bird had used this perch before – it was bare of foliage, polished by use. It stared at the intruder, its colours glowing as though it had been dipped in an iridescent palette. A bee eater! The bird wiped his bill rapidly back and forth over the branch, keeping one glistening wary eye on him. He ran through what he knew of them – colonial nesters, making tunnels in sandbanks, intensely social, altruistic behaviour between neighbours with non-parental older siblings feeding young – no, no, not that, fool. Go back, go back. Sandbanks by *rivers!* He gave a silent cheer, and bade the bright jewel move on. It did, having dismissed him as not threatening or even very interesting.

Mark followed its direction.

: ▢ :

In just half an hour he stood, grateful and exhausted, knees shaking, by the south bank of the Dja River, staring, bemused and unbelieving, at the muddy water, at the bee eaters, turquoise gems darting in and out of tunnels excavated in the opposite bank, busy, noisy about their own business, indifferent to his trials. His mind ran along familiar, comforting tracks as he watched them – he recalled, in full now, the recent study, which had tugged at his memory showing how older siblings would look after the fledglings of the next clutch, foregoing their own chances to breed. Altruism based on kin selection. These irrelevant thoughts, occupying his brain like a mantra, helped to block others which he didn't want to examine right now. He wanted to savour this small triumph.

He creakily bent his knees to fill the canteen. The water looked silty, but was it clean, free of parasites? Could he risk it? Bilharzia? No, he bloody couldn't, and he had no water purifiers with him – they were probably still in the Landy. Something nagged at him – had he overlooked something else like the insect repellent? He searched around in his pockets again – eventually came across the little envelope of splinters in one breast pocket, but underneath that was a twist of paper, like the tiny blue salt packet you used to get in packets of crisps. The second item he'd overlooked in his frantic inventory.

Clumsy fingers gently unwrapped the waxy twist of paper. There nestling at the bottom, like dark shiny crystals of amethysts, were a few grams of potassium permanganate. Why had he included these? Think, think.

His thoughts were sluggish and his survival training rusty, but it was there somewhere. Must be. Yes, it was a fungicide – trench foot, a bleaching agent. And…and a water purifier!

" Ha! Ha!" he yelled in triumph, as though he'd defeated some implacable foe, sending up a cloud of bee eaters like brilliant confetti.

He filled the canteen from the river, poured the crystals into the narrow neck of the canteen and shook it. As far as he could recall, only a few grams were needed per litre. He poured some water into his cupped palm. Clear! He kissed the canteen and drank some of the water, trying to restrain an urge to swallow the lot.

He slumped against the bole of another tree, the noise and busy early evening drama of the bee eater colony a backdrop fading further into the background, until it disappeared altogether.

He fell into a dreamless void.

Some time later, a subliminal sensation woke him – the sensation of being lightly touched on the leg. He looked down without moving his head, an awful dread beginning to blossom, to see a large hairy spider, a species of tarantula, mount and calmly begin to traverse his thigh.

Shit, shit, shit.

His very own worst childhood nightmare, alive and on his leg! The muscles on his leg twitched, and goose pimples rose on his skin, he gagged as if his very body was repelled; no, no - he had to keep utterly still, no movement.

One of the thick forelegs rose defensively in response to the twitch. He clenched his teeth. He recognised the rust-coloured freak – it was supremely aptly named *Hysterocrates gigas*, about six inches across, apparently said to be quite shy unless aroused when it transformed itself into an aggressive monster. He bit his lip to stop pathetic whimpers escaping. Wait! Wait! Wait for Christ's sake! Sweat formed on his forehead, threatening to drip on the freak's back, as he tried to keep himself as still as possible.

What if it chose to crawl up his body, over his chest, towards his face…!

He could feel a scream building inside him.

Presently, the fearsome one moved off slowly with some dignity, taking its own time, and made its way towards a hole in the ground while Mark's sweat dripped onto his trousers and he unclenched his jaws.

"Urgh, urgh, urgh." Bile was rising in his throat. He felt like throwing up.

His stomach heaved and he retched drily, eyes fixed fearfully on the dark hole.

He sprang up, brushed himself off as though the remnants of spider essence would contaminate him and stamped his feet for no particular reason. He'd rather poke a pin in his eye than go through that again. He was definitely going to have to do a systematic desensitisation course if he ever got out of here in one piece. The ridiculous situation of a comparative psychologist with arachnophobia embarrassed him, but it didn't dilute the irrational fear one iota. That's phobias for you.

Presently, breathing deeply, fighting to regain some composure, he stirred himself to look up and down the river, and was strangely unsurprised to see the shape of a shallow-draught motor-driven craft moving towards him, a peat- coloured bow wave at the prow. He stood, feeling a little awkward at the edge of the bank, and waited. Calmly.

In this place, somehow, he was beyond surprise, anything and anywhere was possible. As in Douglas Adams' Hitchhiker's Guide to the Galaxy, he was rescued by the infinite improbability drive.

The sun was beginning its fast descent in the west, painting the sky a garish overblown orange with streaks of green. A whole day had passed since the dreadful discovery this morning.

The boat turned towards him, and a voice sang out over the water.

"Hey! You alright, man?" It came from the burly figure by the stern, holding the tiller and turning the craft towards the bank. The accent was Afrikaans. The man at the prow was slighter, taller, dark. Bantu maybe.

Mark waved them over. As they reached the bank, he bent to hold the bow in place against the bank.

"Thank you for stopping, but not really, no. I'm afraid I've been left stranded. My driver went off some time last night with the Land Rover. We were camped back there some way, by the track." He waved his free hand behind him.

The two men exchanged looks.

"You marched all that way, man?" Definitely Afrikaans. A large burly figure, the brim of his hat pulled down low over the upper half of his face, Mark couldn't see all his features clearly. Just a blondish goatee and full lips twitching slightly with amusement.

A great ham of a hand shot out to pull him into the boat, the setting sun highlighting golden hairs on a muscular arm.

"Get in, get in, man. You can't stay here. It'll be dark soon."

As Mark hesitated, the hand flapped at him impatiently.

"Come on, come on. We can put you up for the night, no problem, till you get yourself sorted out."

Mark murmured thanks as he tried to get into the narrow boat. He was never very well coordinated at the best of times, and hammocks and boats seemed to sense this. He saw it was laden high with goods – fruit, bottles, cans of beer, packages – and wobbly.

"I really want to thank you – oops - you may just have saved my life. I – I had no food, little water, no map..." He plumped down gratefully on the narrow seat, and wiped an arm across his forehead. Rescued from the Vogon space ship.

The hand was held out again, this time reaching to shake Mark's.

"Piet Muller. Look, we couldn't leave you there, man, abandoned." There was a wheezy chuckle. "You looked like a lost kid, standing there."

"That's just about it." Mark shook the proffered hand. Piet had a strong grip, calloused palms. "Mark Rees. And?" He gestured over Piet's shoulder towards the prow where the silent figure sat staring forward.

Muller ignored this, and said "What the hell are you doing in this area, anyway? It's not the safest of places. Didn't anyone warn you?"

"I'm over here to research chimp behaviour. We were on our way to Somalomo to pick up a guide, and..." His voice faded away. How the hell could he have forgotten Colin Wingent? But he had, he had. Preoccupied with his own trials and tribulations, the poor man had been completely forgotten while he trudged on. His own survival occupied centre stage and left no room for anything else. He had to tell them. He squinted to look past Piet at the dark figure at the bow, but with the fast gathering dusk it was hard to make out anything.

"Look, I think what scared the driver I was with was finding a body, some way off the track."

91

"A body." More a statement than a question.

Muller was staring at him from under the brim of the hat but it was getting too dark to see his expression. Ahead, Mark could feel a movement from the front of the craft – but nothing was said. The silence lengthened.

"It was...," he swallowed, paused and restarted. "Anyway, the thing is, I think I know who he is - was, even though he was badly..." Mark gestured, futilely.

"You *know* the man? Out here in the middle of the Congo Basin – you come across a body of someone you know?" Muller sounded highly sceptical, then, after a pause, added. "Was he a friend of yours?" He signalled to the silent figure to get the boat going.

"Not really. I'd met him briefly back home. We had a chat." Mark tried to get more comfortable on the seat, wriggling himself a space between the packages.

"Did he say what he was doing here? I mean why he was where you found him."

"He said something about going south-east, looking at the, um, forests, I think." For some reason, a tweak of caution tempered his words, making him sound vague.

A stream of some local language, neither French nor English came from the dark figure at the prow. Piet replied in kind, rapidly, curtly, and then turned back to Mark.

"He's warning us of the hippos in this part of the river. Keep your arms in, eh? So, I suppose you have to get to the police, notify them of this?"

"Yes, of course, as soon as possible. Would you have any means of communication? My mobile's useless, of course."

There were some more rapid-fire comments from the prow, which Muller cut off abruptly with a 'ja –ja'. He turned back to Mark.

"We'll see what we can do. We're returning to our camp and you can come with us. We have to offload our provisions. It's too late to get you to Somalomo now – dark's coming fast – and too dangerous. Stay overnight, have a good meal, a drink or two – and maybe a shower. How does that sound, eh?"

Chapter
10

It was like something out of the Wild West - a rough, tough mining town, except this was a logging camp in the twenty first century. But for the night heat, the exotic flora pressing in and noisy nocturnal fauna, it could have been the Klondike at the turn of the twentieth century. It had that ramshackle temporary look of unfinished buildings, crude cabins really – and an indefinable scent of barely suppressed violence, although, as he looked around, Mark could see no obvious reason to feel this, except for a prickle at the back of his sweaty neck.

These were cabins thrown up rather than constructed, made of corrugated aluminium roofs and logs of unfinished wood, either side of a rutted unpaved road of yellow-brown mud that sloped down to the river. Makeshift lighting was loosely strung between the cabins, creating bright yellow pools between the increasing charcoal darkness. A pervasive stench suggested that the sewage system left something to be desired.

Some pretty rum characters were wandering around, in and out of the cones of light, one or two with shotguns slung over their shoulders.

Piet took his upper arm in a firm grip. "Come along, let's get you sorted out." He led him down the middle of the road, shouting greetings to one or two armed types, dressed in cod cowboy style with wide-brimmed hats pulled down low like Muller's. They grunted indecipherable greetings back.

Piet's companion on the trip down the river had melted away into the deepening gloom when they docked, apparently to arrange the unloading of the provisions.

They approached a larger cabin, facing the main mud track, with a veranda surround built of halved logs and an aluminium roof.

"Here we are, a guest cabin." He gestured proudly, throwing out a beefy arm. "All mod cons. A shower first, eh?"

"Can't think of anything I'd like more, Piet. This is really very kind of you. I must smell pretty ripe by now."

" I've been careful to stand upwind, man." Piet had a throaty chuckle. Mark smiled for the first time, it seemed like, in days.

: ⌂ :

Some time later after the magical healing powers of a tepid shower, and dressed in Piet Muller's ill-fitting bush clothes, Mark felt a new man. The trousers were a bit short on him and wide around the waist, and Muller must have a bull- sized neck, but it was wonderful to feel clean again. In the shower, he'd discovered a few insect bites that he hadn't noticed before in places nobody but an insect would want to go. Obviously, he'd kept up his course of anti-malarial tablets

— until being marooned. Now, he had just the one strip of tablets with him. He swallowed one. He would have to ask Piet if he had any spare.

He wandered out onto the veranda in his ill-fitting clothes to survey 'Main Street'. It was totally dark now, but a few lights were shining in scattered cabins, and raucous laughter billowed out of one of the larger cabins when the door opened. A woman screamed a high keening cry causing Mark's hairs to rise on his arms. One or two figures staggered through the door, evidently the worse for wear, shouting incoherently. As he watched, a half-hearted drunken fight broke out under a pool of sickly light, with both combatants missing rather than connecting, like a couple of schoolboys, and eventually falling over still locked together, arms wheeling futilely.

A heavy hand on his shoulder made him jump.

"Nervous, eh? Not the sort of place you're used to, I'll bet. A bit rough and ready, but the boys are harmless — unless they get too much liquor. Best to keep to your cabin, though, since they won't recognise you as a guest — might think you're nosey parker, eh?" Muller peered closely at him, lessening the impact of what he'd just said with a grin. "Listen, we have a barbeque going behind my place. Always a bit of a party when we get back with the provisions. You on for that? You'll be safe enough with me."

"Yes, yes, that sounds wonderful, although I feel guilty imposing on your generosity." Perhaps he should heed Muller's advice and not venture out alone into the camp.

Muller stared at him, then burst into guffaws of laughter, slapped him on the back — a little too hard.

"You English," he boomed.

"Well, Welsh really," Mark muttered.

This caused another bout of guffawing, as Piet propelled Mark, with a hefty shove, towards the rear of the cabin and out the back.

Moving along behind the cabins, Mark saw several people were gathered around a BBQ from which rose the smoky smell of grilled meat. His mouth filled with saliva – until he recalled once again the awful sights and smells of the Marche. He swallowed quickly.

Piet was introducing him to a pudgy figure of middle eastern appearance.

"This is my deputy, Farwahl Gaddafi. My right hand man."

"Mark Rees, lost and recently found by my saviour, here." Mark held out his hand.

Gaddafi stopped chewing and smiled nervously, made a small dipping bow, and wiped the back of his hand across a luxurious moustache.

"Don't be fooled, man, he may look a softie, but he's hard as nails. Eh, Farry?" Piet Muller shook the other man's shoulder. The other wheezed an agreement through a mouthful of meat.

Gaddafi's eyes darted back and forth as he continued to nod eagerly as though to underline Muller's assessment of him, but he said nothing. The dancing orange flames from the barbeque reflected off a sheen of sweat on the man's forehead. Surely, it can't be me he's uneasy with, Mark thought. Mark considered himself pretty amiable and unthreatening, but then again this wasn't a usual situation. No, it's not that… humidity was still high and his freshly showered body was getting sticky again.

"So, what do you do in this camp, Mr Gaddafi?" Good grief. Gaddafi?

Gaddafi swallowed his mouthful. "I'm...what you say?... Admin? Paperwork." He heaved a sigh and shrugged, as though expecting sympathy. He quickly popped another morsel of meat into his mouth.

"Come on. Food." Piet shepherded Mark towards the BBQ, grabbed a tin plate and pushed it into his hands. "Build up your strength, man – you look as weak as a bloody kitten."

The barbeque, behind one of the larger cabins at the top of the 'street' – Piet Muller's living quarters - was industrial size, sufficient to feed the five thousand. Mark looked around. There were about fifteen to twenty people there, of all ages, it seemed like, and what in other circumstances one might call white-collar employees. All nationalities. Mark could see some Africans, obviously, some whites, two orientals, several of middle eastern appearance. And a melange of languages. All were dressed casually – but then this was hardly the type of place to encourage formality. Obviously, the manual workers in the camp weren't invited, and Mark guessed this carnivorous spread was for the bosses only.

There wasn't a single woman there. He guessed what women there were in the camp were for one purpose only, and certainly not to sully this macho feast.

Piet had been swallowed into the throng, so Mark peered carefully at the grilled meat. The Yaounde Marche in mind, he didn't want to make the mistake of eating a near relative.

A strange shaped small piece of pork-like meat caught his eye – at least it didn't look like primate. He turned to an African standing next to him, piling his plate with an assortment of meats.

"What's this, do you think?" He pointed at the charred lump.

The African looked puzzled at first, then his expression cleared and a broad smile spread over his face.

"Very good." He made a kissing motion with his fingers. "You try."

"Well…" He smelled it cautiously.

His new friend plonked a piece on Mark's plate and waited.

"You try, you try." His arm was nudged encouragingly.

He did. It was delicious – the meat practically melted in his mouth. He hadn't realised just how starved he was. When was the last time he'd had a decent meal?

"What type of animal?"

"Small, eat *petit fourmis* and – ah." Here he sketched some roundish shapes dotted all over his body. "No hair."

Mark stared at him trying to work it out. "Eats ants? No hair – scales? Pangolin? Not pangolin!"

Christ almighty! He spat it out. Dear God – an endangered species! The small scaled mammal, *Manis tricuspis*, that loved termites, trundling about, living his inoffensive life and dwindling fast, ending up on a BBQ. On his plate! In his mouth!

"No, no! We can't eat this! It's endangered. Few left…" He waved his hand around, agitated, knowing that he was not understood, while his companion stood there, uncomprehending and appearing slightly hurt that anyone would refuse some tasty grilled pangolin.

"Christ, it's like eating panda. You know? Panda?" His new companion displayed a nonplussed expression and suddenly the steam went out of Mark, leaving him deflated and exasperated. Who was he to berate this guy? Good job Sue wasn't here – she would have been apoplectic with rage. He patted the other's arm in an attempt at apology.

"Sorry."

And he needed to eat.

"Look, what else is here?" He pointed to the other pieces of grilled meat, hoping there might be something here not on the verge of extinction, because his stomach was protesting.

"Ah, monkey, duiker, chicken." He pointed to various shapes on the long grill.

"Thank Christ for that. Chicken." I bloody well hope, he added under his breath.

: ☼ :

Several strong bottles of beer later, with any lucid command of English, let alone any other language, rapidly deserting him, Mark decided it was time to hit the hay. He'd overdone it – a self-indulgent compensation for his privations, he told himself, and a celebration of his survival against all the odds. More than that poor pangolin managed. He drank a last toast to it, feeling a bit maudlin.

"'Night, Piet. Going to hit the sack. Knackered. And thanks again for all... Real diamond." This time he slapped Muller's solid, beefy back, and staggered with jellied knees up the steps to the veranda of the guest cabin.

"See you in the morning, Professor. Sleep well."

Laughter followed him up the steps.

Mark waggled his fingers, and stumbled through the door to more laughter. He found the bedroom at the back and flopped, face down on the bed, pulling the mosquito net around him.

There was something he had to do – but it could wait. He couldn't remember what it was anyway.

Soon, he slid down into deep sleep, his body exhausted.

Chapter
11

Sometime in the night, phasing into a lighter stage of sleep, Mark thought he heard rustling. It must be some large six-legged type shimmying across the floor, he reasoned; a beetle maybe. Or a snake? Either way, he wasn't too bothered, as long as he kept still. Then it occurred to him that the number of legs might be eight. Immediately, he was less sleepy.

He opened the one bleary eye not buried in the pillow, and tentatively swivelled it around without moving his head. He definitely did not want a repeat of that horrific episode in the forest.

He saw a dim, slowly sliding shadow on the wall created by the flickering ruby light of the dying barbeque and a nearby yellow 'street' light filtering through the blind. That's either a seriously large grade eight spider, or...or I'd better keep dead still, Mark thought. His pulse was an audible drum beat in his ears.

This was an attempt at robbery by some alcohol-fuelled roughneck in the camp – probably armed with something lethal. A knife? Or a gun?

He had absolutely nothing worth stealing except under the mattress, and those hardly worth the effort – even his discarded clothes were in a worse state than anyone elses in the camp. Best play possum. The thief would depart once he realised there was nothing of value here.

His ears detected movement near his tattered safari jacket thrown carelessly over a chair. What on earth could the intruder be looking for? He'd left his passport back at CRU – only carried a photocopy with him – and that was in his money belt underneath him. His knife? Compass? Torch?

No - he guessed the pockets of his jacket were being searched for valuables – money, watch, mobile. Well, his watch was cheap, and he had scant money in his belt; the thief could be after the mobe, but he'd put all these items under the mattress he was lying on – more because of the inconvenience of replacement than for any inherent value.

Another small rustle as paper was unfolded. The potassium? He'd long ago finished his mints.

Or maybe the splinters.

More paper sounds – the sound of pages being turned. His notebook!

The frustration of not being able to turn and see what the intruder was doing, what he was examining, caused a twitch to start in his calf muscle. Vainly, he tried to suppress the twitching, but it was as useless as trying to stop your stomach rumbling.

A drop of sweat slid slowly down his temple as he anticipated the thief's next move would be to search under the mattress.

He held in his fear, not breathing. More pages turned.

Eventually the looming shadow slid menacingly down the wall as the figure exited the room as silently as it had entered. Mark waited rigid for some minutes, squinting between his eyelashes, sweat stinging his eyes. Then eased himself up, gradually. His muscles had tensed and gone stiff and his head was pounding with the after-effects of the unaccustomed alcoholic binge.

He got up and walked stiffly over to his jacket. Was anything missing? Surely, no one could be bothered with a twist of potassium permanganate crystals. No, that was there. Another pocket - yes, the other folded piece of paper was there, too, with its contents. Ah, his notebook was still there, too. And his knife and compass and Maglite torch, still lying on the chair. He searched the other pockets and scanned the room.

He skidded back over to the bed and fumbled under the mattress. Yes, great. Both watch and moneybelt with his passport photocopy and bit of cash safe – and the mobile. Of course they were – they were underneath him. He wasn't thinking straight.

Nothing. Nothing had been taken. What the hell was that all about, then? And who? All they seemed to have done was rifle through a few pages of his notebook. Perhaps they thought it was a passport. A British passport would fetch a few bob here, he imagined.

This place was beginning to make him feel creepy. There was an aura of palpable menace. Even at this hour, early in the morning, he could still hear the odd shout, occasional piercing scream, a burst of a furious quarrel which subsided as rapidly as it began, and once a loud splash.

In spite of Muller's hospitality, Mark urgently wanted to get hold of the authorities. He had to relay the news of Colin Wingent's death as soon as possible. The police had to know – and poor Colin's relatives. And he had to contact CRU – let them know he was alright. He felt another stab of remorse that he had recklessly endangered himself to come here. Joe was only a toddler, and he hadn't given enough of himself to him; they'd not had the chance to develop a proper bond. And now, the chance might be lost – unless he got out of this mess unscathed.

He felt under his mattress for the mobile, and without much hope tried the search for a network – dead as a dodo. The radio? No go - Farry the Lebanese had told him, when he inquired at the BBQ, that it was out of action.

He felt suffocated in the heavy humid air. He had to get outside. In spite of Muller's warnings not to stray and in spite of the recent visit, he had to get some air that was slightly less stale, think what to do.

He dressed in his old smelly ruined clothes which at least fitted him after a fashion, hid additional items under his mattress – his knife, compass, torch and after some thought, the notebook - in case 'The Shadow' returned - and glided silently down the front steps of the veranda. He strapped on his old watch.

It was relatively quiet now at – what was it? – 4.05am. An onyx night had settled over the camp, just the occasional call of a sleepy bird, the flicker of a bat, and, even though the moon was setting, the stars were bright enough to illuminate a still monochrome world like a black and white photo. Nothing moved. At last, the camp inhabitants seemed to be asleep. Or fallen into drunken stupors, more like.

Mark watched from the shadows of the veranda, uncertain as to what he was doing. As he stood, indecisive, his dark-adapting eyes picked up a faint light emanating from somewhere up the glutinously muddy track which served as the main road in this strange, temporary, isolated camp. So someone was still up.

What he really wanted was to talk to someone. Too much had happened to him, too fast. He wasn't able to process it all and seemed unable to formulate a proper plan of action. To be fair to himself, he had experienced some pretty awful privations and didn't feel that he'd recovered yet. Stupid to have drunk so much but he'd wanted to wash it all away – the slaughter of Colin Wingent, the abandonment.

His best bet was to try to get to Somalomo, or maybe Yaounde, get hold of the authorities, explain about Colin Wingent – and why he'd been delayed in getting to them. Tell them that he believed Wingent's death was down to the satanic horrors of *muti*.

Warily, bearing Muller's warning in mind, he crept along in the deep shadows of the crude cabins, making his way towards the dim light and away from the river, realising that he didn't know from the front which cabin was Muller's. Still, he might as well have a gander now that he was up and not feeling very sleepy.

He had to skirt a makeshift square-shaped well, about two yards square, which, judging by the rank smell, was full of stagnant water and worse. He didn't want to think about the splash he'd heard earlier or what else might have landed in the well. That water must be totally unfit to drink – choc full of nice amoebae. Anyone drinking that sump water was sure to cop a dose of dysentery or amoebiasis. Luckily, since he'd been here he'd stuck to alcohol, and it seemed as though everyone else did too. This well was likely the reason why.

He wondered at the primitive facilities — if that was the word —provided for the employees. Booze aplenty, judging by last night's merrymaking, and the provisions on the boat. In fact, now that he thought of it, the alcohol far outweighed comestibles on the small skiff — a mini booze cruise.

Well, he knew now, thanks to the grisly variety on offer at the barbeque, where most of the meat came from — the bush. So the camp didn't have to provide much by way of food, just guns. Keep the happy campers tanked up with copious supplies of alcohol, supply the shotguns and ammo, and Bob's your Uncle, save money on expensive basic services like a proper water supply.

He crept on, throwing glances around. 'The Shadow' could still be out there, lurking. As he moved forward, the light resolved itself into a yellow square — a blind drawn down over a window. The sound of a low voice. Good, someone was awake and talking, Piet maybe, or Farry.

A burst of static white noise brought Mark to a halt about a yard from the wall. Was that a radio? But the radio was out — Farry had said. He waited, holding his breath. The voice was murmuring again — it sounded like the wheezy Lebanese deputy. He couldn't make out what he was saying; his French wasn't good enough, especially when overlaid with a strong middle-eastern accent. He crept stealthily up to the covered window of the small cabin. There was no glass, just a blind pulled down. He reached up to gently lift a corner of the blind, just... There was a sudden scrape of a chair across the wooden floor. Mark froze. Bugger, some one had heard him — how embarrassing was this, to be caught creeping up on someone's private conversation?

The door to the cabin squeaked open and feet clattered heavily down the veranda steps, accompanied by barely discernable breathy muttering, as though the other was annoyed. Maybe he hadn't been spotted. Squashing himself into the side wall of the flimsy structure, Mark squinted into the dark, detecting the squat bulk of the Lebanese waddling away from the shack.

He wondered why he hadn't just greeted the deputy and asked to use the evidently now-mended radio. Because of largely unacknowledged suspicions, lurking at the back of his mind, the feel of this place, the barely contained violence.

He leaned back into the wall.

Why had he not faced up to what this place was? Why had he pushed it to the back of his mind? Because they had rescued him from possible death, dusted him off, set him on his feet again? For God's sake, it was a roughneck's logging camp, hard up against the boundaries of the Dja reserve, where evidently the employees shot bush meat with a rare abandon, drank themselves into a stuporous state, possibly because the drinking water was dysenteric. And who, no doubt, would not welcome outsiders poking their noses into their business. Muller had hinted as much.

But it was even more urgent that he contact somebody about Colin Wingent, and by now CRU and Sue would have expected some sign of life from Somalomo.

He peered round the corner of the cabin, intending to go in and use the radio. A deep breath, a loud crack ...and everything went black.

: Ʊ :

His vision was blurred, when he awoke. Even as the scrappy thought entered his mind that he should never have drunk so much last night, an acute pain sliced across the back of his head. He gasped and reached around to the back of his head. An egg-shaped wound in the occipital region, tender to the touch, some blood on his hands. He couldn't remember how that had happened. He must have fallen out of bed, concussed himself and blacked out for a while.

He was on the floor – a crude wooden floor. He squinted up at the ceiling. It was different. No fan turning sluggishly – he could see some light filtering through crudely arranged corrugated iron panels. Where was his chair? Never mind the chair, where was the bloody bed? And his other stuff. Gone. The only thing was a filthy, stinking blanket tossed carelessly over him. He threw the reeking thing aside.

He didn't understand. This wasn't his cabin bedroom.

Turning his head to scan the tiny space – more of a cubicle - brought another agonising slash of pain. He gritted his teeth. Get up – he had to stand but he wasn't sure why he should.

Making grunting noises and cursing, he forced himself up, inch by agonising inch, using the wall as a prop. He took some deep breaths to clear the thundering in his head, and mentally transported himself back to the night of the BBQ – last night? Think, think.

Yes, he'd gone outside the cabin they'd assigned him, for some air, wandered around. The radio shack! He'd gone to the radio shack. Then darkness - nothing.

He'd been whacked! Some bastard had slugged him. He vaguely recalled another smack on the head not so long ago. It was getting to be a habit. He felt around his head more gingerly - he had matching lumps, one at the front and one at the back.

Why? What the hell was this one for? To steal something? He had an idea that wasn't it – there was some reason why not. A memory flickered - a shadow on the wall. A shadow, and him lying possum-still while the Phantom rifled through his things, yet nothing taken. He wasn't mugged for his possessions.

So then, attacked just because he'd wanted to use the radio? The radio he'd been told was out of action.

He tried pushing against the door. As he'd expected it was locked. No way out.

He slumped back again, put his head in his hands. It felt like a herd of gnu was thundering through his head.

Why? He'd said he ought to contact the police. Why should they want to stop him communicating with the police? Or was it CRU? Obviously, because they had something to hide. Which was...? Of course - the appalling living conditions. No, unfortunately he suspected that the state of this place wouldn't raise too many eyebrows. Many people lived in worse conditions, many had no employment. Here, they had work at least.

He felt a bit nauseous. Dehydration was adding to his woes. His tongue was sticking to his palate. He desperately needed a drink of water – clean water.

Suddenly, he knew, thought he knew, with absolute clarity what their big secret was. Why had he been so dense? Bemused by their human kindness, awash with relief at being rescued, he had denied it to himself. That good old ego-defence mechanism - denial. The longest river in Africa. Christ - his thoughts were wandering all over the place. Focus.

What had that big insight been? It was gone now.

He had to get away. But first, he needed water.

"Hey, hey! Anyone! I'm sick! Get me water, please!" He banged on the sides of the hut and made his head spin.

Nothing. Just the sounds of the bush – insects, birds, the faraway chitter of a monkey. Not even the camp noises which he'd now be pathetically thankful to hear.

What time was it? He had no watch – so it was either stolen, or was it back in his cabin with his jacket? He couldn't remember where he'd put it.

"Hey, you fucking pathetic excuses for humanity, you'll be sorry..." He said the last bit more quietly.

No one came – it was tomb quiet. Where was this hut anyway? Was this – a prison – inside the camp? Too quiet. A horrible thought occurred to him that he'd been left here, abandoned – no one would come, ever. Years later, his skeleton -

He had to get out. He scrutinised the hut more carefully. Sturdy wooden frame with corrugated iron panelling. Just seven feet by eight, he reckoned. A door.

He crouched down on the floor. There was a small gap between the corrugated tin and the wooden floor. He lay flat and put his eye to the gap. All he could see was dense vegetation. This he did with each of the four sides, squinting into tiny gaps. Only on the side of the sturdy wood and corrugated iron door, could he glimpse, in the cracks around the side, a small overgrown path, barely discernible, leading off into the dense foliage and curving away. No sign of life anywhere.

Except, now he detected a persistent high-pitched whine like a chain saw nagging at his hearing. The saw mill attached to the logging camp. It hadn't been operating when he arrived at the camp – obviously, because it was night. No one will hear me with that racket — even if they were inclined to respond.

He tested the strength of the door by throwing himself at it, but the restricted space prohibited getting up any momentum. He could tell from the rattles that the door was padlocked. He gave it a futile kick.

He looked for the hinges on the door. Unfortunately, he had nothing he could turn the screws with. And, hinges were on the outside of doors.

It was like a roaring kiln now, the hot air drying his throat. Sliding down the baking side of the hut, there popped unbidden into his mind the scene from 'Bridge over the River Kwai' where Alec Guinness playing a POW, was incarcerated in a tin box, slowly roasting in the searing, suffocating heat as punishment for something or other. Did he die in there? He couldn't remember. He pushed the scene aside.

Presently, he tried another shout. His voice was getting hoarse without liquid. His headache had intensified with the dehydration.

No answer. The silence of the bush surrounded him, the whine a constant background noise, masking his shouts. Now that he thought about it, since the saw mill had started the bush was too quiet. There should be more noise — grunts, squeaks, cries of birds, noises of animals rummaging about. Silence wrapped itself around him.

Why? His eyelids closed. Why was the bush so quiet?

: ☼ :

Sue put down the phone, worried. What was she able to tell Jeannie, Mark's ex-wife? She wasn't certain of the current state of their relationship, but thought they were separated. Mark wanted more access to his son and Jeannie was dragging her feet; at least, that was *his* version on the one occasion he'd disclosed anything. But whatever the degree of separation – and it was no business of hers, really - Jeannie had a right to know what was going on, except there was nothing she could tell her. She'd heard nothing herself. Without much hope, she'd tried his mobile number, left a message. He should have been in touch yesterday, from Somalomo or somewhere else. There had been no communication either from Mark or Tchie Nkemi, the warden.

There was something wrong. It prickled at her skin.

Ekoko had tried to get through to the police in Somalomo. The chief was out and about, he was told, but the duty officer, or whoever passed for such, promised to pass on the message.

Perhaps it was time to contact the British High Commission in Yaounde. She decided to ask Ekoko first, since he was *au fait* with the customs and ways of going about things. She certainly wasn't, and she didn't want to put her foot in it and offend someone. That seemed all too easy to do with officials here.

She found him preparing meals for the 'guests' as he called the bonobos and chimps.

"Our Caro has a big appetite now that she is pregnant, Sue Clarke. We must watch her weight." He sliced a juicy mango and added it to the other fruits, the dense sweet aromas filling the air.

"Ekoko, I'm getting worried about Mark. His ex-wife has just phoned wanting to speak to him." She paused. "They're late, aren't they?" She watched him prepare the fruit as she fiddled anxiously with her pendant, feeling the familiar pulling sensation in her guts she always experienced when afraid. "I couldn't tell her anything, so I stalled - just said

Mark was out on a field trip, and that he'd contact her as soon as he got back." It wasn't that she felt guilty about lying to Mark's ex, just that she wasn't very convincing.

Ekoko paused in the act of sprinkling vitamin powder over the chopped fruit. A frown appeared on his normally cheerful face.

"*C'est vrai*. They must be there by now. I will try the police in Somalomo again?"

"Thank you, Ekoko."

"Let me finish our guests' meals, and I will be with you."

Sue needed Ekoko's help with long distance communication in case the party on the other end spoke one of the local languages, like Bakole. Cameroon had 286 languages, and Sue was fluent in precisely one. Her GCSE French was rusty, and not up to dealing with the local dialects.

Ekoko got through again on the phone to Somalomo and a salvo of speech followed. He listened, drawing down his brows, spoke some more and slammed down the phone. He'd got the same indifferent answer, that the Commissaire was away, and the speaker claimed to have no knowledge of how to contact him. He blew though his teeth in frustration.

"What about the Yaounde police, Ekoko? Would they be able to contact the Somalomo Commissaire for us?"

"*Gendarmes*?" He looked doubtful, pursing his lips. Clearly he didn't have too high an opinion of the police. He looked down seeing her anxious face and relented. "We can try. Yes, we can do that."

He picked up the phone again. There followed similar rapid-fire sharp-sounding exchanges as Ekoko fought to get past the officer on the duty desk to speak to Commissaire

Beti. Eventually, after raising his voice, he succeeded, and he resumed in English to explain that they were very concerned for Mark's and Nkemi's safety, as they hadn't contacted them from Somalomo.

Ekoko listened, his face creasing with annoyance. Sue watched him closely, was praying it wasn't bad news.

"I know you warned him of the dangers, Commissaire Beti. But that is not the point. He is a professor, a *very* important person, most eminent in his field."

Mark would be severely embarrassed at this.

"And," Ekoko ploughed on, "Professor Rees must be able to do his research in the bush, even if it is dangerous. This is very important research on our great apes – which I am sure you know are essential to our ecotourism trade. Would we not be *ashamed* if anything happened to this important personage whilst he is our guest?" He was about to add other glowing credentials to Mark's magnifying status, when he was interrupted by the Commissaire.

Whatever Commissaire Beti was saying, was evidently not what Ekoko wanted to hear, as he rolled his eyes towards the ceiling, sighing.

"Yes, yes, you have told me you gave him a warning of the Dja, but..."

Sue pulled at his sleeve, and mouthed 'Colin Wingent' at him. Ekoko nodded at her.

"You realise that another citizen of Great Britain has gone missing, too? This is strange, is it not? Three people altogether with my warden, Tchie Nkemi, who was driving the professor?"

He waited, holding his hand over the receiver.

"He's saying there is no connection between the disappearances."

"Well, he would, wouldn't he?" Sue hissed

Ekoko removed his hand from the receiver and spoke into it. "That may be so, Commissaire Beti, but other people might make a connection, and this cannot be good for our ecotourist business in Cameroon. All we respectfully request is for you to contact your opposite number in Somalomo, who has, I believe, a responsibility for overseeing the Dja Reserve."

He listened. Sue watched his face, searching for clues.

Ekoko sighed, and then said into the phone – the *coup de grace* – "Then we shall have to notify the British High Commissioner. He will, I am sure, be in touch with you."

The response even Sue could hear, as Ekoko held the receiver away from his ear, then gently put it down.

"Well, that was not very respectful, but I think now he will do something."

"So there has been no word yet from Colin Wingent, either?"

Ekoko shook his head, pulled at his lower lip. "Nothing. Nothing at all."

Chapter
12

Mark woke from his uneasy doze with a start, but this time re-oriented himself quickly. How long had he been asleep? It was light now and the headache was a more distant booming. He glanced at his wrist. No watch.

"I know where I put it," he muttered, "under the mattress – but I put it back on again before I went out, so it's been nicked". His voice had that rusty disused quality.

He was wryly pleased with this progress in his mental capacities. But he figured he wasn't imprisoned because someone had stolen his watch; that had been taken after he'd been put in here, when he was unconscious, he was sure of that. They didn't want him to know the time.

He had to devise a way of getting out. Urgently.

He crouched down, as before, to peer under the small gap between the side and the wooden floor. He realised for the first time that the hut was on short stilts – like the cabin he'd been allocated – but much smaller and shorter. So, there might be a veranda and about one or two steps to the ground.

He examined the flooring more carefully. Rough planks, and underneath, spaced floor joists.

He tried to pry up one of the planks, but soon realised that wasn't going to work – they were firmly nailed down. Think, think laterally. If they won't be pried up, then they can be bent down. Perhaps.

He backed into one corner, and inched up the two adjoining corrugated iron walls by bracing his boots against the two sides. He would use himself as a pile-driver, low level headache notwithstanding. He took a deep breath and jumped as hard as he could onto the floor. There was a splintering sound.

Mark listened carefully in case the noise had alerted someone. But there was no sign of a soul and the saw mill's whine provided a useful mask to his attack on the cabin. He bent to examine the plank. Although it didn't break, he thought that with repeated jumps he might just be able to weaken the floor.

There would be a good time to break out and a bad time. The cover of darkness, that's what he needed. But then what? Where to go and how to get there? He had nothing with him. He'd need food, water, a knife at the very least. His compass. Christ, all that stuff was back in his cabin. Even if he escaped, he'd have no option but to try to sneak back there, retrieve his stuff and get the hell out of this shithole.

He'd have to wait until dusk to try again, even though his thirst was now a raging torment. Having decided on his course of action, he was hoping perversely that no one would now come along and screw up his escape plan. He felt that if they fed and watered him, his resolve might falter, and his fate would be in their hands. But he was Director of CABS, unused to not being in control and it grieved him to be totally helpless, vulnerable. Worse still he'd put himself in their hands, willingly, gratefully. Would Sue have got herself into this situation? Probably not - she was more wary and prudent. And Paul? He was more suspicious, an occupational hazard. He thought, though, that perhaps Colin Wingent was more like himself, gullible and trusting, and, frightening thought this, that was how he'd ended up murdered.

What did they intend with him? There was that undercurrent of lawlessness in the logging camp that inclined him to think that they wouldn't hesitate to dispatch him. No qualms. That was the tidy option. And probably he wouldn't be the first. Who was there out here to police things?

He slammed his foot into the corrugated side of the cabin in fury and frustration. It rocked as if in a gale. He paused, thinking, and repeated it, putting all the force he could muster behind the kick. Something cracked loudly – his earlier jumps must have weakened the structure of the cabin. At first he thought he'd broken a bone in his foot, but it only throbbed with the effect of the kick. He pushed against the structure, and this time it rocked a little further. One of the back corner struts had partially split lengthways – it had been weakened with his first 'pile-driver'. Triumph flooded through him, threatening to make him reckless, but he knew it would be foolish to attempt a breakout now. He had to be patient. Wait for dusk.

He sat back down on the odious blanket and listened for any sound of someone approaching from the camp. The atmosphere had grown suffocatingly humid, and the bites he'd suffered during his wandering in the forest were itching. He tore off his shirt and rashly raked at two of the worst areas under his arms with his nails.

Plops sounded echoingly on the roof. Plop-hiss, plop-hiss - as drops of water boiled into vapour on the searing roof. Rain! The frequency increased. The drops resonating on the roof produced a cascade of reverberating sound. It was as though he was inside a metal drum being beaten with a stick.

With the rain his desire to quench his thirst became well-nigh impossible to bear. He looked around to see if there were any leaks and spotted a dribble of water filtering down between the corrugated roof panels. He put his shirt underneath the slow drips, and sucked the water off the soaked material. His fractured, divergent thinking immediately summoned up the image of chimpanzees using handfuls of crushed leaves as sponges to mop up the rain, and then sucking the water from them. When it came down to it, where was the difference?

The moisture greedily sucked from his sweaty, filthy shirt was pure nectar.

: ☼ :

Once again, he awoke with a start not intending to have fallen asleep, vowing to stay alert and vigilant. It was dark – no, almost dark. A peek under the sides and floor of the hut showed a low crescent moon's glow emerging mistily through the dispersing rain. With sunset at about six, he estimated the time as about seven o'clock, maybe half seven, With the dusk the rain had eased and was now more like a summer shower at home.

Time to do it. He limbered up a little to get the kinks out of his muscles, and put his shirt back on. Then, thinking of Beckham taking a penalty kick, aimed at what he thought was the weakest point – again and again, careless now of the sound.

"**Come on!**" Kick. "**Come on!**" Kick. "**Come on!**" Kick.

He built up a rhythm. Just as he was beginning to tire, his calves and feet protesting, the back corner of the structure crumpled under the assault – the strut holding up that corner cracked loudly, the hut tipped and the corrugated iron bent outwards. With further well-aimed kicks, he made the hole larger.

He crouched down and struggled out of the tight-fitting hole into the open, ripping his sorry shirt, taking large gulps of air, free from the suffocating, fetid miasma in the cabin. He lay on the ground, face to the clouded black sky, gazing at the low moon, gasping and feeling the balm of light rain on his face.

He knew he couldn't afford to linger there – there was always the chance that someone had heard the repeated banging and crack of wood splintering, or even that someone might take pity on him and bring some water. He had to get going.

First, though, he had to find out where he was in relation to the camp. Stiffly, he pushed himself to his feet and loped creakily alongside the narrow camping trail, through the sopping undergrowth, stopping now and then to do the chimp-sponge thing. In spite of the obvious extreme danger he was in, he was elated – freedom was a strong, heady wine. He began to laugh – and stopped himself suddenly, clamping a hand over his mouth. The laughter had an unsettling hysterical note to it. He didn't like the sound of it.

Presently, the path opened out into a wider space and he sobered up. Peering through the wet bushes, crouched down, sucking on some leaves, he could see the camp laid out in front of him; some lights percolating through window blinds, adding to the low moon light, provided sufficient illumination As before, as likely on every night he imagined, some figures lurched drunkenly about — now in a sticky, gloopy mud. As before, there were shouts and arguments, grunting sounds of fighting. Screams. He tried not to think too much about those — but prostitution was rife here. He'd been here long enough to notice poor, always black, always desperate-looking, women - no, underage girls really, breasts barely formed - forced into the sex trade. And even some pygmy girls, faces blank and eyes empty. What choice when you're starving?

Mark assessed the situation. He would have to skirt around the glutinous 'high street', over to the other side to get to his hut, retrieve his stuff.

"The game's afoot," he muttered. His stubborn streak was asserting itself - he wasn't going to be denied, not now that he had come through all the shit that had happened to him. He wasn't a Major's son for nothing. If little else, the old man had bequeathed him a certain pigheadedness, not always a lovely trait but here, now, it would see him fight tooth and nail to get out of this benighted hellhole.

He doubled his precautions now that he was so close to the centre of the camp, making a long loop to the north, which took him close to the looming hulk of the saw mill, towering like a decaying ghostly ship stranded on an eerie skeleton shore, a darker shadow against the night sky. It emanated an ominous air. He shivered.

He hadn't seen it before and stopped to assess whether anyone was around but the machines were silent now. The pungent resinous scent of newly-cut wood floated on the rain-sodden air. Massive logs were piled up in towering stacks beside the mill, their diameters exceeding his own height. In spite of himself, Mark crept closer, fearful yet fascinated by the end product of this whole enterprise. In the gloom, he detected the looming shapes of two massive vehicles – juggernauts, ready-piled with logs of wood chained down on the flatbeds. While some of the logs were impressive, others were clearly younger trees, not yet mature. He wished he knew enough botany to identify the species.

In the light of the moon, as he ran his hands over the sawn ends of the logs, he saw numbers and a name stamped into the wood. He could just make out the name on both logs - Rouge-Bolles – the logging company. He moved his fingers, feeling as much as seeing in the dim moonlight - these were the log numbers, each log being assigned a specific number, Bills of Lading numbers, if he recalled correctly. Forgetting his own predicament, he peered closely at one log then at the other – they seemed to share the same number – 498152. Which was odd. He was no expert but one thing he was fairly sure of was that each log should have its own BoL number – that much he'd retained from a phone chat with Colin Wingent after the VP's dinner. That and the stonkingly enormous prices some trunks could fetch.

He felt the log ends again, thinking. They were up to some sleight of hand here in the camp, giving two separate logs the same number. He remembered Colin said he suspected various tax dodges went on. That was it - a levy had to be paid on each log felled so giving two logs the same number slashed the amount to pay by half. *Was* that it?

On an impulse, not sure why he was doing it, he dashed between the piles of log, through the puddles and picked up some of the sawdust. As he held the fine chips in the palm of his hand, the discarded connection, begun when he was imprisoned in the hut, spluttered to life again. The splinters collected from poor Wingent's face, and this. Logging connected the two…

A nearby rustle brought him back to his plight.

He quickly shoved the sawdust into his shirt pocket, chiding himself for letting down his guard, swivelling his neck around like an owl. He waited, straining to hear something, but he was impatient, desperate to get out of this camp. Presently he crept on, crouched almost double, more wary as he got closer to his goal. There! There it was, the third down the row, and no BBQ tonight – too wet. Suppose they'd posted a guard outside? But why would they? He was safely incarcerated in the tin coffin.

There was no one he could see. Bent double, keeping to the inkiest shadows, he mounted the steps up to the cabin, praying they wouldn't creak, grasped the handle of the door and turned it gently. No squeak.

He let out the breath he'd been holding.

Inside, it was darker still, but he mentally recreated the layout of the furniture in the small cabin – using the method of loci, made famous by the Greek poet Simonides to identify the location of guests in a collapsed temple - and entered the bedroom. Here some light allowed him to see the chair with – miraculously – his tatty safari jacket still lying across it. He fumbled in the pockets, and, yes – the two pieces of paper – the twist of crystals, and the splinters which were assuming ever more importance. What else? Just two anti-malarial tablets left. The money belt with his passport photocopy, knife, compass, torch, mobe and note book, all still there under the mattress.

He was disproportionally elated to discover almost all his possessions, excepting his watch, as though this guaranteed he would make his escape.

"Bathroom – might as well use it, clean myself up a bit – I stink like a drain." He pushed aside warnings of the rashness of this decision as though his freeing himself from the hut and having got this far had bestowed upon him some invincibility. Besides his skin was crawling.

In the dark, he spotted his water bottle lying in the sink where he'd kept it handy. He put it to one side and ran water from the tap, splashed it over his face, arms, bathing the insect bites, all the while keeping an ear open for any sounds. He soaked his torn shirt and rinsed it through – he'd have to wear it wet. He debated whether to take a drink from the tap, but desperate though he was, the last thing he needed right now was a dose of dysentery. He filled his water bottle with the dubious water. He'd use the remaining permanganate to purify it when he got the chance.

He felt refreshed, soothing his bites with more cold water, pouring water over his head.

"Now what? Trek to Somalomo? By land? Or take a boat? If I take the boat, I'll be going upstream – would they catch me in another faster boat? If I go by land, would I make it? How long will it take them to realise I've gone? How far is it to Somalomo?" He was muttering all this to his haggard, unshaven reflection in the spotted mirror above the sink. He leaned close to the mirror trying to see better in the dim filtered light. His amber-coloured eyes were itchy and bloodshot. He was a sorry mess with the forehead lump still visible, plus the mozzie bites. Still, no permanent damage unless these bastards caught him.

Questions, questions, no answers. He scrubbed at his damp scalp, undecided, and winced as he touched the matching contusion at the back of his skull. His usual indecisiveness must not be allowed to hold sway.

Right. Right. He breathed deeply. Boat it is.

: ◻ :

The motorised pirogue, empty now of provisions, was stubbornly sticking to the treacly mud, and Mark was frightened, if he pushed harder, of the clinging mud making too loud a sucking noise. Inch by painful inch, it slid reluctantly into the river, Mark praying to the river gods there would be no splash.

Once it was floating at the edge of the brown river, he crawled carefully in and crouched on the bottom, breathing heavily. Obviously, he couldn't use the engine yet – he'd have to propel it by hand, somehow. Although he'd rowed at Uni, he had little experience of navigating small boats alone, but at least he knew the right direction to head in. He fumbled around on the damp bottom of the skiff, searching for an oar. Nothing. He began to panic. Where the hell was it?

He got out into the water's edge again, fearful of being discovered any minute, and scanned around the boat, swishing his feet around. The shouts and screams from the camp seemed too close. His hand connected with a solid long dark shape. An oar! Just the one, though.

He clambered back into the skinny canoe-type boat with his prize, trying to figure out how best to do this. The shape and structure of the pirogue was so different from a rowing boat. He recalled the dark figure standing at the bow when he'd been picked up – too visible. He settled for a kneeling position at the front with alternating left-right pulls through the water. As he left the bank behind, he remembered this was the position adopted by First Nation kayakers; it was not meant for this heavier motorised skiff. But he was moving at least. He glanced over his shoulder. All seemed quiet, for now.

He needed to put as much space between himself and the logging camp as possible.

On he pushed through the dark waters, stretching his shoulder muscles, the clearing sky now filling with sharp stars and the moon, higher now, gleaming on the silvered water ahead of him, beckoning him on.

Chapter
13

Theophile Djomo stared wide-eyed and open mouthed at the crumpled side of the hut where the man should have been. He crept silently closer, fearful in case the man was hiding, waiting to pounce. It was quiet. No one! There was no one there! No, not possible! Muller had hit the man hard with his sjambok, he'd said, when he found him nosing around the radio shack. He should still be staggering like a drunk, bouncing off the hut walls.

A sudden chill assailed him as he gaped aghast at the corner of the ruined hut, gently touching the jagged hole with the corrugated iron bent outwards. He'd come here late at night to check that all was well - he knew the penalty he was likely to pay if the man escaped, but he hadn't thought he could. He was just doing what he'd been told – his duty – putting the man in the hut. Many others had been put in here. None had escaped, some had died - eventually. This man was to die, anyway. He couldn't last long in the hut without food and water.

Now he had to be found, quickly.

He scanned the wet ground around the hut, playing his torch over the grass and shrubs, and immediately spotted a depression where someone had lain down on the ground. Peering ahead of the depression at the foliage and angling the torch beam, he could see that the man had passed this way – bent stems, disturbed ground. He rested the back of his hand on the ground, trying to estimate when he'd passed this way. No heat – the passing was some time ago, the early part of this night, he guessed, but it had rained and this made it difficult to be sure.

He peered closely from ground level all round the slight, almost invisible depression, and the signs showed the man had followed alongside the path back to the camp. Why? Why would he go that way? Djomo himself, in that situation, would have run as fast as possible the other way.

Hunkering down, he stopped to think, trying to put himself inside the strange man's head. There had to be an important reason why he'd go back towards the camp, why he'd put himself in extra danger. He closed his eyes to think. Then he had it –of course, he needed his knife, his compass. He'd gone back for them. Without those he wouldn't get very far, wouldn't survive. Ah. And his notebook – *that* was it.

He should have stolen those items earlier when the man had been asleep but since he was to die anyway there was no point, no hurry.

He ran swiftly back to the camp, and lurked a while at the back of the third cabin where the man had stayed, watching from the bushes. He could still be in there and maybe he was more dangerous than the other one, the one who watched over the trees – he was certainly tall, with lion-coloured eyes which stared at you, piercing your thoughts, making you feel uneasy. The other one had been easy to deal with, but he wasn't sure about this one.

He would be very careful.

All seemed quiet, so he crept stealthily up the steps to the veranda, close to the railings, avoiding the creaking part of the steps and stopping there to listen again. Nothing, just drips of water falling from the roof, and the usual camp sounds - a harsh cry, a dog barking, a loud argument. The cabin was empty – he could feel it.

He opened the wooden door for the second time – he knew it wouldn't squeak - and went quickly to the bedroom. He didn't really expect to see the man sleeping there, but he knew what objects were there in the bedroom.

His gaze scythed the room, taking in the chair. Now, there was nothing.

Yes, the man had come back here after escaping, but where had he gone then? It had been raining, so it wouldn't be easy to find where he went from this cabin as the camp tracks were a churned mass of muddy footprints. But wait, Djomo, in his place, would have left by the back door where he had just entered. Less mud, more vegetation. That wouldn't fool him, though. He was the best tracker in the camp. In the *arrondissement.*

He left the cabin and scouted carefully around, looking closely at the ground. The moonlight revealed boot prints going down the backs of the cabins towards the river. The river! The tall man, the Professor, had taken a pirogue, escaped by the river! He would have to tell the boss, no way to avoid that now. Anyway, was it really his fault that the man had destroyed the hut? He should have been put somewhere stronger, safer. That was the Afrikaans' fault. Better, much safer, they should have killed him straightaway.

: ⌺ :

His shoulder muscles were screaming, lactic acid building up. His kneeling position in the pirogue was all wrong. The rowing he'd done at Uni was very different to this left-right, dig-down style – anyway he was much younger and limber then. Although his strokes were fuelled by fear, the damn boat was too heavy, and he was fighting the current, sluggish though it was.

He'd been going for two hours now and his body, bruised, bitten and dehydrated, was betraying him. He'd have to stop soon, try to pull the boat up the bank, but this was hippo and croc country – perhaps that wasn't the most sensible course of action. He'd been listening for the signs but so far all he'd heard had been a hoarse roar from a grumpy hippo, and that was distant, and the persistent nocturnal insect chirrups. No silky sliding noise of a large reptile entering the water. In fact, the water was not exactly overflowing with river life. He dipped his hand in the water and palmed some. Rubbing his fingers together he felt the grittiness of silt - it was far too silted for much plant life, like the water hyacinths the hippos consumed in vast quantities.

The moonlight had illuminated no tympanic reflections of eyes peeking above the water-line, so hopefully no crocs in this particular stretch and anyway what he could see of the banks, silhouetted in the faint moonlight, were too steep; crocs liked the sloping banks from which they could stealthily and ominously slide down into the water, making no ripples, unseen until the final charge. Would they go for a pirogue? He thought they would.

He tried to steer the canoe towards the bank, but it was fighting him as it swirled in a strong eddy. He grabbed at an overhanging branch, causing the boat to wobble. With some difficulty he steadied the craft and clung on. He should have brought some rope to tie up the canoe. What the hell was he supposed to do now, with the boat bucking under him, his shoulders and arms creaking with fatigue?

: ¤ :

The face before him swelled with anger, growing red. Djomo watched with oddly detached interest, his Dutch courage bolstered by a swiftly drunk bottle of beer.

"What?!" The face bellowed. The veins were standing out on his forehead, and his neck. Djomo watched the throbbing veins. Muller had had more than a few beers, too, and it never improved his already short temper.

"How can we know he breaks out of the hut?" he asked. "Others have been there, not got out." He was being reckless in challenging, but he'd made the cold, correct calculation that Muller would need his skills more than the desire to punish him – for now, anyway. And the beer fortified him.

"Fool!" Muller spat and swung his sjambok, a stout whip made of rhinoceros hide.

He saw the sjambok descending and turned sideways so that it glanced off the greater muscle mass on the top of his shoulder and rebounded to hit the wall of Muller's cabin; it made a dent. Muller had a foul, murderous temper – he didn't think as clearly as he, Djomo, especially after drinking, and that was most nights. He needed reminding of the priorities. He rubbed his shoulder but was quietly gleeful about the fat pig's wall. One day soon, Muller would be made to pay a very high price for that. He, Djomo, would exact revenge. Meanwhile, he could wait.

"You should have checked the hut before, idiot!" Muller shouted, his face inches away, spittle speckling his face.

"Look, boss. We are wasting time while that white man gets away. We must start now. He has taken the pirogue…"

"How long? How long has the bastard been gone?" Muller growled, the vicious sjambok clutched in a meaty fist.

"I think he…not long ago, maybe two hours. But," he paused, looking slyly at Muller, "maybe he does not know we have other pirogues. We can catch him."

"Well don't just stand there – get the best one ready, make sure the motor's got enough fuel. I'm getting my gun and equipment. Go, go!" The sjambok was waved furiously, in dismissal this time.

Djomo dashed towards the boathouse, pleased at the way he had successfully diverted the boss' thoughts away from real punishment; he had seen some who had experienced Muller's temper apart from the Woodman. *If I can track the strange one with the yellow eyes then this will be forgotten.* Muller was volatile, but lived in the moment. *Once Djomo's lapse was sufficiently past, and other events had overtaken this, well then Djomo might even be rewarded*, but he, Djomo, would not forget. *No, his time would come and Muller would pay.*

He smiled in the dark as he prepared the canoe, checking the engine, tapping the fuel gauge.

The yellow-eyed one was dead.

: ♡ :

Mark took several deep breaths and bent over. He had to do this now – he could feel the lactic acid reaching deadening levels in his muscles. Then he wouldn't be able to hold on, and he'd drift backwards, the way he'd come.

132

He hung from the overhead branch while the pirogue danced under him, swirling in the eddies.

The motor! What was wrong with him? Stupidly he'd forgotten all about the blasted motor – surely it would be safe enough to use by now. He let go of the branch. Immediately, the small boat whirled once and joined the current – taking him downstream the other way.

He threw himself toward the stern, grabbed hold of the casing of the motor and tugged at the cord. These accursed things never, ever started first time.

It started first time!

"Hah, got you, you bastard!" he said triumphantly. But, as the motor got into its stride, he grew scared. The chugging reverberated back from the banks and the dense foliage and seemed to focus the noise like a sonic beam, straight down the river, seeming far too loud in the dark.

There was a slight bend up ahead, and he aimed the boat towards it, urging it forward. He had to make up time, put more distance between himself and the camp. Of course, he didn't know for certain that he would be pursued. Maybe they hadn't been to the little hut, or if they had, they wouldn't know which direction he'd taken. But even if they did, maybe they reckoned him better left to his own devices – they might figure that he'd be the instrument of his own downfall, the state he was in – a reasonable conclusion, that. Save them the trouble. He couldn't kid himself that his field crafts were up to scratch – they were too rusty, no doubt about that. But some of the training was coming back to him. It had done no harm, either, that he'd been forced to do the army's rigorous survival training. Oh yes, he'd eaten his fair share of fried earth worms, drunk nettle tea and learnt to make fires in the rain. The Major was no doubt looking down with grim satisfaction, enjoying this. What he had preached about survival disciplines to a young, petulant Mark, more concerned with saving than hunting animals, might now prove vital.

Here and now, one major problem was that he didn't know how far it was to Somalomo, didn't know how far he'd come or how much time he'd need.

He looked back nervously over his shoulder, down the long pathway of rippling quicksilver cast by the luminous moon. Foolishly, he'd not reckoned on there being more than one pirogue. Obviously, they'd need more than one to bring provisions, booze, into the camp – probably had a fleet. He should have stopped long enough to sabotage the rest. Squinting at the fuel gauge in the moonlight, he saw that it was low – very low.

The small boat rounded the bend, and gave him some respite from his anxiety. The chugging became a monotonous comforting rhythm. Presently, in spite of his dire situation, his head nodded down onto his chest as, exhausted, he shifted into the half-world of disconnected, shifting images.

The dreadful demise of Wingent. A *muti* killing to provide special powers. A lot of blood was missing. The liver. Little 'Adam' floating in the Thames. River gods. Splinters showing where he was killed? Not where he was found. Where was the killing done?

That semi-conscious stream of thought ended abruptly, as Mark's thoughts skittered to the stinking hut. Why was he put in there? Did Muller know he was there? Did Muller hit him? What would they have done with him, if he hadn't escaped? Was there any connection with the 'Shadow' who searched his room, nothing taken? The radio shack – not out of action. He could have used it. They – who are 'they'? – didn't want him to use the radio.

The 'Shadow' had read his notebook! That was it. There was something in his notebook…

His head lolled and jerked, lolled and jerked, like a puppet's.

: ⵔ :

"Can't you get more out of this thing?"

The flat vowels offended Djomo's ears.

"She don't go faster." In this dark night, Djomo could risk a glare at Muller.

They had been fighting the current for two hours or more, and Muller's temper was worsening, ordering Djomo to stop now and again so that he could listen to the night sounds.

"Stop. I want to listen," Muller would order, then stand up in the boat, slowly turning his large head, trying to catch a sound, as the pirogue drifted gently backward.

Stop – go faster – stop – go faster. On and on.

This time, Djomo dared to say, "I hear nothing. He has gone." A note of truculence had crept into his voice – he could be back at the camp enjoying a warm whore and a cold beer, in that order. This was a waste of time. The man was long gone, and he did not really care. Of course he said none of this to Muller.

He lit a cigarette, while Muller stood, a looming presence, at the bow, his heavy breathing audible.

"Hey, Djomo, you lazy bastard, unclog your bloody ears and listen. We're not going back until we get that nosey *baster.*"

If he had escaped, Djomo knew the man stood little chance of survival and almost none of getting back to Yaounde. Djomo knew his bush.

He blew out the smoke in a long stream, stained blue where it caught the moonlight, and turned his head. There came a very faint rhythmical sound. He listened, his head cocked to one side.

: ♡ :

Mark jolted awake. A microsleep, sufficiently long to disorient and confuse him, not enough to refresh. What had awoken him? A change in the engine's beat.

The engine! He looked at the fuel gauge. As he'd dreaded, it had run out of fuel. It was running on empty. Even as he stared at the gauge, the engine gave one last burble and died. Immediately, in the sudden descended silence, the boat began to drift with the current.

Mark fumbled for the oar in the bottom of the boat, then stopped, frozen. A shiver of fear passed through him as he detected what sounded like a faint throbbing sound.

He should have risked the motor sooner, made some distance between himself and – who? He had to assume that it was Muller or one of his sidekicks. Maybe there was more than one boat. Even if there was only one, and the pirogues held no more than three, he was still outnumbered.

He squinted down the river. There was just the quivering silver line of the moon, angled differently after the bend. It was difficult to assess how far away they were behind him – it sounded the same level now as when he'd first detected it, but sound was distorted and reflected by the lush, river-dipping foliage that lined both banks here.

He made a decision – he'd be better off out of the river.

He steered the boat towards the north bank and made a grab at the overhanging branches. They swept gracefully down into the water rippling the surface, and he was able to grab a handful. At least there were no eddies here.

Now what? If he could just bring the boat tight in to the bank, there was a fair chance the sweeping branches and leaves would hide it.

He steadied himself, digging the oar forcibly into the muddy bottom, where it stuck upright and held the boat fast against the bank. He broke off several slender whippy branches. One, he slid through the ring at the bow and tied the ends together, his fingers like awkward sausages, not at all sure if this would work.

He took another branch, threaded this through the first and tied those ends together, daisy-chaining a makeshift anchor rope. All the while, his ears were cocked for signs of the approaching boat, sweat slid down his neck and his sausage fingers stubbornly refused to work fast.

He couldn't tell if he heard his heart thumping or an engine.

Finally, after five loops, he thought he could risk it. He was just able to reach over and grasp another handful of trailing branches, and quickly put one foot on the bank. Holding his daisy-chain in one fist, he grasped a tree trunk and wound his 'anchor' around a sturdy-looking branch. It held.

He crouched down, panting with the effort and fear, his mouth dry, and listened again. The engine noise was more defined now – they must be closer but with sound absorption and reflection slicing off the higher frequencies it was impossible to tell how close behind they were.

No time to waste, he set about hiding the boat behind arranged boughs. Of course, he couldn't see how effective this was from the riverside, but it would have to do.

He'd no idea how persistent these people were - would they give up after a while or stubbornly keep going? One thing he did know – having got this far, he was buggered if they were going to get him.

He backed away from the riverside, stumbling deeper into the bush, leaves whipping against him and dislodged irate insects whining about his head. His shoulder muscles were screaming in protest from the unaccustomed poling, and his legs, anaesthetised from the prolonged kneeling in the boat, refused to work properly.

He slapped at a persistent mosquito which had managed to draw blood, and prayed that missing out on his anti-malarial tablets whilst imprisoned wouldn't make him vulnerable. That was ridiculous – what was he worried about? He had to survive another bout of jungle trekking first, and in worse condition than the first time.

He checked the Silva compass hung round his neck. There was no path here, but he reckoned if he kept going north, at right angles to the river Dja, he must intersect at some point the track that would lead to Somalomo. What he had to do was put maximum distance between himself and his pursuers. Pursuers! He stopped. Something was wrong. There was no sound, no regular sound. No engine noise.

They'd stopped.

Would they be able to find where he left the river?

: ◘ :

"It stopped."

It was another of their halts, and Djomo, by now thoroughly bored and irritated by the whole chase, strove to keep the delight out of his voice.

Muller grunted. "Keep quiet."

They both listened, Djomo trying to keep the boat stationary with the oar.

Silence, except for the usual nocturnal suspects, but they were both adept enough in bush lore to distinguish between man-made and natural sounds.

"He got out of river," Djomo offered.

" *Hou jou bek* — shut up - we'll see who chickens out first."

Five minutes later, still nothing.

"Definitely stopped. Right — use the oar. Slowly." A hoarse whisper.

Muller swept the banks with a powerful light from a heavy torch, cutting swathes through the darkness.

They were barely making way against the current, inching forward, sliding quietly through the water.

After several minutes, Djomo decided to offer up his considered opinion since he was doing all the hard work, and drinking time was fast slipping by.

"That man can't survive. He doesn't know this place. You have to know this place like I do. It will be very hard for him."

He paused trying to gauge Muller's emotional temperature, which was variable at the best of times, and could erupt volcanically.

"Let's go back," he finally ventured.

"Too many whores, man. That's your problem." Muller gave a sharp humourless bark. "You'll get the clap – if you haven't already. Keep your mind on the job."

: ☐ :

He felt suffocated. There was no movement of the humid air under the thick canopy – the moisture was trapped, along with the pockets of whining aggressive insects. He had no idea how far he'd staggered along, but he sensed he was at the end of his endurance. It wasn't just this jaunt – it was everything else that had gone before, which was having a cumulative draining effect upon his stamina. His clothes were soaked with sweat, intolerably itchy, and he had to resist the temptation to rip them off and rake at his flesh with his nails.

Had he made the biggest error of his life in leaving the river? The river, a tempting vision of silky water running over his fevered body took over his brain. He half-turned to go back, but looked up through the greenery.

A sullen dawn was just breaking. It had been hours since he'd left that noisome camp, hours rowing and and hours trudging painfully, with swollen, throbbing feet. He daren't take his boots off – his feet would swell further and he'd never get them back on again.

There was no path to follow, but soon he would have the rising sun on his right to keep him oriented. Would it be on his right? He didn't know anymore.

His feet moved automatically. Why were they so determined to get him? He thought he'd figured it out earlier, a lifetime ago, but now nothing was clear and his memory was still fogged. Maybe because he'd caught them out in a lie, when he'd discovered that the radio was working after all.

So bloody what? Was that any reason to whack him? Then there was the business of the 'Shadow' searching his room, and that happened *before* the radio incident. It hadn't looked like straightforward robbery, either. Was that all of a piece with the radio?

The happy campers must have been suspicious of him from the off. Why? What had he said...? That he had to tell the authorities about Wingent asap. That's when they'd claimed the radio was broken. And then the Shadow had stolen nothing but had flicked through his notebook, his description of the corpse of Colin Wingent...

He lumbered into a tree trunk and, too exhausted to go round it, slid down, his eyes closing, and descended into a dark well of dreamless sleep.

Chapter 14

They all sat round the veranda table. Ekoko had gathered everyone together, from the most senior to the most junior - a slight lad of seventeen with large eyes and a wobbling adolescent voice, contrasting with his skinny frame. Ekoko's nephew, Honore Njitapa. There were five altogether, Ekoko, Sue and two other wardens, plus Honore.

A war council. But a puzzled, bewildered one.

They sat there, mute, everyone by now seriously worried about Mark and Nkemi's disappearance.

"Tchie is my brother." This came out of the blue from a serious, quiet warden. Like Tchie, Louis said little except what needed saying.

"He is your cousin, Louis." That was a statement rather than a question from Ekoko.

"He is like my brother," conceded Louis. "Same blood." He fingered a raised scar running along his left cheek. It was the twin of Tchie's scar. The other warden nodded sympathetically.

Sue decided they must get things moving.

"They've been gone four days now, and we've heard nothing. Nothing at all. We have to decide what to do next."

"The Commissaire in Yaounde says the Commissaire in Somalomo heard nothing, too." Ekoko looked around at the other four, a sombre expression on his normally amiable face. Since it was so unlike him, Sue guessed he wanted the others to realise the importance of what he was saying, and not dismiss Tchie Nkemi's absence merely as casual absenteeism. After all, it was not entirely unknown for relatives to suddenly absent themselves for a time for family duties. But this was different because both Tchie and Mark had vanished.

"We have to decide what we're going to do now." Sue repeated herself, looking over at Caro anxiously. Now that she was near her time, Sue wanted everything to go smoothly; she didn't want her picking up tensions on her quivering emotional antennae. Sue had debated sending an email herself to Caro, purporting to come from Mark. She'd seen Caro checking the computer for messages.

She chewed a thumbnail, seriously troubled.

"Should one of us follow their route, do you think?" Sue asked Ekomo.

"That could be very dangerous – like throwing someone else into the river after a drowning person." Ekoko squeezed his eyes shut as soon as he'd said this. "Ach, I am sorry. Not a good thing to say."

There was a throat clearing from the far end of the table, and an adolescent voice, wavering between bass and falsetto piped up.

"*I* will go. I know the Dja River. I will find them."

They all looked at the teenager.

"No, Honore. I know you are brave boy and want to help, but we need you here with our guests. Anyway, your mother would kill me if I let you go." Ekoko's diplomacy in gently letting down the adolescent showed why he was senior warden. Although the lad looked crestfallen, he accepted the truth of Ekoko's statement without comment.

"I'm going to the High Commission." Sue had decided. "They need to be told, and there must be something they can get the Cameroon government to do – like mounting a large scale search."

"Don't be too sure that the government will do the bidding of your Embassy." Ekoko said somewhat sharply.

Sue squinted up at the senior warden, realising that she had sounded like some old Africa hand from colonial times, who only had to click their fingers to have some government lackey rush to obey. Those times were well past, and good riddance. She hadn't meant to sound that way, but she hadn't thought how it might come across to Ekoko. Maybe that was a problem hung over from French colonial times, that unthinking, insensitive assumption, falling into a reflexive way of acting without a thought as to how it was perceived. She should have known better, as a psychologist.

"I apologise, Ekoko. It wasn't meant that way – I just thought the HC might have more contacts, and perhaps more influence than us mere scientists."

She watched Ekoko's face relax, and the awkward moment passed.

"Yes, of course. You should contact them. They need to know if one of your people is in trouble." He put a hand gently on her shoulder.

"Two, if Colin Wingent still hasn't turned up."

"And where the Professor is, my brother is," stated Louis with finality, nodding.

"Let's hope so," Sue said. She got up, glancing over again at Caro, sitting some distance off out of hearing, rubbing her swollen abdomen, looking thoughtful.

: ⏣ :

The message sent from the Rouge-Bolles camp deputy manager was disturbing. The previous little difficulty had been dealt with, but now here was another one to take its place. And one which might prove harder to sort out. He would have to do something. Not the same solution as before, though. That wouldn't wash twice. So – what, then?

He adjusted the cuffs of his immaculately white shirt, considering.

It would have to be quick, but the troublesome Professor would have to be found first. He had to trust that that lumbering dolt Muller could find him and dispatch him – this time making sure that no one else could find him, or his remains. Supposing he didn't, though – what then?

Then things would have to be arranged here – a welcoming committee. Swift and sure – and above all trustworthy. Yes, he knew just the person.

He dug out his mobile phone and scrolled down to the number.

: ⏣ :

Djomo swept the powerful beam over the river banks. Muller was taking his turn at the tiller.

Djomo suddenly stiffened, pointing.

"Go back, go back. There, there."

"What? There's nothing there. That moonshine you drink's made you blind, man."

Just as Muller said this, the beam struck a sharp light off something shiny. Not croc eyes - just the one reflection.

"See? I was right." Djomo was triumphant.

Muller grunted.

"Take this tiller and give me the torch. Get us in to the bank over there. Come on. Hurry."

The arrogant Boer never acknowledged Djomo's contribution. It was as though he couldn't bring himself to do it – as though he would become a smaller man if he had to thank a black man, Djomo thought as he changed places. He ground his teeth. His time would come, he knew – he would bring Muller down. He must take steps to ensure this. Muller would realise that he was nothing without him.

But not now – now they had to deal with another white. He dug the oar savagely into the silt. The river, it occurred to him, had got more muddy over the years as the bank soil, released by cutting down the trees, washed into it. Fewer fish to catch, too. Part of him thought, fleetingly, that this was a pity.

Muller's beam showed a static reflection, which resolved itself into a hidden pirogue as they approached. They swept aside the veiling branches. Yes, there it was. The one the tall professor had taken. Djomo recognised it immediately – it's dents, the oars with the patches of paint still clinging to the wood. An odd-looking makeshift rope had been improvised to tether the boat to the bank.

Muller whistled through his teeth, satisfied.

"He can't be far away. Tie up quickly."

Djomo secured their boat, and they both scrambled up the steep bank. The Boer stopped to check his rifle, then pushed Djomo forward to go ahead of him. He, Djomo, was the best tracker in the area. Muller would have to follow his lead, wherever Djomo led him. He savoured that thought.

He bent to feel the ground and examine the immediate area for any signs. He could see in the grey light that the man had crouched here, where the ground was slightly damp; and – he laid the back of his hand over one of the faint impressions - recently. He straightened to scrutinise the surrounding vegetation. He was looking for broken stems, bent leaves, signs that would indicate the direction the man had taken.

Chapter
15

The low murmurs, like wispy paper rustling, disturbed him in some undefined threatening way. There was the stink of menace lurking in their voices. What were they saying to him? And where were they? He tried to look around, but he was restricted, muscles heavy as lead, and the light had an ominous yellow-ochre tinge as though from a diseased sun. The voices went on, murmuring, now more malevolently, closing in. He couldn't make out the words — they ran together, blurred, overlapped. And separated — became the hideous poem — he knew these words, sickening words, as they hissed sibilantly into the foul air...

I had a dream, which was not all a dream.
The bright sun was extinguish'd, and the stars
Did wander darkling in the eternal space,
Rayless, and pathless, and the icy earth
Swung blind and blackening in the moonless air;
Morn came, and went—and came, and brought no day,
And men forgot their passions in the dread of this their desolation, and all hearts

Were chill'd into a selfish prayer for light:

Cold crept over his body, pinning him down with paralysing fear as he watched the sickly sun dim. Where had he heard those terrible, fateful words? Why did he remember them now? The voices weren't human! Now they spoke about him, cursed him, but they weren't human. Terror washed over him but he still couldn't move, couldn't make a noise. Then the insane liquid sounds cleared and he knew – he knew! – what they were saying, these dark inhuman voices.

"See what you have done," another hissed.

"Die, you must die," one sibilant voice rose above the others.

"Evil, evil, evil." Others chanted in their spectral voices.

The others whispered their agreement, their voices like a bleak chilling wind. They were closer now – he could hear their raspy limbs scraping along the floor. Something scratched along his face, and there was a shrill, piercing scream that went on and on.

His voice! He was screaming!

His eyes flew open and he saw – two figures looking down at him. They had the wavering insubstantiality of Munch's 'Scream' figure. That haunted expression, like gazing into the endless void of empty space. A realisation that you are nothing...

But even as he cringed, they too stepped back, seemingly more frightened of him, eyes wide and fixed on his face.

His heart was hammering, rapid in his ribcage, thunderous in his ears, as he continued to gaze at them fearfully. Two inconstant spectres.

The figures began to slowly stabilise gaining substance. They were real, not dream figures.

He breathed through his open mouth - inhale, exhale, inhale, exhale - trying to calm himself, waiting for his vision to clear. A vivid dream, that's all. Just a dream, its afterimages still polluting his brain. No, it wasn't a dream – how could he have heard Byron's 'Darkness' in a dream? Word for word! He'd been forced to rote learn that desolate poem at boarding school as punishment for something – refusing to do something. He'd never forgotten it. Its hideous images of a dead galaxy, all hope extinguished, had stayed lodged in his fertile mind, insinuating its fearful images into his childhood nightmares. But he'd left those and the poem behind long ago...

What was happening?

The others hadn't moved at all, just continued to stare at him.

Were they real people?

When his autonomic nervous system had damped down sufficiently, he tried to sit up, but his body wouldn't obey. The others immediately moved back in unison again. He tried to hold up a shaking hand, an imprecation, and cleared his throat. His hand flopped back down, useless.

"I'm sorry. Really," he said pointlessly. His voice sounded like a rusty old saw. "A bad dream." Bad dream? He normally slept like a log, scarcely remembering his dreams. None had ever been as terrifying as this. Night terrors, a sleep disorder suffered by some poor souls, he'd never experienced. Just the usual childhood nightmares. This was something of another order altogether, its tattered remnants clinging to his brain like a shroud, clogging his thoughts.

Now he lay back with a groan and examined his surroundings. He was lying down on the ground on a woven grass mat - had given up for now trying to sit up - and he was in some type of shelter, roof, walls, palm leaves. How did he get here? Why was he here? What had happened - before? He couldn't summon up the right memories.

He re-focused his gaze to take in the two standing silently by him. The older man wore an animal skin, diminutive in height but wiry, his face wizened, holding a stick - not a stick, a spear - in one wrinkled hand.

The other was a girl, no, woman, well advanced in pregnancy. As he stared at her abdomen, she placed a protective hand over her swelling. The same build, same wiry strength.

He looked more carefully at their faces again.

Of course. His thinking was sluggish. *Pygmies!* The Baka pygmies of this region.

They were still staring at him as though transfixed – or frightened? He tried a smile and reached out a hand, palm up. His hand moved slowly as though through a dense Junovian gravity. It sank back, defeated, into his lap looking like a dead fish. He stared at it, tried out his other arm, his legs – they felt as heavy as lead, too. Perhaps he was better off just lying here – he was beginning to feel a little more *compos mentis*, the ragged shadows of the nightmare, or whatever it was, the horror that poem always instilled in him, were leaving, dispersing wisps of smoke in his mind.

"How did I get here?" He waved his slow hand around, languorously. How difficult it was to talk without gestures.

The old man – an elder? – spoke rapidly, pointed at the woman, who had said nothing, still gazing, unblinking, at Mark.

He remembered now. He had lain down, exhausted, having trekked as far as he could after leaving the pirogue.

Then what? He must have fallen asleep. How in God's name had he ended up here, wherever 'here' was?

He peered around the elder to look through the entrance of what, he could tell now, was some sort of bivouac made of palm leaves and branches, to see a clearing. Other people were moving outside, going about their business. A vine basket filled with some plants hung down in the entrance to the hut.

These were the Baka people of Cameroon. He had wanted to meet them, these people so close to the forest, so knowledgeable about their forest, living in exquisite balance with their environment. The much-put-upon pygmies of this region, abused, enslaved even, by the more assertive Bantu and by illegal loggers alike, ousted from their villages, left destitute and worse - deprived of their deep spiritual connection with the forest. Mark frowned in concentration, trying to remember the literature. He silently thanked the time he'd spent reading up on the various ethnic groups before embarking on this so-far fateful trip. Right – so think – what do you recall? His brain was as languid as his limbs, slowly sorting through information. Homing in...

"Jengi!" That was it.

This caused a rapid synchronised intake of breath from the two people still standing, looking down on him. The woman took a step back, fear glinting in her eyes. Anxious-sounding conferring followed.

"Jengi," he said again, more softly this time – their name for the spirit of the forest.

Had he made a *faux pas*? Perhaps it was a sacred word, not to be pronounced by insane outsiders. He tried to remember more of what he'd read, but his brain was still fogged.

So quickly that he had little time to react, the woman knelt and stared intently into his eyes.

"Jengi?" She repeated the word with a rising inflection.

Mark thought a little. The beginnings of some form of communication. He moved his head slowly like a nodding dog, trying a smile, hoping it didn't look too strained.

The elder man rushed from the hut, and Mark wondered what was going to happen. He tried to look appealingly directly into the eyes of the young woman, trying a bit of the old Celtic charm. Instead, she reacted with some alarm, drawing back and pointing tentatively to his eyes.

Ah, so that was it. His damned eyes, a startling saffron orange, had caused astonishment before, although occasionally had been called alluring in his better moments. But not repulsion — not so far at any rate.

"Look," he said, and crossed and uncrossed his eyes, then smiled his best, he hoped, enchanting, if slightly strained, grin.

She gazed intently a bit longer at him, then broke into a wide smile, laughing.

As they were both laughing the elder man returned with a younger, well-muscled man. They stood behind the woman, evidently wondering what was so amusing.

She spoke rapidly to them, pointing to his eyes. With any luck, she'll tell them I'm hardly any threat. A harmless, silly person — a clown.

"White man," the young man said suddenly, his brow creased in a frown.

"You speak English?" Mark asked, surprised.

"Mmm. Campers. You from campers?" He spoke in halting English as though he seldom used the language, giving

Mark a suspicious look, the furrow at the bridge of his nose deepened. At this word, there was a hiss from the elder.

"No, no." He shook his head vigorously causing his vision to wobble again, out of synch with his head movements. How to explain the dire straits he'd found himself in. How they'd come to find him – rescue him, as they must have done, though he remembered nothing of it. What he was doing there. He guessed the loggers weren't popular – they exploited the Baka dreadfully, forcing them to endure horrific conditions.

He tried sitting up again carefully. It was a little easier. He inched himself back to rest his back against the wall of the hut.

"I came here," he said carefully, "to watch the animals – chimpanzees – ah, monkeys." Here he pointed to his eyes. "Not to kill, not to eat, just to look." The three exchanged glances at this, ones that were difficult to interpret. Press on.

"Scientist." He pointed to himself. "I am a scientist. A zoologist." That was more translatable than comparative psychologist or primatologist.

. The young man, still with a frown, passed this information on to the others, but Mark couldn't tell from their expressions whether they understood or believed him.

"You look animals?" The young man asked with a lift of his chin, doubt written all over his face.

"Yes, yes. But not kill." He'd underestimated the youngster's grasp of English. This was translated to the other two, and some surprise, or doubt, was evinced.

But now came the difficult part. What should he tell them of what he'd seen – Colin's body, the attack on him, hunting him? He knew there was little love lost between the

Bantu and the Baka, and that the Baka had been displaced, turfed out of their villages by logging companies, their beloved forests destroyed. Worse, some Baka girls were forced to prostitute themselves to the vile dregs inhabiting the camps, odious garbage of the world, catching God knew what STD's. From what he'd read and heard, the pygmy girls were popular because they charged less and were more childlike; and there was this obscene belief that you couldn't get AIDS from a child. His eyes were drawn to the woman's swollen belly. Once again she put a protective hand over her stomach.

"I will try to explain. I found a body – a *dead* white man, killed like –um - like an animal. My driver stole the car, drove away. I was left alone in the forest. I walked and walked to the river Dja," - the others recognised the name of the river, so Mark nodded encouragement, waited for the translation. His throat felt like sandpaper; he'd have dearly loved to have asked for a drink, but he knew he had to try to convey his situation and his place in the scheme of things first. Establish what his position was, his essential harmlessness.

He examined the ground. Yes, that would do.

"Here. The river Dja." He drew a wiggly line with a finger, and a cross where he thought he'd reached the river. "Me." Pointed at his chest.

The young man knelt down and peered at the scratchings in the dust.

"Then a boat came." Blank looks. "A pirogue."

Ah. Knowing looks were exchanged. It seemed he had their attention. He remembered these people had a strong oral tradition of telling stories, stories which were passed down the generations. An oral history. He wondered if *this* story would enter their repertoire. Perhaps a bit more drama was in order.

"Two men – one white, one black, a Bantu – took me to the camp." He drew a circle for the camp near the line of the river.

At the word 'camp', again the reaction was startling. A loud hiss of air expelled through the teeth, and a rapid vocal exchange accompanied by angry expressions, all three talking at once.

Now he was getting some real idea of how things stood here, between the logging camps and the locals.

Now he knew how to play this. Clearly the loggers were the bogeymen. Scarcely surprising.

"I was a prisoner in the camp." He mimed being bound by his hands. "And look." He bent his head and indicated the lump on the back of the head he'd earned that night by the radio shack. The others leant in to peer.

The woman's hand reached out carefully to feel the lump nestling in his curly black hair, and drew her hand back sharply, saying something to the others.

A bit of sympathy won't go amiss, so he put on a hurt expression.

"I escaped." He mimed breaking his bonds. "And ran to the river, the Dja, took a bo – uh - a pirogue, and rowed." He mimed 'rowing' and pointed to the river, running his finger along the line to where he thought he'd disembarked.

The young man, frown gone, animatedly translated this exciting adventure, the other two nodded then three pairs of shining eyes turned expectantly towards him.

"I heard them chasing me, hunting me. The white one had a gun." He acted out shooting at this point, getting into the spirit of the thing. "I left the river and walked – and

156

walked." Another line running from the river into the forest on the north bank.

"No food, no water. Then I fell." He feigned collapse on the floor.

Dramatically, he then sat up and encompassed them, trembling arms held wide against the pull of gravity.

"You saved me, brought me here. And I am very, very grateful to all of you." He hoped this corny emotional gesture could convey that he knew he owed them his life. He didn't know who'd found him, how they'd carried him – or why they would do such a thing, associating whites as they must with the brutal, callous loggers.

"I am *not* a camper. We want to protect the animals of the forest." We? They might well wonder who the hell 'we' are.

He looked at them as the young man translated as best he could, following Mark's mimes, trying to assess their reaction to what he'd said. He rubbed his legs, trying to get more feeling back into them.

When the young man had finished, all stared at him, silently, the elder man pursing his lips either in sympathy or doubt. Which?

Then the woman left, returning with a bowl of liquid, which she passed to Mark. He sniffed carefully at it.

"Water!" He gurgled it down. "Thank you, thank you."

He was feeling more human and recovering fuller use of his muscles with every minute that passed. Now for introductions. He shifted to get into a more upright position and pointed to his chest.

"Mark." Then he pointed to the elder man with a querying expression on his face, feeling he ought to be addressed first.

"Bo-dawa," the old one pronounced with dignity, as though this was something Mark should have known.

But the young man intervened, laughing.

"He say 'people of the monkey clan' – that is who we are, this clan. But his name is Boukou" – at this the elder nodded his head – "and I am Mosakamo, but I was Bo-chantier when I work at camp." Mark recalled reading that social identity was a shifting concept for the Baka depending upon the social context and circumstances – perhaps a more honest reflection of the changing social roles we all assume in different situations. He scarcely dare ask the young woman's identity fearing further confusion. She saved him the trouble by coming forward, and pointing to her chest as Mark had done.

"Bo-dwa." She then reached out to Mark's chest, and said "Maak."

"Yes, yes." Mark's broad smile made her laugh once more.

Again Mosakamo offered an explanation.

"She is person of - what? – medicine, because of you."

"But I thought 'dawa' was monkey. You said - " Mark's head was beginning to spin again.

"Not 'dawa' –'*dwa*'."

"Why is she a person of medicine - because of me?" God, this was getting confusing – these shifting identities.

"Because she work to cure you." Mosakamo turned to Bo-dwa and muttered something. She went to the entrance and brought over to Mark the vine basket containing the plants. She picked out one plant and showed it to him, pointing to his mouth.

"Look." Mosakamo gestured at the plant.

"Ah. I see. She's been treating me, helping me. Thank you, Bo-dwa." He accepted the plant, bowing his head.

"You take little of that," Mosakamo added helpfully. "Big dreams, strong." He sketched out big dreams with his hands.

That's for sure, Mark thought. He examined the plant more closely – the flower pretty, white with pink spots. I've seen pictures of this. I *know* what this is. The pygmies use this to attain a religious state...

"Bloody hell, woman. You gave me a psychedelic!" he burst out. Small wonder he'd had those nightmares – he'd been having a trip not a nightmare. Ibogaine, that was it. From the root of this shrub, *Tabernanthe iboga*. A psychoactive alkaloid. This much botany he did know – there was a whole semi-religious cult built up around this plant in some areas – the cult of the Fang, or some such strange nonsense that seemed more fitting to 'King Solomon's Mines'.

Bo-dwa looked surprised at his reaction, then spoke rapidly to Mosakamo.

"Ah – she want know what you see when you sleep."

"Well she might." Mark muttered. "Talk about being used." He gazed up at Bo-dwa, considering. She'd had the best of intentions, and to tell the truth, he was beginning to feel a great deal better and stronger than he had for a while. He decided to wing it, dress it up a little. A lot. These people valued a good tale.

He smiled at them all, preparing his lie.

"I was in a beautiful green forest, full of animals, bright birds singing, butterflies, flowers, ripe fruit…" He shaped his hands, now more inclined to obey him, in the air above his head.

This was translated.

159

They were hanging on every word, leaning in towards him.

"... there was music in the air. I walked around happy. The animals were not frightened of me. I stroked them, stroked the duiker, the monkey, sat with the gorilla. There was a rainbow glowing in the sky. Then..." Dramatic pause. "Then darkness fell like a veil...no, like the end of the world, all the animals disappeared, the lovely music stopped... It became cold and a drumming sound started."

It seemed to be going down well. They were still watching his face, transfixed.

"Then there were loud voices, chasing me, getting closer, closer – like evil spirits. I was frightened. I screamed, then woke up, and here I am. Saved." That bit, at least was near enough true.

He finished with an expansive gesture Henry Irving would be proud of.

There was a pause, then Bo-dwa exhaled, satisfied, as though this was the outcome she'd been expecting. They relaxed, and evidently began discussing the meaning of the weird person's dreams.

Suddenly, there was a child's yelp of fear, and a young boy came dashing towards Bo-dwa, to hide his face in her swollen belly.

Mark felt the ground shaking, like the tremors before an earthquake. The adult Baka all looked at each other, their faces tight with tension.

The thundering and shaking grew louder, and the pots tossed and danced in the entrance to the hut. There were shouts, anger mixed with fear, from those outside.

Still uncertain of his legs, Mark crawled outside to see what was happening.

The tremors grew, and palm leaves were shaken from the roof. Then an explosive roar came from the single track road near the village as a huge yellow Renault truck, five massive russet-coloured trunks on its fifty foot trailer, burst from the bush and swept past the village, sending children and dogs scattering, leaving in its wake a roiling cloud of fine red-brown dust billowing round the trees and bushes.

The whole scene stunned the senses.

As the dust began to settle creating a film covering the leaves, bushes, huts and people, Mosakamo coughed, spat, and said, "Every day, every day."

Boukou sat with his head bent, muttering and hacking, trying to clear his throat.

"What does Boukou say?"

"They kill the forest, they kill us."

The small skinny boy lifted his head from Bo-dwa's belly and stared folornly at Mark. Bizarrely, given the context, Mark saw he was wearing a red Manchester United shirt, tent-like on his small frame. A reject garment from the sweatshops, undoubtedly.

Other villagers had gathered under the grass awning in front of the hut, drawn by curiosity and perhaps the faint hope that Mark, being also white like the logging bosses, might be able to do something to rid them of the thundering monsters.

"How long will forest live? Animals? Baka?" Mosakamo's question was rhetorical, for he knew, they all knew, the answer.

"From the camp, wasn't it? You get this every day?" Mark was partly talking to himself and partly to those around him – he'd quickly picked up on a Baka habit where speech may not be directed towards a particular person. The young boy crept closer.

"One of those trunks will fetch thousands of pounds in Europe. *You* won't see the profit, that'll go into officials' back pockets."

Mosakamo translated for anyone who cared to listen.

Now others were contributing, talking over each other, a rising, keening sound. Mark looked to Mosakamo for help.

"Logging kills forest, Baka say – kill Jengi. They use bulldozers" – he used his hand to demonstrate a flattening – "do this. Hurt land. Make desert."

Mosakamo tried to quiet the flood of voices, but this was how the Baka discussed important issues, speech overlapping, intermingling.

"He say" – here, he pointed to a scowling younger man holding a long stick – "campers give guns to workers, and they kill all animals. Now there are no animals for us. We who live here. Yes, yes," - he pointed to another older woman with a wizened face and four front teeth missing – " Emaluan says forest is empty. How do we feed our children? And Boukou said river is dying."

Boukou nodded his head vigorously, then his voice cut through the babble, and Mosakamo translated in the sudden quiet that followed his words.

"He say Jengi is dead."

In the profound silence that followed this statement, Mark felt shame sweeping over him. It stemmed more from his own unforgivable ignorance than any feeling that, as a westerner, a white, he was partly to blame. He was, of course – and the whole damn lot of us – for letting this situation go on. It wasn't just his beloved chimps and bonobos doomed by unstoppable greed, but these gentle people who had developed an extraordinary equilibrium with their environment – who trod so lightly on the earth.

He stood, suddenly upset and more angry than he could remember being for a long time, and as most of the villagers hadn't seen him upright, they fell back a pace. They came up to his chest, and this disconcerted him for a second. He needed to walk around, think, get rid of the last vestiges of ibogaine lingering around his synapses.

"Uh – I'm going to pee. I have to think." This he addressed generally to the assembled and bewildered crowd, and dashed off to a nearby thicket.

Chapter 16

He was sitting, exhausted, dispirited, with his back against a large, rough-barked tree, head hanging. All that had gone before had taken its toll on his reserves. He'd acquired the quiet but vigilant attention of the young boy in the ManU shirt — Bo-dwa's child? - who sat nearby, not looking at him directly – just being there – playing something like jacks with five pebbles. He'd played that when he was a child. It was peaceful, the pebbles clicking gently, just some low bird sounds, some insects buzzing, the quiet child. Soporific. He was so drained. He'd been yomping through the jungle, hit, imprisoned, fled in a bloody-impossible-to-row boat and finally rescued and drugged.

His head sank slowly down onto his chin as he descended into the dark chasm of exhausted sleep, this time free of drug-induced nightmares.

: ◻ :

On the fringes of his consciousness, some shouts impinged, sound of lightly running feet. Then – how much later? - Mosakomo was shaking his shoulder.

"Come now. Now, Maak! Your hunters here. You hide."

Mark was awake in a flash. He'd been stupid enough to let his guard down. Why had he supposed the dynamic duo would give up? Their persistence was a measure of how crucial it was to get back to Yaounde as soon as possible, to the authorities – pass on what he'd found. If only he could figure out what exactly was going on.

"What? Where can I hide?"

"You come. I know."

Mosakamo sounded confident, but this was just a small village, of scattered round huts – they were called *mongulu*, he thought. He looked around at the shaggy thatches, meat and herbs hanging up to dry at the entrances, panniers full of tubers, mortars and pestles outside the entrances to the huts. He looked at the children dashing around, squealing, chased by the strange, non-barking basenji dogs. Nowhere to hide.

Now, the adults were more contained, but apprehensive, throwing him sideways glances he couldn't interpret. He looked around – the forest crowded close in upon the village. Where could a tall gawky white guy like him hide? How close were they?

He must go. He couldn't put these people in more jeopardy.

Mosakamo pulled at his khaki shirt sleeve, dragged him over towards the centre of the village.

"Here."

"What is this?"

"We put you here. Cover. Hunters not see."

Mark stopped and gazed, undecided, reluctant to endanger these people who had put themselves at no little risk to help him, not even knowing who he was, asking for nothing while they had so little. He wasn't at all confidant until, dragged inside one *mongulu,* he twigged their ruse. It just might work.

"Fast. Now."

"OK, OK. I'll try." Mark slid inside and lay down curled into a foetal position. Twigs and palm leaves were hastily laid over him, and panniers piled nearby.

: ¤ :

Mosakamo sat on the mat and picked up the seven-stringed angular harp. He could feign being in that state – the dream state – play his instrument, make bright noise. The children could sit around. And Maak would lie quiet – he hoped. But his experience of white men was that they were always noisy, never still, never just listened.

Presently, crashing through the bush came a large, red-coloured sweating man, followed by a scowling angry-looking Bantu.

Ah yes. He continued to play the harp, looking sideways at them through half-closed eyes. Yes, he knew them. That boss and his Bantu tracker. He knew them from before. In the time when he was Bo-chantier in that foul, stinking place, the camp. But he was not Bo-chantier now – he was Mosakamo. He could not be told what to do here, in this place, his place. There, that Bantu had beat him when he did not bring back bushmeat for him. He'd tried to explain, but they were stupid: No animals in forest – no bushmeat.

And that white with a red face. He had seen him smash his large fist into another's face, squashing it, the nose spouting blood in one of the many camp fights. Even now he was waving a long gun about.

He would not use their names. They were bad. Maak was right. But he hoped they would not recognise him; usually they couldn't tell the difference between one Baka and another, because it was not worth the effort. But if they did recognise him, then they knew he spoke the language they used, and they would demand his help. And he would have to get up from the mat, and ...he sighed quietly, kept his head down playing.

There they stood, puffing air. Then the white shouted, slinging his long gun over his shoulder.

"Professor Rees. Are you here? We only want to help you. It was all a misunderstanding. Hey, are you here?"

Boukou calmly walked over, dignified, holding his long stick. Mosakamo was proud of his father; he would be happy if he was like him one day.

The white, now speaking Bantu, was demanding to look in all the *mongulu*, said he was looking for a bad white, an evil spirit. His father's face did not change as he gazed up at the threatening figure.

Some low cries came from the hut behind his father

The Bantu now roughly pushed past his father causing him to stumble, and ran into the hut, but shortly came out faster than he went in. Bo-dwa was lying on the floor inside, writhing, holding her stomach, panting, her cries increasing in volume, clearly in the final stages of a difficult labour.

"A monkey in there – having a baby." He addressed the white one in a loud voice to show he wasn't scared, but Mosakamo knew he was. He knew he shouldn't have gone into the hut; it was not allowed, not with a birth due.

Mosakamo knew the Bantu always referred to the Baka as 'monkeys' as though this made them more important, made them think they were bosses. He kept his head down, plucking the strings and humming.

A loud piercing scream from the hut sent the Bantu scuttling off in another direction. The two searched all the huts in the village, pushing the old and children aside getting angrier and angrier, while the Baka roamed and shuffled around looking confused, getting in the way.

The Bantu kicked over several panniers containing plantains and manioc ready for preparation. In his fury, he ground the vegetables into the dusty red soil.

"If you are hiding someone, we will return and kill you all. *All!*" he yelled in English.

Someone else with the rudiments of English and an air of innocence, said, "What you look?"

"You want bush meat?" Another innocent asked. This question almost all Baka had had to learn.

Frustrated shouts followed. The white waved his gun around menacingly -

"Get those bloody freak dogs away from me or I'll shoot them."

They left.

: Ϙ :

"You're bloody useless, man. Couldn't find your arse without a map. I thought you were supposed to be the best tracker in the Dja. We've wasted a night and a day going after Rees."

"I told you what happen if it rained. A thousand times more difficult." Djomo was feeling very aggrieved; he was proud of his tracking skills and the criticism was unjust.

Muller knew that. "The trail has gone now. We should have killed him when he came," he added.

They were trudging up the nearby logging track, back in the direction they had come.

"How far away can he be? He wasn't that much ahead of us." The telltale signs of Muller's uncertain temper were showing. The throbbing vein in the neck, the reddened face. He hated to lose.

"Listen. *He* go where he want — *we* have to. . .to find where he go. That is difference. That is why it take longer." Djomo knew he was treading on dangerous ground, explaining this as though to a child, but he was annoyed and tired.

"Fucking excuses. What is he? A weedy so-called scientist. What the hell does he know about survival in this hell-hole?" Muller's face was scarlet now. He took out a grubby rag and wiped the sweat off his face.

A rhetorical question. Djomo didn't answer, instead made his own observation, attempting to deflect criticism of his own shortcomings.

"Those monkeys — they behave wrong." Djomo gazed back at the Baka village. "They are up to something. I know."

"Ach — they know nothing, they are nothing. They don't like us going into their village. Brings bad luck, all that voodoo rubbish."

Suddenly Muller stopped trudging and paused staring at the ground.

"Fucking hell. You know what he's done?"

Djomo decided to wait it out, even though Muller wanted him to ask.

Muller poked Djomo's chest with a stubby finger. "He got himself a bloody lift — from the logging truck. Headed that way. Look — these are recent tyre tracks. Nothing else has tyres that size." He jabbed a thumb in the direction of Yaounde.

Djomo stared back down the track. "No. Truckers never give him a lift. They work for us."

"Why not — if he offered them money? Wouldn't you? Anyway, the truckers are subcontracted and they don't know we want the Professor. Why shouldn't they give him a lift?"

Djomo shrugged. "Then we can do nothing."

Muller glared, evidently despising the sound of defeat in the Bantu's voice, and sucked gently through his teeth.

"We have to get back to the camp, warn Yaounde. They can take over. Come on, shift your lazy arse."

: ☼ :

When it was safe, they had giggled and told each other what they already knew — that they had outwitted the white and the Bantu. Each wanted to tell of their prowess as an actor, how they'd fooled the *bo-campiers* but all agreed that Bo-dwa had been the best. Those cries, those screams! How the Bantu had run from that *mongulu*. It had been hard to stop the laughter, keep a serious face.

They had dragged Mark out from under the pile of mats and panniers placed behind Bo-dwa as she lay writhing in apparent agony, and laughed again at his size, his appearance, his dazed expression.

There were too many stories to tell that night by the fires. With some carefully hoarded alcohol and tobacco from the trading with the Bantu, the stories grew and were embellished with the telling and the retelling. The raconteurs tried to outdo each other, voices overlapping, rose and fell in a rhythm, eyes shining in the reflections of the orange flames.

These stories would last, honed with the retelling.

But Mark worried that there might be repercussions if it were discovered that they had sheltered and hidden him. He had seen at first hand the loggers' attitude towards the Baka, treating them like sub-humans.

They were more ruthless and sadistic than he'd realised, and for their sakes he needed to be gone from here as soon as possible.

Chapter
17

Mark glanced sideways at the taciturn driver. He was apprehensive both about being a passenger since his last experience with an uncommunicative driver, and, much much more, about the nature of his - literally - bloody trade.

The Baka, it transpired, had had a plan to get him back to Yaounde, but seemed somewhat embarrassed as they explained, eyes shifting around, not looking at him. Now he understood why.

The only way they could manage to trade with Bantu and others was by making use of their superior skills in hunting. So, depleted of wildlife though the forest was, it was they, if anyone, who could find the increasingly scarce game. It had always been their way to take what they needed, no more. But the desperation of poverty induced by the devastation of their traditional hunting areas had forced them into hunting further afield to supply the greedy bush meat trade – and trading the bush meat in exchange for cigarettes, alcohol, medicines. No money exchanged hands. Nobody ever paid the Baka.

At regular intervals, Mosakamo said, a market trader in bushmeat appeared to relieve them of their smoked duiker and monkeys, taking the meat back to Yaounde in the back of his rattling pick-up.

There should be one the next day.

He'd spent the night in the *mongulu* in which he'd first come round, and awoken relatively refreshed without any troubling Byronic images having plagued his sleep.

Now, as he looked across at the driver, who steadfastly kept his gaze on the track, squinting against the smoke drifting up into his eyes from a skinny roll-up, the horrible irony inherent in his own and the Baka's situation mocked him. And another mute companion. Not that Mark felt like chatting.

It had been upsetting, leaving the village. The young lad in the ManU shirt had gazed up at him, silent and somehow accusatory, gaze unwavering as though everyone, in the end, always let him and his people down, as though, even so young, he'd learnt to expect no more. It was even more intolerable that these people were themselves forced into a horrifying trap where they were contributing to their own downfall, bit by bit.

Mark glanced back through the grimy window at the piles of sad, gruesome corpses with their sunken eyes, pathetic delicate duiker hooves waving jerkily at the sky, slim, long-fingered primate hands dancing gruesomely in the back of the pick-up. He was back in the market - how many days ago? – gawping in horror, a white-faced incandescent Sue by his side, and now here he was accepting a lift from one of these corrupt butchers. It was futile just indulging in the western luxury of anger and grief for the fast disappearing wildlife and the Baka way of life; they were a unique, irreplaceable people, just as the species that, once gone, would be gone forever.

He could feel his anger rising, all the more acute since he was hitching a ride; he could, without any qualms, throttle this degenerate and jam his skinny cigarette down his scrawny throat. But he needed the lift.

The pick-up bounced into and out of a pot-hole, and Mark's head hit the roof of the cabin. The driver's demeanour remained virtually unchanged, eyes narrowed, badly rolled cigarette clamped between thin lips. He spat a stream of brown tobacco-stained phlegm out of the pick-up's window.

He needed to do something when he got back to Yaounde. What, precisely he should do, he couldn't say – yet.

: Ơ :

Here he was again, standing outside the police station, looking at the crumbling façade. When he had been here last, he had intruded on a fierce argument between Commissaire John Beti and an unknown army colonel.

He was more battered and bruised than that earlier self, and maybe a tad wiser to the ways of this world – perhaps a touch more cynical and a little less naive. He looked down at himself, his torn and stained clothing, rubbed a hand over several days' worth of stubble, felt the bump on the back of his head. He sighed and pushed open the door, half expecting to hear a row going on as before, but all was quiet, the duty officer – the same young man – sitting at his desk, flipping a stubby pencil between his fingers, reading a newspaper.

Business, apparently, was slow.

The young man looked up and he started as though a jolt of electricity passed through him, his eyes wide. His mouth made an open 'O' as his jaw fell. Mark thought that an excessive response to his reappearance. Or did he resemble a wild man? He hadn't looked into a mirror since he'd left the camp cabin – and it had been dark then.

The officer jerked upright like a puppet and dashed over to knock on Beti's door, all the while keeping his eyes fixed on Mark. A muffled noise from within and he opened the door. Some mutterings ensued. The door was flung open, and Beti appeared, shock growing on his face. Mark was beginning to get used to this response.

"Professor Rees. Please, please – come in. Everyone has been very worried about your safety. Your colleagues at CRU, your High Commission.

Nobody has heard from you for days." He was too polite to mention Mark's disgraceful attire – or no doubt the aroma that wafted around him.

"That would be because I was captured and imprisoned at a logging camp." He tramped wearily into the office.

Beti stood stock still by the door. After a long pause, now fully taking in Mark's appearance, he indicated a chair.

Mark flopped down on the far side of the desk, the still neat desk, with a heavy sigh.

"You were right, Commissaire, to warn of the dangers in Dja."

Beti nodded his head slightly in agreement as if he'd expected to hear no different.

"What happened to you?"

Mark ran a hand over his face. "I'd better start at the beginning…"

Mark described the drive, the disappearance of the driver, Tchie Nkemi, and being abandoned in the forest. He took a deep breath before describing the discovery of the horribly mutilated body in a clearing, and his recognition of a scar on Wingent's hand. He paused and examined Beti's face to gauge his reaction. He seemed impassive, his face carved of stone, but then perhaps he was used to hearing such gory tales.

In the pause, Beti pushed a cigarette case across the top of his desk, saying nothing. Mark hesitated – people kept offering him ciggies and he was too weak to refuse. Still, he'd had a bloody agonising last few days, suffering all sorts of privations. He gave in and accepted one with a nod of thanks and very little guilt. Beti leaned over and lit the cigarette with a fancy zip lighter.

"Thanks." He took a long enjoyable drag and exhaled at the ceiling. "That's not the end of it, I'm afraid. After the discovery of the body, I had to find my way to the nearest village, settlement, whatever, and figured that I should continue in the direction we'd been driving. Well, eventually I found my way to the Dja river, was picked up by two campers from the Rouge-Bolles logging company."

At this Mark saw the merest flicker of – what? Alarm? Interest? – in Beti's eyes. Beti picked up the lighter and began tapping it lightly on the desk surface.

"You know of this company?" asked Mark.

"It is one of the biggest in Cameroon. They have concessions adjacent to the Dja Reserve," he said neutrally.

"Adjacent? But not *in* the Reserve, I take it?" Mark flicked the ash into a handsome smoked glass ashtray pushed across the desk towards him.

"Why do you say that?" Beti asked quickly.

" Because… Well, nothing really." Mark thought he'd better keep these thoughts to himself, not prejudice the outcome of any court case that might follow from Wingent's murder. Anyway, he couldn't be absolutely sure that Rouge-Bolles were logging within the boundaries of the Dja Reserve – he'd had no map with him – and the fact that Wingent's body was in the Dja Reserve proved nothing since he was obviously murdered elsewhere. So, he'd better keep his counsel for now. He intended to find out, though. He had an inkling of an idea.

Beti put his head on one side, considering Mark.

"You think illegal logging was going on." It was a statement, and right on the button.

"I really couldn't say for sure." Mark hedged. He could sound neutral, too.

"You can't be unaware of the situation here in the Cameroon," Beti persisted. "Illegal logging is big business, perhaps *the* biggest contributor to our economy. Certain companies, perhaps most, are not averse to greasing a few palms to make authorities look the other way." Beti scrutinised him through a cloud of cigarette smoke as he lit his own cigarette.

"Baksheesh is a way of life here. It is, you could say, part of our economy. Has been that way for a long time. The logging companies are – protected, I suppose is the best description."

Mark was surprised to hear Beti talk so openly of the destructive devastation – worse here than in any other west African country – where those holding positions of the greatest authority were taking massive backhanders, amassing vast fortunes, in exchange for permission to decimate their most precious assets, the forests. Why? It was usually not spoken of, even though it was a fact of life here, so why had Beti brought it up? There were strong rumours that the police were in on these corrupt practices. Maybe he wanted to find out how much Mark knew. That was a two-way street, though.

He had to say something quickly. At this juncture best be cagey; pick his way carefully, until he could be more certain of how things lay. How could you know who was straight and who not? He liked Beti, didn't want to think the worst of him, but perhaps it paid in the present circs to be a little less trusting for the time being.

"Perhaps I should just tell you what happened to me at the camp?"

"Please, go on." Beti graciously waved him to continue.

"Right. Naturally, I wanted to contact you – the police – as soon as possible concerning Wingent's murder. Mobile didn't work out there and I was told the camp radio was out of order. This was a lie – the radio *was* working as I found out during a night-time stroll that took me by the radio shack. Unfortunately, I couldn't use it as I was whacked on the head" – he pointed to the lump on the back of his head – "and dumped in a locked hut."

At least, at this, there was a gratifying widening of Beti's eyes. He suddenly stood, which briefly alarmed Mark, but only strode to the door to open it and demand two coffees from the duty officer.

Beti strode back to stand in front of Mark, his arms folded, smoke from the cigarette curling around his head.

"I cannot apologise enough for the treatment you have received here in Cameroon, Professor Rees. It is completely unacceptable that a man of your eminence should be treated so." His somewhat stilted, formal phrasing, oddly did not rob his statement of sincerity.

Mark was a little taken aback at this. It wasn't quite the reaction he'd expected.

"Well, it wasn't much fun and I'm not sure they would ever have released me." Did Beti know how he came to be here? He hadn't asked which was odd. He could only know if someone at the camp had told him – via the 'caput' radio.

What he had to consider, however reluctantly, was that Beti himself might be part of the endemically corrupt system – and if that were the case, would Mark and the rest of them at CRU, not to mention the Baka, be in some danger if he or the police figured that Mark knew too much?

At that moment the coffee arrived, and Beti was taken up with fussing around with milk and sugar. Mark decided he needed the energy boost and asked for three spoonfuls. The coffee was exquisite and strong, reviving Mark's flagging spirits and infusing his brain with energy.

Beti was studying him, he saw, over the rim of his delicate china cup. Mark couldn't figure him out – he had one of those enigmatic faces that revealed little. What he now had to consider, at this point in his narrative, was whether describing the role of the Baka in his escape would endanger them, or bring them well-deserved respect – and perhaps some reward.

"But you did escape – and here you are." Beti encouraged him to continue.

"Yes. I managed to break out of the hut and steal a pirogue. They followed me though, so I had to leave the river. Had to take to the bush." He was chopping up sentences into small bites while he considered.

He took another large swallow of the coffee to give himself more time to judge whether or not, and how, to edit his tale.

"Eventually, I – um – was lucky enough to get a lift with a trader – a *bush meat* trader," he added, glowering over the desk. "But I wasn't in a position to be fussy." Best to keep the Baka out of it for the time being – he didn't know how things stood between them and the police.

"After your travails, you need to be checked out medically, Professor." He seemed genuinely concerned.

"Yes, yes. I will. But right now the important thing is to recover Colin Wingent's body."

"We will find him, don't worry." Beti seemed confident, but there was something wrong here. He didn't seem infused with any urgency.

"He was brutally murdered and mutilated. His body – " Mark took a deep breath, " – his body looked as though he'd been the victim of a *muti* killing."

"*Muti?* Are you certain? That does not occur here in Cameroon, Professor." Beti looked stern. "That sort of thing is more Nigerian," he added loftily.

"Certain - organs had been removed." At this memory, Mark's bile began to rise as he recalled the gruesome scene. He dug out his notebook, flipped through the pages, from which he imagined still the miasma of carrion arising, and passed it to Beti; he quickly grabbed his coffee and took a gulp to obliterate the memory of the smell.

Beti was quiet for a while, reading and digesting this information

Eventually he looked up, his expression unreadable.

"I'd better hang on to this, Professor, if you don't mind. Thank you," he said, waving the small notebook. "We will have to do an autopsy and determine the cause of death, and investigate the motive. Do you think it could have been robbery, Professor?"

"No. He still had his watch on, although no other papers or wallet as far as I know."

Mark touched his pocket. He could feel the outline of the tree splinters – and the somewhat sweat-soaked sawdust through his shirt pocket - but something held his hand. He was reluctant to pass this evidence over to Beti until he was surer of his ground.

"As he was a British subject, Commissaire, I'll have to notify the High Commission. I don't know if he had a family but they have a right to know as soon as possible."

"You can leave all that to the police, Professor." He waved his hand airily. "We will do what is necessary. Your best course of action is to return to the chimp centre, and await developments – Caro's happy event must be very soon and I expect that she will need you there. Do not worry, we will keep you fully informed." He made as if to get up.

"Wait," – Mark suddenly remembered what was odd – "you don't know where to find him, do you?"

Beti remained inscrutable.

"I haven't told you where his body lies."

"I assumed his body was lying by the track to Somalomo. It would be hard to miss."

He was fronting this out well, thought Mark.

"Actually, Commissaire, he lies off the track, about one hundred kilometres into the reserve – an estimate - and about fifty metres into the bush, on the south side. The point on the track is marked with a piece of this shirt tied to a tree." He held up the ragged hem of his filthy shirt. "Not a very bright tag, I'm afraid, but you or your men should be able to spot it."

Beti stared at the torn shirt as if seeing it for the first time.

"Thank you for all your help, Professor, and I trust you will soon be able to resume your studies – at the CRU, if not in the bush. We will proceed with all due diligence, and, as I say, keep you informed of any developments."

And that was that. He was dismissed, coolly and with finality.

Chapter
18

Once again, Mark found himself on the pavement outside the police headquarters, not sure if he'd been given the bum's rush, not sure if he ought to be annoyed, not sure if he ought to be suspicious. Or if Beti and the police just wanted to get on with recovering Wingent's remains without the interference of some wannabe Sherlock Holmes.

He gazed around, somewhat disoriented after his trials in the bush, the busy traffic and the bustling crowds confusing him. As he tramped along, his state of dress – or undress – attracting a few stares, he dug out his mobile and contacted CRU.

The shouts and exclamations coming over the phone caused him to stop in his tracks, holding his mobile a little away from his ear. Only now, hearing their reactions, did he fully realise what they had been through, being thoroughly taken up with his own endeavours.

Guilt suffused with a deep gratitude flowed through him and tears pricked his eyes. He turned away to face a building so that no one should see, putting a hand against the wall to brace himself. After the hubbub died down, he apologised in a shaky voice for what he'd put them through, gave them a précis of what had happened, including the discovery of the body, asked an apparently shaken Sue to phone Jeannie, and arranged with Ekoko to be picked up from outside the British High Commission in three hours' time.

Closing the phone and surreptitiously wiping his eyes, he scanned around for any familiar landmark.

He headed south towards the Place Ahmadou Ahidjo. In hilly Yaounde this was a low-lying area of Centre Ville. He patted his pocket, certain now of what he must do, determination in his stride.

First, the Amity bank — what a misnomer for a bank - near the large Hilton Hotel. Through all his tribulations, he still had his credit card, a bit battered, in his moneybelt. He hoped it would work because he was absolutely skint. He walked from spacious Rond-Point de Boulevard 20 Mai with its ultra-modern oddly shaped showcase buildings down the avenue itself. When he got there he spotted an internet café — the ICC Internet Café — and decided to return there when he'd done what he had to do.

Thank God, the card slid in like a dream. He got out about fifty quid's worth of CFA's.

As he tramped back down the wide Boulevard du 20 Mai, taking in the sights, he wondered at the preponderance of Gallic influences; recall of his sketchy history of Cameroon, taught him that the country was a fusion of French Cameroon and a southern part of the mandated British Cameroon, while a northern portion of British Cameroon had voted to join Nigeria. An old West Africa hand, a devoted imbiber he'd pumped for useful information before he came out, and well-lubricated by a few shorts, told him that this union had serious fault lines, and the dominant political party was francophone, the resentful anglophones being marginalized politically and commercially. Apparently the current president, Emile Bama, spent more time in Paris than Yaounde, a willing puppet of France's Africa policy which consisted principally, the loquacious imbiber claimed, of the determination to oust all despised anglophone influences. The elections earlier this year had re-elected the President, though whether they'd been fairly conducted without the usual intimidation and vote-rigging was moot. Bama, through his French military connections, could be relied upon to keep the flag of 'black France' flying, and his regime could count on substantial tranches of 'aid' from Paris – very little of which found its way to the increasingly impoverished Cameroonians. Post-colonial colonialism.

Bama – that was a familiar name from somewhere else. He couldn't remember and he had other, more urgent, things to attend to.

He stopped. Right, here it was. The Central Post Office. He went inside and saw a post-restante service, but what he wanted was a padded envelope. A rack of envelopes there on the left. And a jiffy bag. He grabbed a piece of note paper and a pen, thought a moment and began scribbling, pausing now and then to gaze into the middle distance.

When he'd finished, he scanned the post office rapidly, more vigilant than he'd been in the past, opened his pocket and gingerly extracted the splinters of wood which had been with him all this time, wrapped in a slightly soggy piece of paper. He gently transferred them to another smaller envelope from the rack, which he scribbled on, and inserted them into the larger padded envelope. A second smaller envelope now, into which he tried to pour from his pocket the damp clogged sawdust from the Rouge-Bolles sawmill; an awkward transaction, but nobody seemed to be taking much notice. This, too was sealed, labelled, and placed in the larger envelope. He was sweating profusely by the time he'd done this and the mosquito bites were itching.

After writing the address on the front, he handed over the larger envelope and paid for express delivery.

This accomplished he heaved a sigh of relief and wiped his face with his shirt sleeve. He had done what he could for poor Colin Wingent for now, and this, at least, was out of his hands. He knew his old friend wouldn't let him down.

: ◌ :

A figure hugging the shadows took out his mobile phone.

"He's in the Central Post Office."

Pause.

"No, I couldn't see what he was doing. I couldn't get close enough. He's very nervous, looking round all the time. If I'd gone any closer he would have spotted me."

Pause.

"He's coming out now… I can either follow him or try to find out what he did in the post office…I can't do both."

Pause.

"OK. You're the boss. He's headed up the boulevard – again."

With that the mobile was clicked shut, and the figure separated from the shadows to follow at a distance. He could allow his target to gain some distance since the avenue was long and straight. He had an excellent view of the tall Professor.

: ◌ :

Mark settled himself at the terminal in the internet café. He was still feeling somewhat twitchy, and turned quickly to look when someone opened the door. It was a slim white man with slicked back dark hair, in neat, newly ironed khakis which contrasted starkly with Mark's sorry state of dress and dense stubble. He nodded briefly in response to Mark's stare and sat smoothly down at a nearby terminal.

Mark logged on. While waiting for the computer to go through its usual rigmarole, he took another sneaky look at the other. He mustn't do that. The guy would think he was distinctly odd, or worse, making a move on him.

Here we go. He logged onto 'Yahoo', used his password – the not very original 'bonobo' - and recalled his friend DCI Paul Draper's email address from memory.

'Paul – I'm typing this in a hurry. You'll soon receive a package from me – at least, I hope you will – which will contain some evidence collected at the site of a murder. The victim is a Brit – Colin Wingent - working for Forestry Watch and, I think, originating from Longstock. I met him before he left – a really nice guy. I came across his remains in the bush, in the Eastern Province near Dja Reserve. As yet his body has not been recovered by the police here – I needn't go into the reasons for that now – but one envelope, labelled, contains the bloodstained splinters I lifted from his cheek.'

Mark paused, reliving that horrifying moment. He sighed, rubbing his face with both hands. What must it be like, so far from home, to find yourself in that split second before the fatal blow, completely alone, knowing with a certainty that you will die? Or did it all happen so fast the poor sod had no time to react? He hoped so.

'The remains were mutilated and had all the signs of a muti killing (see the case of 'Adam' found in the Thames). There was no cut or sawn wood near the body, too little blood in the vicinity. . .'

He stopped again, leaning back and scrubbing at his scalp which reminded him of the still sore bump on the back of his head. He was going to ask Paul to do something which could possibly get him in hot water – even steamy international waters- but he was banking on the fact that the death of Wingent, as a fellow-countryman murdered abroad, must grant the UK police, particularly the Hampshire police, since Wingent had told him he lived in Longstock, a legitimate interest. He was sure he'd heard recently of detectives from Hampshire travelling to India to trace an alleged murderer and initiate extradition proceedings. Surely, there were several instances where Scotland Yard got called in to help police forces abroad when a Brit died in suspicious circumstances in foreign parts.

A couple of young locals came into the internet café, laughing and chatting. Mark resumed.

'…*so I'm guessing that he was killed and mutilated elsewhere, somewhere near cut/sawn wood to which the splinters belong – which would tie in with his work for Forestry Watch – and his body transported, post mortem, to where I found it.*

The other envelope contains sawdust taken from a saw mill where I was abducted and imprisoned. It's OK - I got away - obviously!

Could you treat these two samples as you would any biological forensic evidence? They may already be somewhat contaminated, I'm afraid.

Now, I'm going to ask a big favour of you…Could you contact Prof Steve Frampton at the Botany Dept at the Uni? He's a very affable type and a good friend – and I know for a fact that he'll jump at the chance to do a DNA analysis on these 2 samples. Part of his research is compiling a DNA map of endangered tree species in Africa – this will be right up his street. He should be able to pinpoint where the splinters came from as well as the species. Ditto for the sawdust. Can you explain the situation to him?

And say this is a priority and a chance to test out his team's DNA tree map. I'll explain the significance of all this when we get the results.

I'm sending these samples to you first, as this is a police matter and you can ensure the chain of evidence. I know I'm dumping a lot in your lap, Paul, but there's no one in the police better equipped to deal with bizarre situations!'

He knew his friend. Paul wouldn't be able to resist the scientific puzzles dangled before him, and he would be able, on the basis of the murder of a local and the splinters, to present a solid case to his Superintendent or whoever. If he got the go ahead, he'd be the SIO. Unless he had other stuff on his desk.

Mark flexed his fingers, taking another surreptitious look around. The same three people were still there, the two young men sharing a terminal with much whispering and snickering. Bet I know what you're looking at, Mark thought. The dapper looking guy was still there, quietly absorbed in whatever he was doing, eyes glued to the screen.

Mark glanced up at the wall clock. He must be getting on if he was to be ready for Ekoko's pick-up, and he had another errand first.

He signed off with a plea to let him know the outcome of any analysis asap. He felt sure he would be asking further favours of Paul in the very near future.

Before logging off he typed a quick apologetic email to Jeannie feeling cowardly for not being able just now to phone and listen to her accusatory comments on his ' irresponsible adventuring' as she called it, nor did he want to hear her reaction to his miraculous reappearance on the phone. He'd be trying to gauge the sincerity of her relief. So later, when he was less fragile, but not now.

He was careful to log off properly, got up quickly, paid his CFA 1500, and exited the café. Where was he going now? Avenue Churchill.

How the hell did you get there from here? A wave of fatigue swept over him and that thumping headache returned, catching him unawares, causing him to lean drunkenly against a wall. Then he saw his solution - one of Yaounde's ubiquitous battered yellow taxis with its spots of rust and lead paint resembling an infectious disease, was circling the spacious roundabout. He pushed himself away from the wall and practically stepped into the driver's path in his eagerness.

The taxi's brakes squealed, and the driver with a hangdog face stuck his head through the open window and grunted an interrogation.

"Uh – Avenue Churchill, please."

He checked that he had enough cash, and sank back gratefully into the torn and tattered upholstery.

Thankfully the driver didn't feel inclined to ask questions, he seemed absorbed by his own droning monologue. Normally, Mark quite perversely enjoyed listening to a good whinge by a taxi driver; they were comfortingly the same the world over - they all launched into their favourite grumbles in a babel of languages once your backside hit the leather, but now he was irritated as the monotonic whinge went on, in French. A captive audience.

At that thought, he turned to stare through the rear window. Nothing suspicious, but he was hardly an expert in detecting a tail.

As they passed a shop, Mark, on impulse, asked the driver to stop and wait. He dashed inside and quickly rummaged through the T-shirts, which was all there was on offer. He selected one, and to the consternation of the shop assistant and outraged stares from other customers, changed there and then from his disreputable stained khaki shirt into the new T-shirt with a fetching beer logo on the front. He pressed what he thought would be the right sum of money into the assistant's hand, balled up his disgusting shirt and dashed out again before anyone could react.

The gloomy taxi driver, indifferent as to whether anyone was listening, was still grumbling about something or other.

: ✡ :

In spite of his vigilance, Mark didn't spot the discreet figure who had followed him in a shabby Peugeot from the internet café. The man picked up the mobile phone from the passenger seat.

Chapter 19

They reached the High Commission, and Mark paid off the lugubrious driver with some relief. He paused, trying to gather his thoughts before he went in. Events had been moving so fast he had scarcely time to properly consider what he was doing. He thought about what he'd just done – had he been too hasty? He'd wanted to get the information about Wingent into the hands of the police as soon as possible, but he wasn't entirely sure that he trusted the local police to act on it, conduct a thorough investigation, or even have the resources to do so, so he'd provided his friend DCI Paul Draper with the evidence that might pinpoint where Wingent had been killed – if not why, and by whom. It had the smack of an arrogant westerner about it, but he hadn't the energy to be bothered about that. He could feel his dwindling inner resources leaking away.

Now, he had to inform the High Commissioner as Wingent was a British subject. Beti had said he would do it, but this way Mark would know for sure that the demise – the murder - of Wingent reached the right ears without delay. And importantly, any relatives. Mark hoped fervently that he wasn't married with small children. Also, as he had been reported missing too, he felt it incumbent on himself to appear in person.

The receptionist stared, rather rudely, Mark thought, at his attire. He asked to see the High Commissioner, said he was prepared to wait for however long it took, said it was a matter of the utmost urgency concerning the death of a British Subject.

He must have injected enough fervour into his voice, for she looked startled, picked up the phone and murmured rapidly, listened a while, murmured some more while glancing suspiciously at Mark's T-shirt and unshaven face, put it down – and nodded brusquely at him to wait in one of the luxurious winged leather chairs placed against the wall.

As he was fidgeting impatiently, he saw a pair of shiny brown brogues descend the stairs followed by a pair of exquisitely tailored trousers. That was quick.

"Professor Rees? I'm very glad to see you're all right. I heard you wished to see me as a matter of some urgency?" The High Commissioner glided across the marble foyer, far too courteous to even glance at Mark's ensemble, far less portray any reaction.

"Yes – um – sir." How did you address a High Commissioner? Mark stood.

"Please, let's not stand on ceremony. Jonathan – Jonathan Hyatt. I'm very relieved indeed to meet you." He stuck out his hand, a heavy signet ring on the right ring finger. He was much younger than Mark imagined, an unlined boyish face, about a couple of years younger than himself, he guessed, immaculately groomed in a light grey suit moulded to his shape.

"Well then – I'm Mark. I'm sorry to disturb you without an appointment, but - "

"Please, don't think twice. As I say, I'm just relieved you're alright. I was told by both the police and your Chimp Rehabilitation Unit that you were overdue making contact from the Dja Region. But now I hear your visit involves the death of a British subject. Did my secretary get that right?" As he spoke, he led the way up the stairs to his office.

"I'm afraid so, uh, Jonathan. A man I met shortly before he came here to Cameroon, by the name of Colin Wingent."

Hyatt gestured Mark to proceed him into a well-appointed but not overly lavish room, saying, "I rather dreaded hearing that news ever since I learned Mr Wingent had gone missing. I'm very sad to hear that. Do you know the circumstances of his death?"

He moved a chair for Mark to sit down.

As Mark went on to explain the details of his dreadful discovery, the state of the remains and his speculation that it might be a *muti* killing, he watched Hyatt's face carefully, trying to ignore the persistent throbbing in his temporal lobes.

To begin with Hyatt's expression was bland, imperturbable. As Mark continued, it altered gradually to one of astonishment and repulsion, his mouth pursing, a frown blemishing the smooth forehead.

Mark held back on the posting of the forensic evidence, as he wasn't too certain of the legalities and suspected that Hyatt might be annoyed he'd breached local police etiquette. Perhaps he should have put his faith in the local forensic facilities, but he didn't know what they offered, and Steve's programme was spot on for what was needed here.

"You'll understand why I came to you, as Wingent's relatives will have to be located and notified as soon as possible, but also because it seemed to me that this case might have more aspects to it than I fully understand."

"You'll have to explain that, but first things first." He rang for a tray of tea.

Tea or no tea, Mark was anxious to engage the High Commissioner's interest before being dismissed as some wild scientist whose brain had been scrambled by his bush experiences, so whilst waiting, he launched into his adventures starting with the journey to the Dja Reserve, his abandonment and trek through the bush, discovery of poor Wingent, his rescue by the Rouge-Bolles employees and being taken to the camp.

Hyatt's attention was unwavering, punctuated only by varied vocal expressions of amazement.

The tea arrived, served silently and discreetly by a PA. Mark paused to greedily gulp the Earl Grey. First, strong coffee with the Commissaire, now tea with the High Commissioner.

As he polished off the tea Mark felt himself being scrutinised. Young Hyatt might be young for a post like this but he seemed shrewd underneath the diplomatic polish. Mark sensed he was a confident man, content to wait.

"Sorry. I haven't had anything to eat or drink today – well, a coffee at Police HQ. By the way, I've notified Commissaire Beti of the body's location." Mark paused. "The next bit is difficult – I don't know what my standing is here, in the legal sense, but I need to tell someone in authority, to seek your advice, really."

A low frequency thrumming behind his eyes heralded the spread of his headache.

"Please, go ahead. I'm more than happy to advise where I can." A very diplomatic answer. Hyatt sat forward a little.

"OK. To take up the tale where I left off: Rouge-Bolles, the logging camp where I was taken after being rescued: A disturbing place, menacing, but I was treated hospitably – at first - given a cabin to sleep in, fed and watered." Not so much watered as tanked up, he recalled. "But that night my cabin was searched. I figured in a rough-neck place like that, robbery wasn't exactly unknown, besides I had little worth stealing. Nothing *was* stolen, in fact. Anyway, I pretended to be asleep, but after the intruder had left I couldn't get back to sleep. Perhaps unwisely, I decided to have a look around the camp."

"Definitely 'unwisely', I would have thought." Hyatt rested his chin on his fist.

Mark shrugged.

" Right. No excuse, but after what I'd seen and the ordeal in the bush, I wasn't thinking straight – that state you get in where you're drunk with exhaustion and not a little booze, I have to admit, but too wired to sleep. I'd been told that the radio wasn't operating therefore there was no way I could contact the police here, but creeping around the camp I could hear radio chatter from the radio shack. As I watched from the shadows I was coshed from behind and..."

"You *what?*" Hyatt's head came up sharply, the smooth polish cracked a little. "Who hit you?"

"I don't know – I was slugged from behind." His head pulsated in sympathy. "That alone might not be too surprising in that camp, but when I woke up I found myself locked in a hut somewhere outside the camp confines."

"You were falsely imprisoned? God, Mark, this is serious, very serious, unlawfully imprisoning a British subject. If I may, I'd like to take down some details." Hyatt grabbed an elegant black Parker pen and a yellow legal pad, which gave some clue as to his earlier training.

Mark nodded – gingerly – in the direction of the pad, not wanting to exacerbate the thudding in his brain.

"You'll know better than I the legal niceties, but I couldn't understand why they'd initially seemed so friendly. Anyway, the next night I managed to escape from the hut and just pelted toward the river – I had the idea of taking a boat and rowing westwards towards – somewhere. Somalomo. I don't know really. Anywhere. Just to get away. But – and this is the thing – they actually came after me. This is what's baffling. Why so determined? Sometimes I think I've figured it all out – at other times I'm not so sure. It's confusing…" He tailed off. He wasn't even sure he was telling this coherently.

"Maybe they thought you knew something they didn't want the authorities to know? Something they thought you'd seen?" The pen was poised over the pad.

"It seems like it, but the only thing I knew really was the whereabouts of Wingent's body." There was something else, though.

"And the fact that he was brutally murdered, of course."

"Of course, there is that. You think that someone in the camp could have murdered him?" Not waiting for an answer, Mark went on, "It had the hallmarks of a *muti* killing. Do you think someone in that camp practises that sort of voodoo?" Although he harboured some doubts about the sorcerous connection, he couldn't totally dismiss it on the basis of the presence rather than absence of one bone – the atlas bone.

"Honestly? I don't know. There are regions where some form of magic, voodoo, is quite common. Here, have some digestives and another cup – you look as though you need a sugar boost." He poured another cup of tea and passed a plate of biscuits, peering at Mark's face. "You mentioned earlier that this dreadful murder might have other aspects to it. Would you care to explain?"

Mark munched the biscuit and spoke around it, spewing crumbs onto his new T-shirt. He was beginning to relax for the first time in days; it was almost bizarrely cosy, sitting here drinking tea and eating digestives, relating his extraordinary tale. Except for the banging in his head.

"I've been slow, I think, in trying to put all this together. I only got some chance to think when I was resting up in the Baka village." He figured it was be safe to tell Hyatt about the role the Baka had played in his adventures, without being quite sure why. But maybe, in his state of exhaustion, he was making ill-thought out decisions.

"The Baka? You were accepted into one of their villages?" Hyatt seemed surprised, elegantly arched eyebrows rising towards the hairline.

Mark explained his flight from pursuit, his collapse and coming round in a Baka *mongulu* – he missed out the bit about the ibogaine trip.

Hyatt listened keenly, his own cup of tea forgotten, as Mark related what the Baka had told him about that camp – one of the young men had worked there for a while before becoming sickened at the way his people were treated and leaving. "Apparently, they told me the usual procedure was to push the Baka off their land, which was then logged – and there's no proper supervision, no regulation, no one to whom they can appeal. Young girls are driven into prostitution. They're destitute and impoverished." Mark felt again the desperation of these unique, vulnerable people as they struggled to survive.

Halfway through his second cup, Mark resumed.

"Look, Wingent was working for Forest Watch. Is it possible, do you think, that he was murdered because he was on the trail of illegal logging, and somehow Rouge- Bolles is involved?" He scratched at a bite on his arm. For the first time, Mark had enunciated some of his suspicions out loud. "I can't prove any of that," he added lamely.

Hyatt looked thoughtfully at Mark.

"Then what about the *muti* signs you mentioned? If Wingent's death was connected to the discovery of illegal logging, why a *muti* killing?"

"A cover – perhaps?"

Hyatt sat back. "Or perhaps not. Let me get this straight, Mark. You're claiming that Wingent detected illegal logging by this company – one of the biggest in Cameroon, by the way – and for this he was murdered, presumably by one of their employees, but it was made to look as though it was a *muti* murder to throw the police off the trail."

Mark nodded slowly. "That's about the size of it. It does sound a bit thin, though, when you say it. And I've no real evidence to support it, just that they were so tenacious in their pursuit of me."

"They were aware at the camp that you'd discovered the body?"

Mark nodded carefully.

"And you told them you had to get hold of the authorities and notify them asap?"

"Mm."

Hyatt pulled at his lower lip while studying Mark.

"Do you want any more tea?" He asked eventually.

Mark shook his head, wondering if Hyatt was prevaricating because he didn't know what to say, or if there were some other reason.

Hyatt put down his pen, having evidently come to some decision.

"I'm sure you did your homework before you came to Cameroon, Mark. You know the situation vis-à-vis illegal logging. I'm not giving away any state secrets when I say it goes on – in a big way – and everyone is in on it. The army, the police, the government officials, relatives of the President – all get lucrative backhanders. The logging giants, of which Rouge-Bolles is the biggest – most, I have to say, are European, and I wouldn't hesitate to single out the French - buy a concession, ostensibly at least, legally. They then *extend* that concession into neighbouring illegal areas, like the Dja Reserve, say. I'm not saying, mind you, that I *know* this to be the case here. They may be operating perfectly legitimately in that area."

"If not, though, how do they get away with it?"

"There's no real supervision. Not enough personnel. If there are personnel they have too large an area to cover, or they're in on the deal; many palms are greased along the way."

"What happens to the timber then? I saw one of the juggernauts loaded with timber tear past the Baka village, and they told me they pass by every day."

"They go to Douala, the port." He paused to re-align some papers on his neat desk. "I've heard that there's some forgery or fiddling of the bills of lading."

Mark rubbed his itching eyes. He was feeling hot. The headache was increasing. What he said about bills of lading nagged at him – it sounded familiar but he couldn't grasp it.

"The forests are disappearing fast, Jonathan – they're killing off the golden goose. My particular concern is with the disappearance of the primates – lowland gorillas, chimps, bonobos. Once the loggers invade virgin forest - and they apparently supply their employees with guns in order to save on provisions – that's the death knell for all the animals, monkeys being a particular delicacy."

"Believe me, Mark, we've made representations, and there have even been agreements, but they're not worth the paper they're written on. There's very little desire to curb the activities of these giants as the major part of Cameroon's black economy depends on them – sixty percent of all their exports. Any one who is honest is as caught up in the sticky web as the corrupt officials, and these companies know that very well."

" Jesus. So once Cameroon is denuded, they'll pack up and move on to ravage the next virgin forest – if they can find any left?"

Hyatt thinned his lips and lifted one shoulder in a shrug of acknowledgement.

"And the fact that some of the tree species and most of the animals are on CITES Appendix I or II makes no difference at all?" He was angry but he had to keep it together.

"Perhaps you could refresh my memory on the Appendices?" Hyatt made a note on his pad.

"Of course, sorry. Those species most endangered – on the verge of extinction - are placed on Appendix I of the Convention on International Trade in Endangered Species, like tigers, gorillas – all the Great Apes, in fact. Appendix II is the next level – not quite so endangered but getting there fast."

"Yes, I see. " Hyatt scribbled quickly then got up and paced over to the window, gazing thoughtfully down into the High Commission's courtyard. "HMG would dearly love to expose the criminality in this trade – not that everyone isn't aware of it, they just find it more convenient and lucrative to ignore it – and enforce sustainable logging. We are signatories to CITES after all, and to the Kyoto protocols, and it would do the old PR image no harm at all. If it could be done here, it could prove a model for other places next on the loggers list – frankly, if it could be done here, it could be done anywhere. Cameroon recently had the honour of topping the list of most corrupt countries. Hot competition there, I have to say. But it seems that no matter what evidence is supplied of illegal logging, nothing happens; they remain inviolable."

"You're saying that there's nothing that can be done to stop them?" Mark was aghast. "We just let them level the forests and turn all into desert?" This sounded a bit theatrical, but it was how he felt.

Hyatt remained looking out of the window, but shook his head regretfully.

Mark's shoulders slumped. His throat was raw.

"Do you think I could have a drink of water?"

Hyatt turned.

"You look a bit flushed. Are you OK?"

"I don't know. I think I just need some rest."

Hyatt walked over to a cabinet which he opened to reveal a small fridge, took out a bottle of Highland mineral water and poured a glass. He handed it to Mark and watched with concern as he gulped the blessedly cool water.

"Thanks."

"Have you been keeping up with your anti-malarial tablets?"

"Not… not recently – I just had a small strip with me when the Land Rover…" He tailed off, too tired to bother finishing the sentence.

Hyatt tutted. "Would you object if I got our doctor to look you over?"

Mark, feeling drained, shook his head, suddenly too exhausted to say anything.

His eyes shut as he sank into a grey billowing mush.

: ⌂ :

He found himself in the sick bay, actually a small clinical-looking room in the Commission, being tended to by a very lovely Cameroonian doctor with cool hands, braided and beaded hair and spectacles which somehow enhanced her beauty. He'd always been a sucker for the severe librarian look which he fondly believed masked a passionate nature. What was he thinking? Adolescent fantasies. Must be the fever.

Now he was embarrassed since he seemed to be partially undressed, although still with his fetching T-shirt on. He peeked under the sheet – no, some modesty preserved. He was making a habit of being ministered to by lovely females but on neither occasion was he in a condition to fully appreciate it.

"Doctor?" He croaked.

"Doctor Njock. Sit up, please." She was brisk, applying her hand firmly to his back.

He did as he was told, groaning pitifully, as she applied the stethoscope.

"Breathe and hold," she ordered.

He obeyed meekly.

When she had finished her examination she scrutinised his face, pulled down a lower eyelid, stuck a thermometer in his mouth, and made some notes, while he sat under the sheet, staring at her like a mesmerised rabbit.

She extracted the thermometer, shook it and glanced at it and frowned down at him.

"High but not too bad. You should rest a while, drink the isotonic concoction I'm going to leave with you." She gave an exasperated sigh. "You seem to have dehydrated yourself. You novice tourists never remember to drink enough."

"I'm not a..."

"And I see you have sustained a number of insect bites over your body. You must use insect repellent – *all* over," - an eyebrow delicately raised – " including those areas you think are immune, and if you get bitten, use the antihistamine ointment immediately. Here." She thrust a tube of antihistamine at him. "Use this now."

"Where did you learn your bedside manner, doctor?" He was feeling hard done by.

"University College Hospital," she snapped, turning to her notes and scribbling rapidly.

"London Uni?"

"Where else?"

He was at a loss, but gamely tried to make conversation.

"I hadn't intended to get stuck in the bush. I was – I lost my transport and had to make my way back on foot."

She clicked her tongue, less in sympathy than condemnation. "No wonder you're dehydrated. A cup or two of Earl Gray with the High Commissioner isn't going to hack it, is it?"

Her English was flawless, unaccented. Should he dare to complement her on it and risk getting his head bitten off? He tried a compromise.

"Where are you from?" He asked as she passed him a jug and glass.

"Ealing."

That wasn't the answer he'd expected, and, from her expression – the merest twitch of a smile - she guessed that. Her face was transformed when she smiled, finally taking pity on him.

"I'm specialising in tropical diseases. I've been over here for a year, and I'm the resident GP for the High Commission."

Mark swallowed some of the liquid, and put the glass down.

"No you don't." She pressed the glass back to his mouth. "Refill and keep going. Right, I can look in on you later. If you develop a headache, take two of these co-codamol." She slapped a strip of pills on the bedside table, packed up her bag, flicked the locks briskly and whisked out.

Mark downed another half pint of the isotonic mixture, staring at the closed door. Christ, how was it medics always managed to make you feel like an intellectual midget, somehow at fault for getting ill and if only you'd had more sense you wouldn't need to be bothering them? Occasionally, it irritated him since it took just as long to complete a PhD, if not longer, but he always felt diminished in the face of medical efficiency. What was even more annoying was that he suspected she was right – he hadn't taken in enough liquid.

The next visitor, just as Mark's eyelids were drooping, was Jonathan Hyatt. He entered the room quietly and came over to the bed.

"Sorry to disturb you, Mark, although I must say you look a touch better." He scrutinised Mark carefully. "I was worried for a while there, wondered if you might have contracted malaria. I didn't mean to disturb your rest, but I've checked with our Doctor Njock and she says you should be fine by this evening."

"Lovely girl, great bedside manner. Look - I must apologise for putting you to all this trouble, but you're right - I do feel a lot better. It was really stupid of me to get into this state, particularly after I'd got rat-arsed at the camp. "

Not the most diplomatic expression, but Hyatt didn't blink — he clearly had other things on his mind. He got up and checked that the door was closed and sat carefully on the edge of the bed.

"I contacted your Sue Clarke at CRU as you requested, told her you're fine, just needed to rest. Luckily Ekoko Roger hadn't yet left to fetch you back there. She'll pass the message on to your ex, as she put it. Sue was very concerned and sounded a bit annoyed, too, but I was able to reassure her that you'll be right as rain, and that we'd see to your transport back to CRU as soon as you got the all clear from Doctor Njock."

"I can't thank you enough. I feel a right fool."

Hyatt glanced around again, even though it was obvious no one was there. Perhaps it was an occupational hazard in a diplomat.

"I've had an idea about what we discussed." His voice was low, lending a clandestine air to their meeting. "I want to put it to you and hear what you think."

His eyes were eager as he outlined his idea to Mark.

Mark listened attentively.

Chapter
20

They discussed Mark's collapse, if that was what it was, and the reassurance from the HC himself that he was recovering well from no worse than dehydration, as they were enjoying an evening meal of rice and *zom* – spinach and beef – sitting round the table on the cool veranda. The other wardens were tucking in, listening.

"So, he is at the High Commission, and they will drive him back tomorrow. A VIP," Ekoko said.

"Silly bastard," Sue sighed, putting down her fork. "He's supposed to know better than to allow himself to get dehydrated." Her seeming annoyance masked the relief she felt at his survival.

"We have to tell Caro. She keeps checking the computer."

Before he could move, Caro was suddenly there beside his chair, pulling at his arm. Uniquely, among the apes, she was allowed free access to other areas of CRU for a while in the evenings.

"Paa-paa." She occasionally made sounds which seemed to bear some resemblance to human words, but Sue knew the anthropomorphic pitfalls of assigning English meanings to her vocalisations. Nevertheless, 'paa-paa' *could* be 'papa' while 'nnn' *could* be 'no'. Bonobos had a wider range of sounds to draw on – and to modify? – than chimps.

"What? What is it, Caro?" asked Ekoko.

She grabbed his hand and pulled.

"I think she wants you to see something. Come on, let's follow, Ekoko." Sue rose and took Caro's other hand.

She dragged them towards her computer room and made them sit closely beside her in front of the screen. She refreshed the screen and there was a message written in idiograpgic symbols, and underneath, the translation into English. With a press of a key the voice facility read out the words in an androgenous robotic tone.

"Ah, Mark sent you a message, Caro," Ekoko said. After having her at CRU for almost a year, he was still getting used to Caro's astonishing language abilities. He'd told Sue that at first the other wardens had difficulty believing that she wasn't really a little human inside a bonobo suit. Sue grinned, wondering again at the sound she'd made on the veranda – it would be all too easy and drastically unscientific to conclude that she'd been saying 'papa', although she might see Ekoko in that way.

Caro pointed a finger at Mark's hieroglyphs paired with words on the screen:

'Next – day – I – see – you – and – Sue.'

It was possible to send a message from a PC with a standard keyboard to Caro's computer which the software would translate into idiographic language, and give the original English email in written and vocal forms.

And on the next line:

'love – Mark'

Caro pulled the keyboard towards her and pecked out:

'Mark – OK - ?' The voice intoned the words. This question was directed at them.

"You were right, she was worried," Sue whispered to Ekoko.

"Yes, he's fine, sweetie," she said out loud."He will be here – with you – tomorrow."

To make sure she understood, Sue pecked out the corresponding symbols.

Caro hugged Sue in her delight and excitement. Bonobos were expressive, emotionally more affectionate than their close relatives, the chimpanzees.

Just as quickly she let Sue go and hugged Ekoko, then dashed out to the outdoor enclosure, grabbing her plasticated lexigram on the way, dragging it along the ground as she rushed to tell the others. She tended to show an element of impatience with her conspecifics when they failed to catch on to what she was signing on the screen or the portable lexigram, and Sue was fascinated to see how she might set about this. Because she was so bossy, the others always seemed to take notice of her and what she was doing, and obligingly gathered around.

They watched her through the window. She soon had an inquisitive little crowd around her, heads bent towards the lexigram, Hand lingering shyly on the outside of the group. Would Caro be able to convey to them Mark's return? Of course, his departures and returns were probably of minimal interest to them, but that wouldn't deter Caro. She felt a stab of guilt that she hadn't got on with her research what with all that was happening. She must start in earnest tomorrow.

"We should celebrate his return," Ekoko said, looking relieved.

"I can't tell you how worried I really was, Ekoko." She continued to stare out of the window. "He's — what would you say? — somehow vulnerable. An innocent. He trusts people too easily. In some ways, the world's too cynical a place for him."

Ekoko placed a hand on her shoulder.

"I feel that about him, too. He is a very clever man but there is something of the child in him. But now we should be happy like Caro, and look forward to his return."

"He said nothing about Tchie Nkemi," Sue whispered. "What do you think that means?"

"A mystery. I shall have to talk to Louis, his cousin. I won't be able to give him any news." He chewed his lip.

They returned to the veranda, where the others were finishing their meals and sitting back relaxing with the duty-free Dunhills. The quick African dusk, smeared with a lurid blood-orange, was poised to turn into silky dark night. Ekoko explained to the other wardens what Caro had said.

Sue gazed around and suddenly realised that someone was missing.

"Where's Honore, Ekoko?"

"Ah, I've given him some time off today to visit his mother — my sister. She's very protective — she doesn't believe I'll look after him — she likes him to visit home regularly. But he's seventeen! I tell her, he'll still be a baby when his friends are married, when his friends have babies." This was obviously an old family argument which Sue chose not to pursue.

At that moment there was a piercing high-pitched cry from the enclosure outside.

: ◌ :

"You brush up quite well, considering." Jonathan Hyatt scrutinised him with a critical eye.

"Considering what?" Mark asked indignantly.

"Considering what you've been through, of course. Just stand still a moment."

Hyatt adjusted Mark's conservatively striped tie as Mark gazed down at him. It came to him in a rush, and left him feeling stupid not to have realised before, that perhaps the High Commissioner was gay. Did he think Mark was available? No, surely not. He wasn't the gay man's type really, was he? What was the gay man's type?

He felt his cheeks grow hot.

Anyway, it had nothing to do with what they'd planned.

"You know I'm really not used to these sorts of bashes. I tend to get tongue-tied and drift off to the margins, escape as fast as I can."

"Well, that's not going to be much help, is it? The whole point is that you keep your eyes and ears open, as will I."

Hyatt stood back, raking his eyes up and down Mark's form.

"You'll do."

"I feel like a trussed up turkey."

Hyatt tutted. "You've evidently been playing the wild man for too long. Let's go."

They descended the elegant marble stairs to the plush function room where the HC was hosting a drinks party, introducing businessmen and women to the diplomatic clique. This fortuitous shindig had been arranged some time ago, and Hyatt had put it to Mark that it might be worth his while to join the cocktail party, chat up a few select people, keep his ear to the ground, etc. Who knows what useful titbits he might pick up? He, of course, would do the same.

After some thought, Mark had agreed reluctantly, because while such gatherings were something he usually avoided like the plague, Hyatt was right, gossip can be useful. He'd delayed his return to CRU until tomorrow and he'd used Hyatt's PC to send an email to Caro. So he was trapped here now and he might as well make the best of it.

Mark hoped that their synchronised descent wouldn't be taken to mean that he was assumed to be Jonathan's partner. Reaching the bottom, he quickly grabbed a red wine and a canape from the waitress and plunged into the overdressed melee. But Jonathan was not to be put off so easily. He caught up and took hold of Mark's elbow and firmly steered him over to the fireplace.

"I'll introduce you to some of the movers and shakers," he whispered. A professional welcoming smile appeared on his smooth tanned face, which seemed genuine to Mark. His own smile, in contrast, he knew would look strained, so he dropped it and opted instead for a serious but interested look.

Hyatt approached someone standing, gazing at the book titles displayed in a cabinet.

"Mark, I'd like you to meet a friend of mine, Thomas Griffiths. Thomas, this is Professor Mark Rees."

The other turned around. Mark saw a shorter man of about fifty with bright blue mischievous eyes and a reddened nose. He had something of the dissolute look of Dylan Thomas about him with his greying curly hair and feminine mouth.

Hyatt paused only briefly, then addressed Griffiths. "You've heard of CRU, of course."

Griffiths gave Hyatt a quizzical look.

"That rehab unit for chimps?"

Hyatt nodded. "That's it."

"Of course. Who hasn't?" Comprehension dawned, the eyes sparkled. "Ah, the good professor works there?"

"Yes. Mark and his postgrad student are staying there. He's over here to conduct some chimp research." Hyatt pronounced triumphantly.

"Good god." Griffiths thrust out a hand. "How d'you get a jammy job like that, then?" The Welsh lilt was just detectable.

Ah, yes. One of the two standard reactions.

"Just lucky, I guess."

"Now, Thomas here is an old Cameroon hand. If you need to know *anything*, he's your man." Hyatt said meaningfully, patting Mark's shoulder and gliding quickly away, leaving Mark and Thomas looking at each other.

"Not your usual High Commissioner, our Jonathan." Thomas said eventually, with a sly smile and a wink.

Christ, he thinks I'm Hyatt's latest squeeze, thought Mark. He tried, not very successfully, to control a blush creeping up his neck.

"I'm eternally grateful to him for getting me back on my feet – I'd got dehydrated in the bush, collapsed in his office earlier today. Very embarrassing."

"Oh? How d'you manage that then – to get into such a state?" Griffiths' hand swept out and expertly snatched a passing drink. "Zoologist, aren't you?" Mark nodded not bothering to explain the nuances of the boundaries between Zoology and Comparative Psychology. "You fellows are supposed to be able to take care of yourselves."

That ignored the fact that the majority of zoologists slaved away in labs, but Mark had to consider how much to reveal at this point.

"Well, it's a long story." At this Griffiths' newspaperman's ruby nose lifted into the air like a hound scenting the quarry, and the eyes glinted.

"But first, tell me what an old hand gets up to here in Yaounde."

The glint died.

"I edit the 'Cameroon Times', English language daily. Have done for the last sixteen years. Seen everything there is to see, done most everything, too, and print it when I can get away with it." He took a long draught of the wine, practically emptying the glass in one go. Was he getting a little tipsy? His Welsh accent was becoming more pronounced. Mark had a scientist's deep distrust of the press – in his experience they never reported scientific findings accurately, always putting their own sensationalist spin on everything and muddying the waters.

"So how'd you get yourself into a pickle in the bush, then?" Griffiths wasn't to be put off so easily.

"I got lost, had no water – back in the Dja Reserve."

"Christ man, that's no place to be faffing about. It's one of the most dangerous places in Cameroon."

"You're not wrong there." Mark explained why he'd been there, how he'd come to be abandoned. What should he say about Wingent? He and Hyatt had agreed beforehand that Mark should only mention that he'd come across some human remains – true enough, but sufficiently vague to gloss over the details.

"I'm embarrassed to say I got left high and dry by the driver who legged it, or rather drove off in the Landy, and I had to schlep through the bush with virtually nothing on me." He waited to see how this went down. As with Hyatt earlier, he had Griffiths' close attention. Griffiths was in the know in this little social circle in Yaounde — he must have his ear to the ground.

He lowered his voice, leaning towards the other. "This *has* to be off the record, OK?"

Griffiths said "Of course, of course. Whatever you want." He seemed to be holding his breath, but heady alcoholic fumes drifted past Mark's nostrils. He'd obviously got a head start before even coming to this shindig.

"I came across some human remains — not recently dead, mind, but a white guy, maybe in his late thirties."

"Christ man, have you notified the police?" The little eyes were gleaming once more.

"Yes, but until he's ID'd you can't say anything. He may have relatives."

"Trust me, my lips are sealed."

Trust a journo? It went against the grain, but Griffiths evidently knew Cameroon inside out. He could be very useful if cultivated. Mark had to seem to take Griffiths, uniquely, into his confidence. This is what Jonathan had suggested — if Griffiths scented a possible story that was his and his alone, he was more likely to come across with any info.

"OK. The thing is, after discovering the body and meandering through the bush for some time I was picked up at the river Dja by two loggers from Rouge-Bolles."

"Rouge-Bolles? Count yourself extremely lucky, Prof." Griffiths gently prodded Mark in the chest to emphasise his point. "They're not known for their altruism at R-B. They don't welcome visitors there. Believe me, I know. I've tried. Got the bum's rush, I did. Lucky not to get shot."

Mark leaned in close to Griffiths. "I think I can trump you there. After being slugged, I found myself locked in a hut outside the camp and left. No water, no food."

215

"You're having me on!"

"Not at all. I eventually managed to escape using a pirogue —but they came after me."

Griffiths took a long considered pull at his cocktail, staring acutely at Mark all the while. *Perhaps he doesn't believe me. It does all sound far-fetched, a bit boys' own-style 'Ripping Yarns'.* But he reckoned the old hack in him was well and truly hooked.

"The reason I'm telling you this is not to sound like some idiot hero, but because I'm concerned at the level of illegal logging in that area. You know better than I, I'm sure, what the consequences are — I saw it in the depletion of the forest fauna, the bushmeat, the silty river and the impoverished Baka people." He took a quick scan around — no one seemed particularly interested in their rather intense conversation. "I need to know what *you* know about the whole sick business."

"Hang on. First you tell me about a body in the bush, then you're banging on about the logging. You're making a connection between the two?" Griffiths looked at Mark, his little eyes shrewd.

"I couldn't possibly say. I've no evidence whatsoever — yet," Mark mumbled, still afraid of being overheard, but leaving the idea hanging temptingly in the air for Griffiths to make of it what he cared.

Griffiths polished off his drink in one long gulp, his eyes still fixed on Mark, before replying, his voice low.

"Look, we all know that Cameroon is one of the most corrupt countries in the world, and a lot of that stems from the logging industry. It's made many rich and very powerful men, and many more poor ones, like your Baka. Corruption extends to the highest government level, the army and the police — up and down the social strata. In other words, it's endemic and frankly I don't see how you can do anything about it. I've tried editorials on the matter and all I get is seven shades of shit from government lackeys and blue pencil all over my piece." He paused, scratching the red bulbous nose. "Your best bet is to contact WWF here in Yaounde – see Dave Lancaster. He's much more knowledgeable than me on the logging front – I've interviewed him about the industry a couple of times - although even he can't seem to make much impact."

Once more he poked a finger towards Mark's chest.

"Mind you, if you were able to *connect* the death of that body you won't tell me about to the loggers, *then* you might be on to something very fruity. And I'd want first dibs on the whole thing."

"You'll be the first to know." Mark, backing away from the jabbing finger, was surprised to get such an open statement from a canny old journo.

Stumbling a little as he stepped back, he waved his arm about involuntarily, unfortunately the one holding his drink of red wine, spilling it down the crisp white shirt front and the pale grey suit which Hyatt had lent him.

"Oh, shit. Look, I'd better go and dab it off. But thanks for the advice." Mark turned to weave his way through the throng. "I'll be in touch," he threw over his shoulder.

"Make sure you are," Griffiths replied, raising his glass.

He pressed through the crowd, all monkey suits and over-fussy dresses – he couldn't see Hyatt anywhere, which might be just as well the state the borrowed suit was in - to exit the double doors to the function room, and looked around for any signs of a bathroom. The wine was soaking through the no-doubt horrendously expensive fabric. He knew where one bathroom was – he'd used it earlier today. He loped quickly up the grand stairs and sought out the rooms where he'd rested up.

This corridor was familiar. He walked down, footsteps silent on the absorbent thick-piled Wilton, scanning the doors. As he approached a cross corridor he heard the low mumble of voices, both male. He thought he recognised one of them but couldn't be sure. For some reason he would never be able to explain, he crept up to the junction, feeling foolish but holding his breath all the same.

He peered cautiously round the corner. The corridor was quite gloomy. The nearest figure, about fifteen feet away, his back to him, was faintly familiar; he'd seen him before somewhere. The second further figure was hidden by the first, but it was this person whose voice Mark thought he knew. He jerked his head back round the corner and listened:

"...difficult now...deal with… escape." This voice had an angry whiplash to it, but the speech was broken up by sound absorption. He couldn't understand the gist of it. Then another voice, more sibilant than the first cut in:

"I couldn't follow here…your problem...you're here, not me. When you figure it out...me know." A trace of some accent.

It sounded serious, and more than that, it sounded personal. Where had he seen the first figure? He'd caught, briefly, only a quarter profile but that was enough to jangle a few memory synapses.

"…café...where else..."

"…nowhere...shop..."

Mark stiffened, surprised. What were they saying? Was it *him* they were talking about, lurking about in dark corridors having whispered conversations? He strained to hear more.

"… get back...ready...call you."

The other made a grumbling disgruntled noise which sounded like a dismissal.

The conversation was finished and they would be coming back round this corner any second. Mark groped back behind him and grasped the glass crystal knob of the door. It turned. Holding his breath and pulling a fearsome face, he twisted the knob slowly so that it wouldn't make any noise, opened the door and backed into a darkened room. As he did so, he could sense a muffled footstep nearby. He swiftly closed the door, just in time. A second later the strip of light under the door was blocked as if some one was standing right outside. Mark backed away, scanned the room looking for somewhere to hide but could see nothing in the gloom until his vision dark-adapted.

A weak beam of light leaking through a crack in the curtains caught the glass facets of the crystal - the knob was turning. He'd been spotted, amateur that he was. God, this was stupid and embarrassing, besides they'd probably been talking about something entirely unrelated to him. He was showing signs of paranoia unless - tired joke – they really are after me.

Regardless, he squashed himself against the wall on the hinge side of the door, as it slowly opened.

A click and the light switch came on. Two soft steps into the room.

Mark squinted through the restricted gap. He still couldn't get a good look – until the head swivelled to look around the apparently empty room. He was on the verge of recall – but face recognition had never been his strangest suit.

The figure grunted and retreated, closing the door after him. Mark let his breath out, but remained standing rigidly against the wall, busily back-tracking in his mind. Recent, today. Where? Café…shop. Yes, now he had it! But how odd that he should have looked at this person and actually wondered briefly if he might be following him – then dismissed it as silly. Sleeked back dark hair, poor complexion, slim, dapper – the guy in the internet café! He *was* following him then. Shows one should trust one's first instincts.

If he was one, who was the other? The one furthest away, the one the café guy had seemed to be reporting to?

He let some time pass before cracking open the door and peeking out. All clear. He emerged from the room and rushed quickly to the toilets. There he gazed at the ruby red ruin, the colour of Griffiths' nose, on Hyatt's pale grey jacket. He dabbed ineffectually at it. He'd offer to have it dry cleaned.

Coming out of the bathroom, staring dismally at the mess he'd made of an expensive silky grey suit, he practically collided with Hyatt himself, coming round the same corner. Yet again a guilty flush crept up to his cheeks.

Mark stared at Hyatt, unable to think of anything to say. Hyatt stared at the stain.

Chapter
21

Sue and Ekoko looked at each other, and each saw fear in the other's widened eyes. In unison they ran outside. Other figures, too, were dashing around randomly, uncertain as to which way to go. Torch beams sliced the dark, crisscrossing ineffectually.

There were hoarse cries, rising shrieks as the other animals were infected by the fear and it spread until the air was rent with their frenzied cacophony.

Ekoko said, "The enclosure."

He didn't have to say which enclosure. A claw grabbed at her heart and squeezed.

To her, that first piercing sound was the high pitched cry of a terrified bonobo. Her mind catapulted back to the visit of the army brass, the implicit threats, the swaggering menace they presented, scarcely bothering to hide it. She'd been uneasy and so had Caro.

She rushed into the indoor living quarters first. No one there. Panting with fright, she slammed out the door to the enclosure and looked round frantically. The glowing moon provided a silvery-blue light illuminating the trunks of trees and ropes provided for the bonobos to play on.

There they were, huddling together in a tight group by the fence, their arms grasping at each other, their fur on end making them appear weirdly comical.

"**Caro**! What is it? What is the matter?" Sue yelled as she dashed over to them.

Caro turned and, seeing Sue, waddled over, her arms raised high in horror. When she reached Sue she clasped her tight, fingers digging in. Sue could feel her shaking, her teeth chattering.

"Sweetie, it's all right, it's all right." She stroked the coarse black hair on her back, rocking her gently. She peered down at Caro's swollen abdomen. Everything seemed to be fine down there, though she couldn't see much held in this tight terrified embrace.

By this time the others had gathered around. Sue felt a gentle touch on her arm. It was Hand reaching out tentatively with her mutilated hand. Sue realised that this was a measure of her terror, since timid Hand had not approached her before. She looked over towards the fence as she gently pulled the older female to her side. She couldn't see anything, it was too dark with the bushes pressing in.

But there was a sickening cooked smell.

"Ekoko! Ekoko!" she yelled, gathering the others towards her, making universal comforting sounds. As she tried to urge them towards the indoor quarters, they all moved in unison, clinging to each other and her. The bonobos were making chattering sounds of fear, occasionally escalating the decibel level. We must make a ridiculous sight, she thought, as she shuffled along awkwardly with her retinue, like so many skirt-clutching children, towards the open door.

Ekoko appeared with Louis Nkemi, both carrying torches. She should have thought to bring a torch. They stared a moment in fascination at the strange apparition of Sue and her clutch.

"Thank God, Ekoko! Something out there by the fence terrified them. Let me get them inside and settled and I'll come back and show you."

"No, Sue Clarke, you stay here with them. They are very frightened. They need you with them. We will look." He waved the younger man, whose eyes were wide with fear, towards the enclosure. "*Allez, Louis, vite.*"

Inside, Sue turned to the others, looked around at a loss for a moment, then found Caro's favourite toy, a grubby white rabbit called Snow and the new teddy bear. She tried to disentangle herself from their grasping hands, her terrified retinue of bonobos following her every action. She was fetching straw for bedding to try to settle them down, making crooning noises which she hoped would soothe them, when there came another cry – this time it was human, hoarse and pained.

All heads lifted and fur on arms and backs began to rise again. Sue quickly gathered the apes to her again, soothing, stroking.

My God, what the hell's happening out there?

: ⌂ :

Hyatt actually grinned. Mark couldn't be more relieved. He'd cursed his lack of balance and coordination innumerable times, but usually it affected only him.

"I'm so sorry, Jonathan. I can't tell you how..."
Hyatt held up a hand.

"Actually, it's not my suit – it's a friend's, and to be perfectly frank, I never really liked it. So, don't concern yourself."

Hyatt had been coming round the corner from the direction where the two figures were conferring. Had he been one of the two? Was that the voice he'd heard? He tried matching the two – recalling the one and listening to the other. He couldn't be sure.

Hyatt had been asking if his foray into the midst of the 'great and good' had been worthwhile. He was gazing at Mark eagerly.

Hedge.

"Ah – I'm not sure yet. I have to check something out first, then I can put you in the picture, Jonathan."

" Fine." Hyatt stared at him for a long beat, evidently puzzled as to why he wasn't more forthcoming. "I can get you a change of clothing if you would like, and you can rejoin us."

"To be honest, I'm absolutely whacked. I hope you won't consider me too rude if I hit the sack. That dehydration episode has caught up with me."

"Of course, that and everything else, I expect. You know the way to the room we set aside for you?" His voice seemed a bit distant.

"Thanks – yes. And I'm truly grateful for all you've done for me today. If anyone dares to criticise HMG's diplomatic service in front of me, they'll get a proper tongue-lashing. 'Night, Jonathan."

Hyatt stood staring at Mark's departing back.

Mark walked down another corridor and up a flight of stairs to the bedroom they'd assigned him. He made sure the door was locked. He'd have a long soak in the bath and think about things. Bloody hell, it was all so unclear, and he was too tired to sort it out. Who to trust, that was the thing. It depressed him, since he was a naturally trusting sort, liked to think the best of everyone – and yet recognised that that sometimes made him appear a little naïve and occasionally foolish. But he didn't like cynicism – it was far too destructive an emotion. Was he being paranoid again? Christ knew.

He ran the water as hot as he dared, rummaged about amongst various bottles of smellies and poured extravagant amounts in the water. Well, his taxes probably helped pay for these luxurious perfumes. He stripped off and slid into the steamy foam with a deep sigh.

Tomorrow he'd nip into the WWF office.

: ✿ :

Sue couldn't see what was going on outside now – it was the cavernous enveloping dark of the African night, and the windows just reflected back her pale anxious face. She'd had to settle the bonobos down before she could leave them and go outside. It seemed quiet, finally, out there.

Caro preferred to sleep alone on a straw pallet. It had been a very long time since she'd been able to cuddle up to a warm bonobo mother and she could scarcely remember it. So she'd long enjoyed the luxury of assuming any sleeping position she found most comfortable without having to consider anyone else; at present this was a starfish posture lying on her back, eyelids gradually closing, Snowy clutched in one hand. Sue glanced around at the others. All had their preferred places, and seemed to be settling down with drinks, comforted by her presence.

She'd had to keep calm for their sakes, but her heart was thumping wildly. That second scream – despairing, desolate. Horrifying. Human.

Once upon a time, she might have curled into a defensive foetal ball at that chilling sound, waited for whatever horrors were out there to pass over. Once. Not now. With her charges to protect, there was no way she was going to allow terror to overwhelm her. She couldn't be passive in this situation. She had to find out what was going on.

Impatiently, she waited for the bonobos to prepare for sleep.

Eventually, they settled down with many grunts and groans and tossing around of straw to make a comfortable bed. Sue crept out, closing the door to the outside part of the enclosure gently behind her and exited the enclosure via a locked door set into the fence, using the spare key Ekoko had given her.

Moving along the outside of the enclosure fence to the point where she'd found the bonobos at the fence, she looked for Ekoko and Louis, cursing the lack of a torch. Suddenly she came across them, almost bumped into them. Oddly, they were standing rock still.

"Ekoko?" Sue whispered. "What is it?"

The smell was there again. It was like the smell at the market...

Ekoko seemed to shake himself from an hypnotic state, gaze fixed on the ground, and turned to stare at her. Suddenly, he lunged at her and spun her round.

"*Non, non!*" was all he said.

"You're hurting! Let go!" Sue was alarmed at his intensity.

"Sorry." Ekoko loosened his grip. "I do not want you to see - this," he waved his torch behind him in the vague direction of the ground, the beam slicing across a still sticky-looking form.

Sue turned round and could see, over his shoulder, a shape lying on the ground. Louis hadn't moved a muscle.

"That? What - what is it?" She crept closer. The mound gradually resolved into a body shape. She gasped, a hand flew to her mouth.

The odour was stronger. Charred meat. The same smell as that from cooked bushmeat.

"Please, you must not see." He held her arm again, keeping her back. "*That* is Nkemi – Tchie Nkemi, Louis' cousin," he whispered into her ear.

"No!" Her horrified gaze was now fixated on the shape on the ground – she couldn't tear her eyes away. "No! It can't be. He went with Mark to the Dja – he – *he* was the one who went off with the Landrover, wasn't he?"

"Yes, yes. I did not choose the driver well, and I am ashamed about all that, but this? Why this? He is dead," he added unnecessarily.

"What's happened to him? Why is he here?"

Ekoko suddenly slumped against the fence and sat crouched with the torch held loosely in his hands and his head hanging.

Sue was about to repeat her questions, when he replied in a low voice.

"I wish you had not seen this. It is terrible. I think I know how..." He gestured with the torch unable to articulate.

The beam steadied briefly on a dreadful sight. The body seemed drenched in blood seeping through torn and charred rags, dull ominous gleams reflecting in the low light. But it was the skin that held Sue's horrified gaze. She was unable to look away. The body's whole skin appeared to be blistered, leaking haemorrhagically. And the barbequed meat smell wafted towards her...that did it.

Sue twisted around and was violently sick on the ground, bringing up all her dinner. It shook her so much that her knees buckled and she had to hang on to the fence. Ekoko jumped up and supplied her with a handkerchief.

He yelled for some water, and for Louis, who seemed to have abruptly disappeared. Sue remained where she was, grasping the fence, eyes tightly shut, her back to the horror that had been a young man, albeit a misguided one, perhaps even a thief. Nobody, nobody deserved that sort of death. How could anyone do that?

She knew she would never be able to rid herself of that dreadful sight. Or smell.

Feeling weak, she half opened her eyes and squinted over to the indoor area where she'd tried to settle the bonobos for the night. She thought she could see a palm placed against the darkened window. She'd better keep her voice down.

"I am afraid I know - this is called 'ironing'," Ekoko said swallowing hard.

"What? What are you talking about?" Her voice was a hoarse whisper. She kept her eyes fixed on the dark window.

He knelt beside her.

"He was 'ironed' to death, Sue Clarke. I heard of a thief tortured this way at the 3rd police precinct in Yaounde."

"Ironed? Dear God Almighty! You mean with a hot iron?" She was going to retch again. With great effort she controlled it, holding his handkerchief tightly to her mouth.

After a while she tried again. "Why? Are you saying the *police* did this?"

A younger warden appeared with a bottle of water which he passed to her, eyes enormous with fright and studiously avoiding looking at the bundle on the ground.

Sue thanked him and took a long gulp and passed the bottle to Ekoko. She coughed and retched again. She was in no condition as yet to comfort anyone.

"I do not know for certain. All I know is I have heard of this technique as a...a special method for getting a confession."

"By the police?" she asked again.

"Yes. But maybe that was just that district police." He rubbed his forehead in distress. "This is a message, I think." He took a long swallow from the bottle.

"A message? What do you mean, a message?" Nothing was making sense in this nightmare.

"Tchie worked here. The army visited here, remember. Mister Wingent is murdered. Mark is chased and attacked."

Sue stared at him.

"We're being warned off? Warned off *what*, for Christ's sake?" Her voice had risen in spite of herself.

"What is Mark doing in Yaounde?" Ekoko asked, apparently irrelevantly.

"Well, he's...he's telling the authorities about Colin Wingent. About his murder...oh, God, do you think that's it?"

Ekoko merely nodded.

"If we're being warned off, that must mean...this...this was Colin Wingent's killer?" Sue gestured behind her, not turning.

"Or killers. I think so, yes."

"And Mark has created waves, the killer heard - knows where Mark's based, here at CRU, and..." She waved her hand behind her back to indicate the seeping body, reluctant still to turn around. Then something occurred to her.

"But — but you said it might be the police? Why would the police *not* want a murder investigated?"

"Because they had something to do with it, Sue." Ekoko spoke so quietly she had difficulty hearing him.

Stupidly, she realised that was the first time he'd not used her surname.

"That's monstrous! I don't understand. What could they have to do with the murder of a..." She tailed off, her thoughts in a turmoil.

"Think, Sue." He sounded impatient with her. He'd slumped back against the fence again, evidently fatigued, long legs drawn up and head hanging.

She gazed at him, hands still clinging to the wire fence, trying to piece it together, realisation gradually dawning.

"We have to contact Mark. He could be in danger. And you need to get hold of all those extra men you mentioned."

Chapter
22

Mark was driven out to the CRU by Wilkins the Trade Attache in a spanking new and immaculate Land Rover, pungent with that rich new car smell. My taxes again, he thought. He'd had to wait until the late afternoon before Wilkins was free to take him back, and he was fidgety with impatience.

The news late last night from CRU was upsetting and bewildering, although a strained-sounding Sue had been meagre with detail – Tchie's body had been found. 'Not pretty', she'd said cryptically, adding that she'd explain more when he got there. The pot-holed road to CRU plus his fevered imagination did nothing to help his lurching stomach. Poor Tchie. All the times he'd cursed him as the instigator of all his woes when he was stumbling through the bush, all that had befallen him since that event. He'd even wondered if he'd suffered from Asperger's. Now he was dead. How exactly had he died, and why?

He could feel Wilkins' sideways glances at him. No wonder. He'd presented a pretty sorry picture when he'd examined himself in the steaming bathroom mirror at the HC – pale, in yet more borrowed clothes, wild slept-in hair, with dark rings under his eyes which somehow emphasised their extraordinary hue. At least he'd had a decent shave. And some of the bites had succumbed to the antihistamine ointment, making him feel more comfortable. Except for his guts. Neurotically, he briefly wondered if he might have caught some parasitic worm which was even now eating away at his guts. More likely the apprehension of what was awaiting him at CRU.

Wilkins put the headlights on full as dusk approached.

The beams from the headlights bounced in tune with the pot-holes. Mark clung to the door handle, dreading what they'd find at CRU.

"Not much of a companion, I'm afraid," he said by way of apology.

Wilkins tutted. "Think nothing of it. I was just concerned about you, about your health. I can't begin to imagine what you've been through."

Mark turned towards him in the seat. The Trade Attache seemed more cordial and open than when he'd first approached him at the High Commission to notify them of his presence, and the trip to the Dja. He'd misjudged him as a job's worth desk jockey.

"I can scarcely credit it myself. A simple field trip to observe some West Coast chimps, and it turns into some sort of nightmare, with a murdered body, and me being chased all round the bushes – literally."

"Do you think the pursuit was because you discovered the body?"

"That poor guy, Wingent, had been butchered, not just killed, and – uh – certain organs removed." Weirdly, it helped to talk about it, distracted him from the roiling in his stomach. "It looked like a *muti* killing."

"What? That voodoo business? I've not heard of that being practised around here. It's more of a Nigerian practice than Cameroonian, isn't it?"

"Yes, I was told that. If it had been just that, then I can't understand why I was chased all over the damn place. Doesn't make sense, does it?"

"You said 'looked like'."

"Ah — well, it wasn't quite right for a *muti* killing." He didn't really want to go into details right now.

"You figure it was something more than that? Maybe made to look like a *muti* killing in order to throw the authorities off the scent?"

Mark turned fully towards Wilkins, a little surprised.

"Yes, that's exactly what I wondered." He had expressed some of his suspicions to Jonathan Hyatt, but in the light of his new-found uncertainty about who to trust, he decided discretion was the better part of valour.

"I can understand that, but it brings up all sorts of other problematical questions then — like, why? Why go to all that trouble? Why kill him anyway?" Wilkins said.

He dug around in a side pocket and produced a hip flask, offering it to Mark with a little shake.

"Help restore you to your former pristine condition."

Mark took the flask. Normally he never drank whisky, but now he took a good swallow and felt the warmth spread down his throat to his guts.

"Thanks. I think I needed that." He passed it back to Wilkins who also took a generous slug.

"You asked the right question. Why?" Mark resumed. "The old business of motive – if not to harvest organs for the dark arts, then what?"

They were silent for a few minutes.

The headlights sliced the sky then hit the track with a jolt as the Landy negotiated a ridge in the middle of the road.

"Christ," cursed Wilkins. "Sorry."

"No probs," Mark muttered through gritted teeth as his head rebounded off the roof, probably adding yet another lump to a collection which by now would have had a phrenologist salivating.

"So what do you think the real motive was?" Wilkins asked as they gained smoother ground.

Mark took a deep breath. "I'm not sure. At first when I was picked up by the dastardly duo, a South African called Muller and a Bantu – Djomo, I think his name was - I was treated very well. Taken back to the logging camp, given a cabin to get cleaned up in and rested, a BBQ – the works. It all seemed hunky-dory – I was so pathetically grateful to have been rescued." He paused recalling that night. What a trusting idiot.

"You told them about finding the body?"

"Had no reason not to. More than that, I told them I knew the guy, and must get back to Yaounde straightaway to notify the authorities."

"Then it all went pear-shaped?" prompted Wilkins.

"Did it ever. Someone, I'm not sure who, but with hindsight it might have been the Bantu, snuck into the cabin whilst I was sleeping – and didn't take anything, just went through my meagre belongings. There was nothing a real thief would bother with, anyway."

"Why do you think they did bother then?" Wilkins offered the hip flask again, but Mark, remembering his overindulgence at the camp, shook his head.

Mark sighed. "I can't be positive, but perhaps they thought I had something on me that might implicate them in the murder."

"That begs the question, doesn't it?"

"Precisely."

"Did you have anything?"

Pause. "No." Mark was thinking of the notebook, but they hadn't taken it. It came to him then that they hadn't needed to because they'd intended to kill him.

They were both quiet again, Wilkins concentrating on minimising the jolting by swerving around any troughs detected by the headlights.

"Not far now. As far as HMG is concerned, Mark, you need to be very careful. We have a duty of care towards any UK citizen, but coupled with that no practical means to provide you with bodyguards, or indeed to insist that you accept any, even if we did have the means. All we can do is strongly advise you, caution you, not to stray too far from CRU." He looked over to Mark again. "Where else have you been in Yaounde since your adventure besides the HC?"

"Um – Police HQ to see Commissaire Beti and this morning a brief visit to WWF just to introduce myself." He decided not to bother going into his ridiculous shopping trip or the internet café. "Why?"

"Just trying to get the whole picture. How long was your field trip supposed to last, anyway?"

"I don't know, really. This was to be a feasibility study on the West Coast chimps in the Dja. Sue Clarke, my postgrad student is studying the spread of linguistic abilities among the bonobos at CRU after the introduction of Caro."

"I've heard of Caro, of course."

"And one of the main reasons we came at this time is to be here when she gives birth. Sue Clarke will want to see if she attempts to teach the baby her idiographic language, so she may stay on a while, and make subsequent visits. There've been such instances of linguistic transmission with other apes but not fully researched."

"Hmm. Is her time near?"

"Indeed. Imminent, as far as we can tell."

"And when she's had it? What will you do then?"

"Will I go back, do you mean? I don't know." Mark rubbed at his hair.

"Considering what you've all been through, I would think you'd want to take a step back, at least take a break, let things settle down here, eh?"

"I need to talk it through with Sue. You may be right, but I have a stubborn streak – I don't like to be run out of town. I prefer to go when I choose. But there are other considerations above and beyond my own selfish ones."

"Like your family, you mean? I heard you have a youngster at home."

Mark frowned. He was sure he hadn't mentioned this to Hyatt and certainly not to Wilkins, but then, an uncomfortable thought, they'd likely have all his personal details at the HC. He didn't really appreciate being told he ought to get home to his son, the real reason, he acknowledged, being that he already felt guilty enough about being away from Joe. But perhaps they weren't that up-to-date if they believed he was still with his wife. He wasn't going to correct that impression – they can update their files without my help, he thought.

"Well, yes, of course I want to get back as soon as I can, but I was actually thinking of the great apes, in particular their declining numbers due to their habitat destruction and the horrendous business of bushmeat. Speaking of a duty of care, they're the ones *I* feel responsible for. As well as that, it was brought home to me just how wide the devastation reached when I was with the Baka people."

"The pygmies?"

"Do you know what they told me?" Mark continued without waiting for an answer, gazing fixedly through the window screen. "Their girls are much in demand as prostitutes *because* they're smaller and cheaper! Can you believe that? And if those bastards in the camps can't get them, they abduct them!"

"I've heard rumours, of course. A perfectly dreadful situation. Ah, here we are."

Wilkins brought the Land Rover to a halt outside the main CRU building.

A pale Sue dashed up to the vehicle, apparently undecided whether to scold Mark or hug him. So she opted for both, pulling him out of the car, embracing him, shaking him and calling him a stupid idiot. Didn't he realise how frantic they'd been, all of them, worrying, not knowing anything?

Mark contented himself with repeating "I'm sorry. I know, I know. I'm sorry." He felt genuine remorse as he saw it through her eyes - all they got, after days of silence, was a short mobile call, plus a follow-up call from the high panjandrum himself.

Finally, he extricated himself from Sue's ambivalent angry hug to see Wilkins smiling ironically at him, and Ekoko hanging back, looking stern and stiff, beside him.

"Ekoko?" Mark approached him hesitantly. "I must apologise for putting all of you through this worry." He was concerned that perhaps he'd overdrawn on his friendship account with Ekoko. After all, the guy had more than enough on his plate without some stonking fool getting himself into all sorts of trouble in the bush.

Mark was relieved when Ekoko stuck out his hand for him to shake, although his grim expression remained.

"We have bad news, Mark. There has been a - a murder here."

"*What*? What do you mean?" He turned and glared accusingly at Sue. "Sue? You told me that Tchie had had an accident."

"No, I didn't say that - you assumed."

Wilkins interrupted, stepping closer to Ekoko. "You're the senior warden, right? A murder, did you say?"

Ekoko nodded, flicking his eyes to Wilkins and back to Mark's face.

"Sorry – this Mr Wilkins from the High Commission." Mark made belated introductions.

"Mark, I am sorry. Yes, it was Tchie Nkemi murdered," Ekoko said softly.

"Jesus! And why is he here?" Mark felt the blood draining from his face, looking futilely around. "How did he get here, anyway?"

"Perhaps we ought to go inside?" asked Wilkins taking his arm gently. "You have called the police?" This was directed at Ekoko

Ekoko's face closed down, but he nodded curtly. "Yes, but there is a delay – there are not here yet. Come." Ekoko led the way to the centre's main building, up the wooden steps to the veranda where they'd so often sat together, enjoyed meals and drinks, talking in a desultory, comfortable manner, feeling a deepening companionship wrapped in the dense African night and its sounds. Now, that peaceful atmosphere was shattered, as Ekoko described what had happened.

They sat around the table as still as the heavy night air when Ekoko briefly described the injuries Tchie had suffered, the light from the lantern on the table highlighting the glints in his eyes and deepening the hollows beneath his angular cheekbones.

Sue's head was hanging, and Mark's face was covered by both hands in a parody of shock.

At last, Wilkins spoke. "I'm so sorry for your loss."

Mark loathed that phrase - those formulaic words were as totally empty of meaning as 'Have a nice day', but Ekoko nodded his thanks without replying.

"It does, I regret to say, sound like the police. I've heard of that type of, um, death before, associated with them," Wilkins added.

Again, Ekoko merely nodded. Sue remained silent staring deep into the lantern's light, while Mark experienced another level of guilt about how he'd roundly cursed the unfortunate Tchie, the *murdered* Tchie. Then it penetrated.

"Police? The police did that? But I just saw the Commissaire yesterday."

"You did? Why?" asked Sue.

"I had to tell him what I'd seen. Wingent's body. Tell him where it was. Could it really be the police?" He turned to Wilkins.

"All I can say is that the technique is not unknown to them." Wilkins lit a cigarette and blew the smoke into the rays of the lantern.

"That is what I told Sue Clarke." Ekoko agreed.

"What are we going to do?" asked Sue.

Just then there was another liquid high-pitched cry coming from the indoor area. Mark's blood froze. That was not a human cry.

"Oh my God, not again," Sue whispered.

She stood suddenly knocking over the veranda chair, but Ekoko had already leapt out of his seat and was running over to the indoor enclosure area.

All of them, at their different speeds made their way to the indoor area.

They heard a shout from Ekoko who reached the enclosure first. "She has started!"

Sue and Mark arrived at a rush to Caro's sleeping quarters.

"She's in labour!" Sue said. She dropped to her knees by the bonobo's side. This was her first time – she'd never attended a birth before. Her hands fluttered like birds over Caro as she lay on her bed.

"Please, please let it be alright." She begged under her breath to a god she didn't believe in. All the stress had probably brought labour on.

Caro was lying on her side, making low whimpering noises. Sue stroked the black hair on her head.

"It will be fine, sweetie. It's good. Baby is coming. You will soon have a little baby." She went on making soothing comforting noises, repeating them like a mantra, for want, really, of anything else to do.

Ekoko was on his mobile to the vet who'd been kept on standby for just this event.

When Caro caught sight of Mark she reached an arm up to him, curling her hand round the back of his neck and pulling him down. She planted a loud kiss on his cheek.

"Caro, I missed you. I am sorry. I was away too long." He gently disentangled himself and held her hand in his, rubbing it gently. "But we are all here now, to look after you. You will be fine. We will help you. Do not worry."

But he felt the same anxiety and excitement as when he'd attended his own son's birth. Scared, overwhelmed, tearful, apprehensive, ecstatic – and, Christ, so impatient.

: ✿ :

In the event, the vet got there quickly, bustling into the sleeping area with his bulging bag, an anxious-looking assistant in tow. There was no way he was going to be late for this big event. This was the most important birth he would ever attend. Nothing was to go wrong. For ages he'd had his medical bag packed with everything that might be needed.

He began bossing everyone around, found some task for each of them. In the excitement, caught up in it, they left behind the horror of Tchie's death - temporarily.

Finally – she gave birth.

Caro's labour lasted longer than he would have liked, he said, and she was exhausted but there she was, finally, cradling a baby girl. A perfect, tiny, wizened baby bonobo with questing, wobbling eyes and clenched fists. And Caro was in love as they gazed in awe at each other.

Eventually, in the small hours, as a smoky pink dawn began in the east, they crept silently away, almost as exhausted as Caro. They slumped in their seats where the evening had started with the terrible news of Tchie's murder, on the veranda. The lamp was now out and while the dim light still lent a monochrome tinge, colour was beginning to bleed into the landscape, the ever present cicadas providing the background noise now beginning to cease their stridulations, one by one.

They all had rather silly smiles on their faces. Smiles strained and touched with sadness, though – Tchie should not be forgotten even at this moment. Ekoko dashed inside to get some celebratory drinks of beer.

They raised the bottles to Caro and to the vet who had a wide grin plastered on his face, blissfully unaware of the tragedy. Even the harassed veterinary assistant was handed a drink.

"Never again, but I wouldn't have missed that for the world," Sue breathed.

"Never? You'll find it a tad difficult to avoid your own labour." Mark said, trying to unstick his borrowed shirt from his back.

"You think I'd want kids after that? No way, Jose."

Ekoko looked around.

"Where is that other fellow you brought with you, Mark?"

"Oh." Mark swivelled his head around. "I completely forgot about poor old Wilkins. I should have thanked him for the lift. I imagine he sloped off. Probably a bit queasy. You know what some blokes are like. Not like myself of course, a veteran of the delivery room twice over. Cheers!"

Wilkins was indeed driving back to Yaounde and the High Commission, his thoughts whirling with the gruesome murder of the young warden.

He opened his mobile while keeping a sharp eye out for pot holes.

Chapter
23

D CI Paul Draper laced his hands behind his head and leaned dangerously back in his creaky old swivel chair. His expression stern, he was staring yet again at Mark's email.

What Mark didn't know was that the late Colin Wingent from Longstock, near Winchester, lived with his brother, Adam, and that Adam had already supplied a DNA sample, along with hair samples from Colin's hairbrush. They'd wasted no time in getting his buccal sample following Mark's email, so that when the package containing the splinters arrived the Forensic Science Service could look for a match with the blood stains on them. The poor kid had looked destitute

Blood, which had soaked into the pithy fibres, from what sounded like Colin Wingent's very bloody murder. Paul glanced over at the mysterious padded bag lying innocently on his desk, its dark contents still unseen by him.

It had just arrived by express delivery.

His brother had confirmed the area where he thought Colin was headed for, and what he'd told Adam he was going to do there — monitor the tree-felling, check that it was within the legally defined areas and that the trees were of sufficient size. If it *was* his body lying there in the bush, and that seemed likely, it was no doubt by now ravaged by scavengers and any useful forensic evidence long destroyed or compromised. Unless the Cameroon police had got there PDQ after Mark reported to them.

Apparently the brothers' mother was languishing in a retirement home, suffering from advanced senile dementia, so Adam Wingent had told her nothing of the dreadful news as nothing was proven as yet. She either wouldn't remember anyway, or confuse Adam with Colin as she had so often before. But at least the brother was prepared for the worst, and Paul was very much afraid that would prove to be the case.

He felt sorry for the younger brother. Waiting to find out was soul destroying, not knowing was worse. No one else to turn to, either — except a girl-friend in London. He knew the anguish of waiting — his own sister, Helen, had disappeared when a teenager never to be found, dead or alive. Even now, so many years later, he still found himself scanning crowds for a now-mature woman with a certain way of walking, a turn of the head, his own dark blue eyes. The spear of painful hope when you think you might have seen someone who could be her - and the crashing despair when you know it isn't. Families never really recovered from destruction like that, and his own had been no exception.

He sighed, creaking idly backwards and forwards, stretching his arms above his head. From his point of view it was the next bit of the email that caused ripples - visiting the good professor at the university armed with the evidence in a jiffy bag. With the Super on holiday, the permission of the Acting Superintendent of the Basic Command Unit, based here at the Central Hants. Police Station, was required in order to persue enquiries into the suspicious death of a British subject abroad, albeit one who normally resided in this fair county. But – and this was a big 'but' – it was always extremely tricky when that death occurred abroad. Police forces are notoriously prickly about other forces poaching on their territory. He knew he would be, in their shoes.

Nonetheless, as Paul had put it to the AS, this would merely entail enquiries at this end which might assist in the apprehension of a culprit at that end, and needn't involve either the other Basic Command Unit that covered the Test Valley where the Wingent brothers resided, or the Major Crime Department; he, uniquely, was best placed to deal with this since he knew Professor Rees, and Professor Rees personally knew the genius in the Botany Department at the University. He'd received a cautious 'yes' to the analysis of the samples with the proviso that he incur no expenses, the budget already having been spoken for and groaning as loudly as his chair. And a 'yes' to keeping the inquiry, such as it was, to their BCU, and not at this stage involving MCD.

How the hell was he supposed to incur no expenses? Unless – he peered again at the email – the professor viewed this as a challenge and a valuable test of his data-base. He picked up the phone, prepared to schmooze a little.

Just then his DC, Sandhya Ghopal knocked on the door to his cramped, messy office and entered, looking a little pale around the gills, he thought.

"What's up, Sandy? Look like you've seen a ghost."

She brandished some printouts at him.

"Worse, much worse, sir. You asked me to look up that 'Adam' case – the boy found in the Thames?"

245

How macabre was that? Adam the brother, and his brother, Colin – perhaps – murdered like 'Adam'.

"I remember sketchy details.Only the trunk was found, that right?"

She nodded at him as she sat heavily in the plastic chair opposite him. She was tall, Junoesque rather than slim, rich black shining hair piled up on top of her head, wide deep brown eyes – right now, staring at him sadly. Paul could all too readily understand the attraction she held for George Thynne, his DS.

"That's all that was *ever* found of him. But it was a dreadful case." She rubbed her cheeks, bringing some colour to them. "I'm beginning to think I may be too squeamish for police work, sir."

"Rubbish. We all feel the same way when it's a child. When you stop feeling like you do now, it's time to worry. Let's have a gander." He waved at the papers. "And you can drop all that 'sir' business. Sit down."

Sandy handed them over and sat down on a hard plastic chair. His office wasn't overendowed with decent furniture.

"OK. I'll give you the gist of the case anyway and you're right - I have to learn to cope with this stuff. Right. It was thought to be a *muti* killing because of the tell-tale removal of certain internal organs and the fact that he was only a four-year old child. Children, apparently, have more potent effects, so they're preferred..." She shook her head, took a deep breath and continued. "Anyway, you can read all the gory details for yourself, but suffice it to say that the case became a landmark for the forensic work done on Adam's bones. That's how they located the area where he was brought up in Benin, West Africa - and from his stomach contents, his last meal. The shorts his poor little... his shorts came from a shop in Germany and their orange colour was apparently significant in these voodoo rituals – something to do with river gods. So was the fact that the atlas bone at the top of the spine had been removed." Sandy paused, gazing fixedly out of the window. "Some sort of powerful hex, the atlas bone."

Paul had heard of the case, naturally, but not the dreadful details. He stared at her in horror, wishing he didn't know now.

"Poor little tyke. And *this* was what Mark Rees came across in the African bush. Christ. I bet he saw his breakfast again."

Sandy stood suddenly, still pale, giving Paul a strange look as she hung onto the back of the chair.

"I have to get back to my paperwork. It's still waiting for me," she said stiffly.

With that she exited and shut the door with some finality.

"Oops. Prat." Paul berated himself.

He put the printouts carefully in a folder and picked up the phone again and, once through to the university, asked to speak to Professor Steve Frampton.

: ⛢ :

The School of Biological Sciences held the Botany Department. It was a large, not very graceful seventies-style building with then state-of-the-art acres of bronze smoked glass glinting in the autumn sun. It was probably a sauna in the middle of summer.

Paul, as he always did when he got the chance to nose around laboratories, peeked into this room and that, sniffing the air like a hound. There was that distinctive 'science' smell, compounded of pungent organic chemicals, formaldehyde and alcohol. It both excited him and induced in him an old regret that he hadn't persisted with his science at school – in fact he'd been darn useless thanks to a fearsome Biology teacher and turned instead to History. But his fascination with all things scientific, especially the rampantly expanding forensic sciences which were blossoming out into all sorts of directions – like this unlikely, original one – had never really extinguished.

He was looking forward to finding out about tree maps, and the like.

On the second floor he found Professor Frampton's office, and knocked, glancing at his watch. On time.

A cheerful voice bellowed at him to enter. He found a large imposing figure with a beaming red round face jumping up from behind his desk and pumping his hand vigorously before he'd had time to say who he was.

"This all sounds very exciting," Steve Frampton grinned delightedly, rubbing his hands, as though he'd won the lottery. No preamble, straight in.

"Ah, yes, I hope so. DCI Paul Draper, by the way,"

"Sit, sit. Now, you brought the samples with you?" He had eyes only for the padded envelope Paul was carrying.

"I do, but first I have to ask you if you're OK with this. We are, um, somewhat financially constrained when it comes to…um…"

"Yes, yes. It's fine, fine," the Professor beckoned towards the envelope, his eyes alight with anticipation.

Paul handed it over and watched as the Professor examined the date stamp and the seal and scribbled a note on a pad.

"Have you opened this?"

"No, I thought it better to keep it sealed until you were ready to deal with it, less risk of contamination,"

"Quite right, quite right." Steve Frampton had a habit of repeating the initial phrases of a sentence. He quickly snapped on a pair of latex gloves with all the enthusiasm of an over-zealous customs officer. "Let's see now, what do we have here." He opened the envelope carefully with a scalpel and tipped out the two inner envelopes. One he opened carefully with the scalpel and slid the contents out onto a clean sheet of filter paper. Small wooden splinters, four in all.

Paul leant forward, interested to see what had prompted his friend Mark to go to such trouble. These then were the insignificant chips of wood that might solve a murder?

Steve Frampton poked them about a bit with a pair of forceps, humming the while, and transferred them to a covered Petri dish. Then, peering more closely, he froze, and looked at Paul over the rims of his glasses.

"There are traces of what appears to be a dark liquid soaked into the fibres. Here, see? Is this blood?"

"Yes, sorry - I should have warned you. It is blood." But you barely gave me the chance, he was thinking. "On more than one?"

"Yes, yes. Here and here."

Paul peered at the splinters. "Good. More chance of getting viable DNA."

There were darker stains on two of them, but he might easily have mistaken them for shaded streaks of the reddish wood where the professor's more experienced eye had detected the stains almost immediately.

Frampton glanced up and gave Paul a long considering look, his expression puzzled.

"I think I should get one of those back to the forensics lab, see if they can analyse the DNA," Paul added. "For a definite ID."

"Mm, of course, of course, as you wish." Steve Frampton was already transferring two splinters to a sterilised stoppered test tube, which he placed in another padded envelope and labelled. Paul took it.

"Thank you. More than likely it's the victim's blood, but we need to verify whose it is – and, you never know, there might be another's trace there, too."

At this, the genetic botanist frowned briefly, shook his head sadly, and took up the padded envelope again.

"There should be a wad of sawdust in there, too, according to Mark's email," Paul warned.

Steve Frampton took another pair of forceps and gingerly extracted the second inner envelope, slit it open, pulled out the wodge of still-damp sawdust and placed the mass into a second Petri dish, putting the lid on top. Finally, he sat back clasping hands over a comfortable stomach and considered Paul over the top of his rimless glasses.

"So how much can you tell me about these samples, Chief Inspector? I gathered from your phone call there's a gruesome story behind these chips of wood." No initial echo now. "You must be good mates for Mark to entangle you in this affair."

"Paul is less of a mouthful. Yes, I'd like to think so, and he'll owe me a few jars after this. Well, I'll tell you all I know, and all this comes second hand, as it were, from Mark."

"Listen, I love him to bits but that Mark's a regular magnet for trouble." A plump latex-covered finger wagged, accompanied by a wry grin. "It trails around behind him clinging like a skunk's scent. You'd think, wouldn't you, that we'd lead quiet, contemplative lives here in our ivory towers? Not so," he went on, not expecting an answer. "Not for the likes of Mark Rees — well, you'd know that yourself. He wanders through life in his un-coordinated way, all wide-eyed innocence, with these spectres of trouble floating along in his wake, just waiting for an opportunity to strike."

Paul smiled in recognition of the description. It fit Mark to a 'T'.

"Yes, brilliant, preoccupied, dedicated — and sometimes, all over the damn place."

"Still, you didn't come here to listen to me try to analyse my dear colleague. What's the lad been up to?" He pulled off the gloves and threw them into a pedal bin.

"He's in some kind of trouble, having stumbled across the murdered body of a Brit in the middle of the bush. This is his blood, I think." He waved his own jiffy bag.

Steve's affable expression disappeared. He sighed and put his hands up to his face in an oddly feminine gesture. "Oh, God. It would have to be Mark. It would have to be him."

"He'd met this poor guy briefly before going out there, so he was able to identify him even though the remains were - well. The thing is, the body looked like a *muti* killing — that's a ritual sacrifice."

Steve dropped his hands from his face. "Ah, yes, yes. I've heard of that. Let me think. That case a few years back — the boy - Adam didn't they call him?"

"Exactly, that's the one. So you can imagine Mark's shock. Nevertheless, he was still sufficiently compos mentis to take these samples from Wingent's cheeks." He indicated the splinters in the first dish. "They'd stuck there with his blood. Mark deduced that he'd been killed elsewhere — as there was no sign of cut or torn timber in the area where he found his body and not enough blood in the immediate vicinity – and taken to that spot post mortem."

"Ah, so if we can determine the species *and* do our tree DNA profiling – which is essentially what it is – then we might be able to pinpoint where the unfortunate fellow was actually murdered." The professor's expression was brightening.

"That's what I'm hoping – to make a connection between the body and the killing ground. If that can be done, then there might be forensic evidence to discover at the site of the murder, if it's not deteriorated by now. It could certainly help out the police over there."

"Right, right. An intriguing twist to our usual application. And this sorry lump of sawdust?"

"As I understand it, Mark picked that up from a saw mill. He seemed to think that the place might somehow be connected to the murder. I'm not certain how. But if you'd be able to do the same sort of analysis on that...?" He left it hanging as a question.

Paul was reluctant at this stage to give the botanist the whole story as it could be argued, if this ever went further, to court, say, that the forensic examination had been compromised by revealing the details of the origins of the material.

"Hmm, hmm." The professor was busily writing out two labels which he attached to the lids of the glass dishes.

Then he put his pen down and sat back.

"Now, I ought to give you some idea of what we'll be doing, and what we might be able to accomplish. First, we're happy to use these samples as they may help develop our data base, and may help refine our techniques – and, we'd like to see this further developed for use in the field to prevent illegal logging."

Paul, at this, tried not to betray anything. This was just what he'd been hoping for, and the fact that the beaming professor himself brought up illegal logging - Mark's email mentioned that Wingent worked for Forest Watch - meant that he didn't have to, and also that they were all moving in the same direction. So he contented himself with thoughtful nodding.

"Now, as to what we'll do – and remember there can be no guarantees – it's a form of DNA profiling which can give a very reliable method of determining the geographical origin of the wood. We analyse key sequences of genetic code that distinguish one cluster of trees from another."

He ploughed on as though Paul was a post-graduate student.

"The technique analyses the frequency with which particular genes appear in the samples from each location."

So far so good, thought Paul, frowning in concentration.

"We then use this information on the distribution of specific genes to predict the likely frequency of these *same* genes appearing in other, unsampled geographic areas, a statistical smoothing method, if you like. In other words, we develop a DNA-based reference map to assign timber origin."

Just hang in there, Paul told himself. He nodded slowly, wearing what he hoped was an intelligent expression.

"Good, good." The assumption was made that Paul was following all of this, whereas, in fact, it was more like seventy-five percent, which he privately reckoned was pretty impressive for him.

"So, while we've already sampled 27 areas in West Africa – Gabon, Cameroon, Congo and so on - we can extrapolate gene frequencies into unsampled areas."

Hold on, hold on. He was picking up on the Frampton echo-effect. He held up a finger.

"Are you saying that you don't actually have to have taken DNA samples from particular areas in order to pinpoint where some timber has come from? That you can, with some statistical sleight of hand, fill in the gaps between sampled areas."

"Excellent, excellent. I wish some of my students grasped the concept as quickly."

"Thanks. I think I was hanging in there by my fingernails, but what you've told me is astounding. You don't need to have an exact match between, say, seized timber and reference samples."

"You've got it. That's what we believe. The same technique is used with seized shipments of ivory, so we're developing this for the even vaster trade in illegal timber. And there's not a great deal of time left."

"But I'm guessing you need a good data base to start with." Paul paused, thinking. "You have some samples from the Cameroon, then? I'm not giving anything new away since you just mentioned Cameroon, and, well, I suspect you already knew that he'd gone there."

"Yes, yes, of course, but not where exactly..."

Ah, good, Paul reasoned, that would lend added weight to the evidence if this ever did come to court. If there's any evidence to be got.

"...and we have as many as nineteen samples from Cameroon since it has some of the most bio-diverse and threatened rainforest in West Africa."

"You'll try to identify this hot-spot for us?"

"Certainly, certainly. We'll do our best. We should be able to place the origin of the timber to within fifty miles. It'll be a new direction for us, but any additional application strengthens our hand when it comes to grants."

Fifty miles was still a heck of a chunk of forest.

"Then, we'll both benefit, I hope." Paul stood up and held out his hand. "You'll let me know when you have something?"

Steve Frampton bounced out of his chair.

"Shouldn't be too long. I'll give this priority. It's a terrible, terrible business."

As he was ushering Paul out of the door, seemingly eager to get on with his analyses, he touched Paul's arm.

"Is he alright? Mark? Not in personal danger?" His shiny brow was furrowed in concern. He reminded Paul of an anxious puppy.

Paul paused. In truth, he wasn't sure if Mark was in imminent danger right now. He could well be, judging by his email, with allusions to pursuers and imprisonment, but he had the distinct feeling that the sooner they could get an answer to the riddle of the woods, the safer Mark would be.

"I hope not, but to be brutally honest, the sooner we can have your results the better."

He shook a plump firm hand.

Chapter
24

Commissaire John Beti crouched down beside the bloodied bundle lying beside the fence, his face twisted in distaste as he hastily dug out a pristine white folded handkerchief. He wiped his forehead and covered his nose. He examined the pathetic remains without touching them, leaning this way and that, and then stood slowly, beckoning the morgue attendants forward.

He had arrived at CRU very shortly after the baby's birth, but later than he should have due to the search for Wingent's body in the Dja region.

"You found this body?" He addressed Ekoko, who stood apart a little, his arms folded across his chest. Ekoko's left eyelid was twitching.

"I did. Who do you think could have done this, *Commissaire?*" The title was stressed sarcastically, causing Beti to glance up at the taller Ekoko quickly.

"Ah, I know what you are thinking," he said, rising up on the balls of his feet.

Even at Beti's full height Ekoko towered over him, still glaring.

"This was one of my best wardens, Tchie Nkemi, a young man. He was related to another of my wardens – they were cousins. I tell you there is great disturbance and anger here at this."

Beti held up a hand.

"I understand that, and there was that other unfortunate case of death by this method. That is what you were thinking of."

"Unfortunate? He was *tortured*, Commissaire, tortured by 'ironing'!" He flung out his arm pointing towards the body being lifted into a body bag. "His mother cannot be allowed to see him like that," he added.

Beti flinched at this.

"Yes, yes, but that other case was in the 3rd Yaounde precinct, and the disgraced officer and his thugs were apprehended. They brought shame to our good name, but they were dealt with."

Ekoko snorted his derision at this as though 'good name' and 'police' were unconnected concepts. "These are not isolated cases." He was warming to his theme, neglectful of the possible danger he was creating. "And here, poor Tchie murdered by the same method. Beyond coincidence, Commissaire!" His voice was getting louder, attracting the attention of Mark who had been walking along the fence checking for any breeches.

"Ah, Professor," Beti practically leapt upon Mark as a saviour from Ekoko's wrath. "I want to assure you that neither I nor my men have had *anything* to do with this disgraceful affair of the murdered warden, whatever this warden may think. I demand and expect the highest standards of behaviour from all under my command."

There was another soft snort from Ekoko bringing a glare from Beti.

Notwithstanding Beti's ringing endorsement Ekoko had told Mark the Cameroon police were well known for both their corruption and torture. Any real or supposed infraction of the law, like not getting off the pavement when an officer wished to pass, could land you in one of the stinking police cells, and once there, you were at the mercy of the sadistic police officers; prisoners had died for such an offence. Why should officers under Beti be any different?

Mark could think of nothing immediate to say. He'd be damned if he agreed with Beti – particularly by Ekoko who stood glowering at both of them - and damned if he didn't. Then, staring down at the body bag lying by the fence, about to be lifted into the back of the mortuary van, he realised he owed it to two dead people to try to sort out this whole mess by talking.

"Commissaire, I'm a mere foreigner flailing around in the dark and trying to understand the larger picture here, but it seems as though whoever it is who's trying to frighten us with that poor bloody corpse – and it does look like a warning, left right there by our fence - and whoever it is who imprisoned me and chased after me in the bush, may all be connected in some way."

"Yes. I believe it was a warning, too. I told Sue Clarke. Whoever did this – ," Ekoko shot another hard glance in Beti's direction, " - is telling you, Mark, to say nothing about that other murder."

Beti was switching attention from one to the other.

Mark rubbed at his hair, wondering if he was wise to reveal more of his suspicions. He'd faced the same dilemma at the HC but had in the end felt that he had to discuss it with Hyatt as Colin was a Brit and Hyatt had responsibilities for the safety of fellow subjects. He'd been on the brink of talking it over with Wilkins, too, but he wasn't *au fait* with the set up at the HC and didn't want to tread on sensitive diplomatic toes. Beti had himself raised the subject, but Mark hadn't really taken it up. However, Ekoko and the CRU staff deserved more consideration and Ekoko seemed to have reached the same conclusion as himself.

"There's something else. I don't think Colin Wingent's death was a *muti* killing at all…"

Beti interrupted. "I have read through your notes, which are detailed, but we cannot conclude from the presence of one bone that the murder was not *muti.*"

"You're right, of course, but just suppose that the link was illegal logging. That's the work that Colin Wingent was engaged in - monitoring the forests."

He ploughed on, practically paraphrasing Beti's comments at Police HQ but addressing himself to Ekoko who was looking confused at the mention of notes and *muti.*

"We all know that the illegal timber trade is Cameroon's largest, yes? Sixty percent of all exports? We all know that it's very much like illegal drug smuggling, global, with very much the same characters involved – drug barons, timber barons. No difference. All criminals, all ruthless, all voracious." He held his hands wide, appealing to them to agree.

"I have already said this to you," Beti said.

"I know," Mark agreed. "We now have additional information, though." He counted on his fingers for emphasis.

"Wingent's murder, my abduction, *Tchie's murder* — suppose they're *all* linked to this trade, to protecting this trade — and the people involved in it."

Beti pursed his lips, looking thoughtful, while Ekoko had taken refuge in impassivity, waiting for more.

Mark wanted to trust Beti, but, more importantly, wanted him to look in the right direction.

"Surely, the man who could break up this evil trade by discovering Wingent's murderer would be an heroic figure, a national figure..." Probably that was laying it on too thick, too crass. Beti was now looking at him sceptically.

"I understand what you are saying, but *I* do not need the incentive of fame to do my job properly," Beti said stiffly.

Mark had asked for that with his clumsy attempt to flatter.

Beti now drew himself up indignantly, tugging at the hem of his jacket. "What I need *you* to understand is that my men were not responsible for this atrocity." He gestured towards Nkemi's body, now behind the closing doors of the van.

"Have you not wondered why the body of Mr Wingent was not where you said it was, Professor?" he continued.

"What?"

He'd momentarily forgotten about the police search for Wingent's body although it had flicked through his mind that maybe there had been no real attempt by the police to find it or maybe predators of the four-legged variety had disposed of it.

"No, I see not," Beti went on, a self-satisfied expression on his face. "We did find your tag tied to a tree, and we did collect vegetation with smears of blood and these will go for analysis if they are not too – um – compromised. What we did *not* find was evidence of removal by carrion eaters. There would have been much more of a trail of blood along the ground, signs of dragging, and evidence of tissue and even body parts left behind."

Mark swallowed, his throat dry. "Not there?"

Beti went on remorselessly. "There were no such signs and I therefore conclude that the body was removed by human hands before we got there. Would you agree?"

"That's a fair assumption." Mark said faintly. Ekoko remained silent and stern.

"So, then, we have a body missing at the particular time that I and my men arrived at the marked spot."

Shades of Sherlock lurked in the background. Something there…

"He never believed in coincidences!" Mark burst out.

Both men stared at him.

"Sherlock Holmes. He never believed in coincidences," he explained.

Blank looks.

"There must be some hand behind the coincidence in time between the disappearance of the body and the arrival of you and your men, Commissaire, isn't that what you meant?"

"Yes, yes. Exactly what I was going to say." Beti looked mildly aggrieved that his thunder had been stolen. "But why did the body disappear?"

"There may have been some compromising evidence on the body? Something I'd missed." Mark paused gazing at the spot where Nkemi was found, reluctant to get into a gory description what with that gruesome death so fresh, the mingled metallic scent of fresh blood and the charred smell of cooked meat still catching at the back of his throat.

Could that be it? He looked up again.

The others were piercing him with expectant looks, waiting.

He took a deep breath.

"Ekoko, I haven't had the chance to put you into the picture properly and I apologise. Briefly, what happened when I came across the body was this: when I saw - when I got close, I could see he'd been badly mutilated. His internal organs had been removed. It didn't look like a predator's work – the neat removal suggested some sharp cutting implement. A knife maybe." He paused briefly. "I immediately thought of a case that made the headlines back home a few years back. The trunk of a small boy, African, washed up on the banks of the Thames in London – headless, no hands, no internal organs. Forensic scientists concluded it was a *muti* killing."

"In your country? You also have such evil magicians?" Ekoko was surprised.

"No. Yes. The police thought the boy had been brought to Britain from Nigeria for the specific purpose of satisfying these rituals."

"Barbarians. They bring dishonour on their people!" Beti spat his contempt.

First, shame and now dishonour. Cameroonians had little time for Nigerians and weren't reluctant to express it.

"Where was I? Ah, yes, well, I remembered reading that one of the structures removed from a body in such a ritual was the atlas bone at the base of the skull; it seems to have particularly potent powers." His hand unconsciously drifted around to the back of his head. "Wingent was lying on his back, so I had to reach under his head and feel around at the back of his skull - " He swallowed hard.

"And," put in Beti, turning to Ekoko as though he himself had discovered this, "the atlas bone was still there!"

Ekoko was beginning to show signs of impatience.

"OK, OK. So this bone was there, and you think this shows it was not a real *muti* killing. So why did they try to make it look like *muti*?"

"To deflect us from the real motive." Mark spread his hands.

"And therefore you, Professor, if I understand you, think the real motive is connected with illegal logging."

"I'm convinced of it now – what with Tchie's murder. Why else would they pursue me? Because I'd seen the body – the body of a fellow citizen. They didn't know if I'd be familiar with *muti* ritual killing. In a way it was bad luck for them that I'd read a little about it – enough to make me suspicious. If I'd been deceived – and I was initially - I was uncertain - things might have gone a little easier for Tchie."

"How did they know you were not fooled?" asked Ekoko.

"I've been slow figuring that out. My notebook, of course, which I passed to the Commissaire here. I put in there all the details surrounding the body, and the findings of a cursory and very crude examination – plus the presence of the atlas bone."

Beti was nodding at this.

"Whoever it was crept into my room at the camp read the notes and then, of course, realised that the pretence of a *muti* killing might not work – at least, not if I got to the authorities."

"So they had to dispose of you and the notebook. And further they couldn't take the chance that others might see through their fake *muti* killing, thus the removal of the cadaver from the spot you tagged. I can see your reasoning, Professor, but we still have not addressed the question of the coincidence in time of the body's removal and the arrival of myself and my men to search for it," Beti said in his prim way.

"You think someone knew when you were going to look for it and removed it?" Ekoko was coming round, albeit slowly.

"I do," replied Beti.

"So who knew you were going to Dja when you did?" asked Mark.

"You and I – we discussed it in my office."

"I certainly haven't told anyone." Mark was indignant. He'd not said anything at the HC – he thought. "And what about your staff?" Mark batted the ball back, recalling the scared looking youngster in the outer office when he'd first visited Beti.

"Well, yes, of course. There was the Duty Officer - although he was in the outer office and could not hear what we said - " Beti tailed off, a thoughtful gleam in his eye.

"And other staff must have been told, I presume."

"Not precisely, no. Not *where* we were going exactly, nor what we might find." He stopped and stared into the far distance, muttering something under his breath. Then he turned and addressed Mark.

"I must return immediately to HQ. Professor, might I request a favour from you - that you accompany me? I need an impartial observer." Beti was suddenly brisk.

"Why?" Mark was taken aback.

"It's difficult to explain until we get there. But it shouldn't take long and it may benefit all of us caught up in this tangled web."

"It's a bit tricky right now, what with Caro's baby, and all this." He gestured vaguely around where Nkemi's tortured corpse had lain, the grass underneath still darkly stained.

"I stress it is important both to this case, Nkemi's, and Mr Wingent's." His eyes seemed to implore Mark.

"Go, go, Mark, we are OK to look after ourselves. Anyway, their sick message has been delivered. There will not be another one soon." Ekoko made shooing movements with his hands. He seemed to have abandoned his hostility towards Beti at least for the time being. "Sue Clarke and Caro will be safe with me. My men are ready, I can tell you."

Mark nodded his agreement, nonetheless perplexed as to what Beti's mysterious request was all about.

"Excellent. Professor, I will show you once and for all that neither I nor my men were involved in this."

Mark hoped he was right.

Chapter
25

The brief dusk had been swallowed fast by the mantling night, but the temperature had scarcely dropped. The air was still sticky with humidity and either that, or fear, made it difficult for Mark to get enough air into his lungs.

The two of them crouched outside the Police HQ sheltered by luxuriant foliage, peeking between leaves, like a couple of chicken thieves; the irony of the situation, voyeuristically snooping on the police with the Commissaire, was not lost on him. They were waiting to check that the coast was clear. Beti had insisted on it, although Mark couldn't see why they couldn't just waltz in; after all it was the Commissaire's station.

"Shh. You make too much noise with your breathing. I need to listen." The closeness of Beti's territory made him imperious, thought Mark.

"I can't see any lights on. Anyway, it's your office – why don't we just go in?"

"Who knows who might be watching?"

"*We're* watching, dammit. Look, no one's there – no lights, no cars, just us." This is ludicrous. What am I doing here?

"Mmm," Beki sounded doubtful, but eased himself up gradually from his crouching position. He scanned the area once more, then beckoned Mark to stay behind him as he crept, hunched over, towards the entrance. Mark followed him, defiantly upright.

At the entrance, his mouth close to Mark's ear, he whispered, "When we are inside you say nothing, move quietly. You are not there, do you understand, Professor?" He emphasised the drama of the occasion by placing his finger over his mouth.

"I wish I bloody well wasn't here. What are we doing here?" he stage-whispered. "And what on earth are we looking for?"

"We are looking for evidence which will exonerate me and my staff. I need you as a respectable witness. Remember, no noise. It must seem like just me in the office."

"What sort of evidence?"

Beti produced a chatelaine-sized bunch of keys, evidently a badge of status, and they were quickly through the entrance before Beti replied.

"Some evidence that this office is not as secure as I thought…"

"What? You've been bugged? You're not serious."

"It is my integrity and that of my staff that has been compromised. I want you here as an impartial person of authority to show that I and my men are honest." His voice too was a stage whisper.

"What we need is a scanner device of some sort – a bug detector."

"Well, I do not have such a thing, so keep looking."

Now into his office, Beti pulled down the blinds before switching on a desk lamp.

Beki went straight to his desk and was rummaging about underneath.

Mark turned around in the middle of the room flapping his arms ineffectively. He didn't really know where to begin, or how, so tentatively ran his fingers under the window sill, encountering only cobwebs and dust.

He whipped round suddenly as he heard whistling. It was Beti trying for a semblance of reality – for the sake of some unknown listener who more than likely didn't even exist.

Mark rolled his eyes, then crept around the sparsely furnished office, trying to be as quiet as possible, carefully lifting up a chair and peering under the seat. Nothing there. Well, of course there wasn't. This was a farce and a bloody waste of time.

Still, he'd better appear willing. He lifted up a rug – dust; peered up at the central light fixture – dust that hadn't been touched in years; looked behind the filing cabinet – more dust rising into the air.

Didn't Police HQ warrant cleaning?

He must not sneeze. He pinched the bridge of his nose.

Beti was still whistling and rustling some papers as though he was working late – and alone – whilst feeling around underneath drawers.

Mark pointed at the phone, the obvious place, and mimed unscrewing the old-fashioned receiver. Talk about teaching your grandmother to suck eggs. Beti nodded, increased his whistling and picked up the receiver. He gingerly unscrewed the receiver and peered inside. Mark bent over to look. There was nothing untoward that would catch the eye. Bugs were usually round things – in films anyway. All seemed as it should be.

I Iis eyes travelled down the cord to the phone socket. Hadn't he'd heard of bugs in sockets? He bent down to squint more closely at the socket. Was it larger than usual? One thing he was absolutely sure of – it seemed brand new, and, far more telling to his way of thinking, it had no coating of dust. Mark grabbed a piece of paper off the desk and scribbled rapidly. Beti inclined his head to read,

" Phone socket. Pull it out carefully. Screwdriver?"

Beti's eyes went wide, he held up a finger, nodding, and scrabbled in a desk drawer coming up with a small knife. He got down on his knees, while Mark, feeling foolish, rustled papers, humming the while since he had never been able to whistle.

Presently Beti straightened up and showed Mark the opened socket with a shrug. They both peered inside. What were they looking for, anyway? What he knew about the spook's trade wouldn't fill the back of a postage stamp.

Then Mark froze – that blessed 'eureka' moment. He reached into his trouser pocket and pulled out his mobile. Holding up the phone to Beti and waggling his eyebrows, he tried to convey what he wanted to do. Beti understood and focussed the desk lamp on the socket. Mark took two pictures, still humming – one showing the entrails and one from the outside - with his mobile and quickly transmitted it with a brief explanatory text.

"We wait," he mouthed. He glanced at his watch. What was the time there? Would he be awake? Would he be able to find out?

"Work, work," he mouthed again, flapping his hand at the desk. Beti obligingly began his noisy paper shuffling, banging drawers and whistling tunelessly.

Mark put the phone on mute and waited, chewing the inside of his cheek. Maybe he'd turned his phone off. He'd be asleep. He wouldn't know the answer… Christ, this was a stupid idea. The whole thing was laughable if it wasn't so serious.

He looked at his watch again – 2 minutes had elapsed.

He paced around as quietly as possible.

A text message! He waved the phone at Beti.

"Wait. I'll find out. P"

He almost yelled out loud. Good old Paul. He showed the message to Beti. What a brilliant idea to think of asking him. What would he be doing? Paul must have access to data about spook devices. One thing was sure, though, he'd not be best pleased to be roused from sleep. He had a tendency to grumpiness at such times.

Yes, here we go! A picture. A photo of the self same socket - and what was this? Mark shuffled over to Beti to show him the tiny screen. Heads together they read:

' *3-way outlet mains adapter. UHF Transmitter over 15 m radius. 110v AC/220v AC. Long term monitoring.' Looks like UR spooked! P*

"Bloody hell, you're right," Mark whispered. The photo, probably from a spooks' online catalogue, was exactly the same.

Beti grabbed the phone, eyes staring. He recovered and snatched a piece of paper and quickly scribbled.

"Who is this person?"

Mark's turn to snatch it back.

"Friend. DCI in Hampshire."

Beti gazed at Mark as though he'd performed a particularly adept trick of prestidigitation, so Mark mouthed, "Police inspector."

Beti thought a moment then grabbed back the now crumpled piece of paper.

"Let us replace bug. Use it." He underlined 'use' several times and mimed replacing the socket-bug in the wall.

Now it was Mark's turn to slowly realise that they could employ the bug for their own Machiavellian purposes. He nodded eagerly and hummed a little to keep up the theatre he'd been neglecting. Beti carefully screwed the adapter back in place and beckoned Mark outside the room and into a corridor.

"Now do you believe me? I have been betrayed," he claimed rather breathlessly. His anger at the dastardly intrusion into his holy of holies made him rise up on his feet and his actions became a little jerky. This was quite an extreme reaction for Beti, Mark reflected, a man who took pride in exercising icy control.

Mark was thinking that if Beti wanted to deflect suspicion away from himself, this was an excellent way to do it, planting a bug himself. But he really didn't want to say that at this juncture when they'd just discovered the bug. Maybe it was a reluctance to spoil the conspiratorial moment of discovery. Maybe he didn't really want to believe it. Anyway, if they were to use it to plant disinformation – which was Beti's idea – Beti himself could hardly be the culprit. Unless, of course, that was another way to deflect suspicion away - no, no, too involved.

"How shall we use it if we leave it in place?"

"It is obvious, Professor. We plant false information."

How many times had he read of just such a twist in books. Part of him – the prepubescent boy part – was thrilled with the idea; the more adult portion, which he sometimes recognised was not as developed as it should be, cautioned restraint.

"Of course, but what precisely? Look, let's get out of here now and discuss how we go about it in more comfort." He was beginning to feel that they were stretching their luck, hanging around the Police HQ at this time of night. Or at least, he was – whereas it was Beti's natural habitat.

They left the office as they'd found it and crept out as surreptitiously as they'd crept in.

When they were back inside the CRU Land Rover, Mark heaved a sigh of relief, wiping his sweating forehead.

"My God, I can't believe we just did that. I'm knackered. I'll never make a good spy. Obviously you suspected something of the sort, didn't you? That's how they knew when to move Wingent's body before you got there, isn't it?"

Beti was quiet, staring through the dusty window screen. Mark looked over at him.

"What?"

Beti turned slowly towards him.

"Not 'what', but 'who'. Who planted it? It must have been recently placed there because of the absence of dust."

"Yes, but the only way to find out is do what you suggested and plant false information. See what happens. But we need to decide exactly what we're going to say that will mislead your enemies."

"Enemies, yes. There may be several, alas," Beti breathed. A haunted look came over his face, and Mark realised that in all the excitement he had entirely forgotten that it was the Commissaire who had been targeted here. When he finally returned back home Beti would still have to deal with his 'enemies' who mightn't stop at bugging, if what he'd experienced so far was anything to go by.

"I'm sorry, Commissaire. I'm being selfish. I can't imagine what it must be like to discover that someone has been recording your every word, someone who might be close, even." He paused. "Any idea who might be responsible?"

Beti took a deep breath. "In truth, I have too many suspects." He gazed sadly down at his clasped hands. "Cameroon is unlucky. We have many corrupt officials in the government, army and even the police, as I told you. It could be anyone. Anyone."

Beti looked to be in danger of lapsing into a brown study, so Mark tried to jerk him out of it, bringing the conversation round as to how best to use the bug.

"We need to stage some scenario in your office, and plant false information that will lead us to the culprit." He sounded like a copper - perhaps some of Paul's thinking had rubbed off. "Here, have a polo mint. Might help you to concentrate." He rummaged about in the glove compartment and produced an oldish tube of broken mints.

Beti took one and they both sat back sucking thoughtfully.

"We should try to lure them to my office, spring a trap."

It seemed the discovery of the bug was bringing out the latent James Bond in both of them.

"Yes, good. How shall we bait the trap? Something they can't afford to ignore..."

"No, no, no. You have to leave this to me. You cannot be involved, a visiting professor. It is not correct." Beti waved a hand dismissively.

Mark was shocked. "Look, I'm already involved. Have been right from the beginning. At the risk of sounding self-important, it was me who was imprisoned, slugged and chased. It was CRU that's been threatened. It was a British subject who was murdered. So - what's more likely than that I would visit you again to have another talk about it? In fact, it would be odd if I didn't."

"I cannot deny that." Beti silently sucked on the mint for a long moment. "Accepting the premise that this bug was recently planted, then this all begins with that murder, Mr Colin Wingent's murder, would you agree?"

"Yes, you're right. Whoever's responsible must suspect that I doubt it was a real *muti* murder – if they're the same ones who read my notebook. And they want to discover what you know about it."

"Ah, they may think that you know who the murderer is and told me – outside the office."

"But I don't."

"But they don't know that." Now Beti was more animated as he turned towards Mark. Mark could just make out his eyes, gleaming in the dark.

"So we must convince them that we *do* know, that we have some particular evidence."

"What sort of evidence?" Mark asked. "The trouble is I've only been guessing why Wingent was murdered – that he came across illegal logging operations. No real evidence, not what DCI Draper would call probative evidence."

"What sort of data was he collecting, this Wingent?" asked Beti.

"He briefly mentioned it to me: what species were being felled, what size trees were being felled and – and *where.*" It was Mark's turn to get excited. "Yes, of course, what's wrong with me?"

"I don't know..."

"I found the poor bugger *in* the Dja Reserve which is a restricted area – logging prohibited – although he wasn't killed on that spot. Suppose in our make-believe scenario he actually did discover illegal logging going on in the Dja?"

"Yes, that may be likely in fact. No concessions are allowed in that area. It is a reserve."

"Suppose then in our scenario that he obtained some evidence *showing* illegal logging and conveyed it to another party without the knowledge..."

"Of the murderer! Yes, yes, I see. But who would he send it to? To me? To you? Who?"

"No, no." Mark thought back to Hyatt's stiff little party. Griffiths. Would Wingent send it to the papers? No, the murderers would know that a juicy story like that would have appeared by now if Griffiths had anything to do with it. If Griffiths wasn't censored again, that is. It had to be Forest Watch – if he'd had the time.

"No," Mark repeated. "For our purposes, it doesn't matter whether he *really* had any evidence to pass on or not, does it?"

"We only have to make the murderers *think* we have something..." Beti was quite animated, a wide smile spreading across his face.

"That's it. The question is 'what'? We're back to what sort of evidence?"

"Photographs may be best."

"Ye-e-e-s. Photos showing the species of trees, the size of trees and maybe the location - like a GPS reading."

Mark looked down at his lap — the mobile was still resting there. The mobile he'd just used to transmit a picture to Paul. He held his breath thinking.

"I've got an idea — let's talk it through. Wingent, while he was here, was working for Forest Watch under the auspices of the World Wide Fund for Nature — you know they have offices in Yaounde?"

Beti nodded.

"Well, he was allowed to use their facilities. Now suppose that he had a mobile phone with him similar to the one here — and he did what we just did in your office."

"Sent pictures to a friend?"

"Or in this case, sent pictures to the WWF offices."

"Ah, then our murderer might think there is evidence at the WWF…"

"Unless someone like me — who they may believe is closer to Wingent than I really was — visits the WWF offices and downloads the pictures from a PC."

"You can do that?"

"Oh yes, Wingent could send the pictures from the field to a PC and later print the pictures off. The neat thing, though, is that I *have* popped into the WWF offices, albeit briefly. I went to — well, never mind now — the point is that if I have been watched that part of the story will hold up."

"Excellent. Then tomorrow, you come to my office and you say you have found some evidence…"

"Say, a photograph of the felling of undersized trees, or trees in a reserve area..."

"…about Mr Wingent's murder that may help us find the perpetrator..."

"I don't want to endanger the WWF people — so, I'll tell you that I checked the data on the PC terminal used by

Wingent, found the pictures, saw that they were crucial to your investigation, printed them off – and then, realising the plight this might put WWF in, deleted them on the PC."

"Good. Then we say – no, *I* say I must put them in a secure place like the filing cabinet…"

"Then we wait – see who turns up."

"No, *you* do not wait – *I* wait with some of my men. I am definite on this."

Mark tried to read Beti's expression - it was too dark but there was a stubborn note in his voice.

"OK – reluctantly. What time do you want me in the office?"

"Nine sharp. We will get these devils. You know, these mints are very effective."

Chapter
26

Mark turned up on time at the Police Headquarters, performed his part well, he thought, resisting the temptation to shout so the adapter bug could pick up the conversation and left, giving Beti a quick wink.

As he drove back to CRU, it occurred to him that they may not have found all the bugs. In fact, there might be visual surveillance implanted somewhere else in the room, in which case the whole charade was a bust. 'He/they' would have known that Mark and the Commissaire had discovered the socket bug and just made total pratts of themselves trying to set a trap.

Oh, well, he just had to wait and see what – who – turned up. Or if.

: ☼ :

Back at CRU there was an email from Paul waiting for him.

'What was that all about – the insect? Did you realise it wasn't even sparrow-fart over here? Anyway, your Prof is very keen to help – he has

the samples and will prioritise. Blood traces from wood samples will help confirm ID. Keep me in the picture and watch your back — viz, use the delete key when you've read this.'

A touch cryptic, still he owed it to Paul to give him a fuller explanation. He glanced at his watch doing a quick estimate of the time back home. He would be in his office.

'Police HQ was bugged and seems Commissaire/police set up as fall guy/s for another murder (warden who accompanied me to Dja Reserve murdered as a warning). We planted false info which may entrap real culprit — and possible murderer of CW. Don't know how many involved in whole filthy business of illegal logging though, but do know corruption reaches into highest ranks.'

Mark sent the email and, feeling rather silly, deleted.

He then turned to all the other business he'd been neglecting, especially Sue and Caro and her baby. So he sought out Sue, and caught up on all the news; they'd had little chance to chat since he'd been effectively submerged by events since he'd returned. Caro and the baby were sleeping so best not to disturb them, and feeding seemed to be going well.

He looked in on them quietly, feeling unduly proud and quite grandfatherly, and tip-toed away to find Ekoko.

Ekoko's men, unsurprisingly, had been very disturbed by the murder of Tchie, and Louis, his cousin had returned to the family home to comfort and try to explain to his Aunt what had happened.

"He cannot tell all, Mark, to his Aunt. He will have to lie about Tchie's death. To tell the truth is to ask for more trouble. But he wanted to get there first, before any rumours started."

"I know it's of little comfort to Louis, to all your men, but you can tell them at least that the police weren't involved. You know, in case any hotheads decided to take action."

"This has to do with your adventure yesterday?" Ekoko sounded curious. "Can you tell me what happened?"

"Yes – uh – between you and me, Beti's office was bugged, a listening device had been planted. So we think the murderer knew exactly what Beti was going to do, where he was going to go – that's why his men found no body. Whoever was listening got there first and removed it."

"You are saying that the same person also killed Tchie by ironing to make it look like the police were the killers?"

"I know it sounds a tad unlikely, Ekoko, but it all fits. Right now we have to wait and see who falls into the trap we've set." He was sounding far too conspiratorial, and, yes, eager. He was too childishly pleased to be in the loop. He needed to keep in mind always what these people could do, and what they had done. It was far too dangerous – in that, Paul was right to caution him – for him to slip into boys' own adventure mode like some idiot comic book hero.

'Keep me in the picture. . .' Paul had said. The time had come to tell Paul all that he knew.

When he got back to the PC, there was another email from Paul. So he was probably working in his office, which meant that they could talk real-time.

Do you have any idea of what you're getting into? You could be next, and I don't have another comparative psychologist friend. Go nowhere alone – same goes for Sue Clarke. You can't afford to trust anyone. If any moron daft enough does fall into your trap, let me know who.

Meanwhile – 2 findings:

1.   Trace analysis of blood on splinters has come through; it confirms a relationship to Adam Wingent, CW's brother. AW gave us a buccal sample earlier. Identical with DNA from CW's hairs from his hairbrush, too. On this basis we can search their house to see if there are any indications of what CW thought was going on, what he might have discovered, etc.

2. The tree species is the endangered sapele *and Prof Frampton is 80% certain (using statistical jiggery-pokery) that this tree came from the Dja reserve, and same goes for the location of the trees from which the sawdust came. Sawdust is a mixture of three species — moabi, ayou and sapele.*

Two things follow from this:

1. For the murder, DNA analysis of the splinters is only of use if we can match them to an actual tree. An unlikely prospect, and even then it won't prove who did it — but it's weighty circumstantial evidence linking logging/ loggers and murder i.e. providing probable motive.

2. Whole logging business suggests there are two factions involved:

1) At the Cameroon end, I'm assuming there are well-connected types taking backhanders, granting concessions, overseeing transport, arranging false documentation and generally protecting the loggers, and 2) there **must** *be western-based contacts involved in the illicit timber trade — after all, the timber mostly arrives at European ports.*

We'll try to find out more about destination of Cameroonian timber this end.

*Can you discover - * without *getting into trouble — the concessions that border the Dja Reserve? How long does it take from cutting timber to port? How frequently shipped? Where shipped to (assuming port of origin is Douala)? Etc, etc.*

Hold fast - Paul

Mark was astonished that the analyses had been performed so quickly. Maybe it wasn't so surprising for the blood — except for the fact that it was still viable, not denatured — if they already had his brother's blood analysed and hairs from Colin. But his old friend Steve Frampton was moving at the speed of a tornado. Either the old bugger had nothing else to do, or – or he was seriously concerned – as was Paul. If his good and normally phlegmatic friend *was* concerned, then perhaps he, Mark, should be a little more circumspect. Still, what to do?

Mark sat scrubbing fingers vigorously through his curly hair, a habit when he was thinking.

"Of course, you tosser," he chided himself.

He pecked out a quick reply to Paul, then dashed off to see Ekoko.

: ◻ :

Ekoko was annoyed.

"Why should you go? Haven't you had enough adventure?"

"This will be safe, I promise. I shall be very careful, but I have to find out more, and they should be able to tell me."

"Hmf."

Ekoko, who had been sitting at his desk checking some invoices, didn't sound convinced, and Mark had some sympathy with him. He'd done nothing but dash around getting into scrapes, and spent hardly any time here.

In no time at all he was racing back to Yaounde, leaving a disgruntled Ekoko behind, but certain he would be able to work something out.

As he bounced along the rutted track, his mobile rang with that ridiculous mooing sound that he had neglected to alter. It always startled him, always made him look around, until he remembered.

It was Beti.

"I wanted to check that you are not coming into town for any reason, Professor."

Mark stared at the mobile. Was the man psychic?

"No, of course not. I leave the police work entirely to you, Commissaire. You're the professional - you know what you're doing. I'd just get in the way." Actually, he felt that he'd earned the right to be somehow involved, but he was the outsider, the bumbling amateur.

"What's that noise I can hear?"

Christ, the man was paranoid. He could hear the engine growling over the rough ground.

"Look, I'm doing work – the work I came to Cameroon for, researching culturally transmitted behaviour in chimps."

Perhaps that would shut him up.

"I have to go now, but I will contact you when we have some news," said Beti, apparently reassured.

"You do that." Mark dropped the phone on the seat. He couldn't really figure out why Beti appeared to be so worried about him. Or was it that he wanted him out of the way when, if, things started happening?

He took a large swig of water from the plastic bottle. He had other things to think about.

Chapter
27

He should have had a proper chat with this lot long before this. Got a few things clear. Now, because he'd left it for so long, he was feeling awkward, partly because he had, albeit unknown to them, indirectly used them in the deception cooked up with the Commissaire.

He got out of the Landy and looked around, checking for surveillance — and he thought *Beti* was paranoid - aware that if there was any, he'd be unlikely to spot it. WWF was located in Bastos, a quiet residential area in the north of Yaounde. Their office was a smallish affair. Unprepossessing was the word. Perhaps discreet was a better word.

No doubt it was wise not to adopt too high a profile, which might come across as overly aggressive. They seemed to go about their business quietly, publishing reports about the depredations wrought by illegal logging and bushmeat, and the consequent effects on the wondrous but depleting biodiversity of Cameroon, and apparently managing to avoid, so far, the fate that befell Wingent, and, almost, himself.

As he'd phoned ahead, he knew the most senior member of their three-person team was waiting for him, and he was a little apprehensive about this meeting. Earlier, when he'd been hanging around waiting for Willkins to give him a lift back to CRU, he'd barely popped his head around their door. Unfortunately, David Lancaster had been out at a meeting, and he'd just had a brief word about what he was doing with a younger team member from Colorado. What was her name? Julia? July? He'd spent only about five minutes there, and he'd relied upon that visit to lend credence to the story he and Beti had concocted about Wingent's evidence.

As before, he poked his head around the door and called.

"Anyone home?"

A gruff voice answered.

"Come on in, Professor Rees".

Mark entered all the way into the small chaotic office, to see a large figure seemingly trapped behind leaning piles of paperwork. The figure stood to reveal a giant, reddish beard peppered with white, thinning ginger hair on top and chest hair poking out of the unbuttoned neck of his khaki shirt. Several sheets of paper drifted folornly off in the draft.

"I'm pleased to meet you, finally," the voice boomed.

Mark felt himself reddening.

"I must apologise. It was unforgivable of me not to see you first. I can only plead that we were swept up in a confusing tide of events, and this is the first opportunity I've really had. I did pop my head around the door earlier, and spoke to — ah — Julia from Colorado — but I missed you."

It sounded feeble even to him, but the giant seemed satisfied, smiling.

"Please don't feel bad, Professor, I know how it is, and also something of what happened to you from our mutual hack friend. And it's Julie-Ann from Carolina."

" Sorry. Julie-Ann. I'm poor with names. Thomas Griffiths, the hack? Of course. He told me to come and see you, ask your advice. It's Mark, by the way."

"Dave." He said poking a thumb at his chest. "Tom said you'd had some adventures in the Dja Reserve." He indicated a chair.

"You could say that. It all seemed to stem from the death of Colin Wingent whom I'd met before coming over here. All I was setting out to do was observe some chimps in the Dja area." He hoped that didn't sound too querulous. To his shame, he felt some prickle of resentment at having discovered the body. Everything had come off the rails since then.

He took the chair.

"Colin. A bad business. I doubt the culprits'll ever be caught – after all, it's not like it's the first time a conservationist has been attacked or simply gone missing, although it is the first time it's happened to a Brit."

"And maybe it's the first time it was made to look like a *muti* killing."

"What?" Bushy eyebrows rose above deep set faded blue eyes. "That's new – and nasty. Maybe the bastards are getting more inventive. Tom just said there was something deeply fishy about the whole affair, but I didn't know it was that."

Mark gave him a potted version of his discovery of the body and the disappearance of Nkemi, and the eventual appearance of Nkemi's body at CRU.

After some more frowning and sympathetic growling, at the mention of CRU Dave's expression suddenly brightened.

"I'd heard that Caro had a baby."

"Yes, a girl - just about the one good thing that's happened since I got here. How did you know so fast?"

"Bush telegraph – well, our friend the vet really. Remarkable – Caro." A big grin split the beard. "Eh, forgive me. Would you like some tea?"

Mark was thirsty after telling his tale and agreed eagerly, still mindful of his bout of dehydration. Dave bustled ponderously around with a teapot and enamel mugs, while Mark marvelled at the precariously balanced piles of papers wafting gently in the breeze from the window. Reading upside down, he could see one was concerned with monitoring elephant numbers – Monitoring Illegal Killing of Elephants (MIKE). Yet another species teetering on the edge, at least in West Africa.

"Ah. I see you've spotted our recent paper," the voice boomed from behind Mark, making him jump.

"Sorry. Couldn't resist a peek."

"No probs. We have to monitor the elephant numbers since Senegal and the Ivory Coast – ironic name, considering – killed off their own elephant populations and are now importing tonnes of illegally poached ivory from here." He plonked a large mug of lethal looking tea in front of Mark, sloshing some over the sides.

"This paper – you presented it to the government here?"

Dave pulled a face.

"We tried. But when we sup with the devil, we need a very long spoon." At Mark's puzzled look, he added, "I mean, we have no choice but to work with this government, however corrupt, if we want to stay here. So we have to tread a very fine line between gentle cajoling and subtle threats about aid." He sighed. "It's uphill work – sometimes I like to think we're getting somewhere, inching forward at the pace of a snail; other times, I think we're slipping backwards."

"If you went too far, you'd be chucked out?"

"*Persona non grata.*" Dave nodded and took a noisy large slurp of tea. "We'd get the bum's rush, or worse, before we had time to pack a toothbrush."

"You need a large dose of tact and diplomacy, then." He saw Dave as more of an activist than a diplomat.

Dave just grunted. Mark guessed that tact didn't come easily.

"Dave, um - Thomas Griffiths, as I said, suggested I come and talk to you, that you knew what went on better than most. I just wanted to be put in the picture re illegal logging – and, also," he paused - awkward this – "to find out if Colin Wingent had a base here – a desk, terminal, filing cabinet, that sort of thing – where he kept his data."

Dave squinted at him over the rim of the mug.

"Why do you need to know that?"

Mark wriggled uncomfortably on the chair.

"It's an involved story. But to cut to the chase, it might just be possible that there are clues somewhere amongst his papers or files as to what happened to him and who did it."

"He barely had time to plant his posterior on a seat here, poor bugger, but we had assigned him a spot in the Resources Room."

It was disappointing, but more or less what Mark had expected.

"Come on, I'll show you." More sheets of paper drifted off as Dave stood and clumped his way out of his office along a corridor to a spanking new room, more like a library, kitted out with a conference table, stacks of files and books – and computer terminals.

Several faces looked up as Dave passed, rumbling greetings.

Mark gazed around, surprised.

"This is impressive. Why on earth didn't I come before?"

"It's open to all honest researchers, Mark. You're welcome any time. Here we are. Colin was to have worked here, no filing cabinets, I'm afraid." He indicated a desk with a monitor, clear of papers or books tucked into a corner of the Resource Room.

"Can I?" Mark sat at the terminal.

Dave gestured that he was free to search the PC as he wished.

It became apparent that nothing was on file, no password, and Colin may not even have used the terminal. Mark opened the drawers. Nothing but paper clips and rubber bands and a small dead insect.

"I'm at a loss. Did he take a laptop with him, do you know?"

Dave dragged his fingers through the beard, obviously an aid to thinking.

"Don't remember seeing one. He did have a mobile, though."

Mark sat up a little.

"Are you sure?"

"Yeah, one of those nifty ones that take digital pictures, internet access, email – all that. And triband, so he could phone home."

Mark dug his own out of his pocket, a nudge of excitement in his guts.

"Like this?"

Dave nodded. "Looks like it, but I'm not up with the latest mobile gadgets."

"They don't work everywhere in the Dja region, though."

"I told him that, but he said he was pretty sure from what others had told him that it *would* work where he was going. It's very patchy, the service in that area."

"But he sent nothing from that mobile to this terminal, so if it was working and he used it, where?"

"Some other terminal, then?"

"Yes, must be. If we can find it, we just might discover something about where he was when he was killed and if the location of any call can be pinpointed."

"You said you found him, near the track into the Dja Reserve."

"Yes, but he wasn't killed there – that was fairly obvious. It might be that *where* he was killed is crucial. For example, was he in the Reserve area, and maybe discovered logging going on there? That would be a likely motive."

"And any photographic evidence could prove vital. Yes, I see."

"Did he say exactly where he was going?"

Dave inhaled deeply while he tried to recall.

"I'm pretty sure he was going to one of the concessions bordering the Dja Reserve. Maybe Rouge-Bolles. They've got most of the concessions around there."

Mark felt blood drain from his face. Them again!

Dave peered closely at him.

"What's wrong?"

"Rouge-Bolles. Those bastards imprisoned me – and left me to die. At least, I think they meant to." He looked up at Dave, his gaze unfocused. "Anyway, after I escaped the Baka gave me shelter and - ."

Dave hauled him by the arm out of the chair and virtually frog-marched him quickly back to his office saying nothing, and looking grim.

"Best talk in here. Like I said that Resource Room is open to everyone. Get my drift?"

"Oh, sorry. Do you think anyone heard?"

"Hope not. But was that part of the long story you mentioned earlier, what you said in there?"

"Yes, yes, it was." Mark now gave Dave an edited version of his tribulations at the hands of the loggers. He was getting quite good at this now, having related the tale a number of times.

"Whew!" Dave, who Mark guessed, was normally fairly impassive, seemed satisfyingly impressed. "Those bastards are among the worst offenders, and aggressively protective of their areas – and I do mean aggressive. There have been other disappearances over the past few years, you know, like I said. Nothing provable, of course; after all, it's a hazardous place and people have 'accidents'." He sketched quote marks in the air. "You should count yourself damn lucky to get out of there in one piece." He picked up the mugs and prepared another pot of tea.

"I'm beginning to realise that. I certainly wouldn't have survived without help from the Baka."

"Those poor sods have been the worst affected by rapacious timber barons. Virtual enslavement, and, of course, sexual exploitation." He shook his large shaggy head.

"I saw some of that in their camp – heard, rather. Repugnant. Is there anything else you can tell me about their operations that might help finger the murderers? For example, what happens to the logs when they leave the concessions?"

"Here." Another mug of tea, the colour of Devon soil, was thumped down on the desk. "Ah, yes. We've attempted to monitor the progress from sawmill to – well, the EU eventually, but the port of Douala, where the timber is usually shipped from, is very tightly controlled. I can tell you from personal experience strangers aren't welcome to go nosing around."

"Douala? Right." Paul had mentioned Douala in his email. "But before that?"

"The logs are usually initially processed in the saw mills sited in logging camps or towns, loaded onto juggernauts and taken to Douala."

"I saw one of the lumber trucks pass by the Baka village. The vibration and noise and dust were terrible, blanketing the village. The Baka were, well, afraid of it. I think it's become almost a symbol of all the ills threatening their way of life." Then Mark remembered something from the night of his escape. "How do they go about disguising the illegal timber? As I understand it, each log should have a mark, a number, some sort of certification."

"A number of ways. False certification. Duplication of numbers. Even the marque used by a sustainable forest watchdog, Forest Stewardship Council."

"Should each log have its own particular number?"

Dave leaned back against his desk and gulped his tea before replying.

"Yes, it should. Each log is subject to tax – in theory, anyway."

"I've seen logs with the *same* number at the saw mill in the logging town."

"Ah, that's just the sort of evidence needed to trap the bastards. They try to avoid paying full tax that way."

"Christ, I wish I'd taken a photo at the time. I've no hard evidence but those scum are up to no good." At that time he didn't have his mobile on him.

"They've been up to no good for years.Pity about those numbers, though."

"I can remember the number I saw on two logs, if that's any help."

Dave gave him a surprised look.

"Well, you never know, I guess, when it might prove useful."

"498152." He reeled off the number which Dave wrote down on a pad.

Stubby fingers pulled at the lush beard. "You know, if you were able to tie the murder definitively to Rouge-Bolles, there'd be an excellent case for closing down their operation, and curbing the excesses of the rest of the greedy - loggers. If nothing else, pressure could be applied to the EU to stop importing this timber – which most states are fully aware is illegal – and stop providing EU funds to build logging roads."

"What? You're kidding! EU funds for roads? Frigging funds to rape the forest and decimate the wildlife, more like!" Mark was outraged that under the guise of providing funds the EU was, as ever, serving its own interests vis-à-vis gaining access to fresh timber while simultaneously loudly decrying the felling of the forests. Breathtaking hypocrisy.

"You'd better believe it. EU funds are more often directed at helping the EU than the country they go to – if it's outside the EU. And especially if they can assist strong lobbying groups like the timber barons or oil companies. Did you know the EU subsidised fishing policy has led to over-fishing by European boats down here, forcing the local populace to turn increasingly to bush meat? One of the many factors driving the wildlife to extinction."

Mark was beginning to realise he was pretty clueless when it came to the unholy machinations of big business and politics.

"Well, we have one possible ace up the sleeve, Dave. Maybe. Colin had splinters of wood stuck to his face and these were undoubtedly from the area where he was actually killed – freshly cut timber. And there's a friend of mine back home who can do DNA analyses of the wood to pinpoint its location within a certain radius."

"Hey, hey, hang on." A forefinger jabbed in his direction. "Don't I know that old reprobate? Steve Frampton? Got to be."

Mark was taken aback.

"Why, yes. How...?"

"We've used him on MIKE. Tracking the origin of the ivory. TRAFFIC was involved – the information was passed to them – and the evidence presented to the governments of Cameroon, Ivory Coast and Senegal. It proved that those last two were selling illegally poached ivory from elephants killed here. Well, well, old Steve, eh. How is the old bugger?"

" Blooming when I left. I remember him mentioning the original use of his program for ivory sources – but I'd no idea you were involved as well. Anyway, he's expanding it to cover timber."

"Of course, I'd forgotten – he was over here with a team a couple of years back, taking wood samples all over the place - but I didn't realise it was up and running. That's great." A wide grin split the beard.

"Well, *old* Steve has identified the splinters as having come from the Dja region – with an eighty percent plus certainty." He fished out Paul's email and showed it to Dave, tapping the relevant paragraph. "See? If we can tie down the site of the murder to an area where one of these companies operates illegally, then we have evidence of motive."

Dave read it silently and got up and went over to a map cabinet holding rolls of charts and maps. He checked the labels and snatched one roll out, laid it flat on the desk after sweeping the neglected piles of paper aside and put his mug of tea at one end and Mark's at the other end. Spots of bush tea slopped onto the chart.

"Here we are. The Dja Biological Reserve and the concessions bordering the northern boundary… let's see… hah, as I suspected – look."

Mark peered at the map, mentally traced where he thought he had staggered around in the reserve, and settled his gaze on Dave's large stumpy finger. There were a series of adjacent blob-shapes with dotted boundaries, numbered -39,40,41 – hard up against the northern boundary of the Dja Reserve, and a key naming the company that held each concession.

"I see what you mean. Rouge-Bolles holds several legal concessions neighbouring the northern boundary. And – God, it must be so easy, Dave - they're making inroads into the reserve. Must be."

Dave nodded agreement. "Either with or without the knowledge of MINEF- the Ministry of Environment and Forests. Monitoring and enforcement of legislation is very weak, and there's little political will at the top to tackle the high levels of illegal logging."

He took a long draught of his bush tea and put it down, gently this time, with a glint in his eye.

"'Searching for power is to search for wealth, and searching for wealth is to search for power, because one leads to the other and vice versa.' – as some bright chancer once said. It's this attitude which explains the large number of the elite, both local and national, in the forestry industry. They see it as a way to both enjoy the spin-offs of political-administrative status, and to grab more loot to ensure their status is maintained or improved. That's the way administrative functions are distributed to friends, family or clients as payments, in order to sustain their own position, and extract the surplus for themselves."

Dave stood upright, and smiled wryly.

"There's an old Cameroonian saying which deftly explains this situation: 'the goat grazes where it is tied'. Corruption effectively prevents implementation of the law. Resources are scarce. In this East Province" – his finger circled the south eastern section of Cameroon – "the area we're concerned with, where logging companies based in Europe are dominant, there is on average just one poorly-resourced government monitor – a sole *chef de poste* with a motorbike - for each 20,000 hectares of concession."

"Mm – the High Commissioner said as much."

"My, my, you have been rubbing shoulders with the high and mighty." Dave's brows rose. "Anyway, if the *chef de poste* does send in a report on infractions and corruption, chances are it'll be lost or ignored. It's a desperate situation, Mark, but perhaps we have a chink of light at last – if we can prove Wingent was murdered by these bastards because he'd discovered illegal logging." He paused, seeing Mark bend closer to the map. "What have you found?"

"I'd bet this spot was where I was held." Mark stabbed at a symbol marking a small logging settlement plus sawmill. "But none of this proves anything. It doesn't *prove* who killed Wingent. Like I said Steve's pretty sure that the splinters came from the Dja Biosphere Reserve – which means trees are definitely being illegally logged; we have the likelihood that Wingent was murdered because he discovered this and was prevented from informing Forest Watch and yourselves. We have a lot, but it's still only circumstantial."

Dave was quiet, thinking and slurping his tea, until the silence stretched. He must get through gallons of the stuff, Mark was thinking.

"Perhaps we can do better than that," Dave said eventually.

"How so?"

"Trace the actual log!"

Chapter
28

Mark snorted and grabbed Paul's email, passing it to Dave once more.

"Here, look again. That's just what a DCI friend of mine hinted at, but he also said it would be impossible, just about. That's why I didn't bring it up."

Dave read the rest of the email, then frisbeed it back to Mark.

"Your 'tec pal doesn't know how it works over here, though. How can he?"

"OK. So put me in the picture."

"Let's get out of the office a bit. I could do with stretching my legs." He gave Mark a wink and scraped back his chair and stomped over to the door precipitating another paper avalanche.

Outside in the sleepy residential area behind the BAT factory, they walked along. The road was still empty of traffic – at least there was no obvious watcher as far as Mark could tell.

"I mentioned that the logging trucks travel to Douala – a tightly secured port. All timber is shipped from there to its destination. Sometimes the ships stop en route to Europe, picking up other cargo at Liberia or Nigeria, for example, but then make their way to Europe. Southampton may be a stop along the way. Rotterdam is the usual final port."

"I still don't see how…"

"The thing is, Mark, there's only one shipment of timber every eleven days. There has to be sufficient cut timber to make it a worthwhile cargo – one truck load doesn't do it. So some timber, arriving early from a concession, is offloaded from the trucks and stacked at the dockside waiting to be loaded up. And – this is important - it's stacked in an ordered fashion, according to time of arrival at the docks and loaded in the same order." Dave emphasised the point by stabbing his finger in the air.

"How do you know this?" Mark asked again.

"High powered bonocs. Used in bird watching, of course."

Mark grinned, then stopped, an understanding dawning.

"So all I have to do is work back in time to when the murder took place which is most likely when the log was - " His face fell. "But when's the next sailing?"

"I can find out. I know the name of the ships used by the West Africa Line - Castor and Pollux – and their movements ought to be traceable. Douala Port has a website – that might be helpful."

"Let me think. It seems like an eon ago when I discovered the body and the days seem to flow together. I think it must have been eight...no, nine… days ago but I don't know exactly when he was killed."

His gaze drifted up to the blindingly blue sky, eyes unfocussed. "Wait, wait. Why didn't I remember this before? I made a record of the blowfly maggot infestation. I guessed that these were second instar maggots. Too many variables, though. I'm no forensic entomologist, so I couldn't tell you the exact species of *Calliphora*, and that makes a difference in estimating time of death."

"So does the temperature and humidity. But second instar, that would be...?"

"*Could* be two days. So add that to the nine and we have eleven. What do you think, Dave? There could have been a sailing in that time, eh?"

"Well, if the log was transported and loaded in the last ten to eleven days then it could be close to docking in Southampton. Come on let's try the Douala website."

: ♻ :

Mark used the WWF terminal originally assigned to Wingent to email Paul about what they'd learnt of the timing and route of the two ships. MV Castor was due in Southampton docks in two day's time. He wasn't sure what if anything Paul could do at his end, but he ought to know anyway. If the log wasn't on that ship then the next visit by MV Pollux in eleven days might be the one.

After a lot of scratching of heads and scribbled numbers on scraps of paper, taking into account the size of the sister ships' cargo holds courtesy of the Douala Port website, the usual size of the timber cargo and, by careful scrutiny of the photo kindly supplied on the Douala website, counting how much timber there was in the separate stacks on the docks awaiting loading, they came to an estimate. While they couldn't be absolutely sure, they reckoned that MV Castor *might* be the one transporting the load of timber which *might* include the felled *sapele* log against which Wingent slumped when his throat was cut, the splinters from which adhered to his cheek.

There were several ticklish unknowns, though. The crucial log might be loaded onto MV Pollux, the sailing after this one. Conceivably, it might not be used at all – it might have been left to rot in the bush. Perhaps the perpetrators had seen the blood and burnt the evidence. Any number of things could have happened to the timber, ensuring that it never reached the port. It was a very long shot, but Mark felt that he owed it to Wingent, at the very least, to exercise his best efforts, and behind that, lurking barely acknowledged, was a desire to – in some small way – shaft the logging barons. The dark anger he felt at their infinite greed in selfishly exploiting the fabulous forests of the world for their own short-term benefit seethed through him – to his way of thinking the planet was better off without them, they were as evil if not worse than Hitler, Stalin or Mao. He well knew the likely time left to his beloved apes – less than fifteen years before our nearest relatives were wiped out – unless something momentous stopped the decimation of their habitat.

And how likely was that? Maybe this way he could do something, at least make the bastards uncomfortable and raise the profile of the debate. It was too much to hope that those in charge would change their spots, but those on the periphery, those who happily took their shilling...

The moo sounds made him jump again.

"Damn and blast it!"

Beti again. What was it with the man? Did he have to keep checking up on him?

Mark waved the phone at Dave in apology.

"Yes," Mark barked into the phone.

Beti's voice, high and excited, came back.

"We have him! We caught him red-handed. He's awaiting interview right now. He - "

"Whoa! You mean our...bug man?" He was about to say 'bugger', but thought the rather prim Beti wouldn't appreciate it.

"Yes, yes, Professor. He's here!"

"Congratulations, Commissaire. A splendid coup for you and your men." He was sincere in his congratulations as in truth he hadn't really held out that much hope that their little ploy would pay off.

"Yes, yes, I know this" said Beti again, impatiently this time. "I want you to come here, to see him. You might be able to identify him."

Mark had to think quickly. As far as Beti knew, he was on his way to pursue his long-neglected studies, not in Yaounde.

"But I'm travelling. It will take me awhile to get back to Yaounde."

There was a pause.

"I don't hear your engine noise," said the ever-suspicious Beti.

"That's because I've stopped, Commissaire, to answer the phone. I'm not driving at this moment," Mark said truthfully.

"Well, will you come as soon as possible to see this person?"

Chapter 29

The next day DS George Thynne and DC Sandy Ghopal stood there, in front of the battered metal desk covered in grubby papers and the greasy remains of a take-away burger, and stared at the squat toadyish man sitting behind the desk. He, in turn, squinted up at them through smeared glasses, dug a dirty rag out of his pocket and wiped a glistening forehead.

The DCI had finagled their approach to Rayner, here in Southampton, by persuading the vacationing Superintendent to chat-up his golfing buddy and opposite number in Southampton and allow them to follow enquiries that had begun in Cameroon. 'A matter of courtesy to our brother officers in West Africa. . .to assist in a murder investigation. . . Hampshire resident, blah, blah.'

He was a timber trader – *the* timber trader – who facilitated the transfer of timber from logging giants in Cameroon on to the timber merchants in consumer countries within the EU. The traders were in a key position to influence the state of the EU's logging industry and help clean up the timber trade, yet almost without exception, these pivotal players chose to knowingly continue laundering timber from illegal sources to complacent consumer countries.

Following an email from the DCI's pal in Africa, a bit of deft work with the internet and port websites had revealed that two ships of the French-owned West Africa Line alternately docked here every eleven days or so, and the self-certification from the Cameroon timber company, stating that the timber was from sustainably logged forests, could be waved about if anyone asked – which, usually, they didn't. Once in the EU the timber could be transported along to any other EU country safe in the knowledge that the wood was legitimate. No questions asked. Sandy, with a very proper and fairly immutable set of moral standards, had been outraged that rules could be flouted so openly without, it seemed, any consequences.

"I don't understand what you're on about," the toad wheezed.

"It's quite simple really," Sandy said in her precise way. George had said she could lead on this and she was going to make the most of it.

She'd grown in confidence working with him. Of course, it hadn't hurt that he was clearly dotty about her and allowed her considerable leeway. She'd kept him dangling for a while now, sweet George, not through any desire to torment, but because, while she was flattered and attracted, she was wary. There was so much to consider, not least the family back in Leicester, some of whom were of the traditional mould and not likely to look too kindly on marriage outside her faith – let alone her race. At the same time, she felt bad because she knew he was confused, sometimes uncertain of her feelings towards him and she dreaded hurting him. She slid her gaze sideways. There he was standing there, all gangly, pretending to put things down in his notebook, a frown on his freckled face and his lower lip stuck out.

She sighed inwardly. Back to work. She stared down at the worst comb-over she'd ever seen.

Mr Rayner appeared intimidated as he gazed imploringly up at her. Good – this should go well.

"Mr Rayner, do you or do you not act as a timber trader?"

Rayner nodded with palms held out, evidently glad to have something to agree with.

"Do you receive timber from Cameroon?"

It might have been easy to miss, but a fleeting glimpse of caution passed across the sweaty features of Mr Rayner. George had caught it and gently touched her foot with his.

She waited, staring at the figure slouched behind the desk. Mr Rayner was not a sophisticate in matters of prevarication - he assumed a hunted look, casting his eyes about left and right. That business about only glancing to one side when lying was a load of old cobblers peddled by charlatans. In fact, when trying to be economical with the verite, interviewees' eyes invariably cast about left and right as though seeking for some elusive truth which would convince their tormentor.

"I might." He eventually offered.

"Of course you do, Mr Rayner. We have information that you act as a trader for timber brought from Cameroon. In fact you're the main timber trader for Rouge-Bolles, aren't you?"

He wiped his forehead again, then slumped a little further in his seat.

"OK, OK. Sit down if you like." He waved at a couple of rickety metal chairs that he imagined, no doubt, went well with the desk.

"I'm fine standing, thank you. DS Thynne?"

George raised one eyebrow at her – a warning not to overplay it – and shook his head.

"Look, all I does is buy the wood and sells it on to a third party, a timber merchant."

"And this third party would be?"

"Well that depends as who wants it at that time." His expression was wary.

George's pen tapped impatiently against the side of his notebook.. He glared down at Rayner. They waited.

"OK. It goes from Southampton here to – mostly – Rotterdam." Rayner resumed, shrugging.

"Why doesn't it go straight to Rotterdam?"

"There's other stuff as has to be off-loaded here at Southampton."

"Like?"

"Cocoa, palm oil, um - and some of the wood goes to joiners before Rotterdam."

"What joiners?"

"Depends. Different joiners." He fiddled with some grubby papers on his desk.

"So what's your role?"

Rayner took a sip from a smudgy glass which Sandy, sniffing the air delicately, reckoned held something alcoholic like gin.

"I facilitates the passage of the timber through the EU. That's all."

He must be beginning to suspect that there was something wrong with the timber shipments, unless he was a total idiot

– which was a possibility. Their DCI's email from that friend of his, the eccentric Professor with the wild eyes, was about the murder of a Brit over in Cameroon, and it seemed that there was a link between the timber being shipped over here – illegal timber – and the guy's murder. So here they were, putting the squeeze on this pathetic dope.

"What we need, Mr Rayner, is to look at your paperwork."

At this a twinge of almost panic passed across Rayner's features.

"And determine what your procedures are. Think of it as a type of audit."

At that fearful word, enough to make the blood of any businessman run cold, Sandy thought she'd gone too far as Mr Rayner's eyes slid upwards, but he was only imploring any heavenly being to come to his aid. He took another much needed gulp of his potion.

"OK," he sighed wearily. "I've nothing to hide. I does exactly what I told you. It's all legit and up-front. You ask HMRC if it ain't."

"Oh, we will. Her Majesty's Revenue and Customs have to be involved." After another glance in George's direction and getting an affirmative sign, she decided to go further and involve the timber agent more actively – make him feel a part of their investigation rather than a suspect.

"Mr Rayner," she lowered her voice confidingly, "I can tell you this in confidence, I hope." She waited.

"Of course. The soul of discretion, me." Rayner sat up a little straighter.

"Well, the fact is that we have to examine the next load of timber coming from Cameroon in two days time because we have reason to believe that we might obtain evidence relevant to the commission of a very serious crime."

Let him stew on that awhile.

Rayner's mouth assumed an 'O' shape as he stared up at the DC. Then he grabbed his glass and took a thoughtful and substantial swig of his firewater, brow furrowed in concentration, no doubt trying to figure the odds that he might be implicated. After digging a little into the murky world of logging, legal and otherwise, Sandy and George had banked on someone in Rayner's position throwing in his lot with the police rather than clamming up if they put a little squeeze on him. In fact, HMRC had no statutory right to confiscate timber – which astonished both of them – as long as the country from which the timber came claimed that it had been legally logged – self-certification - and it wasn't likely to do otherwise.

"It's nothing more or less than an open licence to import dodgy timber," Sandy had objected, when she and George and their DCI, Paul Draper, were sitting crushed together in his cramped office.

Paul had said, "Yes, I know but we can't change the law overnight, Sandy. We can only stay focused on the problem in hand. Keep in mind that this is pertinent to the murder of a British subject, albeit on foreign soil. We need to be able to get a look at that timber, take samples, see if we can get a DNA match. You've got to convince our friend the timber trader that we have the legal right to do a search of his logs apparently for one purpose – when, in fact, you'll be doing the search for something else entirely. We want to avoid waking the monster before we're ready."

Sandy wasn't sure that this ploy was going to work, but here they were now, waiting on the perspiring Rayner. So she'd told the truth as far as it went, but the timber man could have no idea what they really wanted.

George decided to push him along a little with a pinch of reassurance.

"Mr Rayner, we can assure you that the crime mentioned – a most heinous crime, but one we can't go into detail about yet – does not involve you in any way."

Rayner still looked doubtful.

"I'm sure that the police would consider it a great favour if you could see your way to letting them examine the cargo…"

He let the sentence dangle invitingly.

Rayner pursed his lips, perhaps drawing some small pleasure from keeping them waiting.

"What ship is it you want a shufty at?"

Sandy flipped open her notebook, the essence of efficiency, and said crisply, "We believe the MV Castor is due in port in two days' time. Is that right?"

"The Castor? Yes, she was delayed a bit, but she's en route from Douala – that's in Cameroon."

"Yes, we know that, Mr Rayner. What we want to do is examine her cargo for the evidence."

"How does you know that this evidence is in the timber part of the cargo?" Rayner asked, screwing his eyes up in what he no doubt thought was a shrewd look.

But a fair question, nonetheless.

George stepped a little closer to the desk and lowered his voice for dramatic effect.

"That, Mr Rayner, is something we can't divulge at this stage. Suffice to say that we have solid information and high expectations of finding incriminating evidence."

"Indeed, we would be *very* surprised if that evidence were not there," added Sandy with a meaningful look.

Rayner was shifting his anxious gaze from one to the other. Perhaps a gleam of understanding was there – or did they have to spell it out?

"Are you in contact with the Castor, Mr Rayner?"

"Listen, I'm saying nothing to anyone. I have a legitimate business to protect here." Now, spreading his palms, he seemed eager to convince them of his openness and honesty. "We deal only with sustainably grown timber."

"I see." Maybe time to apply a little more pressure. "So your timber will have this mark, will it?" Sandy removed a sheet of paper, onto which she'd photocopied the Forest Stewardship Council's tree-shaped logo, from her notebook and flourished it in front of Rayner's face.

Rayner stared at it, mesmerised as it floated down onto his desk.

"You know what that is, don't you, Mr Rayner?" asked George silkily. For such a fresh-faced innocent as he seemed, George could inject implicit threat into his voice with all the facility of a hammy actor.

Rayner recovered. "Of course I do." He poked the paper away from him.

"Then you'll know that this symbol can be found only on sustainably logged timber, mm?"

A nod from Rayner.

"And so we'll no doubt find this FSC symbol stamped onto your timber, eh?"

"Now look here," objected Rayner, "I knows what you're trying to do, but I imports only wood that the country of origin says is legal and from sustainable sources. See here."

He scrabbled around in a wire tray sitting on his desk and finally waved a sheaf of papers at them.

Sandy leant over and gently took the papers from his pudgy fist. George peered over her shoulder. The four Cameroon certificates each bore a caduceus at the top of the paper and several florid unreadable signatures at the bottom of the sheet. Clearly, the papers had been faxed over to the agent from the Liberian-registered shipping agents and a certain company called Rouge Bolles.

Both Sandy and George had come to learn that such assurances weren't worth the paper they were written on. Moreover, everyone in this murky business knew it, too. They'd consulted Greenpeace about the whole dirty business, and were told that Greenpeace themselves had managed to obtain blank copies of these certificates already complete with all the necessary official stamps and signatures

"And you believe these to be genuine, of course."

"No reason not to, have I?" Rayner pronounced triumphantly. He well knew that this was sufficient, that HMRC could do nothing, appalling though it was, even if the wood was from fast-disappearing Brazilian mahogany. Totally inadequate self-certification was the order of the day, and this played right into the hands of unscrupulous logging companies. An honest and upright logging company was as rare as hen's teeth.

They had one more card to play to ensure the fat worm's cooperation.

Sandy's turn to twist his arm.

"Would you like to tell us what species of tree you're importing, Mr Rayner?"

"Ah, well, as to that I'm not too sure about this cargo coming in." His eyes darted about again then glanced up at

311

George still looming over his desk and he evidently decided to expand. "But I think it's what they calls *ayou*."

"Mmm. *Ayou*. Not *sapele*, then?" asked Sandy.

"Uh, *sapele*?" You could practically see him turning the odds over as he pursed his lips in thought. Clearly he was wondering 'Did they know something?'

"You do know what CITES is, don't you Mr Rayner?" George employed his hard-man silky voice again.

"Of course I does. It's the, ah, Cooperation on Trade in – ah - Exposed Species." He looked up more in hope than expectation.

Sandy shook her head regretfully, while George looked down to hide a smile.

"Tut-tut, Mr Rayner." A theatrical sigh. "The *Convention* on Trade in *Endangered* Species. It says which species cannot be traded – and while, say, *moabi* or *ayou* can be, subject to certain conditions, *sapele* has had the export ban renewed. So I trust that we wouldn't find any of the latter in your cargo." They'd both consulted the CITES list of endangered species of trees with the assistance of the Forest Stewardship Council and made sure they knew the species of the logged trees from that region.

Rayner shuffled a few papers round on his grubby desk then dropped them.

"Look here," he said resignedly, "what is it exactly you want from me?"

"I knew you'd want to do your civic duty, Mr Rayner. It's simple. Two things – first, we don't want you contacting the Castor until she's docked – or if you have to for some reason, say nothing of our visit. Remember that we are expecting to find certain evidence in the timber. If they were forewarned in any way, they might wish to dispose of said evidence overboard and then, well, we'd know where the blame would lie, wouldn't we?" Without waiting for an answer, George ploughed on. "Second, we want access to the timber but we don't want the shipping agents, the logging company, the timber merchants or anyone else to get suspicious beforehand, so the access must be portrayed as a random check on timber, an exercise – not under the auspices of HMRC but the Department of the Environment - checking for possible parasites, fungi – that sort of thing – that might find their way into the country via imported timber. Remember Dutch elm disease and the devastation that caused?" He waited for Rayner's nod. "Well, it seems there's another deadly little virus which could attack our oak trees unless DEFRA is very vigilant."

"This way," Sandy took up the story, "nobody need be suspicious, nobody need blame you, because it's simply a random unannounced check made on all timber coming in at Southampton – and one that all can appreciate the need for."

"Naturally, we will, in the course of the inspection, discover which species are being imported, what their size is, and so forth."

Rayner paled and wiped his forehead again.

"But I'm sure, as you've told us, you have nothing to worry about," Sandy added sweetly.

Suddenly something clicked with Rayner and a light of possible salvation gleamed in his eyes.

"Ah, look, wait – I got these – what d'you call 'em –" he rummaged frantically around the in-tray again, "here they is –" he squinted at another four pieces of paper and slowly pronounced, "'Phytosanitary Certificates'. See? Anti-pest treatment of timber."

"Let me see that," George snapped. He grabbed them from Rayner's fist. Sandy tried to maintain a neutral expression while she felt a sinking feeling. Damn, damn, she knew this wasn't going to work. These certificates were precisely the ones required in order to protect the importing countries from the introduction of harmful pests, so they could hardly use the cover of checking for pests in order to gain access to the timber without arousing the suspicions of the shipping agents, logging company, Uncle Tom Cobley and all.

There was a tense silence as George perused the papers, frowning.

"Well, well," George breathed eventually, a sly smile creeping over his face, "what have we here? Some *very* poor forgeries, I'm afraid, Mr Rayner. See here?" He leaned over the desk to point out something on the certificate. "Clearly a colour photocopier was used there, and here - a simple bit of cutting and pasting of official stamps and signatures."

Rayner's brow furrowed as he tried to see what the DS was pointing out.

"Oh," was all he said, faintly.

Sandy let go the breath she'd been holding.

In fact, Greenpeace had warned them, such forged certificates were difficult to distinguish from the real McCoy, normally issued by the federal authorities or the Chamber of Commerce in the country of origin.

Rayner rallied half-heartedly. "Well, they looks OK to me. If they's forgeries, it's nothing to do with me, is it? I can't be held responsible, can I?" He peered up at George hoping for reassurance.

"Maybe not, but clearly these don't cover the viruses we're searching for anyway. They certainly won't do for DEFRA." George threw the sheets down onto the desk dismissively.

"So, Mr Rayner, we keep to the original story, eh? DEFRA must check the timber to keep out any possible infective agents, yes?" He tapped the side of his nose.

Rayner nodded, seemingly defeated, but gave it one last desperate try.

"But as I said, all the wood is sustainably logged – the company in Cameroon assures me."

"Mmm, I think we all know how valid that is, don't we?" said Sandy archly.

They swept out leaving a worried Mr Rayner, and his weary agreement to cooperate in any way. They promised to return when the Castor docked and the timber was unloaded, adding that they were keeping a close eye on all proceedings in the dock area and especially on Rayner's Timber Traders.

Rayner's hand crept reluctantly towards the phone on his desk.

Chapter
30

He placed the phone carefully on the receiver, frowning. A set-back, undoubtedly, but how much of one? It depended on what pressures might be utilised. In the end, he knew, everyone talked, without exception. It all depended on the buttons one pressed. The question was, how *much* might be revealed? He'd had to rely on the discretion and loyalty of those who worked for him, and as long as the money kept flowing into deep pockets they, in turn, could be relied upon, but that could only stretch so far.

He steepled his fingers and brought manicured nails up to his mouth, pouting in thought, expensive buttery gold cufflinks gleamed in the soft light from the green-shaded desk lamp, immaculate cuffs glowed white.

What to do? When push came to shove, you looked after your own interests, sacrificed the pawns to protect the king. That was the fall back position.

Yes, he'd decided. It was drastic but necessary. Once again, he looked at the phone. Was it wise to use this phone? Probably not. He got up and stood in front of a mirror, fussily pulling at his cuffs and sweeping back his prematurely greying hair. He recognised that he was delaying the inevitable with these little displacement activities. He hoped he'd be able to contact his useful little 'mole' in time. He was confident he would do as asked if the price was right but he was having to act more precipitately than he liked.

He checked that he had his mobile in his pocket and exited the room, looking around warily.

: ♡ :

"Stand here, Professor," Beti commanded. "He will not see you here."

Mark wasn't convinced. After a suitable interval during which he'd had to pretend he'd travelled from a nearby, vaguely described research site straight to the police station, having locked himself into the lie that he wasn't in Yaounde meddling in matters that didn't concern him – and barely able to remember how that had started in the first place – here he was reluctantly standing in the corridor outside the interview room whispering urgently.

"How do you know that? If I can see him, he can see me. Don't you have any one-way mirrors?"

"We are not so blessed as your police, Professor. We have to make do with what we have."

"But he might know me. If he sees me ID him – well," he finished not quite sure what he meant.

Beti sighed and looked at his watch.

"It will be dark shortly. We will switch the light on in the interview room and you can stand outside the window, unseen."

Mark pulled a face. "OK, I guess that's about the same as a one-way."

They crept outside and took up suitable spots in the lush shrubbery from which they could peer into the interview room.

"This should do."

"It reminds me of the other night when we searched for the bug."

"Well, now I think we have the bug owner."

"The original bugger," Mark sniggered.

An exasperated hiss came from Beti as he consulted his watch again.

As the swift African night claimed them, the light was turned on in the interview room, shafting a beam of yellowish light onto the bushes but falling short of where they crouched.

"Right. Now you can see," whispered Beti.

Mark shifted his position a little to get a better view. There was the table, two chairs, the dim yellow light bulb burning above and a smartly uniformed policeman standing impassively by the door, facing directly towards them.

The man's face was turned away from the window apparently staring towards the policemen. Mark scrutinised the shape of the head, the dark hair, the posture. He couldn't be sure. There was some far bell of recall tinkling – but -

"I need to move over here, get a better angle," he whispered.

"Careful."

The caution was a little late as Mark, usually as coordinated as a puppet with tangled strings, was already on the move, crab-walking in a crouch, eager to get a full-on glimpse of the suspect.

Beti tried to grab Mark to prevent undue noise and movement but missed his shirt.

The suspect was now looking down at the scarred table surface as though he'd spotted something interesting there.

"Almost, almost," Mark was talking to himself.

He moved closer, not noticing in his eagerness that he'd entered the rectangle of light emanating from the window.

"Get back," hissed Beti.

As he said this, the figure inside turned his head slowly towards the window and stared intensely straight at Mark.

Mark shrank back immediately behind a screen of leaves, but was it soon enough? His heart was hammering in his chest.

He heard Beti hissing furiously at him.

"He saw you. I said stay still. Now you may be a marked man."

The figure was still staring straight at the spot where Mark had hunched down, just broaching the rectangle of yellow light. He had seen before that slicked back dark hair, the lightly pock-marked areas under the cheek bones – legacy of a turbulent adolescence? - the narrow slate-grey eyes peering intently from deep-set shaded sockets. And now the man was smiling slowly, showing large, even, very white teeth – the smile of a predator, Mark thought. A smile to send shivers down your back.

In the safe velvet black of the shrubbery, Mark took hold of both of Beti's arms, holding tightly.

"I know him! I know him! I've seen him at the High Commission!"

"At the British High Commission?"

"Yes, yes. I'm sure it was him."

"What? What's his name?"

"I don't *know* – I never heard it. But he was also in the internet café."

"What was he doing in the British High Commission? Does he hold a post there?" Beti's voice was tight with suspicion.

"He was in an upstairs corridor talking to someone else – someone I couldn't see." But whose voice seemed familiar. Jesus, it could be his nibs, himself. "It makes sense now - they *were* talking about me; I heard the words 'café' and 'shop', both of which I'd visited earlier in the day."

Beti blew his lips out derisively. "You think no one else goes to cafes and shops?"

"Well, of course they do," Mark hissed, irritated. "But in that context...anyway, *he's* the one I saw in the internet café. Add to that the fact that he was in the BHC corridor whispering away to - someone else, I think you can safely say he was following me and reporting back to someone at the BHC." Mark thought again about Hyatt. Could it have been him? He was in the corridor shortly after Mark had overheard the conversation.

Jonathan Hyatt struck him from the beginning as highly intelligent in an understated sort of way – but more than that, there was perhaps an element of deviousness about him. And yet that was an essential prerequisite for diplomats, so could mean nothing.

"You realise the implications of what you're saying, Professor?"

Mark, crouching in the charcoal shadows of the shrubbery, could see only the gleam from Beti's eyes.

"Christ, yes. If the BHC is involved in bugging the police, it becomes a diplomatic incident. A nightmare, I should imagine."

Beti took a deep breath and let it go slowly.

"That is an understatement. Right, I must go and interview this man and, thanks to you, we now have more ammunition against him. I'll get a statement from you later. And you can now go, Professor, but quietly, please."

Beti moved stealthily off, silent as a cat.

Mark, however, decided not to go just yet. He wanted to see what transpired when Beti entered the room. He wasn't sure why – just curiosity perhaps about how the man would handle himself, his body language and facial expressions. He struck Mark as impassive, with the cold air of a professional, and guessed that he had been in this situation before, knew full well how to handle himself.

Shortly, Beti entered the plain interview room and nodded to the young police officer to leave. He stood a moment just staring down at the man.

If Beti had hoped to intimidate him, it wasn't working. The man sat there, unmoving, somehow supremely confident. It occurred then to Mark that he probably had powerful protectors, not least in the BHC, but probably also in the Cameroon government and God only knew elsewhere. He acted untouchable, impregnable. Maybe he was even a professional spy. Could he be MI6?

That would mean that he spied with the complicity of HMG. Was that possible? He wasn't so naïve as to believe that MI6 never spied on its own citizens, all spook organisations did – or was that MI5? - and all other nationals, too, including their allies.But it would mean that, however indirectly, Hyatt, and by implication HMG itself, was involved in the murder of a British subject. Christ almighty! It would have thunderous repercussions.

Mark shifted his position, his knees cracking – and then froze. Was that a nearby rustle? He could see nothing in this cave-like blackness in the shrubberies. There it was again. He held his breath. He'd be safer inside the Police HQ. He backed away, stood suddenly, and dashed round to the front of the building. He banged open the doors to stand there feeling a bit foolish - because, on reflection, the soft sounds in the undergrowth were probably non-human - but certainly safer. The young duty officer was emerging from the shadows somewhere in the rear, behind his desk – the same one as before, when he'd first come to see Beti. As before, he stood wide eyed, his default expression apparently, staring at him fearfully, an enamel mug of tea clasped tightly in one hand. No doubt by now he connected Mark's appearance with trouble.

Should he wait here to find out what Beti got from the man? He knew nothing about how long police interviews were likely to take, but then, unbidden, came the image and the barbequed odour of Tchie's scorched body. Please, not that.

Surely Beti, an essentially decent and honourable policeman trying to keep his integrity in a deeply corrupt force, wouldn't resort to such methods. It was ridiculous. Nonetheless, against his better nature, he found he was listening for screams and howls. Nothing.

He waved a feeble apology to the startled duty officer, and a little embarrassed, backed out of the headquarters. What should he do now? Return to CRU? That would be the sensible option, leave it all to Beti as he'd suggested, but he felt too wired, too restless to settle. He had a hunch that things were nearing a critical point.

He wandered round a corner towards the CRU Land Rover, hands in his pockets and head down weighing his options. He'd parked it some distance away, as a precaution.

The corridor conversation at the HC nagged at him. Two confidantes were talking about him, one the present prisoner – and the other? Was there some way in which he could find out? It was the evening of the function, the BHC was full of people from other embassies and the so-called 'movers and shakers' in Yaounde, as Hyatt called them. A mixed bunch, diplomats from several embassies, Griffiths the hack, and, of course, Hyatt himself. He'd scarcely had time to connect with anyone else apart from Griffiths before spilling wine down the borrowed suit.

If he didn't know who the other was, how could he possibly confide in anyone else, or request their help? But, he realised, he knew one who it wasn't, so he could afford to trust that person.

He'd reached the Landy and was just inserting the key, when he heard a loud yell. He whipped his head around, scanning the area. Yaounde was not very safe at night, and he'd stupidly let his guard drop.

Without a torch he could see very little. His suddenly sweaty fingers fumbled with the key, and yanked the car door open.

More shouts and the sound of running feet. The glove compartment resisted his tugging – it must have got jammed when he was run off the road. As he cursed, the little door gave way and he scrabbled around for a torch; finally, his hand closed on something cylindrical and he snatched at it. Now if only the battery was still charged.

"Sod it," he swore as a weak gleam leaked from the torch.

The footsteps appeared to be approaching fast.

Mark ducked out of the vehicle, clouted the torch on the roof of the vehicle to jolt the waning battery into action and swung around. The beam sliced across a figure – a fearful panting, running figure which swerved off to one side then the other when lanced by the beam of light, like a zig-zagging hare pursued by whippets.

Suddenly there was a loud ringing clang from the roof of the Landy, and splinters of paint flew off with a little puff of dust.

"What the hell..?"

Mark stood there, with the feeble torch beam focussed on the gouge for several seconds, or so it seemed to him, before recognising a bullet hole – well, not a hole really, he thought irrelevantly. A furrow. A bloody bullet had ploughed along the roof.

More hoarse shouting brought him around. More shots, if that's what they were – he couldn't be sure. He shrank back

"Professor, professor!"

Beti?

"Get in your vehicle! Now!"

Where was he? More stampeding of pounding feet came from the direction of the police station. One shadow, black on black, resolved itself gradually into a heavily panting Beti, followed by several other officers.

"Get into your car. Quick." Beti flapped his hand.

Mark quickly ducked back into the Land Rover, belatedly realising the danger he'd been in. A rush of anger quickly followed.

"What the hell are you shooting at me for?" he bellowed out of the side window.

By this time Beti had made it to the vehicle. He stopped but frantically waved his men on.

"Go on. Catch him - but stop firing all over the damn place!"

Several *sub voce* curses followed from the normally constrained Beti, reinforced by a hefty bang as he slammed shut the car door on Mark's side. Beti then bent and peered inside.

"What's going on? I was shot at." Mark was justly indignant.

Beti took several deep breaths.

"No — not you. I saw your torchlight catch him — we were chasing him." He bobbed up to assess the situation.

"A shot hit the Landy!" he protested.

Bobbed down again. "I must apologise, Professor. One of my men — a little too eager, I'm afraid, and not a good shot."

"Oh, well, that's all right then. Think nothing of it."

"You were going to ask me who we were chasing." Beti ignored the sarcasm, still catching his breath, his eyes darting all over the place.

"Who were you chasing?"

"You won't believe this — and I will feel eternal shame. Let me get inside." Beti raced around the car, got into the passenger seat and rolled down the window the better to hear any sounds of the chase.

It reminded Mark of the evening they had sat here, like this, planning what to do about the 'bug', how best to use it. Eons ago, seemed like.

Beti gazed at him for a long beat before going on.

"One of my men killed the suspect." He breathed this softly as though he had difficulty believing it.

As did Mark who jerked back in surprise.

"What? Killed? The suspect? Hatchet-face in there, the one we..?"

Beti nodded.

"I'm sorry, yes. His ID gave him as Norbert Kremmel but it was probably an alias."

"Bloody hell. How'd he die?"

"Poison in his tea, I think. It will have to be verified, of course."

Mark gaped at him. His mind flashed back to the scene at the station. Him, bursting through the doors and facing the startled and frightened duty officer – holding a mug of tea. Poisoned tea! And the nanosecond glimpse of a face in the beam from his torch, not recognised at the time in the midst of excitement.

"Not the DO?"

Beti nodded resignedly.

"I should have realised. Not only were we bugged but there was a – what is the saying? - cuckoo in the nest."

"Some cuckoo. So your DO spiked the tea and hatchet-face drank it?"

"That's it. It worked fast, the poison – I think it may be abrin. Abrin works very fast. Naturally, I deduced that it must have been the drink and that the DO had to be the culprit. He, too, must have known that he would be the prime suspect and so ran."

"Abrin? Isn't that the stuff that comes from the Rosary pea?"

"We sometimes call it crab's eye here – it's a red bean with a black eye. All you have to do is soak one bean for about 15 minutes in water and there it is. He made the tea with the poisoned water."

Beti stuck his head out of the window to track the progress of the chase.

"How do you know all this so soon?" Mark was impressed.

Beti ducked back in again.

"Ah – as soon as Kremmel fell ill I went straight to the kitchen and saw the bracelet of these beans on the counter by the kettle. It was undone in order to remove one bean. Besides, I have heard of this way of getting rid of your enemies."

"So he ran – ran past here." Mark thought awhile. "How do you see this, Commissaire? Your DO was working for whoever was behind the bugging of your office?"

"Yes. And this was a desperate measure to prevent the suspect telling us what he knew."

"Desperate is right. Your DO blew his cover and is now on the run from his own colleagues."

"Do not keep calling him 'my DO'? But you are right – if his colleagues catch him, which I doubt, I have to hope they will obey their instructions to bring him back to me intact." He didn't sound absolutely convinced.

"Well, that's that," said Mark, callously. "One possible lead cut off. Now we'll never know who Kremmel contacted at the BHC – or if his contact had anything at all to do with the BHC. This thing, it seems to me, is getting bigger and nastier all the time, its tentacles spreading."

"It is also getting more dangerous – for you. The criminals behind this – perhaps even in your own embassy - are becoming more desperate; they will stop at nothing. If I urged you to return home, would you take my advice?" There was a note of pleading in his voice.

Mark turned in his seat. He'd come to a re-assessment of Beti from his initial perception of a martinet-like figure, very correct but ultimately ineffectual in the context of a deeply corrupt society, to an honest man with a strong conscience and determination. A man, in short, of rare qualities, and priceless in this context. More than that, he had come to respect and like him.

"I think you know better than to ask," he said quietly.

Chapter
31

The timber was warehoused in a newly-built large structure by the docks, pending an onwards journey to a saw mill, awaiting his attention. His and the good professor's attention.

They'd discussed how they were going to go about the search. Paul had stressed that what he needed was a chain of custody, much like tracing the passage of drugs from the 'mules' who ferried the drugs concealed in various bodily orifices to the big guys who made the serious moulah. From humble bottom feeders dredging in the mire of humanity to the voracious predators at the top of the food chain. In this case, he wanted, if possible, to trace the passage of this actual log if it was here, a very long shot in his opinion, parts of which had stuck to the victim's face. Its destination would help them crawl up the chain of command and define the extent of the criminal activities involved with illegal logging.

If the whole sorry mess – Wingent's murder, Mark's near murder - was to make any sense at all, they had to follow the route of this and the other logs to see where they ended up.

Penny Morgan

What made them so important? Money. Had to be – it always was. Like the ivory trade or the horrific trade in wild species and their various bodily parts – including powdered tiger penis bones, for God's sake, sold for vast sums to boost the flagging libidos of inadequate priapics. It was all about rapacity not to mention stupidity - stupidity that couldn't see the fast diminishing resource from which they made their fortune. The purpose was to make as much as possible, then get out fast, find another forest to decimate, and so on and on. They never thought about 'until'.

So just like the other trades that preyed on the vulnerable, nothing must get in the way of the profits. No holds were barred when it came to protecting their *milch* cows. And Wingent first, then Mark, had got in the way, not to mention the indigenous peoples like the pygmies. He felt a shivery fear for Mark's safety. He really ought to get back home pronto.

When he'd said he had no other comparative psychology friend, he was awkwardly expressing his affection for Mark. At first sight, they were an unlikely pair, the gawky scientist and the intense copper, but they had in common a fierce desire to get at the truth and a ruthless determination in pursuit of it, while enough differences to make their friendship interesting. Mark was disorganised and likely to go off on tangents of apparently unconnected thoughts producing wildly lateral, often fertile ideas, while Paul believed himself to be focussed but perhaps missing things on the peripheries. Divergent and convergent thinkers.

Besides, he'd grown fond of Mark and he didn't make close friends easily. Mark projected, entirely unconsciously, an air of vulnerability, and this prodded a protective instinct in Paul which, had it been for anyone else apart from his daughter, might have embarrassed him.

330

Well, time to fight back, time for a bit of ingenuity.

: ⌖ :

The place emitted the rich pungency of resin with overlying notes of chemicals – the chemicals used to treat the woods against fungal and bacterial pests; the timber had to be treated once it had been unloaded, but, should anyone question their bona fides, they were examining the lumber, under the aegis of Department for the Environment, Food and Rural Affairs, for a virulent new fungus that attacked oak trees. The mingled aromas made Paul feel quite heady, even though they all stood clustered by the open entrance.

The customs man, there for appearance sake, stood some way off, hunched into his anorak, gazing studiously out over the cranes and the docks. He wouldn't be taking part in the search and wanted to know as little as possible about the whole thing.

The stacks stretched into the depths of the newly-built Dutch-barn warehouse, presenting a Canaletto-like perspective. So much wood, so many hundreds – thousands? - of trees. He was in awe of the sheer quantities diminishing into a hazy distance – it didn't do to dwell too much on the devastation left behind.

He turned to Steve Frampton.

"There's too much here, isn't there?" Wanting to be reassured.

Steve was standing gazing around, grinning like a child on Christmas Eve, his pink face alive with anticipation.

"No, no. We'll do it."

The professor seemed to be a perpetual optimist. Nothing daunted him. Paul, however, liked to think he was more realistic, even if others labelled him more brooding and gloomy. That way you were less likely to be disappointed.

"There's bloody tons of the stuff." He waved his arm in the general direction of the vanishing perspective.

"Yes, 3,500 cubic feet, but we only want the recent cargo off the Castor, and of that we only want the *sapele*."

Steve beckoned over his research assistant, the wonderfully named Stanford Puleman the IIIrd, from Connecticut. He was in his second year of a PhD, working on further applications of the genetic mapping program.

"Hey, Stanny, bring over those charts, would you? Let's get everyone familiar with the appearance of the *sapele*." His booming voice echoed down the corridors of aromatic logs.

Whatever the ivy-league Stanford thought of being called Stanny, he gave nothing away. Straight-faced, compact and neat, he handed over the laminated charts to Paul, George and Sandy, lingering a little too long before relinquishing Sandy's hand, and earning a glare from George which he affected not to notice.

"Good, good. Now everyone look at the *sapele* – *Entandrophragma cylindricum* - in contrast to the other woods on your chart. It's a hardwood, a reddish-brown mahogany colour, medium to dark with – and this is distinctive – lighter streaks. Beautiful, beautiful wood and therefore very desirable." Steve stroked the picture fondly. "A mahogany substitute. This is what we're looking for, so ignore anything else."

"We should be able to do this in an organised way. The timber's stacked in a regular manner." Stanny's voice was light, unconcerned, as he adjusted his designer specs. Paul wondered whether or not he was taking this seriously - or was it a welcome jaunt, a break from his postgrad grind?

"Rayner came up with the goods, finally," said George, "and gave us the warehouse location of Castor's latest cargo – the one Professor Rees thinks might contain the log. According to his sketch –" he tried to flatten a crumpled, grease-stained piece of paper from which rose faintly the stale smell of old burgers to challenge the chemically laden air - "our load should be roughly over there somewhere." He stabbed at the paper resting on the bonnet of the School of Biology's mini-van. "Look, here's the date of unloading." They all bent forward to gaze at the diagram.

Sandy then walked briskly off down a wide aisle to the left of where the van was parked at the entrance to the gigantic warehouse.

"That should be about here," she said, turning in a circle holding her arms wide. "The date's right, too," she said, examining a label stapled to the end of one log.

The others moved as a group into the warehouse, and silently stood beside her staring up at the stacked logs, each cut end stencilled with a jumble of indecipherable letters and codes. Close up they were massive, some five feet in diameter, some more, some less – these last ones, Paul guessed, should probably not have been cut. He tried to imagine what these magnificent giants were like in place in the forests of Cameroon. Stripped naked as they were it was impossible to see them as vertical living beings, the very framework of a forest, supporting all the other life.

"Well, well." Even Steve was in awe.

"Perhaps we can find a real *sapele* so that we all know what we're searching for?" asked George, his voice hushed as though he were in church.

"Good idea." Steve paced around and disappeared behind the stack. All the others could hear was some mumbling, then a shout of "Stanny! The equipment!"

Stanny scooted off back to the minivan. George, Sandy and Paul started inspecting the logs, and making comparisons with their charts.

"This looks like *ayou*, don't you think, George?" asked Sandy, consulting her chart.

"To tell you the truth, my love, I haven't a clue. Barely know me birch from me beech ..."

"Or your arse from your elbow."

"Oh, I wouldn't say..."

A triumphant yell from Steve. "Over here."

They all dashed around a stacked pile of logs, wove past another stack to find Steve, grinning and pointing at a one yard diameter log, the wood a rich russet colour.

"Come on, come on. Take a look, all of you."

"Quite distinctive when you see it in the flesh," Paul muttered, peering closely at the dendritic rings. The hue that came to his mind was the colour of dried blood. How strange that that should spring to mind. Watching Sandy stroke the wood, feeling the texture, he saw again the splinters of wood soaked with Wingent's blood.

"OK? Right everyone, let's get to it." Steve was brisk now the hunt was underway.

Stanny returned holding a clutch of markers. Steve then assigned them to different piles of logs, all with the same date of unloading.

"Remember, when you spot a *sapele*, use your purple marker – can you give them out, Stanny? - make a small mark, a letter, near the cut bark at the sawn end because that part won't be used by the joiners – note the position in the stack, and sing out to let everyone know. To make sure we don't give the same letter to two or more logs, we'll start with 'A' and make sure it's crossed off on Stanny's clipboard as we go. OK?"

They all nodded.

Steve turned again to Stanny who was handing out the markers. "You've got the magic water ready, Stanny?"

"Sure, all present and correct, Steve." Stanny smiled winningly at Sandy.

Paul decided to inspect his side of the stack starting at the top and working along. Those at the top were more difficult to see and he didn't fancy clambering over what might prove to be a precarious pile. Then, peering upwards, he saw one likely candidate – checked his chart. It looked like *sapele*, but no. Bugger. He sucked in his cheeks. There was nothing for it – clamber he would have to. He'd climbed enough trees as a kid, albeit upright ones. At least, he'd had the foresight to wear old jeans and a faded sweatshirt, and his disgraceful trainers gave him a good grip.

It wasn't as bad as he'd thought, feet seeking out footholds in the rough bark, although he was glad he'd taken his anti-inflammatories earlier. His low-level arthritis was mostly kept in check by medication, although he dreaded the occasional flare-up in his knees. His natural inclination was to keep his condition to himself – figuring it was nobody's business but his own, and fearing and abhorring signs of pity on the faces of colleagues; nonetheless some had to know, including Sandy and George. And the brass. They had the sense and sensitivity to ignore it.

As he heaved himself up onto another log, there came a triumphal cry from Sandy, and guessed she'd found one.

" Letter 'A' here!"

335

That gave the search a competitive edge, more like a kids' game. His left knee popped and his foot slipped a little – his nose scraped against the rough bark.

The chemical odour from the pesticides was stronger this close up, and it made his eyes water. But present also in the general aroma was the strong harmonic of cedar.

He blinked twice. Was that it? Yes. Check the wood chart. Yes.

OK. Letter 'B'...

He shouted to Stanny to let him know which letter he was using.

He dug the marker from his pocket, but as he crabbed slowly sideways to make a 'B' mark on the edge of the sawn trunk, his skin came up in goose bumps. What if this was *the* one? The tree whose splinters had stuck to Wingent's face. He recalled what Sandy told him about *muti* – and took some deep breaths as his imagination conjured up horrific images.

Blood wood.

He made the mark, and climbed down as fast as he could. He'd actually felt a bit nauseous up there, and told himself it was the greater concentration of fumes rising up into the air.

Another cry of discovery, and another.

: ◻ :

It took three hours, and when they'd finished they'd marked nine *sapelae* and given each a letter from 'A' to 'I' using the purple marker. In the blizzard of codes and numbers stamped into and marked onto the ends of the logs, the purple number was virtually invisible. 'Can't see the wood for the trees,' George had said.

Steve Frampton pronounced himself well pleased, rubbing his hands and, Frankenstein-like, called again for his faithful Igor, Stanny.

"We'll need samples taken from each, Stanny." As the postgraduate hurried off yet again to get some equipment from the back of minivan, he turned to the police officers who gathered round to listen.

"Right. Good, good. Nine altogether then. What we'll do is this: We take a small virtually unnoticeable sample about this size" - he held up a plug of wood about one inch in length and the diameter of a match – " for DNA testing from each *sapele* log.

Stanny scurried back with a tray of plastic tubes with red and green stoppers, taped together in a dozen pairs, and a second tray containing some implements in the shape of an 'X'. Steve picked up five of the paired tubes and handed them round then picked up the instrument.

"Each of you will use this implement – an increment borer - to dig out a small core. They're simple to use. The slender arm bores into the wood when you turn the red-coloured arm." He demonstrated on one of the nearby logs. "OK?"

Obediently, silently, each nodded.

"Lovely, lovely. Now, put each wood sample in a separate *labelled* sterile tube – the ones with the green stoppers - and, most important, if you're doing more than one log change the borer, once you've used it, to avoid cross-contamination. We've got a dozen borers here so there's more than enough to cover our nine trees."

" Now – and this is the good bit – ," Steve paused dramatically, "– we have this nifty stuff in the red-topped spray bottles that I want you to spray onto your *sapele* logs. It's called smart water..."

"Ah - we know what that is," interrupted Sandy, eager to show that the police weren't entirely ignorant when it came to scientific matters. "We covered that in a crime prevention course. Um..." She blushed faintly as everyone had turned towards her, looking expectant.

"Yes," agreed George, coming to her rescue as she tailed off. "The police recommend its use in councils and schools. It's cut theft rates of IT equipment quite dramatically."

Paul, who had been staring vacantly at the ground, now looked up at Steve Frampton, grinning.

"It's brilliant. Do you think it'll work?"

Steve, bright eyes alive and round cheeks gleaming, just nodded. Sandy and George were still evidently puzzled until Stanny pointed out that as each red-topped plastic spray bottle containing a small amount of smart water, was paired with a green stoppered tube that would contain the wood sample they could track the ongoing journey of their log in question. *If* it was here.

"Gloves first," he ordered, handing round a box of them from which each took a pair.

As they struggled with the purple latex gloves, Sandy was evidently putting two and two together.

"So the idea's to take the wood sample, put it into the green tube, label it 'A' to 'I', then use the smart water from the red spray bottle it's matched with to spray the log?"

"You got it. Each of these sprays contains a differently forensically coded sample of smart water," added Stanny with a wide orthodontically perfect grin, giving her a hand to get the gloves on.

"So each log will be given its own invisible spray," added Paul.

"When we've found the log we want — *if* we do - through DNA analysis, we'll know the code of the smart water that we've marked it with." Steve Frampton busied himself handing out the tubes and sprays, taped together as pairs.

"And that will allow us to trace its progress?" asked George.

"Well, we'll know where it ends up - with any luck," said Paul. "And get the bastards that buy this illegally felled wood. They may well be implicated in some way in Wingent's murder."

Steve then demonstrated how to take a small core sample from the timber, place it in the stoppered tube, then use the spray — not just on the bark which might be lost when the wood was processed, but also on both cut ends, ensuring that everyone knew exactly what to do.

"How long will this stuff last?" asked George.

"Long enough for us detectives to track it to its final destination." Paul added 'hopefully' under his breath.

Chapter
32

Paul was flicking through the catalogue, trying to get some inspiration for his daughter Emily's twentieth birthday in October. He never was blessed with originality when it came to picking pressies for her. Without his late wife's advice, he'd got it badly wrong in the past – a doll for a girl who loathed the things, and the clothes! Pink – God, that was a total disaster. Stay well away from fashion. So, something twenty-first century and shiny and techie – much safer.

He sipped his single malt – he was pleased he was keeping to just the one each evening. An indulgence, but he'd read that the occasional dram de-activated free radicals and helped prevent cancer – or was that coffee? Besides, since his wife's suicide, he had a responsibility, which he'd not always properly observed, to look after himself, being Em's only parent. So he'd given up smoking. More or less.

He took another sip.

He flicked another page over. Mobile phones might fit the bill. She had an old one, purple and chunky, with none of these functions – Waps? Triband? It could have been written in Farsi for all the sense it made. He'd managed to send a picture to Mark from his own mobe, so maybe his mobe had triband. Or not.

He blew out his cheeks. He was fast becoming an old fart left behind by the umpteenth technological revolution. He glanced at his watch – he was due to meet George for a drink at the Mayfly this evening. They had the occasional jar together, trying, usually unsuccessfully, to stay off work-related topics. They were both sad Saints fans – so they could always commiserate with each other about the parlous state of the Saints' game as their team sank rapidly to the bottom of the Championship league. Hard to believe they'd been in the FA Cup final against Arsenal just a few years ago.

He'd ask George's advice; he was *au fait* with gadgets of all sorts, the newer and more complicated the better. Whereas he'd never mastered how to programme the now out-of-date VCR, never mind grappling with the DVD thingy which was supposed to be easier, and now iPods were a complete enigma. At least he was computer literate.

Was he all right to drive? He'd sipped the amber liquid over a period of time – he should be OK. But it'd never do for a DCI to be fingered for drink-driving. He'd clean his teeth and use a mouth rinse before he left.

Looking back at him from the bathroom mirror was an intense, serious face – had it always looked as grim as that? - with frown lines between navy blue eyes and dark blond hair, the scar through his right eyebrow a livid contrast – looking a bit pale and careworn for forty-five. Pulling his face about he wondered if he should resort to some of those moisturisers that youngsters went in for, but he doubted it would do much good now. The door on youth had well and truly slammed shut behind him.

By and large, he wasn't too unhappy about that as his young married life had been racked by the unbearable swings of his wife's bipolar depression, which led to her inevitable decline as they cycled faster and faster. He'd no desire whatsoever to revisit those years which had stretched his own sanity to its limits. He just felt that ever-present guilt for Em, for her precious childhood lost. He believed her wanderlust – where was she backpacking right now? North Vietnam? - was part and parcel of her need to resolve the anger that had consumed her after her mother's suicide, that anger being directed at him but more damagingly at herself. But the last couple of years since she'd started at Edinburgh Uni, things had improved; now, soon-to-be twenty and eight years after her mother's death, she seemed to have reached some sort of resolution with her own demons, and they'd drawn closer, battered survivors of the same catastrophe.

He opened the bathroom cabinet and shook out one of his anti-inflammatories from a pill bottle. After clambering around those blasted logs, his knees had been protesting.

: ✿ :

He enjoyed the setting of the 'Mayfly' at least as much as the beer. Perched by the side of the lazily flowing Test, the water gently eddying near the weir, swans gliding imperiously by, you could see and hear the occasional swirls of a trout lunging to the surface. It was idyllic early on an autumn evening.

"I thought you were going to help me out here, instead of crowning me some sort of Luddite because I'm not up to date with all these trinkets," Paul grumbled.

George took a long pull of his bitter, and grinned at Paul over the table. He sighed theatrically.

"What are we to do with you? You're a right grumpy old codger, you are."

"There are things I could tell Sandy..."

"My life's an open book. Come on, then. You're thinking of a mobile, eh? Let's have a gander."

Paul handed over the catalogue he'd brought along.

"First you need to decide what functions you want — what functions do you think Em would want."

"Um — triband?" Paul asked not really sure what it did.

George sighed gently. "That was a guess, wasn't it? Em likes to travel, doesn't she? So being able to contact you if she's in out-of-the-way places would set your mind at rest, yes?"

George had known her since she was about fourteen and knew well what the two of them had been through after the loss of her mother when she was twelve. Paul, naturally reticent, had nonetheless opened up to George about Em's difficult relationship with him during her early adolescence. He was a sympathetic and discreet listener.

Em had itchy feet, and while Paul admired her restless adventurous spirit, he worried about the safety of his only child when she was abroad. Besides she shunned the usual back-packer routes, favouring paths less trodden. Having consulted the itinerary she'd left on the PC at home, he thought she was in Vietnam right now, but she hadn't emailed in a while. What was the likelihood of finding internet cafes in North Vietnam?

"It'd be a relief — though there's no guarantee with Em that she'll actually use it to phone her poor old Dad."

"That's settled then. Now the camera function..."

"Camera...yes," Paul echoed. He recalled the picture Mark had sent of the plug-bug in the Police HQ and the one he'd sent back from the 'spook's catalogue of bugs'; lucky that George had shown him sometime earlier how to work a mobile phone camera.

"....obviously she needs a built-in camera."

"Obviously. Look, how much is all this going to sting me?"

"There you go again. What else are you going to spend your vast salary on? Anyway, all modern phones have a camera. Just think, she'll be able to take a piccie of herself in wildest Borneo, communing with the orang utans, and send it to you. It'll give you some peace of mind. But if you want to get her the latest...," George licked a finger and flipped over more pages. "Yes, here we are – the full works. She needs a WAP function..."

"Oh, please." Paul took a desperate swallow of his beer.

"No, with the WAP – that's Wireless Application Protocol to you - she can access her emails. And if you open your moth-eaten wallet, she can get the Multimedia Messaging Service – MMS - and send you a video."

Paul frowned.

"A video to my email address?" Something tickled the back of his mind – a worm-like thought that wriggled away as soon as he tried to grab it.

"Show me that model," Paul snatched at the catalogue. A Vodaphone.

"Go on – splash out. You'll feel good about it."

But Paul's eyes had adopted a faraway look, pupils dilated.

"Uh-oh. I know that look." George lowered his glass gingerly, fearing some onrushing idea that would sweep away his comfortable evening supping and sitting by the river.

"Come on – finish that half. We'll take your car." Paul was up and walking rapidly towards the car park over the bridge.

"Fuck." George drained his glass.

: ✡ :

It took about ten minutes to get to Longstock from the Mayfly, with Paul fidgeting impatiently all the way, and George muttering that this was the last time he drove Paul anywhere, and what's more he'd have to take him all the way back to the 'Mayfly' afterwards as well.

They got out of the car, gazing up at the typically Hampshire flint and brick cottage. It was secluded, a neat two-up, two-down – the type of cottage a child would draw, with simple lines, four windows, a central front door with a small porch - at the end of a small lane at the edge of the village. In the warm autumn dusk, even though the shadows were deepening, the garden still hummed with late insects darting round golden rod, roses and phlox, but the grass had grown long, strewn with dandelion clocks and daisies.

It was tranquil.

With their mother in a rest home in nearby Winchester, both boys used the cottage, although Colin had been absent much of the time, wandering the globe for Forest Watch. Adam, the younger brother, about thirty and single, had a girlfriend in London, and went back there regularly. Perhaps with his brother's death, he'd left to be with his girlfriend; much better than being here all alone, brooding, and no comfort to be gained from the poor old lady.

Paul had phoned ahead from the car, but even getting the answer phone wasn't prepared to be deflected.

The dandelion clock seeds were sent spinning as Paul and George went up the crazy-paving path to the front door. Paul banged the brass lion-shaped knocker without much hope that anyone was in. The sound echoed through the house with that empty-space resonance.

"We're out of luck." George stuck his hands in his pockets and revolved on his heels to scan the area.

"You're probably right. Let's go round the back anyway, now we're here."

A low side gate led round the back. They rounded the side of the cottage, and both stopped at the same time, staring. The back door hung open, the wooden frame splintered round the lock, naked wood glaring pale in the setting sun.

There was that familiar mix of excitement and anticipation that Paul felt in the pit of his stomach. He got out his pencil torch and played it over the drunken door.

"Go on, then. I admit it. Right hunch." George pulled a face as he bent to peer inside.

"Didn't expect this. Crime scene," Paul warned, meaning they should touch nothing and disturb as little as possible.

"I'll get some gloves from the car."

George loped off back to the car, while Paul pushed gently against the skewed door with his elbow.

He listened, standing still in the kitchen. The air was heavy with silence, menacing, he thought. Robbing an empty house, whilst Adam Wingent was in London? A tempting opportunity, and Paul had noticed no red burglar alarm boxes on the house wall. But wasn't it too coincidental — that a robbery should take place just now?

When did this happen? Paul turned to peer more closely at the split door frame. Very recently, judging by the newly-exposed wood.

He trod forward warily, shining the torch ahead, and paused on the threshold to the hall. An unmistakeable, immediately recognisable ferric tang stimulated his nostrils, simultaneously raising the hairs on his arms, and freezing him into position.

Where the hell was George? At that moment George appeared waving gloves, about to speak.

Paul put his finger to his lips, and beckoned him forward, signalling stealth. Together, they donned the gloves.

Paul whispered "Smell."

George raised his head, sniffed the air, and brown eyes widened, nodded.

"Got your torch?" Paul whispered.

"Yup," George mouthed.

Paul signalled for George to proceed down the dim hall towards the front of the small cottage to the front room, while he would examine the back room, next to the kitchen.

He approached the door to the – what? – dining room? back parlour? – and gingerly turned the handle. It moved easily enough, and, with some trepidation, he began to push open the door. He was objectively aware of his dry mouth and increased heart rate, sympathetic nervous system in overdrive, the emotional fright-flight response.

The door resisted.

He pushed again, gently. It gave a little, enough for him to apply one eye to the gap. Thick curtains were drawn over the windows, the room in deep gloom. It took awhile for Paul's eyes to dark adapt after using the torch. The room seemed still, waiting, and the air even more oppressive than outside – the smell more pervasive now. Objects gradually resolved themselves into dim shapes.

Paul heard George's steps clumping up the stairs. If there had been someone here, they would have skedaddled by now. He dropped his gaze to the floor. There, the other side of the door, blocking it, he could just discern a white arm.

He switched on his torch.

"George. Get down here." He was still whispering, though he was sure there was no one apart from themselves in the cottage.

"What?" Muffled. Footsteps thundered back down again.

"Help me shift the door. Something's blocking it."

Together, they pushed, the door protesting. By now, they'd foregone all attempts to keep quiet, grunting and swearing.

The door suddenly gave up the struggle and they almost fell into the gloomy room. George flicked the light switch.

They both stared down at a prostrate form lying behind the door, white shirt stained with blood. Paul looked at George - his face was blanched, the freckles across his nose standing out clearly.

"Is it who I think it is?"

Paul knelt cautiously, careful not to disturb anything, and peered closely at the bloodied face.

"'Fraid so – Adam Wingent." He applied two gloved fingers to the jugular area. "Dead." He felt the cold, clammy cheek and examined the fingers for flexibility. "Not too many hours ago, I'd guess." He'd last seen Adam briefly when a buccal DNA sample had been taken, and Paul had had to tread the delicate line between conveying the impression that this was just a formality to confirm the body in Cameroon as Colin's, and giving false, and ultimately, futile hope. Adam had seemed a stoical body, though clearly close to his older brother and worried about him. Paul had felt for him - he knew first hand what the waiting for a missing relative was like.

George gazed around the room. It was as though a hurricane had roared through. There was paper strewn everywhere, an office chair and desk overturned, and box files scattered over the floor.

"It looks like it was used as a home office. I'd say someone was looking for something."

"Brilliant deduction, George." He turned in a circle. "I think they found it – where's the computer?" asked Paul.

"Ah. I'll just have another poke around in the other rooms. The brothers may have had more than one."

Whilst George clumped up the stairs again, Paul called up Tristram Harrier of the Forensic Sciences Department based in Winnall Industrial Estate and Charles Terman, the pathologist. By rights he ought to get in the Major Crimes Unit, but not yet. He was, as he'd told the Acting Super, uniquely qualified to deal with this investigation as he'd been in on it from the beginning and was best placed to know how things were going in Cameroon – where this had all started. He was determined to run this himself. He'd square it up top later, if need be.

He gazed down again at the body.

"You poor bugger."

He crouched again, his knees behaving perfectly, and examined the body more closely, without touching anything. He could see scrapes on the knuckles of both hands.

"Put up a fight, didn't you?" He whispered to the corpse. Adam Wingent had been stockily built, with the thickset stature of a rugby prop forward. Paul suspected that he must have been tackled by more than one assailant, but succumbed in the end to a knife attack – two superficial slashes on the arms and three deep stabs. The dried blood was the colour of *sapele* wood. He was beginning to hate that wood.

Paul sat back on his heels as George came back.

"No sign of any other room which might have been used as an office."

"OK." Paul pointed to the wounds. "Knifed. What do you think, George? Any clues there?"

"On the body?" George crouched beside him. "I can see three stab wounds – couldn't say which might be fatal."

"Isn't that maybe significant?"

"How d'you mean?"

"If you wanted to kill someone, would you go for those areas – upper abdomen, right shoulder?" He gestured at the areas

"Maybe not. I'd go for the throat, or aim for the heart – that stab there." He pointed at one wound, left of the sternum.

"And if you'd done that, you wouldn't need the other wounds."

"Right. You mean his assailant didn't surprise him, otherwise he could have moved fast, got just the one killer blow in, and Bob's your Uncle," George said.

"He'd have heard that back door going, so no element of surprise -maybe they expected it to be empty anyway. But likely there was more than one killer. With two of them they weren't too bothered about getting in quietly. One to hold and one to stab, but we'll wait for the PM. Hands," Paul said quietly, indicating the hands with his chin.

George squinted at the hands, lifted one with his pen.

"I see. Defence wounds. Poor guy fought."

"That would explain the chaos, but not the missing computer."

"Are you sure there was a PC here?"

"Look around."

Trying not to disturb the crime scene, George took in some cables dangling over an upturned desk, a few CD-Roms scattered about – and a smashed printer.

"Yup, OK."

"I'd say we were on the right track, wouldn't you?"

"But too damn late. There's nothing upstairs – no signs of disturbance."

"So they got what they came for here, but had to fight for it. Adam resisted – and paid the ultimate price."

Chapter 33

"There was something on that PC that 'they' wanted."

George was now driving Paul back to the 'Mayfly' to pick up his car. Paul was slumped in the passenger seat, looking morose.

"You don't say. 'They' being...?" George managed to open a Marathon bar with one hand and offered it to Paul first.

Paul shook his head. He wasn't hungry, besides George had one of those high-burning metabolisms that required regular doses of sugar - and without adding any weight. He needed the whole bar. He could only envy him his gangly ectomorphic frame; by contrast, he had to exercise stern will-power to keep his weight in check. Except for the occasional tot.

"Got no idea. No – that's not true. We know there must be a UK end as well as a Cameroon end to this business. Somebody at *that* end warned somebody at *this* end that Colin Wingent's PC might well contain incriminating evidence."

"And they came to the same conclusion as we did..." The voice was slurpy with melted chocolate.

"But beat us to it."

"They realised that you could send a piccie from your mobile to your email address back home." The bar was half eaten.

"Clearly not as slow on the uptake as we were."

"Let's look at this. Colin Wingent — we think — may have taken incriminating pictures with his mobile — we still don't know that for sure, mind - pictures that would definitely screw that company's logging operation. But what?"

"Well, cutting undersized trees for one," said Paul, remembering the smaller diameter of some of the logs in the warehouse. "Or trees with an export ban like *sapele*. Or cutting in a reserved area. Yes, that could be it — the Dja Reserve where Mark found Colin Wingent's body is a world heritage site. Imagine the furious international reaction if that got out."

"Never underestimate the public's apathy. Thought you'd be more cynical at your age."

Paul grunted.

"OK. Then what?" George was on to licking chocolate off his fingers.

"The loggers spot our Col using his mobe's camera, realise the game is up if this guy, working for Forest Watch, gets the pictures back to them, or some similar organisation, like World Wildlife, or whatever. So what do they do?"

"Naturally, they kill him — what else?"

"Of course. And destroy his accursed mobe."

"Yes, but then what? At some point, later, it occurs to them — or possibly to someone further up in their nasty timber mafia — that that may not be the end of the trail."

"Someone with a bit more technical nous than the muscle men, and who probably wasn't there at the time, asks them about Wingent's equipment — what did he have with him? Our goons mention his mobe, give details. It clicks with our exasperated guy that incriminating pictures might already have been sent on to poor old Col's email." Paul sat up a little. There was that little tug again.

"And brother Adam gets it while preventing them trying to steal Col's PC," George added.

They were both quiet for a while, digesting this. First, that this criminal organisation — for undoubtedly it was that - had very long tentacles, and, second, that the crims had been a step ahead, effectively stymieing their efforts to recoup the pictures.

Paul twisted round in his seat. Tristram Harrier in Scenes of Crimes Unit's large well-equipped van would be some time behind them yet. They had the whole house to process, and it was — what? He peered at his watch. Nearly ten already; they'd had to await the appearance of the Scenes of Crime team and the pathologist. Once they'd arrived, he and George were able to leave them to it. Tris wouldn't be thanking him for finding a dead body at this hour.

With any luck there might be some trace evidence to indicate how many were involved, the odd bit of epidermis lurking around to give them a DNA profile. Even, should they be so lucky, a fingerprint.

They were silent in the car for a few miles, the dual carriageway speeding past, trees crowding the central reservation and strobing the headlights of cars coming the other way.

Eventually —

"Something's missing." Paul growled into the dark.

"What?" George, his sugar levels restored to normal, had now gone into that suspended state of thought that afflicts drivers on straight stretches of road.

"We need to contact Mark asap."

"Go ahead – you've got your phone. He might get a signal. But why?"

"Think about it. There's clearly close communication between the loggers' – what shall we call it? – two branches?"

"That's terrible, even for you."

"It's likely that the Cameroonian branch now know all about what went down at Wingent's house."

"They're feeling safe now, you think? With Wingent's hard drive destroyed, there's no direct evidence to link them to illegal logging - and murder."

"Mmm. Safe-ish, but Mark's still a threat to them, and therefore in danger. He was the one imprisoned by them and who escaped."

George looked over at Paul. He could tell by his tone that he was masticating some idea - his voice went dreamy and slow while the elements of a plan coalesced.

"He needs to spread the load," Paul muttered. "The more people know, the less the threat focuses on Mark."

"What do you suggest?"

"Broadcast what he knows. Once it's out there, there's no point in going after him."

"You mean go on the radio?"

Paul tutted.

" 'Broadcast' in the original sense – disperse."

"Until we've got some firm, preferably probative evidence, that could be professional suicide. If he gets it wrong, he could be sued from here to hell and back," George objected.

355

"Only one thing for it then, we'll have to get that evidence."

He slumped down in the seat again trying to get comfortable and closed his eyes, turning over in his mind what seemed to be a tangled knot – a criminal cast of God knew how many, here and in Cameroon – and they hadn't fingered one single person yet. It was likely that involvement reached the highest levels of the Cameroonian government with individuals either getting substantial kickbacks from the French-owned logging company, Rouge-Bolles, or more directly involved in their logging activities. There wasn't much they could do about that from this end, except expose them and their predations. Would that bother them? Not likely. Organisations like that with their numerous contacts in high places tended to be armour-plated. They bought themselves out of trouble.

But at this end – they now had a murder on their hands here. The second brother. They'd virtually wiped out a whole family. It was a blessing in the most poignantly sad way that their senile mother wouldn't suffer the knowledge that her two sons had been murdered. He'd been told she was in that late stage of dementia where she didn't always recognise her own children as they were now. For her they were still small boys. Paul could think of nothing more tragic. If he ever sensed his memory leaking away like a dripping tap, he'd take an overdose – if he was able to remember what pills to take.

He surmised that whoever had killed Adam had been caught off guard – even if Adam hadn't. After all, what they were after was the computer or its hard drive, and Adam's presence was unexpected and unwelcome – maybe he surprised them in the act of stealing the computer. Perhaps they'd expected him to be in London. A fight must have ensued judging by Adam's knuckles - and they had to silence him. A mistake, certainly. So they could be rattled.

'They'? Yes, there had to be two. Adam, stocky and muscular, might have been able to overcome a single individual, but not two. Anyway, more than two was too many to have haring around a quiet Hampshire village looking for the Wingent abode; they'd be noticed. Perhaps they were noticed, even though the cottage was isolated. He sighed at the prospect of no doubt futile house-to-house enquiries. The next cottage was some way away, at the entrance to the lane.

Suddenly, he sat up. "You stupid twat," he shouted, causing George to swerve.

"Thanks for that. Is that going on my assessment?" George managed to get the car back in lane.

Paul ignored him and reached back over the seat to the catalogue that he'd thrown there on getting into the car back at the pub.

"Not you, me." He flipped quickly through the pages, mumbling to himself.

"Aha! Here we are." Paul peered closely at a page, following the text with a finger, trying to make out the details in the intermittent moonlight flashing through the trees.

"I wish you'd stop making - "

"Right. Turn round. We've got to get to London as quick as you like."

"What? You've got to be joking! No chance – Sandy and me have a date all fixed up. Cinema and a curry. Perfect. Why the hell do you want to go to London all of a sudden?"

But Paul was thinking. He checked his watch.

"OK. Look – drop me off at Winchester Railway Station. If you put your foot down, I can make the next train in – um – twelve minutes. I'll explain as you barrel along. Go on, shift!"

: ♡ :

George was a skilful driver, Paul had to give him that. He made it to Winchester station with two minutes to spare. The ticket office was closed, but Paul could use his warrant card if need be, as police on duty were exempt from paying fares.

When the short three-carriage South-West train arrived it was practically empty, and he had no trouble finding a seat. After looking around to check that no one was near enough to overhear him, he dialled a number back at headquarters to request an address, and a name.

He was going to arrive in London at some ridiculous hour, but at least he could check out the premises, and then contact someone there in the morning. He'd have to find a place to stay. He often used a convenient but reasonably-priced hotel near Hyde Park when he stayed in London. He had the number in his mobile, so dialled and arranged a single room.

Now, for Mark. He could try texting him – he wasn't really into the tortuous linguistics of texting; it was usually quicker for him to spell out the words properly so his text messages tended to be his own mangled version.

'*Mark – worried UR in dnger. U must get 2 press now; publicise what U know. Paul*'

Would he get the drift? Would he realise what Paul was getting at – that the only way to deflect unwanted attention was for Mark to spread the information around? Once it was generally known, there would be less point in targeting Mark - if the bastards reasoned rationally, that is.

What if he didn't check his messages? What if there was no signal in Cameroon? Belt and braces, then. Email. While he grappled awkwardly with, but eventually managed, the mysteries of the texting process, he couldn't remember using his mobile to send an email, although he'd sent the bug-plug pic to Mark's mobile – and that hadn't been too hard. So he scrolled uncertainly through the functions and after some fumblings and false starts, thought he'd conquered the damn thing. Wait a mo' though – this was no good, because he only had Mark's email address for the Centre for Advanced Behavioural Studies – CABS - in the University Science Park. Did he also have a hotmail account? He did have the CRU phone number…somewhere… later, though. He'd work it out later.

He rubbed tired eyes, and his thoughts drifted off.

He thought he'd have liked to go to Cameroon, see what they did at CRU, travel into the interior to see some wild chimps or bonobos. He was curious about just what Mark did in the field. Perhaps he could take Em with him if she was around. She'd be fascinated, he knew. The idea was growing on him.

The gazed out the window. Reflected images flickered in the darkened window hypnotically.

His head drooped onto his chest.

: ☿ :

He awoke with a startle response and a gasp when the train ground on loudly protesting curving rails into Waterloo.

There was something he'd meant to do. What the hell was it? Why did he fall asleep like a narcoleptic? Age was creeping closer like a spectre. Next, he'd be drooling out of the side of his mouth. Surreptitiously, he glanced around like a self-conscious teenager to see if anyone had noticed. At this late hour, there were only two others, blank-eyed, in the carriage.

He shook himself more alert and walked down the long platform outside to the taxi ranks.

At this time of night there were plenty of taxis, and, happily, the one first in line didn't balk at going to Shoreditch, N1. Paul was surprised when he discovered the address was in East London; in his experience many such NGO's were pretty well off for cash, even though relying on donations, but N1 was hardly the green-treed fastness of St John's Wood.

He tried the CRU number hoping to contact Mark. Someone else with a strong accent answered. The reception was filled with static so Paul yelled loud enough for the taxi driver to give him a sour look.

Professor Rees wasn't there, as far as he could tell. He thought of his post-grad student, Sue.

"Sue Clarke? Is she there?" He wasn't at all sure he was being understood.

Static filled the void. At least the phone hadn't been shut off.

A rustle? A breath?

"Hello?" A far-off voice, a slight echo on the line.

"Sue? Is that you? This is Paul Draper – Mark's friend? The DCI?" He finished on a note of query, full volume, not sure she'd remember him. He hadn't seen her for almost a year.

"Yes…of course… is it?" The tight anxiety in her voice brought to mind the rather reserved brittle girl with elfin features hiding behind a curtain of light brown hair. He found it difficult to imagine her surviving the rigours of fieldwork. Perhaps he ought to reassure her – she'd obviously had a lot going on there, what with Mark having gone missing and all the rest of it.

"Just wondered if I could have a word with Mark. Nothing to – er – worry about." That sounded about as genuine as a nine bob note.

"He's not ..." The pitch had risen slightly. She was worried about him. "He's…Yaounde. You could … mobile…the reception's ..." More whooshing noise. The reception was deteriorating.

"Is everything OK there – with you?" Shouting, he heard his own voice as a faint echo, distorted from the way he thought he sounded.

A pause. "Not really. I – I don't know…much… but …murder …CRU..."

Another one? An icy chill flowed through Paul's blood. It was just as he'd dreaded – Mark was in danger.

"Look, Sue. I'll try to get hold of Mark, but if I don't, you can pass on the message when you see him. He needs to get all the suspicions he and others have about Colin Wingent's death – especially the motive - out into the mass media – TV, papers, whatever else - pronto. That way, we can be pretty sure whoever's behind this will see it's pointless to continue – er – persecuting Mark, if everyone knows what he knows." He paused to see what she thought. Had she got all of that? The echo of his voice pursued him down the phone – 'he knows'.

"…see." The voice was distant. Or thoughtful?

Before he could prompt an answer, she continued.

"I understand…saying…" The voice faded and came back intermittently. "difficult…censorship."

He shifted the mobile to the other ear and caught the sharp curious eyes of the taxi driver through the rearview mirror.

"What? Censorship? He has to try, though, Sue. Get it out there, in the open, then he'll be safe, I promise." He paused. Why on earth did he say that? He wasn't in a position to offer any guarantees. "I'll explain in an email."

He finished the call with Sue Clarke promising — as far as he could tell — to do everything she could. But he was troubled by news of a murder at CRU. Who was it? A warning, had she said? Presumably directed at Mark, to back off, say nothing about Wingent?

He then phoned George and left a voicemail asking him to get hold of the CRU email address and phone him back with it pronto. He knew he was treading on someone else's patch here, but to hell with that right now.

The taxi arrived at Shepherdess Walk. Paul got out, paid off the taxi-driver, clearly suspicious of Paul's motives at coming to Shoreditch at this ungodly hour, and looked around. He'd not been in this part of London for a very long time. Battered during WWII, and a centre for blackmarket activities, it became notorious for turf wars between various gangs, the Krays among them. More lately, though, it had become the preserve of artists, seeking cheap studio space. This was then followed, in that saltatory evolution of London boroughs, by a surge in cafes and bars. The onward march of the bohemian bourgeoisie. But scruffy old Shoreditch in the East End was never going to attain the anodyne gentility of its neighbour Islington. It was always going to cling stubbornly to its edgy, seedy character.

Paul walked along and turned left into a smaller street, dark and deserted at this time of the night — very early morning now. Looking left and right, he could spot no one. Walking on, his footsteps echoing back from the brick walls of the narrow street, he found the address of the Forest Watch offices – first floor, converted warehouse building, it seemed to be.

He crossed the street to get a closer view of the premises. As far as he could tell, the building appeared intact. No sign of a break-in. He breathed out, daring to hope.

He would return here tomorrow, first thing.

Chapter
34

I n the clean washed light of an early September morning, the streets of Shoreditch showed only an innocent face, a world away from the faint, lingering odour of gangland menace that still infused it at night.

Paul pressed the buzzer on the warehouse door marked 'Forest Watch'. A yawning voice answered, as though roused from a deep sleep. When he identified himself, a long silence followed during which he imagined the keeper of the gate trying to process the information.

Silently, he was buzzed in.

Inside, it was like stepping into the Tardis – a complete break with the outside - all ultra-modern minimalism, brushed steel and gleaming black marble tiles. An open spiral staircase graced by an ornate wrought iron banister and an upper gallery completed the must-have look for all thrusting 21st century outfits. There were several organisations based here, of which Forest Watch was only one.

Paul scanned the board inside the door. There were small computer software firms, PR outfits, agents for something or other – and, there, on the first floor, Forest Watch.

He took the spiral stairs up one floor, and there at the top was a rumpled-looking, unshaven young man with ruddy cheeks and tousled sandy-coloured hair, whose first words were:

"I wondered when you were going to get around to us. Hi, my name's Ian Campbell – 'Jock' around here." It fitted. The accent was soft, maybe Edinburgh rather than the harsher Glaswegian accent, although Paul was pretty ignorant of the nuances of Scottish accents.

"DCI Draper."

Jock, apparently faintly embarrassed by his appearance, futilely smoothed his shirt, and said, "One of us has been sleeping here since – you know – just in case something comes in from Cameroon."

"Has it?"

"Oh – just a phone call from Dave Lancaster from WWF in Yaounde where Col was going to have a desk." He shrugged. "He couldn't tell us much. It was good of him to phone, though."

In answer to Paul's question, Jock said that Forest Watch had been informed first by the High Commission that 'Col had been murdered and they said they'd contact his brother'.

"Adam was stunned, but somehow I got the feeling not too surprised. Resigned, really."

So, it seems he didn't know about Adam.

"How's that then?"

"Well, apparently he told Col he ought to take a desk job. It was safer, and then there's their mother's illness. Anyway, that wasn't going to happen – Col was dedicated to his work. He'd wither and die behind a desk..."

Too late, he realised what he'd said, swallowed hard and turned abruptly.

He indicated for Paul to follow him along the gallery to the FW office - a small suite of three compact rooms, one with a couch and mussed up blanket, clearly recently the just-vacated bed of Jock who hastily balled up the blanket and invited Paul to sit while he made some coffee in the next office.

Evidently no one else was in yet – it was still quite early, but Paul, impatient as ever, hadn't been prepared to wait any longer.

He checked his messages on the mobile, and entered an email address into his phone.

When the rich pungent odour of percolated coffee permeated the two rooms, Paul realised he'd missed breakfast, and was suddenly famished as well as thirsty.

Jock returned with sugar and milk and two steaming mugs on a tray, and an uncertain smile. He seemed apprehensive.

Paul grabbed one of the mugs eagerly, ladled sugar into it and gulped down the hot liquid. Hot and strong.

"Jock – can I call you Jock?" A nod. "My visit's to do with Colin's death."

A wince from Jock as he peered down into his mug.

"I guessed. Like I said, I thought you'd be round sooner."

"I'm sorry. You must have been friends as well as colleagues in a fairly small, dedicated organisation like this." Paul waved his hand around.

Jock breathed in deeply, and gazed straight at Paul.

"He was a great bloke, Col. Yes, good friends. We all miss him, not just because he was our friend but also because he was a skilled field-worker. He's going to be difficult to replace." He ducked his head and sipped his coffee thoughtfully.

Jock, idealist he might be, nonetheless had a very practical Scottish streak.

"Since Colin lived in Hampshire, I'm trying to ascertain more about the circumstances of his death." Paul judged it wiser at this juncture to keep back the news of Adam's death. If Jock or FW heard about it through the press, so be it. But it could, at this point, simply confuse the picture and frighten FW staff needlessly.

"His murder, you mean. Anything I can do to help." Jock added some more sugar to his coffee. His hand was shaking.

"His home in Longstock was recently broken into and his PC taken. Now I wondered why since he'd already been murdered in Cameroon, unless someone thought he had something of importance, something damning perhaps, on his computer. Something sensitive he'd sent to his own computer here from Cameroon."

Paul waited.

Jock frowned into his mug, stirring steadily, considering.

"He could, I suppose, have sent something to his PC, but Dave said he'd hardly had time to get his bum on the seat at WWF and he'd not used the terminal there." He sighed and examined the ceiling. "Let's see. He didn't have a lap-top – unless he'd got one over there, or borrowed one. He did have a mobile – ."

"And was it one of those with a camera?"

He attempted to tidy his unruly hair with his fingers. "I think so," he said slowly. "Most of them have cam..."

Suddenly, his eyes opened wide and he dashed from the room, coffee slopping over the sides of his mug.

From the next room, Jock shouted, "Come here, DCI."

Jock had stopped at one of several desks crowded together in the third room and was activating a PC, muttering, "Password, password." He passed his hands beneath the desk top, reaching far back.

"You're not going to tell me you keep your password under the desk, are you?" demanded Paul, astonished.

Jock just looked up, as he retrieved from under the desk a small scrap of paper with a blob of Blue-tack on the back. He handed it over, having the decency to look abashed.

"Col did."

"Good grief, you deserve to be robbed." Paul read what was written. "Keeper?"

"Ah. 'Keeper', yes. We're on 'K' this quarterly – we each choose a password beginning with that letter." Jock typed it in, pressed 'Start' and 'My pictures'.

"This is Col's work station – was. He might have sent a picture from his mobile to his computer," Jock added. "Stupidly, we never thought to check his own terminal here. We just checked our own emails."

"When we saw a PC had been stolen from Adam's house, it was clear that someone else thought he might have used his mobile phone to send a picture to his home PC. And we assumed that was that – dead end. Belatedly, since I'm not up-to-date...try that one." Paul bent down to get a better look.

Jock clicked on the picture squares, but they were of landscapes – very English landscapes which were familiar to Paul. The New Forest in all its autumnal glory. Some fallow deer in the misty distance. He stared. These were good photos.

"Anyway," Paul resumed, "we realised that you can send to *more* than one email address at a time…oh, Christ, what are we doing? We're looking in the wrong place." He nudged Jock's arm.

"Shit, you're right." This came unexpectedly from Jock's lips. Paul was mildly surprised; he'd detected a barely perceptible ecclesiastical flavour - a whiff of Calvinism - about Jock, but maybe that was the nature of activists striving to save the planet. Particularly Scottish ones.

He clicked on the email, and they both waited impatiently for the broadband connection.

There were several unread emails. They scanned them rapidly. Spam, spam and more spam.

A sharp intake of breath from Jock.

"Yes, yes. Look, one from Col."

He clicked, and the email came up. No words – just a picture.

They waited impatiently, then scrolled down.

A picture of two men standing in a bush clearing emerged. A red-faced burly individual with sleeves rolled up over muscular forearms and a sort of cowboy hat jammed low on his head, and a tall African wearing just shorts, his chest well-muscled and gleaming, and, dangling loosely from his right hand, a machete. The African appeared to be glaring at the white, while the latter was staring towards the camera, eyes shadowed under the brim of his hat.

Jock seemed a little deflated.

"Just the one picture. Who are they, do you know?"

"Oh, I believe I know very well who they are. Can you print out two copies for me?"

Jock pressed 'print', and turned to Paul, scrutinising him closely.

"You think they've got something to do with his death, don't you?"

"Possibly, Jock. Look, here's my email address at home." He handed over his card with all his contact numbers printed on it.

"I'd like you to forward this email to me at that address, and also send it as an attachment to this email address." He scribbled down Mark's email address at CRU that George had earlier phoned to him. "Professor Rees was the one who discovered Colin's body and now he may be in some danger, so can you add this message '*suspects – avoid at all costs - show police*' in a large font to his attachment?"

Jock's sandy eyebrows rose as he began to forward the two email attachments.

Paul wanted Mark to have this information as quickly as possible, but reckoned it best not to put too much in the email as you couldn't know who might pick up at the other end.

He owed Jock more explanation than that, though. He sat on an adjacent swivel chair and faced Jock.

"I promise to do everything I can to help find Colin's killer or killers, Jock, but you have to realise that his murder is outside my jurisdiction, to say the least. All we can do this end is provide the police over there with as much information as we can – and see if there are any leads this end that we can follow up."

There was a glint of tears in Jock's eyes as he nodded and turned back to the screen.

Paul picked up the two prints and folded them away in his jacket pocket. Thank God he'd not told Jock of Adam's murder; obviously with him this upset, it was not the right time. Soon enough.

"You know why he was killed, don't you?" Jock's voice was so low, as he turned off the computer, Paul wasn't sure he'd heard.

"Why don't you tell me what you believe?"

"We know illegal logging goes on in Cameroon, and in that area in particular – the Dja Reserve. That's what Col was investigating. Banned woods, undersized woods, but worst of all logging in forbidden areas."

"He knew it would be dangerous?" Of course he did. That was his work but he wanted Jock to disclose whatever he knew.

Jock nodded slowly, face still turned towards the screen.

"Personally, I thought it was foolhardy to go alone without any protection, and I said so at the full meeting we had to discuss it, but Col was determined; he's – he was – very stubborn. We argued about it – I could tell he had his doubts, but he felt that if someone didn't go in there fast and get the evidence, it'd be too late. Once they'd made sufficient inroads into the Dja Reserve, all would be lost – it would be too late to turn the clock back. Besides, we were hoping for some – er - specific backing if we did get evidence."

It wouldn't be the first time that some well-intentioned and courageous activist had lost his/her life to the savage agents of logging companies. He'd read of some saintly seventy-year old American lady in Brazil who'd been barbarically slaughtered for facing up to the timber barons. Colin's death probably wasn't the first one in Cameroon either. He wondered how many others might have died to protect the logging company's lucrative concessions.

"Do you know the names of the logging companies working in the Dja area?"

For an answer, Jock got up and turned to a row of filing cabinets, tapping the top drawer of one.

"This is where we keep information on the companies," he said.

Paul watched as Jock opened the drawer and sorted through a number of hanging files.

"This one - the low-down on the two most notorious timber kings in West Africa."

"Could I have photocopies of those?"

"Don't see why not." Another voice made him jump. It came from behind him.

"How long have you been there, Sam?" asked Jock.

Paul turned to look behind him. Leaning against the door jamb was a tall slim figure, smiling in a lop-sided manner, legs casually crossed, arms folded. A confident pose.

Paul waited to be introduced, but Jock stayed rooted where he was, files still held aloft. Sam came over, stuck out a hand as Paul stood.

"Samantha Ball." They shook hands as she nodded a greeting, her dark fringe falling over her eyes. She flicked it back with a graceful head movement as she held onto his hand. She had one of those short, flapper-style bobs that really only suit brunettes. The black jeans were tight and the bright red top with a V neck-line of the softest wool, Paul noted.

She favoured him with another smile, this time a knowing one.

"Jock and I are colleagues. And you are some sort of policeman?"

"I'm helping to investigate Colin Wingent's death, yes. DCI Draper. Jock's been very helpful, Ms Ball."

The dark eyes flicked quickly over to Jock and back to Paul. Then the full smile was switched on, scarlet lipstick and large white teeth with a small gap between the front teeth completed a compellingly stunning look. Not all men would find her conventionally attractive, but none would dare overlook her.

But she hadn't shown too much emotion at the mention of Colin's death. Jock hadn't moved or said anything, looking a bit like a hypnotized rabbit.

"Sam," she corrected. "Good. Was there something useful on the computer?"

"Not really," said Jock too quickly.

Samantha Ball examined him coolly, head on one side.

"We were just checking whether Dave Lancaster had sent an email," added Jock. "Whether there were any new developments…"

Paul said nothing, trying to gauge the undercurrents of what? —suspicion? — hostility? — resentment? - that wafted to and fro, in all but visible waves. Clearly, all was not as it should be chez—FW. Well, not really his business, but Sam was an elegant brunette and Jock might be quite presentable, when he got his wayward hair sorted out. Most likely, they'd dated and then had a falling out. To his way of thinking it was almost always hazardous to mix work and love, as he'd mentioned more than once to George, but of course he took no notice of him.

"And?" asked Sam, delicately arched eyebrows rising.

Jock shook his head.

Was this some form of rivalry — why not tell her what we'd found?

"Nothing." He shrugged, but he wasn't a convincing liar.

As Jock said this, her expression of scepticism grew, her mouth forming a moue. So Paul decided to jump in on behalf of the hapless boy who seemed to be swimming out of his depth.

"Well, it all had to be checked out. A matter of routine, ah, Sam." He smiled reassuringly at her. "And then these notes Forest Watch have accumulated on the logging companies may well prove fruitful for the investigation, if not at this end, then at the Cameroon end. If you're sure about it, point me towards the photocopier, Jock."

"Let me do it. I'll be faster. Our photocopier Mabel is a little temperamental," she said. Sam stepped forward and smoothly took the files from Jock's unresisting fingers and went next door to a small room off the kitchenette.

Paul studied Jock who was staring after Sam.

"Correct me if I'm wrong, but do I detect an atmosphere re Sam?" He spoke in a low voice.

Jock, reddening a little, mumbled something about trustafarians – a term Paul guessed referred to rich kids with trust funds, and asked if that was right.

Jock shrugged again. "More or less. They've never had to work their way through Uni, the decks stacked in their favour from the off, and they expect the real world to dance attendance on their every need."

This was delivered with such bitterness that Paul wondered again if some other emotions weren't mixed up somewhere in there as well as resentment – a reluctant, guilty longing? Was it directed at the undoubtedly lissome Sam? Or was it simple jealousy that the privileged seemed to swim effortlessly through life's turbulent currents. He'd felt that often enough himself at university in Bristol where a fair proportion of undergrads came from public schools – and he a humble comprehensive product.

"You had a job to get you through Uni?"

Jock nodded. "Yes I did. And it was a damn hard struggle. No way my parents – my Dad's retired - could really afford for me to go to Uni. I read Environmental Sciences at UEA, one of the best for that." A touch of pride there.

"But you can't blame the likes of Sam for having money."

"I don't, not really. It's stupid of me I know. And Sam's nice, really, very – helpful. Sociable. Sorry - I sounded like some proto-anarchist ready for the peoples' revolution there." He stooped to pick up his cooling mug of coffee.

"It's more the assumptions that come with money – and Sam has more than Croesius - that they should rise to the top like cream." He blew out his cheeks. "Oh, dear. There I go again, like some rent-a-mob Trot."

Paul wondered at Jock's upbringing. A strict moral code, he guessed, none the worse for that, but overlaid with a censorious inclination.

"Jock, why did you say there was no email from Wingent?"

Jock's pale freckled skin flushed again.

"I – uh – thought it was police business by then."

A feeble lie.

"It strikes me that Sam has a normal healthy curiosity and will shortly be scanning the emails on Colin's terminal."

Jock grinned, and fished in his shirt pocket for the piece of paper he'd retrieved from under the desk with 'Keeper' scribbled on it.

"She won't be able to find Col's password, and when I get the chance, I'll delete the email."

"You haven't answered my question – why?"

Jock tucked the paper away again, looking uncomfortable.

"I'd rather not say, if you don't mind."

"Fair enough. You have my mobile number on the card should anything else occur to you, or anything untoward happens. I want you to contact me at once, anytime. OK?"

"Sure." Jock tucked the card away with the password paper.

Sam sashayed in with the warm photocopies which she pressed into Paul's chest with an entrancing smile, and handed the files back to Jock.

"There we are. Mabel was good as gold. Must have known there was a copper on the premises," she said, grinning.

Paul returned the smile, feeling the tactile after-image of her fingers on his chest, gave his thanks and bade the two of them goodbye, adding that he might have to be in touch with them again.

"Don't leave it too long, DCI," said Sam.

Out of interest, and because he wanted another look, Paul walked right around the gallery peering at the other businesses and returned back to the stairs. As he clattered down them from the first floor gallery, he glanced aside at the room where Colin's desk was, and saw Sam leaning forward peering at the screen, the mouse in her hand.

She didn't see him as he left.

Chapter
35

Sue hadn't been able to get hold of Mark. He was hopeless, never checked anything – emails, texts, phone messages - when he was preoccupied. Likely it was because he was in a dead spot, or had his phone turned off. It couldn't be – could it? –that he was in trouble yet again.

She didn't know what to do. That DCI, Paul, had sounded so urgent and insistent. She chewed a thumbnail while watching Caro and the baby.

Suddenly, Caro unceremoniously dumped the baby in her lap and wandered off to her computer terminal. Sue looked down at the wobbly head, the eyes searching but not focusing steadily on her face. She bent closer so that she was within range of the baby's limited focal length, and cupped her hand behind the baby's head and cooed at her.

Caro was fed-up; no doubt she was expecting to see more of Mark and Sue was a poor substitute. Her stomping stride over to the computer, the banging of the keys said it all. In another context it would be comical, Caro flouncing around like some cross diva.

"Mummy's in a strop," she whispered to the baby.

"Mark will be back soon, Caro," Sue said aloud, without much conviction.

She tried again.

"He is visiting a friend." A small lie which she hoped would reassure the bonobo. She smoothed the baby's fine fur on her head. The round skull was fragile, like fine bone china.

Just then her mobile rang with the silly warbling bird sounds that she thought were amusing some months ago, but were now just as irritating as Mark's mooing ring tone. The baby's arms flew up in surprise at the sound. Caro, after curling her lip at stupid bird noises, stopped to listen as Sue answered.

"Sue Clarke? This is Yaounde Hospital. We have Professor Mark Rees here in the emergency ward."

Sue sat down heavily on the floor, the baby still cradled in one arm. Caro watched intently, then came over. Sue handed over the baby, faintly mewing a protest, into Caro's arms but her keen gaze was fixed on Sue's face.

"What?" she said faintly. She felt light-headed.

"Please do not worry, Miss Clarke," said the brisk voice. "He has only been in a minor road accident." The accent was familiar, but she couldn't place it.

"He's alright? How is he hurt? What happened?"

Caro pulled at her sleeve, wanting to know what was being said. Sue remembered too late to censor her conversation. Caro would guess it was about Mark. Like most intelligent animals she was adept at picking up on tone and inflexions

"He's dislocated his shoulder, but he is alright now. He is ready to go home. Can you come to pick him up?"

"Yes, yes, of course. Which ward?" Her hand went up to her forehead.

There was a silence at the other end for a while, a whispered aside, then –

"He will be in the hospital entrance, waiting for you."

"I'm on my way right now." God, that man was impossible! Couldn't be left alone for a moment without getting into some sort of schoolboy scrap. She turned towards the anxious bonobo who'd been keenly observing Sue's reactions.

She tried to clear the anxious frown from her face and gave her a tight smile.

"Caro – I am going to get Mark. Bring him back here." She started to search for the Landy keys before realising that Mark had them. She gritted her teeth in frustration.

Caro, baby cradled in the crook of her right arm, slid over to her computer, activated her program, squinted at the hieroglyphic keys as she always did, then picked and pecked.

'Big – trouble - ?'

"No, no," Sue reassured her. She hadn't fooled the receptive bonobo. But a dislocated shoulder should be just a matter of a couple of analgesics and some rest. "Mark is OK, Caro. I promise."

The flaming idiot. The second road accident. First, he's run off the road by some tosser, and now this.

Where the hell were the other car keys? Caro seemed calmed and started playing with the baby.

Ekoko. He had the key board in his office.

Before she left, she cuddled Caro and the baby, murmuring reassurances, put a Lucozade for Caro nearby, and dashed off to Ekoko's office.

He wasn't there. She racked her memory – where would he be now? Any one of a number of places around the site. One of the chimps had a mysterious ailment – he was probably over at the chimp enclosure. She didn't have the time to go searching for him. A note. She quickly scribbled a post-it note explaining where she'd gone and why and placed it on top of a copy of 'Ancient Gods of Egypt', lying on his desk. You never knew about people's reading preferences.

Ekoko would be back in his office soon and spot it.

She looked up at the key board, and selected keys for the Toyota pickup.

: ¤ :

She'd driven like a bat out of hell to get to the Yaounde Central Hospital. Reckless and hypocritical, too – considering that all the way over she'd been rehearsing the tongue lashing she'd give Mark for his slipshod driving when she got there.

She was in the Briqueterie district, just to the west of the centre of the city and north of Camp du Lac. It was quiet as she squealed the Toyota into the darkened hospital parking lot. Few visitors at this time of night. Only one other vehicle parked in the corner nearby.

She leapt out of the pickup, and paused. It was very still, very quiet. Her experience of hospitals, limited though it was, was of continuous bustle. There was some light leaking from the front entrance of the hospital but she couldn't see anyone waiting. She'd have to go inside and ask.

She turned to lock the driver side door. As she bent she felt a movement of warm air behind her, and, simultaneously, the side mirror reflected a shadowy figure. Her eyes widened in shock, her thoughts detonating, even as she dodged to one side, crouching and turning.

Two of them. One white, one black.

It's a trap! Where's Mark? Is he dead? Have they killed him? As her inner screams collided in panicked confusion, it triggered a totally alien fury.

"Bastards!" she shrieked at them.

It never even occurred to her that she ought to shout for help – so totally focused was she on self defence. The hospital entrance was over on the far side of the nearly empty car park. Help wouldn't get here before these tossers could do some damage.

She gathered herself and assessed the situation, backing up a little. Her shriek had briefly startled them – a big beefy white and a well-muscled black guy. Now the beefy one started forward, cursing under his breath.

She wasn't going to make it easy for them.

Sue calculated, swung swiftly around and thwacked 'Beefy' in the gut with a leg-kick. He doubled over with a loud 'whoosh'.

Her solid trekking boots had delivered a hefty kick.

The self-defence lessons she'd taken might actually pay off. Lee had been so right to persuade her to take them after discovering that she often stayed late at work at CABS. And she'd found – an unexpected bonus, this - that they boosted her confidence, too. She was going to be no pushover.

Stupidly, she spent too much time admiring her handiwork while the other had snuck behind her. A hand snaked round to grab her round the chest, squeezing her breasts and making it difficult to breathe.

She bent quickly from the waist, unbalancing the other, and gritting her teeth, twisted to one side. The black guy fell on the ground with a gratifying thump, looking surprised.

That was satisfyingly easier than she'd thought it would be. She'd never had to do this in hot blood before.

She knew she wasn't of a build to impress for long in this sort of arena, willow thin and not tall, but she was fast, supple, and she had a dancer's agility. But there were two of them.

She backed up further, dancing on the balls of her feet – difficult in boots - to get the both of them within her field of vision. Where was 'Beefy'? Just now he'd been gulping air near the pickup.

She scanned the area quickly. No one.

He emerged from behind the pickup at a run, relying on weight to overpower her. She dodged around him like a matador facing a charging bull, and then made a decisive error.

She'd figured it was best to try to get inside the pickup – she had to be realistic, this was a fight she was never going to win. She hadn't had time to lock the driver's door before she was attacked, so there would be no need to fumble with keys to open the door, and she was faster than them; she could swing inside, lock the doors and then have a second or so to get the keys in the ignition…

She swung open the door, but the black guy, his composure recovered, if not his slighted male pride, grabbed her again, this time so tightly that, struggle as she might, there was no angle, no leverage she could use. She couldn't even get the breath to scream. All she could do was kick backwards at his shins with her heavy, sensible boots. At least she had the satisfaction of hearing grunts of pain, but the hold did not slacken. She knew then that she was beaten and in deep trouble.

Ekoko would find her note – eventually – saying where she'd gone and why, but he wouldn't be anxious for a while. Please, please find it fast – look at your Egyptian gods. Get here. Then, her mind tripping fast, she knew the trail would go cold at this hospital – they wouldn't kill her here. Too open, too close to help. Not here, then where?

The hold round her chest slackened slightly.

She took a deep breath to scream, but 'Beefy' guessed what she was about to do, and slapped her hard across the face. Sue staggered as the other one let her go and she fell heavily to the ground. Eyes streaming, she glared at the tarmac.

An inspiration flashed through her thoughts as she lay there feeling the sting, eyes watering, but most of all furious at these two thugs and herself.

She ripped off her necklace under the cover of her body and as she rose to her knees, deliberately slowly, contrived to slide it under the Toyota pickup with her hand as she struggled to get up. She was banking on them taking the pickup as well as their own vehicle.

They confirmed it for her when they roughly grabbed her and the black guy began searching her for the keys, hands lingering, while Beefy kept his hand over her face, his fingers digging into her skin.

"Bitch. You'll pay for what you did," he hissed into her ear, stale beer breath wafting over her.

Chapter
36

Mark and Ekoko stared down at Sue's note, dumbfounded.

Ekoko had found it after he'd completed his final rounds of the enclosures and ensured that his expanded staff were alert and security was tight. He'd clucked his tongue in sympathy. Mark seemed to be a very unlucky person.

Not five minutes later he'd heard the Landy engine and got up, curious. He'd watched with growing incomprehension as Mark had descended from the vehicle, no sling in sight, and waved merrily over at him when he'd spotted Ekoko peering out of the lighted window.

To Ekoko, he hadn't appeared to have anything wrong with his shoulder. He'd rapped on the window and beckoned Mark in urgently.

Now, here they stood, trying to puzzle out what was going on.

Ekoko, ever the more suspicious of the two, said, "It is a trap. They have Sue Clarke."

"They? Who for God's sake?" Mark heard his voice rise with the fear. "What do you – I mean – why Sue? Why would anyone - ?"

Ekoko gazed steadily at him, and said slowly, as though the realisation had just come to him.

"To get to you."

Mark stared back.

"No – that's ridiculous. Me?" He paused a beat, peering into Ekoko's worried dark brown eyes. "Ah – ," he breathed, realisation dawning.

"Sue Clarke is – what do you say?"

"Bait," Mark croaked.

: ⌂ :

They stood, scanning the immediate and unpromising surroundings of the hospital car park, the only light spilling from the front entrance and illuminating a limited circle of ground.

Mark reached inside the Landy, just as he had only two days ago when a bullet gouged the roof, an echo of the same movement staying his hand momentarily. Determined not to flinch, he grabbed his temperamental torch and slapped it in his hand. He'd forgotten to change the batteries.

It deigned to offer a weak beam which Mark swung around.

Ekoko loped over to the front portico to find a receptionist. There was always the outside chance that Sue Clarke was still in the hospital looking for Mark, or that someone had seen something untoward in the car park.

But there was no sign of the Toyota pick-up.

Mark began to search the area more systematically, alternately slapping the torch and various exposed parts of his body. The night-time blood-sucking denizens were on the warpath and he hadn't thought to spray with repellant.

Ekoko hadn't wanted Mark to come with him. It was falling into the kidnappers' trap, he'd said, but Mark had been adamant. The more opposition, the more adamant he became, until Ekoko gave way with ill grace. Mark could hardly blame him for being exasperated – he'd been nothing but trouble since he'd arrived in Cameroon.

Something pale on the ground caught his attention. He dashed over only to find a crumpled up piece of paper. As he bent to retrieve it, something glinted at the edge of his vision. Rods, to detect low light levels at night, clustered more densely at the periphery of the retina, he thought irrelevantly, approaching the object. When he got to within two yards, he knew what it was, and it shocked him into stillness. He didn't want to go any closer. He glanced back at the lighted portico. Ekoko was nowhere to be seen.

He turned back and walked slowly towards the lapis lazuli pendant with its broken gold chain lying gleaming softly on the tarmac. Crouching, he picked it up, examining it as though he'd never seen it before.

He heard Ekoko's quiet footfalls coming up behind him, and silently held the necklace out to him.

"Sue's. See – the catch is broken." His voice was curiously flat.

Ekoko sucked in his breath sharply. "She was taken from here, Mark!" Ekoko looked around. "A *hostage*. I told you!"

"The hospital?"

Ekoko shook his head. " Nobody came in with a bad shoulder. The staff saw nothing, heard nothing. No, they are not here. Not now."

From his crouching position, Mark swung the torch around slowly.

"This immediate area is where she was kidnapped, so this -," he stopped. "What's that over there?"

Ekoko approached the feebly lit spot about another two yards away from where the necklace had lain.

They both bent over to examine a whitish area.

"Not powder," Ekoko said.

Mark gently touched the coarse pinkish-white substance holding the imprint of a heel, pinched some between his fingers and rubbed it.

"No, it's sawdust." Sawdust again. It kept appearing, like a dread omen. Of course, it might be totally unconnected to Sue's disappearance, but, intuitively, he knew it was related somehow.

He peered up at Ekoko.

"Sawdust. Sawmill," Ekoko said.

"You're right." He nodded, thinking.

In the gloom they stared at each other, both evidently arriving at the same conclusion. It was the cement that bound this whole misadventure together, what the whole thing was about — wood. As he had before, Mark absently put some of the sawdust in his shirt pocket, and buttoned down the flap. How long ago had he done that before, at the sawmill in the Dja?

"That's where they came from."

"And maybe that's where they're going to take her."

"A sawmill."

"Yes, but where, for God's sake." It was a despairing cry born of frustration — now that they'd leapt one hurdle, they were faced with another.

"Wait, wait. Your friend at WWF? The one who showed you maps."

"Dave Lancaster. Dave – yes, he would know where the sawmills are located. Brilliant, Ekoko!" He slapped him on the shoulder. "C'mon, let's go." He was off towards the Landy at a fast run, leaving the warden standing, glowing briefly in his own brilliance.

As they settled breathlessly back in the vehicle, Mark rang Lancaster's phone number from the card he'd been given. Obviously, he'd be at home by now. He waited impatiently. Two rings, three, four five, si...

"Hallo?" The deep voice sounded grumpy.

"Thank god you're there." Mark had been holding his breath and now it all came out in a whoosh. He explained what they needed, tried not to gabble.

Dave would be there pronto – with what they needed.

As he closed the phone, careful this time to keep it on stand-by, it rang. He stared at it, mesmerized. A text message.

'If U want 2 C her again – 9pm @ Marche Mokolo alone'

Mark swallowed, his throat tight and dry, and silently handed the phone to Ekoko. How had they got hold of his number? He couldn't think right now - later. As he read the message, Ekoko sucked in his breath with a hissing snake-like noise.

"I told you. They want *you* .To change you for her."

Mark was very still, fearful for her, for himself, too. He could feel his stomach cramping. "They can *have* me. How much time do we have?" His voice was almost soft.

"It is near eight o'clock now. It does not take long to get there. We have almost an hour before..." Ekoko paused as though the echo of Mark's voice had just filtered into his brain.

"No, no. You cannot. We can trap them at the Marche."

"Look, Ekoko, there *is* no other way. Sue's my responsibility just as the wardens like Honore are yours. I cannot allow her to be harmed by not going...but...first..."

Mark fell silent, unmoving, his posture rigid, staring out the windscreen, anger and terror co-mingling and colouring his thoughts, interfering with his reasoning. Then he appeared to wake himself.

"Right. Change of plan. An hour, you said. We call Beti right now, so he can put his men in place at the Mokolo market by nine. Meanwhile, we...," he turned stiffly at last to look at Ekoko, " *we* will find her with Dave's help."

As Ekoko began to protest that this was police business, obviously forgetting his habitual hostility to them, Mark interrupted.

"Listen, she's not being *held* at the market, obviously - too crowded, too many opportunities to escape. They're holding her somewhere else, and as you cleverly put two and two together — it's a sawmill. That's where they're holding her. They're going to take her from there in time to reach the market by nine." Mark grasped Ekoko's sleeve to emphasise his point, trying to persuade him. "We get Beti's men to cover the market, while *we* find that saw mill before they move her. Her best chance, Ekoko. Dave will help us."

Ekoko gazed for a long time at Mark, his jaw muscle jumping.

"Why did they not want us to go to the saw mill to get her back?" he asked finally.

Mark stared fixedly out the windscreen, but he had an answer ready. "Too easy to surround with police. A market, you can slip in and out, even at that time it'll be busy. You'd be hidden in seconds, impossible to follow." He stopped, struck by another thought. "And maybe, *maybe*, they're still protecting their masters – trying to keep them at arm's length from the dirty work, uncontaminated, away from the sawmill..."

Mark's voice faded into silence, while, once more, Ekoko examined him closely. Eventually, he gave the briefest of nods.

"And if it goes all wrong – I'll let them take me and you get her out of there. Right?"

Ekoko sucked through his teeth again.

"Right?" Mark asked again, putting his hand on Ekoko's shoulder.

Ekoko nodded briefly but said nothing. Mark squeezed his shoulder encouragingly.

"Thanks."

Mark called John Beti and explained the whole situation – that Sue had been kidnapped, probably by the murderers of Wingent, that they'd demanded he present himself at Marche Mokolo at nine, that they undoubtedly wanted to exchange Sue for him. Beti offered his men without being asked, and, yes, of course they would be discreet, in plain clothes. He would be there himself to oversee things, he had been undercover before, he knew exactly how these things were conducted. There were plenty of places for concealment in the market.

Another call.

They sat in silence, Mark consulting his new watch impatiently, listening to the night sounds until, minutes later, another, more mechanical, sound joined in.

: ⛌ :

Dave spread his map over the Toyota's bonnet and focussed a strong torch beam on it. All three men bent towards it.

"These symbols are the sawmills in this province." Dave began without preliminaries, trying to lower his rumble to a sound more like an elephant with indigestion.

"There are too many," said Ekoko, a note of despair in his voice.

"Not if we figure that they wouldn't take her too far, my friend." Mark and Ekoko had explained the situation to Dave.

"Yeah, I agree. It would be impractical to move her any great distance to the market, besides they gave us about an hour so let's concentrate on the mills closest to Yaounde, up to about an hour's drive away," Mark suggested.

"Here is one." Ekoko stabbed at one of the symbols south west of Yaounde but close.

Dave shook his large shaggy head.

"No, that one closed down fairly recently. The owners found they could get much cheaper labour closer to the logging source. Didn't want to pay city wages...what?"

Mark had grabbed his arm.

"Closed?"

Dave whistled between his teeth.

"Ah, of course. Ideal hiding place."

Ekoko's face was inches above the map.

"I can see some signs near the saw mill symbol, but the light is too low. Shine your torch there." He pointed a skinny finger.

Dave obliged.

"Yes, they are letters..."

"Let me guess." Mark's face was shadowed, lit only by reflected light from the map. "The letters are 'RB'."

"Yes, they are."

Furious, Mark banged down on the bonnet with his fist, making a dull ringing sound.

"It must be that one, then," Ekoko stabbed at the symbol with his bony forefinger.

"Everyone's favourite logging company – Rouge-Bolles. That figures." Dave peered at the map again as they decided which route to take.

Fifty minutes.

As they prepared to leave the near empty hospital car park, Dave paused in the act of opening the driver's door of his WWF Land Rover.

"Did you think to bring any weapons along with you? You know... just in case."

Mark gaped at him, stupefied. He felt foolish not to have thought of weapons, but then he was equally repelled by the thought that there might ever be a need for them. He'd never felt the need to arm himself even when doing field work. Anyway, he wasn't sure he'd seen any guns at CRU, although Ekoko had mentioned armed men after the army visit. He'd never thought to ask. Apart from any of this, he was rusty. As an army brat, he'd been dragged along by the Major, his father – mentally, he always referred to that remote man as 'the Major' - to target and clay pigeon shooting, with distinct reluctance, it had to be said. That was long, long ago. Now – he'd be a danger to all and sundry if he started wildly popping off with a pistol.

Dave smiled.

"You should see your face. I know what you're thinking, but in this instance it's best to be prepared. It's not the first time I've encountered this sort of sticky situation, and more than once I've found that the mere sight of a rifle can often do the trick."

Mark, trying to sound as though it was second nature, asked "What have you got?"

Dave reached under the front seat.

"Well, a rifle, obviously, and a hand gun." He pulled them out and brandished them in front of Mark's face.

"Ekoko, I reckon you'd be more use with guns than me." Close up, it was difficult to disguise his distaste for such weapons. It was alright for the others, they'd both had some experience of having to threaten to use the damn things, but once he'd escaped patriarchal control, he'd stayed well away from them.

Ekoko seemed pleased at this and took the pistol that Dave offered and examined the weapon as though he knew what he was doing. Mark was becoming increasingly anxious about the direction this all seemed to be headed in, a direction he'd instigated himself. Beti would be incandescent if he knew.

They took both vehicles with Ekoko driving the CRU Landy and Mark as passenger, and Dave going on ahead in his.

As they left heading south west, Mark was wondering how on earth they might play this. They'd all got their mobile phones on standby, vibrate mode, to keep in touch should anyone become separated, but without some plan they were just tilting at windmills. All they had so far, by way of a loose scheme, was to drive near, but not right up to, the sawmill, kill the engines and creep closer, get the lie of the land and then think of something. It sounded bloody amateurish!

Mark reached under the passenger seat for a plastic bottle of water and took a healthy swig. In the act of passing it over to Ekoko, his hand suddenly stopped as though of its own accord, and he froze, bottle in mid-air between them. Ekoko grabbed it off him, giving him a puzzled look, as he gulped some water.

An inkling of an idea had occurred to Mark. He was trying to work it out, examining various angles. It would be risky, perhaps even foolhardy, but if it came off maybe they'd all get out of this in one piece.

Chapter
37

The deep thumping sound grew in volume until it suffused her being – her body was shaking with the rhythm. There was a loud rasping sound, too, desperate, incoherent. What was it? Her eyelids, closed until now, sprang open.

Nothing. Nothing there. It was night. Ink-black, hell black, Dylan's Bible-black. Where? This black it could only be a cave. Why was she in a cave? Did she walk here? Was she lost?

The thumping was still there, in her ears now. The rasping had died down a little. She wanted to clear her throat, - it was dry as sand. She tried. It didn't work. It was all wrong. Her mouth wouldn't open!

She tried to bring her hand up to her mouth, but that was wrong, too. Her hands were locked together, acting in unison, and when they got to her face – there was no mouth!

She screamed – but couldn't.

She thrashed around in sheer panic, but banged her head against walls on both sides. She could scarcely move. She tried again, but only hurt herself knocking against the walls, that dreadful baleful sound emanating from her all the while.

She was suffocating – could scarcely breathe. Some residual spark of sense flared, told her to stay still, breathe through the nose, calm the thumping of her heart. Breathe, breathe – regularly. In – out – in – out – in - out. Damp down the sympathetic nervous system which had gone into overdrive, flooding her body with adrenalin and consuming precious energy. Let the parasympathetic take over. The calmer alter ego. Jeckyll, not Hyde.

And do not cry! No tears. If her nose got blocked with mucous, that would be the end…

Then she froze, the dreadful, impossible truth hitting her. A formless dark chaos threatened to overwhelm her once more. She was imprisoned! Or… the other possibility, too terrifying to contemplate, she tried to push away. Not now.

Think, think, *think*.

Slowly now, trying to rein in her terror, she raised her locked together hands once again to her face and felt the smooth tape that covered her mouth. Carefully she picked away at one end until she could get her finger underneath, and another one. Now, tugging, fingers slipping, slick with sweat, she gradually prised one end of the tape free, gritting her teeth against the pain as a layer of skin came with it.

She lay gasping as though sucking down sweet, clean air, rather than this tainted air smelling of her fear and sweat. Her breathing rate reluctantly, slowly lowered. She rested then, thinking, trying to recall the events preceding her incarceration.

Retrograde amnesia. Recall of events immediately preceding a blow to the head may be lost – for a while. Or return in a haphazard fashion. Or not. Nothing was a given with the human mind…

Then, suddenly, a stroboscopic mental snapshot, a flashbulb memory. Those two shitfaces! It was them! At the car park. The hospital car park. Bits of her memory were stuttering to life. And then? They stuck me in this – place. What was this? A box? She felt around her, above, to each side, her feet reached to the end. It was a box – or a coffin. No, no, no – don't think that. Push it away again.

What was that? Some sound outside.

Suddenly and completely inappropriately, she was filled with joy. If I can hear a sound from outside, then I'm not interred in the ground. I must be above ground, surely. *Surely?*

She strained to listen. Steps, she was sure they were, muffled by the confines of her prison – and, please, please God, not earth above her head. Something else – low rumbles, stopping, starting, rising, falling. Speaking!

She took a deep breath ready to cry out. And stopped, just on the brink of a scream. *Who* was speaking, that was the question? Was it the two shitfaces? Or someone else?

Now she held the same breath, that had been about to explode from her taped mouth, with all the force she could muster; she exhaled, gently. She strained to hear, willing the thudding of her heart, endlessly circulating her blood, her rasping breathing, to stop.

More rumbles. Closer, closer they came. They were voices – she could tell that now, but not easy to distinguish what was said or who was saying it. She strained to hear. Something about telling someone. Then the voices cut off.

What now? She lay immobile. What if they opened the box? What could she do? Her hands were still tied together.

She tensed her thigh muscles, ready to lash out with her legs in what she hoped might be a vicious kick. Would her muscles work? She'd no idea how long she'd been kept like this.

Nothing happened. Steps moved away. She lay still, holding her breath, the better to hear.

When just silence remained, she grew fearful again. Was she just to be left here, undiscovered, until one day, years hence, the box would be opened and a grotesquely mummified body found? How much oxygen was there?

She tried using her teeth to pull away the tape binding her wrists, but it proved impossible in the small confines of the box – she couldn't get the leverage. A lone tear trickled down one side of her face.

Try something else, you wuss, she told herself.

: ✿ :

The track down to the abandoned saw mill had grown neglected and was beginning to get overgrown as nature assumed supremacy once more. Dave, at the front, killed the headlights some way in, and using only the weak sidelights, proceeded gingerly along the deep ruts gouged by timber trucks.

Eventually, his brake lights flashed briefly as he pulled over to the side, taking advantage of overhanging boughs. Ekoko followed him, pulling in tight, but then jumped out to approach Dave's vehicle. They conferred briefly and Ekoko returned and began to turn the vehicle round.

Of course. Turn the two 4-wheels around for a quick getaway. Obvious, but I wouldn't have thought of it, Mark realised. It could save precious seconds. His heart thumping, he worried that he might prove to be a liability in this sort of situation. Dave seemed, by contrast, competent and calm.

Once the vehicles were positioned so that it was difficult to see them in the sooty blackness beneath the thick drooping canopy and creepers, they crept out and, huddled together, Mark outlined a possible plan that had occurred to him when he was about to swig some water. There was some whispered, hissing argument back and forth but, reluctantly, the other two could see the advantage of surprise in his plan, even if it exposed him to no little risk, even if it resulted in someone's death. None of them in this moment had any compunction about taking the life of one of these kidnappers and putative murderers. Besides, more importantly, no one came up with a better idea, so that was it.

Ekoko and Dave would cover him.

Mark filled the plastic water bottle from a jerry can in the Land Rover, and they crept in a tight group towards the saw mill.

The track, fairly straight but with one curving bend which, once rounded, gave them the first glimpse of dark looming irregular shapes, darker black against black, was muddy enough to muffle their progress.

They stood under covering foliage, examining the massive structure, which emanated an air of gothic menace, looking for any gleam of light which might indicate the presence of life.

"Maybe we're wrong. It's not this place at all," Mark murmured.

Nothing moved, even the nocturnal insects and the odd sleepy protests of dreaming birds were absent. They remained crouched for some time, senses alert for any stimulus, sheltered by the night.

As Mark went to shift his position and relieve cramped calf muscles, Dave grabbed his arm and pulled him down.

"See? Over there."

Mark's gaze followed his pointing finger, but could still see nothing. He tried his visual trick as before in the hospital car park — and, yes, there it was at the edge of the visual threshold, a faint spot of reddish light. A glowing cigarette, the ember growing bright as the figure drew on it. Now he could detect the lighter smoke drifting against the black void of the saw mill.

"Smoking." The barest whisper caught in the dark web of night.

Mark tried to think — if it was one of the dynamic duo, which one would it be? Did Muller smoke? Djomo definitely did. He hadn't seen Muller smoke at the camp. So if it was Djomo, his weapon of choice was the machete rather than the gun.

They couldn't use their guns at this point because that would alert Muller. Where was Muller? Inside? Was Sue really here, held hostage?

He quickly pushed away the thought that they might already have killed her.

Too many unknowables. They had to proceed as though she were here, as though she were alive. Mark turned anxiously to Ekoko at his right — the thin face revealed only sphinx-like patience. At his left, he could just make out Dave's profile and bushy beard.

"Time to make a move," Mark whispered.

Just then the red glow arced to the ground in a miniature spray of sparks, and a dim rectangular-shaped aperture appeared in the structure, grey against the implacable black.

"He's gone inside," murmured Ekoko. "That Bantu." The word was loaded with cold contempt.

So it was Djomo. They were right – this was the place.

In a crouched file, they ran silently towards the wooden wall where the door had opened. Through gaps between the planks, Mark squinted.

A long way off, it seemed, a lantern cast a faint sickly light over a table where two figures sat – male figures, he thought, by their bulk and posture. But where was Sue? Was she already dead? Had they killed her, with no intention of exchanging her for him?

They'd been duped – and she was dead.

A low rumble of a voice reached him from inside, muffled as though transmitted through water. He couldn't make out the words, but there was a note of complaint in the tone. Djomo – he thought he recognised the voice from the camp.

The reply was heated, peremptory, and a loud crack made him start.

"Leave her!" That came through loud and clear, echoes bouncing round the immense void.

Muller – he'd just slapped the table. Asserting his authority once more. And raised his arm to – what? – peer at his wrist.

'Leave her' he'd said. He must mean Sue. Sue *was* here – but alive? Please, please, dear God.

In a quieter voice, Muller added something else which Mark couldn't make out.

Djomo rose and went off into the shadowed recesses of this gloomy cathedral to dead trees. Mark couldn't tell if he carried his trusty machete with him.

He was trying to absorb what was meant. Was Sue alive, then, or were they leaving her because she was dead? He rested his head against the rough planks of the door, gritting his teeth. He could hear the other two breathing softly behind him.

Just then Djomo returned emerging out of the gloom and the two of them went off together into the hidden depths of the mill. Presently, the listeners detected an engine. A 4x4 engine, the noise receding down the track they'd so recently come down. Would they spot their parked vehicles?

They waited, tense, scarcely breathing.

"They are going?" asked Ekoko.

There was a gradual diminution of the engine noise with no sudden cut-off as if it might have halted. It reminded Mark of the river pursuit, listening to the sound of the pursuing pirogue.

"Let's hope so," Mark replied relieved that he wouldn't have to try out his plan.

"Right," said Dave presently, "they're off to the market rendezvous – *without* your colleague."

Mark turned to gaze back at the building – if they left without her for the rendezvous, that could only mean one thing – they had no one to exchange for himself. He began shivering, terrified of entering the black void of the mill.

"Go," urged Dave, taking out his mobile. "I'll tell the Commissaire they're on their way to the market. Should take them about 20 minutes from here. Quick."

Ekoko touched his arm gently, and together they entered the gloomy realm. He used Dave's torch and the beam sliced through the dark to reveal the true immensity of the mill, scarcely reaching the walls or roof.

He pirouetted slowly, illuminating massive circular saws and conveyor belts seemingly arching high above them like the distant beams of a cathedral roof.

Underfoot, Mark noticed the damp sawdust that must have adhered to the soles of the dynamic duo in the hospital car park. He didn't want to know, didn't want to go further, didn't want to find out…

"Over there," whispered Ekoko. "Look, what is that?"

"No need to whisper now. I can't see - some reflection. Glass?"

They crept carefully, quietly towards the faint gleam - actions as pointless as whispering but forced by habit and the vastness of the menacing space. With his gaze fixed ahead on a dim square shape reflecting sparse light, Mark suddenly cracked his shin on an object lying on the floor.

He cursed loudly, nursing his leg, while Ekoko took the torch and shone the ray of light on a long rectangular wooden box. Just the shape of a coffin…

Oh, no, no, no. Mark couldn't move. He stared at the shape, limbs frozen, bruised shin forgotten.

What was that? Faint scuffling noises. From inside?

Jerked into sudden frantic action, they knelt, tugging at the hasp which was secured with a padlock. Frantically, Mark cast around for some tool to force the lock.

"Quick, quick, shine the torch over there!" His chest felt tight. He wouldn't think, wouldn't hope – not yet.

A workbench with tools. There were plenty of items lying around – including a crowbar. He grabbed it.

They set to work frantically, prying open the lid. No sounds emanated from the box. Perhaps he'd imagined it.

He was gulping air, frantic.

Mark flung the lid triumphantly back - then doubled over, air whooshing out of his lungs and toppled over. A furious noise, like an angry bellowing issued from the open box. Ekoko now peered cautiously over Mark's bent back, tucking his gun into his waistband.

"Sue Clarke! Sue Clarke! Look, look — it is us! We are here to help you!"

The noise died down as Mark tried to recover his breath, inhaling deeply. In the beam from the torch, wide furious grey eyes glittered at them from the shadows of the box. She had been bound at wrists and ankles and a piece of duct tape was dangling from one side of her face. Her nails were broken and bloody. She was breathing harshly, staring wild-eyed.

Undefeated and determined, she'd done the only thing she could to protect herself, not knowing who she would see when the lid was raised — kicked her legs out with as much force as she could muster in the general direction of the midriff or better, balls,of whoever opened the lid.

"You've ruined my chances of having any more kids," Mark wheezed pulling himself upright using the side of the box, trying and failing to smile, but relief was flooding through him.

Sue was still breathing hard, mouth open, unable to say anything.

They worked quickly now. Once Ekoko had lifted her out, sitting her on the lid and started using a penknife on the bindings, her fury erupted like an uncapped volcano, the ripe language shocking the sedate and rather prim Ekoko, who paused and held up his hands to stem the flow.

Sue spit out the taste of the tape, coughed up some phlegm and took a few deep breaths which seemed to calm her.

"You're damn lucky just to be nursing bruised balls." Her voice was hoarse, the words rushing out. "I'm *so angry*. I fell for it. I should have realised. Such a patsy. They told me you'd had an *accident*," she accused Mark, as though it was his fault.

"I know, I know. You were the lure." He was struggling to remove the wrist binds with one hand while still nursing his assets with the other, as Ekoko worked on the ankles. "And that certainly seemed plausible, eh?" His voice was still a gasping wheeze.

Sue coughed again, still trying to clear her throat.

"They could have killed you, Sue Clarke," said Ekoko, clearly concerned and puzzled that she wasn't more frightened.

"No, it was obvious that it was Mark they wanted." She was recovering her composure. "Hurry up, will you? Get this stuff *off* me!" She struggled.

"All right, all right. We're going as fast as we can." The tape was still clinging to her ankles. "They were going to leave you here, Sue. Honestly, I think they would have left you to die – just as they did with me in the hut."

"My necklace. Did you find it?"

Ekoko reached inside his shirt pocket and dangled the lapis lazuli in front of her.

"I mended the clasp."

This brought a shaky smile to her face, her chin wobbling.

Finally, they helped her out of the box – her intended coffin – and she snatched the necklace from Ekoko, still furious and not yet prepared to be mollified by her rescuers.

She stumbled around, stamping her feet, trying to get the circulation going again. She was muttering to herself.

"Wait just a damned minute, though." She stopped her circulating stomp. "How the hell did you know I was *here*, in this hell hole?" She pointed at the ground. "I could have been anywhere."

"Ah," Ekoko said, beaming. "Mark saw the necklace and then sawdust in the car park at the hospital, so we looked for a saw mill. This one was not used and was near town."

Sue, for the first time since they'd released her, really looked at both of them, eyes shining with tears. She kept her hand over her mouth.

"Thank you," she mouthed, and turned away quickly, moving towards the entrance. "Come along, Sherlocks. I really, really need a long cool beer."

"We have to tell Dave," Mark said.

At that moment, they heard a shout echoing in the cavernous space.

"Over here, Dave. We've got her. She's OK!"

Dave and Sue hadn't met before, so after introductions made in the oddest of situations and a brief explanation of his presence, Dave scanned the area, rifle sloped over one shoulder.

"We can't ignore this opportunity," he said almost to himself.

"What?" Mark asked.

"They've obviously been using this place as a base; you were right on that score, Mark, that's why they wouldn't want the exchange to take place here. Let's have a look around, see what we can find."

"I ought to get Sue back. She's had…"

"Do you mind? I am here. I want to get these *fucking bastards* more than you do, so if we can discover anything here that'll nail them, let's do it. Now!" Her face was still ashen, but her grey eyes burned fiercely.

In the dim light the three men stared at her furious face for a beat.

"OK, OK. Let's split north, south, east and west," suggested Mark.

"Wouldn't want to get on the wrong side of her when she's angry. Mad as a box of frogs," whispered Dave.

Sue was already stomping off, northwards, determined and grim.

: ♡ :

Ekoko's shout brought them rushing to his part of the compass at the far end of the mill.

"This is an office. There will be papers in here," he said, sounding pleased, when the others arrived breathless. It was where he and Mark had been headed for when Mark stumbled over the box.

"Excellent," Mark breathed.

"If they haven't cleared everything out," added Sue.

They were examining a glassed in square-shaped area in one corner of the mill, well away from the machinery. The door was unlocked.

Two empty beer bottles standing in damp puddles on a desk testified the dynamic duo had had a beer each before leaving. Mark spotted a small cooler in the corner and flung it open. Full of icy beer, it gleamed invitingly like an Aladdin's cave of treasure.

"Whey-hey!"

They fell greedily upon the bottles, prising open the tops against the table edge. Sue glugged down the contents in record time; as she lowered the empty bottle, wiping a hand across her mouth, two bright spots appeared on her cheeks, followed by a discreet burp. The others giggled like silly school children, the tension draining away as they tipped back the bottles.

Mark's mobile vibrated against his chest. He picked the phone out of his shirt pocket and listened.

The others watched him acutely as his facial expression changed rapidly to one of delight.

"Beti's got them!" he said to the three watchers. "He's got them! Well done! That's great!" He was shouting into the phone. "No, we'll be here awhile – there's an office here which might yield something useful by way of paperwork. OK, yes, we'll wait."

Dave squeezed Sue's shoulder gently, reassuringly.

"That's that, then. Finito."

"I wouldn't be too sure, Dave," Sue cautioned. "From what I could glean of their talk through that…that…bloody coffin, I reckon there's someone else out there, someone who gives the orders. What Beti has are just the foot soldiers."

"Who?" asked Ekoko. "Who is it?"

"No names I could hear, unfortunately, Ekoko. It was a bit muffled. But perhaps there's a clue here somewhere." She swung around scanning the glassed in office.

There was a battered looking three-drawer grey filing cabinet standing in one corner.

"I'll take this, guys." She bent towards the bottom drawer.

Mark gazed at her a moment, both proud and astonished at her resilience, as he shoved his mobile back into his pocket. Moments earlier she had been entombed in a box, bound and gagged, expecting to be left there to – what? – starve to death. In her position, he'd be traumatised. He *had* been traumatised, in almost the same situation, and, like her, ferociously angry, too, at himself, at his jailers, at the world for abandoning him. But he wasn't sure he had her recuperative powers.

Still, he must keep a watchful eye on her – adverse reaction to her incarceration might be delayed. It wasn't unknown for post-traumatic stress disorder to be triggered after such a horrendous experience.

Meanwhile, Dave was occupied tugging at the desk drawers, and Ekoko was examining loose papers on the desk. Where should he look?

Mark looked around. Surely, they wouldn't leave anything too incriminating behind, particularly any indications of their chain of command. That would be hoping for too much. Unless...unless... they were *very* sure it could never be found.

By the looks of this place, they were in the habit of using it as a regular base, at least when they were not at the Dja camp. This could be their Yaounde base.

So where would you hide important stuff?

Chapter 38

"What have we got, then?" Paul Draper demanded, gazing at his two colleagues, eyebrows raised in expectation.

As a change from the 'Mayfly', they were sitting at a wooden table in the long grassed garden of 'The Boot', sweeping down to the serene Test River. They gazed at the fringing weeping willows, a Canada goose standing on one foot just a yard away, and coot bustling about feeding on river weed. Paul preferred, when he could, to mull over salient points of a case in a more congenial atmosphere than the Lyndhurst Station, which he believed stifled his thoughts, beautiful though the New Forest setting was. Truth was he enjoyed sitting here in the pub garden more than his cramped office.

"OK. Starting at the beginning – always the best place: Adam Wingent – killed because he surprised someone who was after his brother's computer." George was flipping through his notebook trying to find the right page.

Sandy sat back, trying to assemble the parts of this case together. There were still too many pieces missing, too many 'blue sky' bits in the puzzle, so you couldn't quite see the whole picture. She sipped her fizzy tonic water and studied the profile of her George, her mind wandering away from the case.

He, oblivious of her warm attentions, was hunched over his notebook, a frown of concentration on his freckled face.

As a light breeze ruffled his auburn hair, Sandy thought he looked far too young – and sometimes too vulnerable - to be a DS. I'm being too maternal, she chided herself, and he certainly wouldn't thank me for it. He was quite capable of taking care of himself. She sighed gently, and caught the DCI gazing at her with a knowing smile as though he'd read her mind. She ducked her head to take another drink.

George, oblivious to all, continued to study his notebook.

"Here we go. Charles Terman's PM – this is only his prelim report by the way, and you know how he hates being pressed too soon - found he'd died as a result of a stab wound right to the heart – perforating the right auricle, to be precise. The other two wounds weren't fatal. As you thought - professional. Quick, seconds really – a fatal haemorrhage with little external bleeding. Straight in and out. Forceful. Someone who'd wielded a knife before." George looked up from the page. "Someone prepared to kill to get what they wanted."

"Or to prevent others finding something out," prompted Paul.

"Yeah, that emailed photo of the two guys to be precise, which I'd guess was taken close in time to when Colin Wingent died. The likely candidates for Col's murder," George added.

411

He finished off his pale yellow lager, some continental 'gnat's piss', Paul had called it.

"That very same photo I forwarded to Mark with a warning, but he checks his email or mobe…," he grinned at Sandy, "…about as often as George stands me a pint."

"Eh?" George said.

"And those intellectual giants didn't realise that pics taken by mobile can be emailed to several addresses simultaneously. More fools them, because they totally missed the Forest Watch photo." Sandy raised her glass of tonic water in mock salute. As she didn't touch alcohol, she always ended up being the designated driver, but, consequently, always in demand.

A sheepish look came over Paul's face.

"Yes, well, I only caught on to that because I was combing the catalogues for a pressie for Em's birthday, and I was reading the specs. Didn't click at first."

"You're telling me. His treacle-like brain processes are the reason we missed that film." George had been absolutely clear to Sandy that it was Paul's fault that their date had been ruined. But she knew, too, that George regarded his DCI's abilities with something approaching awe, mixed, of course, with a good dollop of irreverence.

Actually, Sandy wasn't too disappointed; she hadn't been that keen on seeing the latest Hollywood action blockbuster with lashings of CGI. Anyway, a film like that would be out on DVD in short order. One never knew, she might be able to persuade George to watch a more thoughtful film next time.

"The point is," Paul continued, addressing himself to Sandy and ignoring George, "that we have somebody – two people? Several people? Who knows? SOCO may be able to tell us - somebody *here* every bit as ruthless as those in Cameroon, prepared to do anything to protect their interests."

"Those being logging, which we now know to be worth billions." Sandy added.

"Sure, if you're prepared to devastate a region and leave it a wind-blown desert," added George.

"Which they are, seemingly." Paul took a pull of his rich brown beer, Bishop's Finger, and ostentatiously smacked his lips in appreciation. Apparently, he lived in futile hope of providing a role model for George's appalling drinking preferences.

"I think Rayner knows more than he lets on." Sandy said.

"Yes, but an unlikely candidate for our killer, I'd have thought. Adam Wingent was young and fit, while Rayner - ," George shrugged.

"Nonetheless, Sandy's right - we should go back to Rayner, put more pressure on him with the recent findings from the professor. Carrot and stick — serious matters involving murder, fraud, etcetera, but obviously we appreciate *he* hadn't a clue as to what was really going on, an innocent caught up in a tangled web of deceit and deception, cooperation with the police looked upon judiciously, blah, blah. If he doesn't want to cooperate, then we can threaten a search warrant — that should whip him into line. However, I don't want to use one unless we have to — it's not that we'd have any difficulty getting one: He has a contract with Rouge-Bolles, which seems to be implicated, directly or otherwise, in the murder of a British subject. He imports their illegally felled logs and facilitates their passage onwards to a joiner or some such, which, once they're in the EU, is quite straightforward."

"Hooray for the EU." George held up his empty glass and waggled it in a meaningful gesture.

"Amen to that." Sandy handed her empty glass to George. "And a packet of salt and vinegar, freckle face."

He queried his DCI with a tilt of his chin towards Paul's glass. "In spite of insults about my being tight as a duck's arse."

"Better not, thanks George. No, as I was saying, it's best to avoid alerting any other parties involved in this, if we can. We flourish a search warrant and Rayner'll be on the blower in no time to any associates. We want to appeal to his better side, if he has one, and get him to volunteer some names of contacts within the logging business."

"Our DEFRA cover should've quelled the suspicions of any RB watchers," George pointed out.

"Well, it was a stop-gap measure at best and there's nothing to prevent Rayner contacting whoever he wants to now he thinks we're out of his hair. In fact, I'd be very surprised if he hasn't. From his point of view, he'd want to keep whoever-it-is sweet, particularly if he knows about Adam's murder."

"If I was in the killer's position – Adam's killer, that is - I certainly wouldn't let on to the likes of Rayner what I'd done," said Sandy.

"You could be right there. There'd be more to lose than gain."

"If he's going to contact someone further up the line of command in RB anyway, then why don't we use a search warrant?" said George.

"It's always better if you don't have to, besides you have to reveal exactly what you're after. It tends to make suspects clam up. And the likelihood is that he's already cleared away any incriminating evidence. No, the fact that he's already helped us and given us the names of joiners where the wood's being sent sets a precedent. Makes it more likely he'll do so again." Paul pushed his glass towards George. "I've changed my mind – a half of the same, please."

"I'll get them in." George strode off, ruffling Sandy's hair just to annoy her.

Paul gave Sandy a shrewd look as George went inside to the bar.

"How are you two?"

As she opened her mouth to answer, a little surprised he'd asked, Paul suddenly held up a hand and rummaged in his jacket pocket bringing out his mobile phone.

"Christ, it must be infectious. I keep forgetting to check my own messages."

He examined the screen, frowning. He was silent for a while studying the abstruse language of texting, then a gradual smile spread over normally stern features.

"Well, would you Adam and Eve it? It's the absent-minded Prof. himself. A text message. I take back all I said about him." He held up the mobe.

He bent to the screen again.

"There *is* a God," he breathed.

"Good news?"

"The best! They caught those two in the email photo!" He grinned. "I don't know if they've enough evidence to charge them with murder. Colin Wingent's picture alone doesn't prove those two were the killers, but the timing and location are strongly suggestive of them being the last to see him alive. Then there's Mark himself - unlawful imprisonment and pursuit by the same unholy pair. And something about Sue

Clarke." He squinted at the screen. "Can't figure that bit out – was she imprisoned too?"

Presently, George returned, tray laden with crisps, nuts and drinks, to be told the news.

"That's great – they must be mightily relieved - but we're no nearer knowing who's pulling the strings." George plonked Sandy's tonic and packet of crisps on the table. "Either here or there."

He folded his gangly legs under the table and gave Sandy a dazzling smile for no particular reason. She felt her stomach flip. Aunty Bindiya, her father's bossy older sister, keeper of the family morals, would be scandalised – he's not even a Christian, as if that weren't bad enough anyway, but an atheist to boot. Practically spawn of the devil. She didn't care, though. She thought she knew what she wanted, and a small rebellious part of her wanted to shock Aunty, wanted to see her face transform into that disapproving just-sucked-a-lemon look; she almost welcomed the showdown that would inevitably follow. Was that enough, though? Enough to sustain a commitment?

Determination to plough her own furrow had carried her through all sorts of family objections, although her doting father would deny his beloved only daughter little. He had demurred at first, but caved in when he saw she was serious. Now, he was unduly proud of her progress in the force.

Looking from George to her boss, she knew she'd made the right decision. She'd been extremely fortunate. For that very reason she was wary of disturbing the delicate equilibrium between the three of them, superstitious that any change would fracture the developing relationships.

"That's true, but it increases the pressure on the likes of our plump pal Rayner. We can squeeze a little harder," Paul was saying.

"I don't like the image that conjures." George pulled a face. "What about our marked timber? Any news on that front?"

Two days ago Steve Frampton had given Paul the amazing news that log 'J' was *the* log: Improbably, the DNA from this fateful log matched perfectly with the splinters taken from Colin Wingent's cheek. Awash with neglected paperwork and trying to make a dent in it, Paul had only given his team the briefest email on the subject. This meeting was his way of bringing them up to date.

"Ah," Paul beamed, looking smug. "We've been able to trace it to the east coast…"

"Who's 'we', if I might ask."

"Me and our good friend Professor Frampton."

"Are we collecting them?"

"What?"

"Professors."

"Very droll. He's taken a keen interest, and I'm not going to look a gift horse. Anyway, as I say, *our* log resides contentedly in a joiners' yard waiting to be made into doors, apparently."

"How do you know all this, sir? I take it you avoided a search warrant there for the same reasons as Rayner?" asked Sandy.

"Yes, anyway it's well outside our jurisdiction – near Felixstowe. Couldn't touch it. Our tame professor waltzed in under the guise of a nouveau riche and slightly eccentric businessman looking for a special wood for custom made furniture for his newly acquired manor. A great loss to 'am

417

drams', Professor Frampton, because the way he tells it, he had a grand time. Strolled pompously around the yard until he spotted a *sapele*, surreptitiously checked the smart water bar code with one of those UV torch gizmos when no one was looking. Luckily for us, there aren't too many *sapele* around which shortens the odds."

It still seemed incredible to him, that they'd managed to do this. To track the origins of a given sliver of wood which had been stuck with blood to a murder victim's face in Cameroon to a joiner's yard in Felixstowe. Of course they couldn't know which *sapele* log any given joiner would get, but there were only nine logs and four joiners involved, according to Rayner. Steve Frampton trod the metaphorical boards twice before hitting paydirt.

"He checked. It was *the* one, same DNA. Log 'J'. He gave it another squirt of that same specific bar-coded smart water – he had the 'J' tube in his rucksack. Then, in true lordly fashion, he demanded that that wood was the only one that would do for him. He was told it and the other *sapele* log in the yard were already spoken for - designated for a pair of very large double doors. A very prestigious contract, apparently, but the joiner would say no more than that – just tapped the side of his nose."

"Fantastic. So we should be able to discover the final destination of the wood - who ordered the banned wood?" asked Sandy. "Or commissioned the doors?"

"With luck. Be interesting to see where the doors end up."

"How are you going to track it from Felixstowe?" George was shaking the little blue packet of salt into his crisps.

"Not sure yet. There's bound to be paperwork in the Felixstowe joiners showing where it'll fetch up, but I don't want to tip our hand just yet." He put his elbows on the wooden table. "Let's put that to one side for the moment. We need to concentrate on Adam's murder. Anything else from Tristram?"

George was crunching greedily, so merely nodded, until he'd swallowed down the crisps. He consulted his trusty notebook lying on the table and read out the rest of the preliminary results from Charles Terman and Tristram Harrier, combining the two, trying to build a picture. The pages riffled in the light breeze.

"As I said, died from a stab wound straight through the right auricle. Nothing unusual in the type of blade, single-edged blade serrated along one side – the blunting at one end of the entry slit suggests this. About five inches long and not too much blood from that wound. Other two stab wounds not critical or fatal. Defence wounds on the arms, contusions on the knuckles. Tris may be able to give us more on the type of knife, and if there's anything under the fingernails."

George took a deep breath and shoved in another mouthful of crisps.

"While he stuffs himself, I'll take up the tale," Sandy said. "Terman estimated time of death between five and six pm. When did you two get there?"

"We left at about nine thirty when SOCO turned up having spent about fifty minutes there. I timed the discovery of the body at eight forty."

"Right," Sandy resumed. "That would put his murder at between two to three hours forty before you got there. They didn't get any prints other than Adam's and, we think, Colin's. This is the best guess since we don't have Colin's body, although we do have a car registered to him and there's a match for prints there. Plus the spread of these other prints around the cottage and on personal effects suggests someone who lived there - Colin. So our friends probably used gloves."

"Our? Plural? It's definite?"

"Sorry, I should have said. Mr Harrier reckons it would have taken two individuals, like you said, sir. Seems like Adam was on his back when the fatal wound was made – the straight in-out vertical movement of the knife - which lead Mr Harrier to assume one was holding him down – bruising to the upper arms – while the other did the dirty deed. Adam struggled with two intruders and managed to hold them off for a time sustaining two superficial stab wounds and some defence wounds on the lower arms, but getting in one or two blows - hence the bruising to the knuckles; it took a while judging by the state of the room – Mr Harrier reckons he only succumbed when one held him down and the other stabbed."

She could visualise the hideous scene all too easily, and dipped her head quickly to take a long draught of her tonic. He hadn't really stood a chance.

"Two brothers, two violent murders on different continents. It beggars belief, except that the deaths are related to Colin's work. *All* this is related to Colin's work." Paul waved his hand around vaguely and then rubbed his face, leaving his hands there.

"This is going to get worse before it gets better," he mumbled.

Sandy was a bit surprised. Her DCI wasn't normally given to expansive gestures and exaggerated comments. Very much the cool customer, self-contained – usually – if a bit too intense sometimes.

"Well," she began tentatively, peering at his glass to see how much the level had fallen. "Yes, that's the consensus. I mean about the murders being related, not..."

She looked over to George for help, still happily munching and unperturbed.

She gave his shin a sharp nudge with her foot under the bench.

"What? Oh. Yes, it begins to look like we have some sort of group over here prepared to take extreme measures to protect RB's interests – even up to and including murder. We don't yet know the composition of the organisation, how many in it. It could be quite small, like a terrorist cell," he said cheerfully.

"Lovely. That's all we need." Paul sighed and drank from his glass, which was still only two-thirds down, Sandy saw. Either Bishop's Finger was seriously strong stuff – or, he was getting a bit 'tired and emotional'.

"Paul, is all this OK with the AS? Major Crimes not angling to get hold of it?"

Paul gazed over towards the silky river. "Let me worry about that. Trace evidence?" Paul asked.

"Waiting on it. Tris took samples from under Adam's fingernails, and some skin swabs. He reckons in such a violent struggle it's likely that spittle will fly around, and it has to land somewhere."

"An arresting image." Paul said as George and Sandy groaned. "Won't help us, though, unless we have a comparison. Anyway, you're going to put the squeeze on Rayner. If he gives us nothing about any associates within RB I want him to know we will use a search warrant if we have to, and, between us, we'll look at his phone records – but don't tell him that. Threaten him with HM Customs, and a full audit.

An audit always scares the hell out of dodgy organisations. Eventually, of course when all this is over, that's exactly what will happen. Right. Who do you think he'll open up to more easily?"

George said, "The blokes tend to fall for DC Ghopal's pulchritudinous charms. I seem to leave them unmoved for some reason."

She tutted mildly at George.

"That I can understand. OK. He's all yours, Sandy. Be gentle with him." He paused. "You, George, research the commercial connections RB has over here. They must have representatives in the UK, apart from Rayner, who's likely a low-level functionary anyway. We now know part of the chain followed by the illegal timber. We know they own the shipping line and the two ships, MV Castor and Pollux. The wood's offloaded at Southampton, then passes to Rayner, the timber agent, who stores it in his warehouse – a nice, new, big warehouse, so he's doing quite nicely, thank you. He, in turn, passes the logs to a timber merchant for processing. Then there's the buyer. I'd dearly love to nail the buyer of those doors."

Paul stared into the bottom of the empty glass as though this glorious prospect resided there.

Chapter
39

"Thank Christ we didn't have to go through with your hare-brained plan." Dave was still rummaging around in desk drawers.

"I don't recall anyone else coming up with a better idea."

Now that Sue was safe, they had taken to bickering amiably while Mark was wandering aimlessly about the office, searching for something, anything. "I'm going to have a search around out here — there might be another office or something somewhere in this gothic horror."

"What did you mean?" asked Sue when Mark had wandered out. "About Mark's plan."

Dave explained to her that Mark had intended to go in first armed with a water bottle filled with petrol, and at the first opportunity squirt who ever he got to first, then, with a flourish produce his lighter.

Sue rolled her eyes and sighed. "Dear God! Close call. What then?"

Dave shrugged. "That was it more or less; he wouldn't have used the lighter, of course. Seemed like a good idea at the time, under the influence of an adrenalin rush. Ekoko and I were to be ready to pounce..."

There came a loud crash and a curse from just outside the office.

Sue rushed through the open office door to find Mark sprawled full-length on the planked floor.

"For goodness sake, what the hell have you done to yourself now?" She was feeling irritable, waspish, with everyone. A delayed reaction, she knew, the sheer elation at her release having died away. She should probably get back to CRU, have a couple of aspirin and get her head down.

She realised that Mark was still lying on the ground, silent.

"Oh my God, you're hurt!"

He made a huffing noise, raising little puffs of fine dust; it took her some time to recognise it as a laugh.

"What is it?"

"I trip up and land with my nose an inch from a ring. A ring! Look!"

The others had rushed over to see what was going on. A ring? Sue had momentary silly thoughts about Gollum and Frodo.

Mark brushed some of the covering sawdust away whilst sneezing loudly, the noise echoing through the cavernous structure. What emerged was the type of inset ring that is usually attached to a trapdoor – and, with further brushing, a three-foot square door appeared. Without his fall it would have remained virtually undetectable under the layer of dust.

"Hey, let me." Dave, as the burliest, grabbed the ring and tugged.

The trapdoor came up quite easily and noiselessly, sending up clouds of dust and a rank exhalation from the dark hole beneath. This is what Dante's seventh circle of hell would smell like, thought Sue, but she knew it wasn't carrion or putrefaction; that was a different odour. This miasma was corruption, rottenness of an entirely different order.

"It has been used before," observed Ekoko, reeling back from the hole as the air escaped.

"Yeah, and probably recently - oiled hinges. Torch," demanded Dave.

The beam showed steep wooden steps leading down into a murky darkness that the light did not penetrate. They all looked at each other, thinking the same thought.

Ekoko retrieved the torch and, wasting no time, started down the dusty steps, ducking down to avoid the edge of the trapdoor.

The others followed. Sue was last, reluctant to put herself in fathomless blackness so soon again, but drawn on just the same, gaining courage from companions.

The flight of wooden stairs wasn't too long, ending with a concrete floor.

"Why would this be here in the first place, unless it was going to be used to conceal something?" Mark whispered dodging a particularly low and menacing hanging cobweb.

"You can talk normally," Sue said. "No one here but us idiots."

There were scuttling sounds receding into the corners. Rats. Dripping water was a distant liquid punctuation.

Ekoko swung the light around. They were in a cellar about fifteen feet by twenty; the ceiling was barely higher than six feet causing the men to crouch. Off one corner was a narrow corridor where the scurrying noises came from. Sue scanned the room and thought it was empty of any interest – a dead end? She toed a dead rat aside.

In one direction, Ekoko's torch beam threw back a dull glint from a far corner.

"What's that over there?" asked Dave.

They all shuffled over, a strange quartet in synchrony, and stood silent before a large grey metal box. No – a safe!

"Bingo!" Mark breathed.

"This is what we have been looking for?" asked Ekoko doubtfully.

"Well, it's a fair bet that this is where these guys keep their confidential stuff – if anywhere."

"Who – Muller and that Bantu?" asked Ekoko, not favouring Djomo with a name.

"Them certainly, and if we're in real luck, those further up the food chain," answered Dave. "They're the ones we really want." He touched the metal side of the safe. "The puppet masters."

"So guys," queried Sue impatiently, her voice wobbling a little, much to her annoyance – reaction was definitely setting in. "Are we going to stand around admiring this safe – or open it?" She whacked the side, and it resounded with a dull empty-sounding echo.

There was a long pause as they listened to the sound die away.

"Anyone know anything about opening safes?" asked Dave.

Silence.

"Wait a minute! Wait a damn minute!" Mark sounded excited. "We don't have to know how to open it."

426

"What do you mean? If we're to find out what these bastards are up to, we need to get into the safe, take a look at what I'm assuming – *hoping* - will be fairly sensitive documents in there," objected Dave.

"Yes, they'd hardly have tucked this safe away down this stinking hole in an unused sawmill unless there was something of critical importance they had to keep concealed," Sue added.

Ekoko, though, was peering at Mark, in the reflections from the torch.

"Mark? You have thought of something."

"Yes, I have a plan..."

The others groaned in unison.

: ✺ :

After he'd explained what they could do, and received grudging acceptance along the lines of 'it had better not turn out to be as stonking useless as that last plan' from Dave, they returned up the steps, replaced the trapdoor carefully and smoothed sawdust and other debris over it.

When they were satisfied with the effect, they examined the office, leaving it looking ransacked, collecting any of their belongings – especially, of course, Dave's rifle – debated over what to do with the empty beer bottles – they left them there - and returned back to their vehicles.

The most important thing now, thought Sue, was to get back to CRU, reassure everyone that all were safe and sound, and – bliss – have a precious balming shower and get a good night's sleep – with the light on. She suddenly felt bone-tired to the point of nausea and consciousness loosed its reins as her head rolled gently on the seat of the 4X4.

: ✿ :

"Beti's approved our suggestion," said Mark, coming off the phone.

"*Your* suggestion, and *your* fiasco if it all goes belly up," Sue retorted.

They were back at CRU. Sue had had a shower and briefly slept, but restlessly and shallowly. Not, she'd told Mark, restorative stage four sleep with those lovely slow delta waves. Mark thought she still looked tired, the skin under her eyes swollen, and she was certainly irritable which she'd every right to be, but she'd not wanted to continue resting during the day. She would go through the day and flop tonight, she'd insisted. How could he blame her? He'd been in almost the same situation, except his box had been a damn sight bigger than her coffin, and what's more he hadn't been in total darkness. She'd had the genuine Edgar Allen Poe experience. It could take a while before she was fully back to normal.

He laid a comforting hand on her arm. He noticed she was wearing her lapis-lazuli pendant once more.

"Why don't you just take it easy today? Potter around. There's no time pressure on your research, Sue."

Sue passed a hand over her forehead, sweeping back her fringe.

"Really, Mark, it's OK. The police have got those two imbeciles — they're no threat now. I think the best tonic is to get stuck in, immerse myself in the research." She paused. "When you've got a moment, I'd like you to look over my experimental design for the pilot study."

"Of course, no probs." One part of his mind registered what she'd just asked him and mentally sketched out what he thought she should do, but another detached part was planning the next step. It was as if this - this urge to pin down the illegal loggers, to stop their predations, to see them smashed — superseded all else. It totally occupied him. He felt fiercely resolute — a driving need to obliterate them and their foul business — to the extent that his own research, and Sue's, was suffering. He was getting obsessive.

Abstractedly, he watched Sue go outside to the bonobo enclosure armed with a dictaphone and a simplified lexigram to present to Caro's group. It was hoped that Caro would prove the catalyst for the acquisition of new cognitive abilities but for the present her time was fully occupied with the baby, so Sue was going to have to modify her approach to the study of the group's gradual enculturation through observational learning. She would have to be careful to avoid experimenter bias, though; he thought, on balance, it would be preferable for her to watch from behind the window to the outer enclosure, a non-participant observer.

His own field research project was a total bust. It had come to a screaming halt before it ever really got out of the starting blocks. How dare those bastards presume to prevent legitimate and such crucial research. On top of everything else.

He picked up the phone again. Now for the next phase.

He used all his considerable powers of persuasion and gained agreement. It took only a few minutes.

: ✡ :

All of them at CRU in their various ways were impatient for the morning, not sure what the day would bring.

Nightmares of entombment plagued Sue's sleep. She allowed herself to sob occasionally but quietly; she'd never admit to crying and certainly never in front of the others.

Her broken nails, jagged from desperate attempts to escape from that coffin, snagged on the sheet. She blew her nose, wiped her eyes and turned over and cursed the evil pair.

Ekoko dreamt of his beloved primates romping around in a pristine and luridly green forest, free from fear, free from being hunted and skinned by poachers from the logging camps. The logging camps were gone... No bush meat in the market...

Mark, even after the exertions of the last day, couldn't get off to sleep. The bunk bed felt hotter and clammier by the minute, the one damp sheet getting tied in knots. He got up to get a drink of water, padding through the sleeping quarters, quiet except for the sound of vigorous snoring from Ekoko's room.

He took a plastic water bottle from the fridge and went out to sit on the veranda. There was a grey-aqua smudge, toning to pink on the eastern horizon, but yet enough darkness to distinguish the strange constellations in the darker quarter of the sky.

Mark gazed at the sinking crescent moon as the dawn gained ascendancy in a roseate sky.

If they could stop the venal predations of the loggers here, would it make any difference? Would it really bring about any changes? What these criminals were doing was nothing less than the rape of the land, after which nothing would remain the same. It could never return to what it was – 'all the King's horses and all the King's men couldn't put Humpty together again'. What would be lost was beyond reckoning; it could not be priced – the indigenous people, the inspiring diversity of wildlife and plant life, all extinct. A crime, to his mind, that ranked alongside genocide – no, it was worse than that – it was happening all over the world. What would you call the death of a planet? Terricide?

He sighed and looked at his watch. Time to check in.

He got up and went to Ekoko's office, filled with apprehension. He didn't know if this would work. His track record for cunning plans wasn't exactly shining, but he would do what Paul suggested.

He took a slug of the water, wrote the email and sent it, then sat back chewing his thumb nail and staring, eyes unfocused, at the screen, mind freewheeling with 'what-if's' and 'what-if-not's'.

When the 'ping' came, his startle response nearly caused him to fall off the chair. Nervously, he opened the inbox, and read:

'The game's afoot. TG.'

" Outstanding," he breathed into the dawn air.

Chapter
40

That morning the editor of the 'Cameroon Times' sat sipping his excellent strong coffee outside his favourite café, paper held up to his face to hide a smirk of satisfaction.

From the cover of his paper, Thomas Griffiths glanced furtively left and right but no one was watching him. He was savouring this moment, having harboured such ambitions in his callow youth of becoming Fleet Street's premier investigative reporter – dreams never realised and, over the years, the sour taste of failure washed away with drink. Now, here he was, in the declining years of his trade, stuck in this backwater, confined if not banned from revealing the deep corruption that pervaded every transaction, small or large, like a viral infection. Unless, that is, he fancied a spell in one of the reeking jails, daily pummelled into painful submission by one of the various inventive methods employed by the Gendarmerie, and ending up with permanently broken health, if not much worse. Better the anaesthetic of drink.

Contemplating the terrible prospect of jail made him thirsty, and he longed for a drop of the hard stuff to go with the coffee to stiffen his resolve, but he had made a promise to himself. Not this once – not today, not yet anyway.

He turned to the newspaper and read the copy again - was pleased. This was some compensation for past failures and disappointments.

: ¤ :

He shook out the paper again, feeling a prickle of apprehension wash over him, leaving his back chill with a sheen of sweat, in spite of the temperature beginning to soar.

He, too, looked around. There were only two others present in the large airy room overlooking meticulously-kept, artfully designed gardens. Even this early, they were well-sunk into their shabby but comforting armchairs, nicely mellowed with prelunch tumblers of Glennfiddich, seemingly engrossed in their papers. Even these stupid dolts couldn't miss the article. It was on the front page, large as life and twice as ugly. But the other two didn't turn in his direction. There was no sound in the room save the odd throat clearing cough and the occasional satisfied smacking of lips.

Was there yet time to salvage the situation? He bent to the article to glean what further details he could.

Those meddling bastards had found the base they used both because of its convenience, in order to meet… and other things…and, for him, in order to conceal sensitive papers and money. But had they found the safe? Squinting, he scanned the article yet again.

'….nothing was discovered in the office, but several bottles of cold beer in the fridge were rapidly despatched….'

No mention of the safe there. It seemed likely that they'd stumbled on the abandoned sawmill when searching for and releasing the girl.

'. ...*the young researcher had been imprisoned in a narrow box. ...*'

He'd reckoned that their plan always was ill-conceived and doomed to failure, and, now, predictably, the dumb shits were incarcerated on charges of assault and kidnap with the vengeful Bantu eager to tell all according to his police source. So, now he had only himself to worry about – at least he was free of any responsibility for those meatheads' cockups. So far. And there was no mention of the company.

But, the question was, how long would Muller hold out for now he was in the embrace of the Gendarmerie? Muller knew more than the Bantu. He harboured no illusions that sooner or later he'd be bound to tell all - the police were very persuasive. In fact, Muller had copied one of their more gruesome techniques on the driver to deflect blame onto them.

He had to assume it would be sooner. Worst case scenario, they would lead the police directly to him. Once that happened – well, the whole Cameroon end would unravel. It was not too much to say that he was the kingpin, here at least. Others, based abroad, dealt with the firm's affairs at the EU end, in whatever way it took – and if the bush telegraph were to be believed they took no prisoners.

It required ruthlessness, unquestioning loyalty – up to a point, of course – and above all a deep thirst for money. He had been well paid for fixing and fiddling for Rouge-Bolles. Certificates mostly. The meatheads had been the so-called enforcers, but they only acted with extreme prejudice at his behest – except this last time. And look what had happened then. If he was absolutely honest, he had allowed them to go ahead, which had been rash; it was down to that ill-considered blast of fury that swept through him at the interference from the fucking tree-huggers and wanting to be shot of them once and for all. But look where half-baked plans got you; contrast that fiasco with the relatively smooth and timely dispatch of the creepy, although formerly useful, Norbert Kremmel who'd been duped by the police into trying to recover damning evidence. The police and that bloody professor. It was a sweet job in the end though, the Kremmel dispatch, no loose ends - he'd seen to it that the Duty Officer was in a safe harbour. Literally.

He gazed out of the window at the garden, seeing not glowing flowers, the lush greens, the darting insects, but his bleak prospects if he did nothing. If he retrieved the papers from the safe, there would be no evidence to find linking him to the idiots gracing Yaounde's noisome jail. Their word against his. No contest.

As for the rest of the motley crew mixed up in the logging enterprise, well, he had the goods on them tucked away securely in the safe – up till now. It was his little insurance policy, because you couldn't trust any other bastard – apart from two whom he'd felt duty bound to warn. They had acted professionally if a little excessively to stem the leak, but to little avail as it turned out, since the meatheads were now in jail. Nonetheless, given the right incentive, say from a rival firm, or, he realised, for a shorter jail term if caught, God forbid, the others wouldn't hesitate to shop him. But, again, in the latter case, it would be their word against his – and you don't get much more respectable than him.

On the other hand, he could get his stuff from the safe, cut his losses, and with the proceeds still live high on the hog in the right quarter of the globe. He knew the globe very well. He knew just where to go.

Another place. Another name.

All in all, he had no choice — he had to get his stuff.

He levered himself out of the enveloping armchair, straightened his jacket, and strode rapidly out of the room.

He had things to do, ends to tie up, and another warning requiring some prompt action to send, although he himself couldn't act until tonight.

It would be the last time he would sit there, with the bumbling, whisky-slicked fools sunk in their comforting fug.

: ⌨ :

"I've earned the right to be there, Michael. I want to be there. I need to see it through." Mark, with a prickle of shame, heard a pleading tone enter his voice.

He had finally progressed with the martinet-like Beti to first name terms rather than the usual honorifics, and he'd assumed, wrongly as it turned out, that he would be allowed in on the denouement — or what he hoped would be the denouement. He'd been involved, for the most part, unwittingly it was true, right from the start. They'd worked well together, he believed.

"They kidnapped Sue," he resumed, prepared to press his case. "While you caught the culprits, we found Sue — and..."

"Yes, yes, yes! Alright, alright, Mark," Beti said with some asperity, straightening his uniform jacket.

Mark smiled. Beti hadn't actually put up much of a fight. He suspected that it was a token objection, to mollify superiors should anything go wrong, which it easily could.

" I promise not to get in the way, and to follow your orders to a fault."

"A first time for everything, I suppose," Beti said a touch sourly. He didn't smile often, but he had a gentle dry sense of humour.

"You must stay in the background. I cannot allow civilians to be put at risk. I would lose my job," he added.

"Agreed."

Mark had some idea of how much pressure Beti was under, not only keeping to the straight and narrow – which for him was a matter of honour – but to monitor his men to ensure they didn't stray. Mostly, he achieved this by being transparently open and fair, instilling a self-respect they'd seldom experienced before, and thus in turn earning the men's respect. They had for the most part, a quiet pride in doing their jobs better than fellow officers under different commanders, even though the pay was abominable. Thus, the betrayal by the still-missing Duty Officer in poisoning Kremmel had been so much more painful for Beti since he had trained the young man.

All this, he had admitted to Mark in a burst of frankness, after Mark had arrived at the police HQ that very night to confirm the identity of the two culprits as being the very same who had attacked and falsely imprisoned him and Sue Clarke. Beti laughed that the Bantu, Djomo, was falling over himself to lay all the blame for everything on the South African.

They'd had a celebratory tot or two from the bottle of Scotch Beti kept in his bottom desk drawer for special occasions. He must have felt he could confide in Mark, still a stranger after all, here today and gone tomorrow, more easily than a fellow officer, secure that his confidences would not be divulged.

: ♡ :

They were ensconced in the deep shadows behind looming machinery that served God knew what function. The place was dusty and Mark was holding his nose, concentrating on not sneezing.

Beti's men were scattered about outside, covering all sides of the building, with strict instructions not to shoot; he wanted a live body. His sergeant had one of their two radio sets, and was instructed to press the button once rapidly when he sighted any suspicious character – but to say nothing. The persistent nocturnal stridulations of various arthropods should cover the brief static burst from their radios.

Beti confided to Mark that he reckoned the mystery man would be constrained from coming during the day, because of the demands of his work – he had to have a day job - and because it would be too open, too dangerous. He'd have to hurry, though; he couldn't leave it too long in case discoveries were made that would spell the end for him.

They'd been waiting since seven pm.

Mark agreed with this reasoning, but it felt odd, coming back here so soon. It was only last night that four of them were here – and it could easily have been three had Ekoko not pointed out the right saw mill on the map and he not stumbled, literally, into that coffin where they'd incarcerated Sue. But they, too, had had to act quickly to avoid losing an advantage. Thomas Griffiths had cooperated wonderfully in printing, in the morning edition of the 'Cameroon Times', the story that they hoped would be the irresistible lure. He couldn't help but feel a certain satisfaction in baiting the baiters, in turning the same tactics against them – or him.

Griffiths was at first reluctant, but the promise of an exclusive full story later was an incentive and his old news hound's nose had twitched. So it was that his paper had printed a front page story about the assault and kidnapping of Sue, and her rescue from an abandoned sawmill. Enough but not too many details. Enough to tempt whoever – Mr Big? - to come to the safe and remove any papers.

Mark looked up at the far roof and saw the stars glittering through gaps in the slats of wood, and a glimpse of the gibbous moon hanging, waiting. Suddenly, unexpectedly, he felt a wave of homesickness wash though him. He wanted to be home, see the familiar constellations in their familiar places, watch the pipistrelles dance and weave chasing the moths through the long dusk of an autumn evening, sipping a decent beer in his garden recliner. Above all, see his son before he missed too many milestones.

He took a deep breath to steady himself. He wasn't usually subject to such feelings – it must be all that had happened to him, coming to a head at precisely the wrong time.

How many hours had they crouched here, only shifting slowly to ease the cramps?

Startlingly, the radio gave a low squawk. Mark, stomach lurching, touched Beti's arm and whispered, somewhat melodramatically, in his ear.

"This is it."

Beti gently 'shushed' him.

Together they squinted into the dark velvet shadows. They had carefully positioned themselves so that they had a good view of the trapdoor, with a stray beam of moonlight filtering through the planks acting like a spotlight on a deserted stage. They could see the dust motes swirling round in the silver-blue light.

Soft scuffling sounds. More motes stirred up.

And, suddenly, a figure bent over. Mark couldn't see who it was – his back was to them. They watched as an arm reached down to the floor and lifted a ring. They heard the soft grunt as the trapdoor was raised.

Beti held Mark's shoulder, preventing him from moving.

A torch beam slashed the darkness, pointed down into the abyss below the trapdoor.

They still couldn't make out anything more than the silhouetted crouched human shape.

Steps descended, taking the beam bouncing with them.

As the light shrank, Beti tapped Mark's shoulder twice. They stood gingerly, Mark hoping his knees wouldn't crack after the uncomfortable position he'd been in. They tip-toed over to the open trapdoor, then stood, listening , holding their breaths.

They were waiting for particular sounds.

Yes, there it was. A faint whirring sound of a dial being spun, again, a pause, again, a pause….now, of tumblers falling.

Then, finally, a loud creak.

"Now," said Beti, tensely.

They rushed down the steps, Beti first, torch beams slicing the dark, Mark waving away the spider webs clinging to his face.

Beti shouted. Mark had no idea what he said, but as he reached the bottom step he saw the figure grasped in an neck lock, one hand forced up behind his back in what must have been a quite painful position, judging by the outraged bellows coming from the man.

Beti dexterously snapped the handcuffs on him and swung him around.

Mark gaped as he focussed his beam on the reddened angry face of Wee Willie Wilkins.

"*You* – but I…," stammered Mark.

The face formed a twisted snarl of hate.

"*You, you* – what, eh?" it mimicked. "Thought it was someone else, like that *faggot* who runs the High Commission? That it? Fucking tree-huggers, you don't live in the real world," Wilkins sneered and struggled.

Mark felt a hot flash of anger, the culmination of all the humiliations and degradations visited upon him, of the hatred he knew he harboured for these barbarians, and lunged at him, ineffectually, as Beti swung the captive around.

"Mark! Do not demean yourself. And you - *shut up!*" Beti roared at Wilkins.

Beti bundled him, none too gently, up the stairs, accompanied by a stream of invective from a struggling Wilkins, and summoned his men via the radio link, while Mark just stood there, in the small dark space, stunned. He had to admit, as Wee Willie Winkie implied, that, deep down, he'd expected the British High Commissioner himself, Jonathan Hyatt, to be crouched in front of the open safe. He'd been dreading it – it would have lead to all sorts of diplomatic complications, tarnished the reputation of the UK in Cameroon, never mind that a clutch of leading lights in the Cameroon government were in on the illegal logging – the media would have fallen eagerly, and with no little relief, on JH as a handy fall guy. Bad enough as it was, of course, but at least Wilkins was a less prominent figure at the BHC. Of course he was in the ideal position to oversee the illegal logging business from this end – and, no doubt, with excellent communications to the UK. A pang of guilt for suspecting Jonathan Hyatt who, with the wisdom of hindsight, seemed forebearing and generous, was quickly blocked by curiosity about the contents of the safe. He'd make it up to JH later.

Mark turned towards it and peered inside. Papers, files, certificates, and on a lower shelf, stacks and stacks of money, mostly Euros but also other mixed denominations by the look of it. Some of it still in bank bands. He'd never seen so much.

From the upper shelf, he picked out a file at random. Details of shipments of timber to various ports. He spotted the names of the two ships, MV's Castor and Pollux.

Another file. Payments to officials in Douala. A list of names and jobs.

A veritable goldmine. It was going to take Beti and his most trusted men no little time to get through this lot. Did they have forensic accountants in Cameroon?

Then something occurred to him.

Beti, having turned Wilkins over to his men to take to police HQ for questioning, was coming back down the stairs, looking very pleased with himself and brushing down his jacket.

Mark gestured at the open safe. "Michael, this stuff in here is absolute dynamite. There'll be those desperate to get their hands on these papers, not to mention the cash."

Beti bent towards the safe and gazed with an expression of wonder at the piles of notes.

"Aiyee," he breathed, a mixture of dismay and astonishment. "An Aladdin's cave. Yes, it will have to be strictly guarded." He rubbed his hands.

"It'll take ages to get through all this, and in the meantime those implicated will move heaven and earth to get hold of this stuff." Mark dropped his voice, though no one else was nearby. "Who knows how far up the government this goes? What pressures they'll put *you* under to release this stuff..." he indicated the safe.

Beti straightened up and gave a small, self-satisfied smile. Nothing was going to spoil his moment of triumph. "You think I hadn't thought of this? It could be a problem but first, they would have to know that there *were* papers in this safe that implicated them. I'm betting that man – Wilkins – kept these papers as an insurance policy. I am sure of that. He is careful, very careful. So maybe others would not know that there were such papers...maybe not even those two we already have in custody."

"Ah. Right. You're thinking if we can keep this find between the two of us, to begin with," said Mark, not entirely convinced, "possibly – it might help to protect you and your men from undue pressure. And second?"

"We tell the world – through our good friend Mr Griffiths - what we *have* found." Beti beamed widely, an expression he rarely used.

"What?"

"Yes, of course. Look at all this *money*..." He swept his arm across the safe. "The safe is full of it."

Mark felt silly. He shouldn't have doubted Beti's ability and perspicacity. Camouflage.

"Cunning like a fox."

They both grinned.

Chapter
41

George watched the flakes sink slowly down through the water, snapped up by the three golden shubunkin swishing their tails left and right like eager puppies. He could feel himself becoming mesmerised and mentally shook himself.

"You're going to have to do something about that shelf," George offered. He pointed out where the heavy aquarium was bowing the shelf in the middle. "Just think, if the tank fell and swamped all your paperwork."

"I'd be devastated."

Paul squinted along the shelf and shoved the Health and Safety manual under it, to shore it up.

"Satisfied?"

"Perfectly. A very apt use."

Paul gave a rare smile. It wasn't that his boss was dour, thought George, although he could appear to be so, but more that he had one of those faces to which frowns came more easily; even when cracking a joke, he kept a straight face.

George felt more at ease now that he'd been reassured that they could continue with this case, that it wouldn't be whisked away to MCU. The Acting Super had seen the sense in letting them run with it, provided he kept tight hold on the budget. George wasn't sure what it was that Paul seemed to have on the AS, but he usually got his own way.

He handed over one of the coffees he'd brought with him, nicking them from one of the civilian staff rooms which made proper coffee. The rich aroma from percolating Blue Mountain curling tantalisingly up the stair well. The harpies guarding this prize usually softened and succumbed to George's charms with misty glances, at once both maternal and possessive. He wasn't averse to taking advantage when it came to a decent cuppa.

"Nectar. Thanks. Here's Tris' full report from the Wingent crime scene and Charles' PM." Paul flapped a file from Tristram Harrier, and the full post mortem findings from Charles Terman. "Nothing new, really." He turned to the PM report first. "Killing blow, as we thought, confirmed as the stab wound to the left of the sternum – straight down and through the heart - with little blood, so death was virtually instantaneous. Two other knife wounds – right shoulder and upper abdomen. Serrated edge to the knife with a five inch long blade. Bruises to the upper arms and shoulders – as though he might have been held down. Bruises to the knuckles on the right hand. Nothing under the fingernails. Time of death put at five to six pm. Otherwise, he was a fit thirty-one year old lad."

He put down the PM report and picked up Tristram's.

"No other prints which stand out in that room where he was killed – Adam Wingent's obviously, and his brother's. One intriguing finding, though, Tris was dead right about spittle flying in that type of struggle – it did, and he got samples from Wingent's face, which suggests that the attacker leant close in and above for the kill."

"Or he was the one who held him down."

"Good point."

He passed over the report for George to scan and sipped the cracking coffee, waiting patiently.

"The saliva yielded DNA, which in itself isn't much good unless we have a comparison."

"Is that it?" George was disappointed. He flipped through the report. "Not much more than the prelim reports."

"Just one more thing – next page there. A mess of tyre treads emerging from or entering the lane leading to the Wingent place, most of which are probably entirely innocent. The lane itself was too gravely to yield treads."

"Hmm. Might be something, or might not."

Paul slapped the desk gently. "Well, that's me done for now. Have you got anywhere with the Rouge-Bolles labrynth?"

"Somewhere, yes – you're going to be surprised. Here, have a butcher's."

George took a file from under his arm, extracted a sheet of A4 and placed it on the desk facing Paul.

"What am I looking at?"

"It's the chain – well, likely chain of custody - followed by our chunk of *sapele* from sawmill to doors, starting there at the top with our friends R-B."

Paul studied the links in the chain.

Rouge-Bolles, Dja, Cameroon

I

MV Castor/ Pollux (West Africa Line, owned by R-B)
from Douala

I

Rayner's Timber Agents, So'ton
I
Felixstowe Woodcraft, Joinery
I
Jansen Construction (Holland)
I
Doors

He raised his eyebrows.

"That all? This we already knew, except for the Dutch firm here. And there's something missing at the end, there." He pointed to the 'doors'.

George, undaunted, gave a small grin and held up a finger.

"Let me go through this with you, and be patient in case I cover ground you already know, OK? We used the papers you got from Forest Watch and contacts in Greenpeace, World Wide Fund for Nature and other assorted NGO's. And, by the way, this," - he tapped the file he still held — "is as much Sandy's work as mine."

Paul nodded, and sipped his now cooling nectar, hiding a small smile.

"Where is she?"

" Schmoozing the slimy Rayner to give up more of his contacts. She might be here shortly. Anyway, in Cameroon, there are two major players in the logging business — perhaps we should call it an industry — controlling the illegal *sapele* and other woods trade. One of these, as expected the more powerful of the two, is the notorious Rouge-Bolles family business, ruthless, corrupt and violent in defence of their logging rights."

"Illegalities include logging in Nature Reserves, like the world heritage site of the Dja Reserve where our good

447

Professor stumbled across the mutilated body of Colin Wingent, and where he was himself attacked, imprisoned and pursued, etc. They defend their concessions, which they extend illegally, by the way, with guns, and don't hesitate to use them; the guns are also used to shoot bush meat, too. On top of all this, these lands are Baka pygmy lands, so logging is, or *should be*, doubly prohibited, if you like."

"So how exactly do they get away with it?"

George grabbed a gulp of coffee before it got too cool.

"Easy. Fraudulent authorisation papers, and falsifying inventories. By the time it's shipped from the Cameroon port of Douala, the wood appears legal, laundered if you like, and its illegal origins are untraceable."

"So I could go into Harrods or John Lewis and buy a table made of illegally logged wood, and have no way of checking whether or not it's legal?"

George nodded. "Odds are that it's not. At least seventy-five percent of the timber from Cameroon is illegal. The Forestry Stewardship Council – the ones with the tree logo – and the only independent and international system of timber verification, said *no* wood available from Cameroon was properly certified at the present time."

Paul gave a low whistle – just as Sandy entered his office. She hesitated at the door, evidently not sure whether to adopt a severe expression or a haughty one.

"No, no, not you. This stuff here that George is going through," said Paul waving his hand impatiently at the papers littering his desk.

George cleared a space for her to sit on the chair next to him.

" I didn't think for one moment, sir." She sat down and pinched George's coffee, gulping some down and giving George a quick wink.

"Anyway, the prestigious retailers prefer to wear blinkers, and by failing to take steps to end the trade in illegal logging, the government aids and abets high level crime in West Africa," George resumed.

"The market here is voracious, so we and the EU are directly contributing to the destruction of the rain forest, not only in Cameroon, but also in the Amazon and Indonesia," Sandy put in, quickly picking up the thread.

"And that in turn, contributes to the demise of endangered species." Paul added.

"Especially the Great Apes – the orang utan in Indonesia, the gorilla, chimps and bonobos in Africa. The Congo Basin – the last redoubt." George and Sandy had been told by various NGO's concerned with primates, like the Jane Goodall Institute, that the Great Apes had about fifteen years left before they winked out of existence.

Sandy told Paul as much.

"Christ," mumbled Paul.

"To get back to the mechanics of the trade: Normally there's no effort made to ensure transparency concerning the 'chain of custody' of legitimate timber products, and the government can't be arsed to look into it, but now, for the first time, we have the chance to crack that." George's eyes were bright.

"Thanks to poor Colin Wingent, eh?" asked Paul. He took his bottle of anti-inflammatories out of his desk drawer, shook out a tablet and quickly swallowed it with the remains of his coffee. George realised he must be experiencing some pain as he was usually punctilious about taking his anti-arthritis drugs alone, loathing questions about his condition.

"Precisely. We know the actual tree he slumped against as he was murdered. Thanks to our other tame prof, Frampton, we know where that tree came from – the Dja Reserve, where it is definitely illegal to log – and we've traced the passage of log 'J' to here, more by luck than design, I reckon."

"Through Rayner's no doubt very sticky paws all the way to the Felixstowe Woodcraft joinery."

"By the way," Sandy interrupted. "Rayner had no problem admitting he is the main agent here for Rouge-Bolles, which we sort of knew anyway, so most of their timber passes through him. And he knows full well it's illegally logged. He also hinted when I put pressure on him – that threat of a full and exhaustive audit - that he has a number to phone in case of difficulties. It's not operative, though – I tried it. Probably a pay-as-you-go throw-away mobile."

"OK, fine, fine. We now know there's a network over here. We'll deal with that later. Now, after the joinery company - Felixstowe Woodcraft? - what's this Jensen company in Holland?" Paul seemed somewhat impatient, and it showed in the asperity of his tone.

"Ah, well." George, picking up on Paul's mood, knew it would not be advisable to string this out too long, however pleased he was feeling with himself. But he thought he might be able to lighten his mood.

"We know from Professor Frampton's little excursion into amdrams that the Wingent tree is to be made into doors. Jensen's will install the doors." George leaned back in his chair. "In a very helpful article from Greenpeace it states that, apparently, one mahogany tree provides enough timber to make 15 twelve-seater solid mahogany dining tables." He hadn't needed to consult his notes at any point. Somehow the sheer enormity of the cathedral-high trees he'd seen in the warehouse burned such details into the memory.

Sandy gazed wide-eyed at George.

"Just imagine the mark-up on that." Paul said, eyes drifting over to the tank where his shubunkins were staring out, hopeful of more flakes. George sensed he'd better get to the nub of this before Paul's patience wore too thin. The anti-inflammatories wouldn't have kicked in yet.

"Anyway, all of this prologue was to set the context of the whole business. Now," he shuffled a few papers around on his knees, "we come to it. Remember, 'doors'.

"With a tree so massive they could make several large tables out of one, but *this* Wingent tree is to be made into just doors? And nothing else?" asked Paul, tapping his biro on the edge of his desk.

"Exactly. And what does that imply?"

"Bloody massive doors. Heaven's gates."

"Well, not quite. Here's where the doors are going."

George triumphantly passed a paper over to Paul. He studied it for a while, expressionlessly. Then, his face cleared and he broke into heaving laughter as he handed it over to Sandy.

"Oh, that's poetic that is."

: ☾ :

Paul sat quiet, contemplative, after his DC and DCS had left to pursue other neglected cases piling up – credit card cloning at a local petrol station, and that good old stand-by, mugging. He couldn't put his mind to any other case, and he knew he was unfairly leaving the bulk of the rest of his workload to Sandy and George, plus other DC's. This case was special, crept under his skin, nagging at him – he couldn't even put it aside for a few hours. He suspected that Mark, in the thick of it, would be the same.

He swung gently back and forth on his battered leather chair staring at the fish who stared back, seemingly surprised at all the attention. The anti-inflammatories were doing their stuff and he was feeling a lot less achy.

They had a chance of completing this 'chain of custody' from tree to final product, and what a product! If they could follow this through then there was an outside chance of scuppering the illegal trade which seemed to flourish not only through neglect and ignorance on the part of authorities who claimed to know better, but above all, the sheer rapacity and indifference of those up to their grimy necks in killing off the rapidly shrinking rain forests.

He dug his small address book out of his pocket and consulted a number he hadn't rung for a while now. Matt Green. As a young ambitious MP, Matt had all the contacts, and more importantly, he'd want to know what was going on with Mark. Paul had met him about a year ago, an old Sixth Form College and University friend of Mark's. At first, Paul had viewed him as a dyed-in-the-wool political animal - smooth, articulate, persuasive. But once you got under that veneer there was more to him than that. In his maiden speech he'd argued for greater protection for the Great Apes before they disappeared off the face of the planet, and he'd proved a doughty fighter, in spite of his espousal of this cause putting a juddering halt to his rapid rise through the parliamentary ranks. Paul wondered if Matt's adoption of green issues was just down to Mark's influence or a case of his moniker determining his destiny, and whether Matt Green ever regretted the road he'd taken.

His mobile was answered immediately to Paul's surprise. After mutual regrets for not having kept in touch, Paul asked him.

"Matt, I need to pick your brains."

Chapter 42

"I'm using the number you gave me, Chief Inspector." The voice came over the line sounding strained, high-pitched. "You said I could phone you if…" The voice faded away.

In spite of the change in timbre, Paul recognised the accent.

"Jock Campbell, isn't it? What's up, then?"

The voice dropped to a conspiratorial whisper.

"It's the computers. They're gone, stolen and we've lost all our files."

"What? A break-in?" Then Paul paused, thinking. "Hang on, though - you got me a hard copy about RB from your filing cabinet. You must still have those."

"No, no, we haven't. The filing cabinets have been stripped as well. *All* the important files have been taken." The voice was rising again.

"But you must have back-ups of the computer files – CD's, memory sticks?" It was more a question than a statement.

There was a silence punctuated only by line crackle.

"You haven't, have you?" Paul was thinking 'bloody amateurs'. How could they be so lax? Such crucial data you kept as tight as Silas Marner's fist.

"Listen, we made back-ups at regular intervals, but all the memory sticks have gone, and we were a bit behind on the back-ups anyway." Jock sounded defensive.

"I suppose they were in plain sight somewhere?" Again, no answer was answer enough. It was no good listening to what they hadn't done. "What signs of a break-in?"

"The front door's been crow-barred, looks like. Wood's all splintered. The place's a mess."

Paul considered. Similar MO, but then so was every other break-in.

"Jock, did they know what they were looking for, do you think?"

"I — ah — I'm not sure. Hard to say. Drawers have been pulled out, papers scattered everywhere..." Jock's voice died, as he seemed to talk to someone else. "Left the keyboards, though."

"Who's there with you, Jock?"

"There're four of us here — me, Deidre, Sam, Louis."

Paul hadn't met Louis, but thought he'd spotted Deidre down the corridor — a generously-proportioned, gaudily dressed figure. Sam he'd very definitely met.

"Look, I'm sure you know this but it's absolutely essential that you touch nothing, move nothing — in fact, just move away from the office area. I'm assuming you've phoned your local police?"

"Yes, they're on their way — they're just down the road from us. We're standing outside the offices now. We tried to touch nothing." Jock's voice was shaky.

"Good. They'll want to interview you all, so keep yourselves available. I suggest you all go to that café next to the building and get yourselves some hot strong coffee, OK?"

"But what abou..?"

"Listen, Jock, it's just a burglary right now, that's all." Paul still wasn't ready to divulge news of the murder of Adam Wingent at this point, over the phone. "And you're all safe, that's the main thing. I'm going to try to get down there asap," he continued, glancing at his watch – 9.06am. "I'll let you know when. Give me your mobe number."

He cradled the phone with his shoulder as he scribbled down the long number.

: ☐ :

In lieu of the AS who was at some conference or other, the Assistant Chief Constable – nothing like going to the nearly-top - proved surprisingly amenable to Paul's taking a second trip down to London, even though his first one was unauthorised. Besides, the ACC had been involved in the earlier Caro case which had turned out well - and he now rated Paul.

The ACC's woolly caterpillar brows climbed a little, and he grumbled about not letting the paperwork slide. But, as he stared hard at his polished shoes, he admitted the sense of trying to tie up two separate but possibly related events, particularly as one involved murder here in Central Hampshire.

Paul decided to go alone. No sense in turning up mob-handed, more diplomatic if it was just himself.

When he got back to his office, he tried the Shoreditch number. He didn't know anyone there personally, but his title got him an equivalent – DCI Seth. He wondered – could he be a relative of Vikram Seth, or was Seth like the Anglo-Saxon first name?

"DCI Draper? I understand you would like to discuss the burglary at Forest Watch – your superior has contacted mine over the matter. Why on earth might it interest the Hampshire police?" A soft voice, a merest hint of accent, he sounded genuinely puzzled.

Paul told him.

"I don't want to tread on your toes, but would you mind if we discussed this? I'm coming to London, and could meet you, if you're agreeable."

"Indeed, I think we should meet – here. Do you know how to get here?"

"I'll be fine. I'm coming up by train, and I'll treat myself to a taxi."

"I look forward to meeting you, and for a useful exchange of information. We're in Shepherdess Street, near Moorfield's Eye Hospital."

"An interesting area if you've a liking for the history of organised crime. You're a mere stone's throw to the offices of Forest Watch then?" He thought it discreet not to mention on the phone that he'd already been on DCI Seth's turf. See how it went face-to-face.

"Yes, my men are there now, interviewing personnel."

On second thoughts, better prepare the ground as Jock might well give the game away, and it would be more embarrassing if he wasn't the first to mention that he'd already visited Forest Watch.

"I should mention that the Hampshire connection, which I guess my ACC outlined – Colin Wingent's murder - involves Forest Watch, so I've been in touch with one of their number, Jock Campbell. Incidentally, I haven't yet told him or anyone else at FW of Adam Wingent's murder. Did you know about that?"

"Yes, I got the low down. I appreciate you're telling me about your previous visit here, DCI. I assume you have your reasons." Did the voice betray a hint of mirth? "Obviously, Jock Campbell contacted you about the burglary, too, otherwise how would you know about it?" It was a statement.

"Yes. Well, I'll see you very soon."

He then phoned Jock to give him an approximate time, given that he had to parlay with DCI Seth for a while.

: ☼ :

Paul approached the square-shaped white stuccoed building, designed in the uninspired sixties architectural style, and walked up the disabled ramp. It even had a blue lamp outside. Very 'Dixon of Dock Green'. He turned to his left. FW was just up the road.

He was shown up promptly into the DCI's office on the second floor. Much neater than his own, and bigger, too. All box files, colour coded, were neatly lined up along shelves like soldiers on parade. There was a brand new leather swivel chair – he could smell the rich aroma from where he stood - behind a large highly polished desk unsullied with the scrappy bits of paper that littered his desk. No fish, though.

A dapper figure, a few inches shorter than Paul, detached himself from behind the desk and came up to Paul, hand outstretched.

"It's good to meet a colleague from Hampshire."

A warm, firm handshake.

"Before we get down to business, may I get you some refreshment after your journey?"

Paul gratefully accepted some tea having avoided South West Trains' dubious offerings. DCI Seth keyed an intercom and ordered tea for two.

A bit of get-to-know you chit-chat followed, then -

"You mentioned on the phone that this was an interesting area, I think you said, for the historian of organised crime." He indicated a chair for Paul.

"Oh, I was just thinking of the Krays, and that bunch of likely lads. Long time ago now." Paul gave a dismissive wave of the hand as he sat down.

"One could get almost nostalgic for those times. There were at least certainties – boundaries that would not be crossed."

A gentle knock at the door, and tea on a tray was bought in by a young PC who handed it over to Seth. Paul studied the DCI as he fussed over pouring the tea. A precise man, he reminded Paul of Hercules Poirot, even down to the neat moustache.

He was meticulous, economic, in his movements.

"Sugar?"

"Two please. Boundaries?" He took up the conversation again. He'd often heard that sentiment expressed about the gangs of the fifties, but he didn't hold with it. "They were a brutal bunch of thugs. Tortured people who crossed them."

Seth-Poirot passed him a cup of tea.

"True. But at least they kept that between themselves, in-house, as it were – I mean, it was, for the most part, inter-gang warfare, whereas now, anything goes. Drive-bys, indiscriminate use of guns, morons with drug-addled brains, drug gangs, sex trafficking gangs."

DCI Seth, comfortable in his plush leather chair, was obviously riding his hobby-horse, getting into stride.

459

"Lovely drop of tea," Paul offered irrelevantly, hoping to change the subject.

"Yes. I do apologise." Seth chuckled, waving away his last comments. "You can tell what our main preoccupations are here, but that's not what you came to hear." He leant back in his swivel chair, steepling his fingers. "So can you give me any more information about the background to the break-in at FW?"

"Well, it's a long and complicated story, involving more than one country. How long do we have?"

Seth glanced at his watch.

"SOCO are still at the crime scene, although the initial interviews should be over for now. Start at the beginning."

So Paul did.

DCI Seth's face gradually grew more astonished, and, something else - more animated - as Paul went through the discovery of Wingent's body in the Dja reserve, the involvement of his friend, Professor Rees, and the role of Forest Watch. He omitted Professor Frampton's role in the DNA analysis and the tree's 'chain of custody', thinking that it might all be too much to swallow in one go.

"This investigation spans continents — here and Cameroon. Fascinating. Fascinating."

The echolalia reminded Paul of Professor Frampton as Seth paused, sipping his tea thoughtfully. "If I understand you correctly, DCI Draper, Wingent's younger brother was murdered in Hampshire in the course of a burglary in order to retrieve a photo taken with his brother's mobile shortly before *his* murder — prompted, you assume, by his discovery of illegal felling. And forensics gives you reason to believe two culprits are involved in the Hampshire murder."

"Spot on. That's the conclusion we came to. And it's Paul." An impressively succinct summary, Paul thought.

"Ah. Thank you. Anish," he offered. "To continue - they didn't recover what they wanted at Wingent's house, so they turned their attention to FW HQ."

"Exactly – that's my guess. It turned out that Colin Wingent had emailed a mobile phone picture of his murderers, who worked for Rouge-Bolles, not to his home PC, or not *only* to his home PC – we're not sure since the hard drives were taken - but also to his office terminal at Forest Watch. Clearly, those responsible may have thought initially that he'd sent the picture to his home PC so took that hard drive. However, the killers shown in the picture are now in police custody in Yaounde." Paul stopped, paused. Was he being stupid here? Was he missing something obvious? But there was no answering synaptic starburst, no flash of insight. Nothing.

"The burglars at FW were searching specifically for photos then – photos that would implicate the logging company's employees?"

"That's my initial guess, yes. But we had already emailed a photo back to Professor Rees. Those two culprits were picked up soon afterwards."

"Well, this is a welcome change to the ever-present drugs crimes –grow-ops and Vietnamese gangs." Anish was actually rubbing his hands together, eyes sparkling, relishing the prospect of a different type of crime. Paul could well understand the crushing fatigue that comes with dealing with yet another drug-fuelled violent crime, and was only too grateful to have harnessed such enthusiasm.

"What exactly is it that you would like us to do?" asked Anish.

"Well, I'd like to visit the FW offices again, have a nose around, if you don't mind – without getting in SOCO's way, of course. Ask a few questions of the staff."

"Jock Campbell you've already met, of course." Anish had a twinkle in his eye

"Sorry about that. I was in a rush to get to the FW premises before anyone else. I came up from Winchester on the last train. I thought that someone connected to Rouge-Bolles at the European end would very soon realise that Colin Wingent also had an office PC at Forest Watch here in London. There'd be no point in removing evidence on one hard drive if it's also on another."

"And removing the hard drives from the offices here would be the simplest if crudest way to remove all photographic evidence, of course." Anish nodded.

"Right. They took all the computers. Just deleting files always leaves some trace which our computer geeks can get at – they knew that." His tea had cooled. Anish Seth, noticing this, immediately poured him another cup, for which Paul murmured his thanks. He continued.

"The email attachment that I saw showed two men – one white and one black. It was a clear enough picture for an ID and it was imperative we get the photo sent back to Yaounde asap. Not only because these were the likely murderers of Colin Wingent, but also because Professor Rees who discovered Wingent's body, was in constant danger since he could identify those who attacked him, if he ever saw them again. So the police there needed to know what they looked like – I told him to get the photo to them pronto."

Anish Seth had adopted a quizzical look as Paul went on to explain further Mark's role in the convoluted shenanigans that had occurred in Cameroon. He'd brushed over some details in the rough version he'd given earlier.

At the finish, Seth appeared a bit dazed, as though he'd got more than he bargained for. He leapt up and paced around for a while.

"A complicated case, I can see that," he said finally, blowing out his cheeks. "Let's say no more about young Mr Campbell, and get over to the FW offices. We can walk there – it's not far."

The weather was holding, a warm and humid Indian summer. Paul slung his jacket over his shoulder and rolled his shirtsleeves up, and set off with Anish Seth, talking inconsequentialities, about their respective workloads, the ever-increasing bumf and the chonically ungrateful public.

"Once, I would have advised my eldest son that a career in the police was a fine job, but not now, not now." Seth shook his head, sadly.

"Because of all of the above?" asked Paul.

"I can't see it getting any better, can you? Prospects for young Indians have increased markedly of late, but the bureaucracy goes on and on tying us in knots. I know he'd be frustrated."

"What's his preference, then?"

Seth laughed. "Oh, he wants to be a lawyer."

Paul chuckled.

When they reached the premises where FW had offices, Paul examined the broken door, hanging at a slant, the upper hinges torn from their moorings. It reminded him of the splintered cottage door.

He took a step back to get a look at the café next door, and, sitting outside under a golf-sized umbrella, spotted Jock, Sam, svelte as ever, plump Deirdre and another thin, wispily bearded fellow, a bit older than the others, gazing gloomily back at him. He flickered his fingers in greeting at them. He got a rueful smile from Sam and only the slightest of nods from Jock.

They stepped past the ruined doorway and the young constable guarding the entrance. Paul raised his eyes to the galleried area where the FW offices were.

"Were theirs the only offices broken into?" Paul asked.

"I believe so."

" There are several other outfits here – none of them touched?"

Anish shook his head. "Apparently not."

"Mm. So the burglars knew where to go. Just as they knew where the Wingent brothers lived."

Their information was obviously good. There was that connection between Cameroon and here – two branches. Communication.

But there was some anomaly which needed sorting out.

Stepping outside once more, Paul dug around in his jacket for his mobile phone. His fingers were clumsy today.

"We need an update," he explained to Anish.

His mobile slipped out of his hand and clattered into the dusty gutter, coming to rest by the front wheel of a Corsa parked by the kerb.

"Buggeration!" he muttered.

Paul bent to retrieve it. As he was straightening up, his eye caught the silver glint of something buried in the tyre's rubber tread. It looked like the head of a rivet but the tyre still seemed under pressure. He was struck by the robustness of modern tyres that never went flat.

Then - that fleeting, slippery eel-like thought yet again.

Like the tyres, his phone was robust; it was still working. He contacted George and asked him to request the most recent information on the Colin Wingent investigation from Cameroon — had the police there uncovered anything from their interviews with the suspects? He was to phone, email, text, semaphore, whatever - Mark, the police Commissaire, anyone — and to let him know as soon as he found out anything. And he wanted to know *exactly* when the two suspects had been arrested - not just when he'd been sent that text message when they were at 'The Boot'.

"My phone doesn't have any fancy 3G internet access or WAP enabled functions," he explained to Anish, hoping to sound *au fait* with such abstruse mysteries. He was just parroting what George had told him.

"I see." Anish, looking as confused as Paul felt, indicated the shattered doorway. "Shall we?"

All seemed quiet inside when they entered the FW offices but for two Scenes of Crime officers in their rustling whites bent over a computer keyboard. Trying for fingerprints, Paul saw, as he watched the gentle rotation of their brushes puffing up little clouds of fine black powder. Good luck with that. He doubted very much whoever had done this had been stupid enough to leave prints. If it was the same crew who killed Adam Wingent, then it was his opinion that they were professionals, and he was almost convinced that they were one and the same.

He went straight to the filing cabinets from which Jock had extracted a file the last time Paul was here. The whole drawer emptied out. And all the others, too.

Next door, he examined the photocopier, in case any papers had been left on the glass screen. Nothing. Not even stray bits of paper lying on the floor.

465

That left the computers. He returned to the room where most of the work was done. Hard-drives missing as expected. All of them. Leaving just blank monitors and keyboards. Jock was right - the place had been professionally filleted.

Somebody — or two, probably - knew just where to go and what to take. They didn't bother trying to delete files, because they knew there'd be some trace of them on the hard drives, so they scarpered with the whole kit and kaboodle, cleaned out the filing cabinets, and left little trace. The only difference here was that no one had been murdered.

He shook his head regretfully at Anish.

"Unless Scenes of Crime come up with something, there's nothing here." The mention of SOCO reminded him that he ought to take another look at Tris' report on the Adam Wingent murder. He might have missed something.

Then, a spike of curiousity prompting him, he felt underneath Jock's work station for the slip of paper taped to the underside of the desk. It said 'Keeper'.

"May I suggest we talk to the staff?" asked Anish staring at the scrap of paper. "What's that?"

"Wingent's current password for this quarter. Yes, I think we should, though I doubt they'll be able to give us much."

Paul replaced the slip of paper under the desk.

They clattered down the stairs to the ground floor and out into the sunshine.

The quartet were still sitting in the same places, staring into the depths of their lattes, making the odd desultory offering by way of conversation.

Sam looked up as they approached.

"What have you found, Chief Inspector?" She alone looked unruffled by the whole business, her dark eyes guileless. She tapped the ash off her cigarette in the tin ashtray, and brushed at a stray strand of hair wafted over her face by the breeze. She smiled up at Paul knowingly. She's only too well aware of the effect she has on men, Paul realised – me included.

Anish Seth looked questioningly at Paul, who made an apologetic gesture.

"Oh. Ms Ball was at FW when I came down, along with Mr Campbell."

Anish didn't appear too put out, and replied for Paul.

"Very little, I'm afraid, Ms Ball, which makes whatever you may be able to give us all the more important. Now, who was first to discover the break-in?"

The bearded one spoke.

"We've told all this to the police once." He sounded as gloomy as his expression appeared.

"And now you will have to tell DCI Draper of the Hampshire Police all over again," Seth said, sternly, indicating Paul.

Paul watched the faces to see if there was any spark of surprise at the presence of a member of another force. But Jock had doubtless told the other two about his first visit and the recent phone call.

"Right. OK. I'm sorry– we've lost everything, you know? All those months of work, Col's..." He was visibly upset. Deirdre, resplendent in a silky bright turquoise suit, put a gentle dimpled hand on his shoulder.

"I do understand. It's a lot to take in, and you appear to have been targeted deliberately." Paul addressed this to the bearded one, trying for a gentle tone. "Could I have your name?" He'd guessed this was Lou.

"Lou Pierce. I was first in, followed shortly after by Deirdre here."

"Deirdre Hayhurst." Deirdre put in. Her protective hand, crowned with immaculate purple nail polish, was still on Lou's shoulder. She had that rounded childlike prettiness of some plump girls, marred only by a slight frown as she stared challengingly at Paul. She and Lou made a wonderfully contrasting pair.

"Then?" prompted Paul.

"That would be me and, finally, Jock." Sam Ball added, touching Jock gently on the arm.

Jock was the only one who'd said nothing so far, although he'd blushed slightly at Sam's touch. His hair was as untamed as ever.

Paul turned back to Lou.

"You were the one to phone the police?"

"Yes, straightaway. And we touched nothing in the offices."

Everyone's seen CSI Las Vegas, thought Paul.

"Except the phone, eh? Anyone else come in?"

"No."

"You phoned me, Jock." Paul turned towards him.

"Yes, soon after I got there, used my mobile. I hope I did the right thing, but I thought you'd want to know."

Just then Paul's mobile rang. It was George.

Paul listened, his expression darkening.

Chapter
43

aul took Anish Seth's elbow and led him down the pavement, out of earshot of the others.

"That was my DS. He managed to get hold of Professor Rees on the phone. He said that the Cameroon police have now arrested the top dog of the operation at their end. This was after they'd already arrested the two implicated in the photo." He found himself whispering, not quite knowing why.

"When was this?"

"The top dog? Just yesterday, but I can't be sure of the time differences."

"Do you think that arrest precipitated the break-in here?"

"You mean was the motive to destroy evidence that might pinpoint possible culprits here?"

Paul stared off into the middle distance.

"Mmm. Apparently they recovered all sorts of papers over there and stacks of dosh, hidden in an old safe, that this guy kept as insurance in case he was bumped. So, what puzzles me is wouldn't any operatives this end know about that?" He turned back to Anish. "And if they did, then any theft of similar or related materials would be pretty redundant as far as protecting RB is concerned."

"Surely it depends on the level of communication between Cameroon and here, Paul. But anyway it doesn't really explain why, if FW had incriminating evidence, that the timber people didn't act sooner to remove it."

Paul rubbed his stubbly chin, trying to figure out why the robbery had taken place at just this juncture.

"No, it doesn't."

"But still FW was broken into."

"Right. So either R-B didn't know its two operatives were in jail in Cameroon and that it would therefore be pointless to burgle FW HQ - unlikely, I feel- or they wanted us to *think* that they didn't know, and they were after something else – not the digital photo."

"Mmm." Seth sounded doubtful. "It could have been a cover for something else, but it's a bit elaborate, isn't it?"

Paul caught sight of his face in the side window of the car they were standing beside. He looked wretched, accentuated lines of tension bracketing his mouth. Every time he looked in a mirror, he appeared more careworn.

"Doesn't make much sense," he agreed, turning away from the reflection. "And actually I have a photocopy of FW's pertinent file on logging companies. I've only had a cursory glance at it but it reveals something of timber laundering methods – forged certificates and the like."

"But the R-B operatives here wouldn't know *that* would they, that you had a copy of the file? So maybe they broke in to retrieve that file?"

"That makes more sense. I suppose." Paul didn't sound too convinced, gazed down at his feet at the gutter and the rivet stuck in the... and abruptly his thoughts flipped — a rapid reorganisation of thoughts - one of De Bono's lateral thought processes - from which emerged an idea. Tyres.

"Anish, do we have all the addresses we need?"

"Of the staff? Of course."

"And prints?"

"Yes, of course."

"We can let the staff go for now, then. I need to get back to your station and use your fax pronto." Paul distracted was abrupt.

Anish seemed taken aback at this sudden change of direction.

"Well, I suppose there's not a lot more they can tell us right now." He looked back at the forlorn quartet, still sitting round the table, coffees cooling in front of them.

At that moment a white-suited figure carrying a camera exited through the ruined doorway and briskly approached Anish. Two others followed, carrying assorted evidence bags and a portable fingerprinting unit which they placed in the back of the white forensic science van.

"All done for now. We'll be in touch as soon as we've processed this stuff, mostly monitors and keyboards." He flicked his chin towards the van. "Don't hold out too much hope, though. My bet is that this lot used gloves." The figure pushed back his hood to reveal grey cropped hair and a weatherbeaten face.

"This lot?" asked Anish.

"More than one anyway — educated guess, two - judging by the kit they had to lug." He turned to look at the FW staff. "They can go back and clean up the place if they want to."

"Good. Let me know as soon as you have anything, Jerry. You know that this case may tie up with a similar break-in in Hampshire, one that resulted in murder." Anish inclined his head towards Paul as if to explain his presence. "So give it priority."

"As ever." The Scenes of Crime Investigator gave Paul, who was walking back towards the café table, a curious look.

Paul, reaching the group, groped for his notebook in his jacket pocket.

"I know we have your addresses everyone, but could I also have your car make and registration numbers?"

They gazed up at him, perplexed.

"What do you want those for?" asked Jock. "How's that going to help find the burglars?" He sounded more assertive than Paul had remembered from their last encounter.

"Elimination purposes," replied Paul, vaguely, waving his hand around the street.

Jock frowned, looking around.

"There's no CCTV around here, so how does that help?"

Sod's law, Paul was thinking. The one place in London with no CCTV.

"There are other means of recording vehicles in the area. Traffic wardens, beat cops. We should be able to work out which cars are normally parked here and which aren't." Feeling quite pleased with thinking on his feet.

"This happened at night, though. None of us would have been here."

"As I recall, you spent several nights here when Colin Wingent was still missing."

Paul was hoping Jock would just shut up, but he was rescued by Sam Ball resting a pale, long-fingered hand over Jock's. She wore a large dusky green jade ring on her ring finger.

"Mine's a silver Audi, Chief Inspector. Registration MJ08 K YV but I didn't bring it in today," she sighed, and fished for another cigarette in her handbag. "It's in for repairs – something wrong with the brake-pads."

Paul wouldn't know a designer label if one bit him on the nose, but that black patent leather bag certainly looked three-figure costly, the black jacket was beautifully tailored expensive serge, contrasting with the low-cut red silk blouse and…he looked quickly down at his note-book. The registration showed the car was new, too. Jock had been right, she was not short of a bob or two. She wore the classy clothes as if by right.

"Thank you." He copied the registration down, then queried the others with his eyebrows.

Lou Pierce, nominally the leader of their little band, but reticent to the point of taciturnity, asserted that he usually used his bike because of congestion, and for sound ecological reasons, but when pressed admitted he had an old Ford Fiesta. He scratched at his beard, as if troubled by this ownership.

Paul copied down the number.

Deirdre, evidently irritated at the treatment meted out to Lou, said she had a blue Peugeot, and pointed it out to Paul, giving him the registration at the same time. The small hatchback was parked some way down the road from the FW offices.

"And you, Jock?"

"VW Golf. Black. WX51 JOP." He was sullen now, playing with his spoon, not looking up.

"No one else? It seems like a small number of staff for the massive problems you're tackling."

Lou gazed up, morosely.

"We have three more field people – one in the Amazon basin, where the decimation of mahogany's the problem, one in Indonesia investigating the racin scandal, and one on holiday."

Paul guessed that racin was yet another endangered tree species.

"OK. Whereabouts is the guy on holiday?"

"Nepal," said Lou shortly. "And it's a 'she'."

"Thank you. SOCO have finished, so you can all return now if you wish. DCI Seth may, of course, wish to talk to you again to confirm some points."

: ♎ :

He waited impatiently by the fax machine in Anish Seth's office, feeling apologetic, for seemingly muscling in and directing an investigation which wasn't his to direct, and for taking advantage of Anish Seth's hospitality and patience. His affability. Other CID officers he knew of similar rank would display territoriality like demented robins.

As he waited, he sipped more tea, kindly provided by the silent PC, and told himself that he should try to be more considerate, not so indifferent to others' needs, not so brusque. Em, in her umbellished, direct way, often said the same, and he acknowledged the rightness of her diagnosis while privately thinking she was just the same as he. Although it was always easier to see another's faults, and she'd never admit that she was like him. He excused himself by believing

that his brusqueness was due to his total focus on a problem
– a psychological form of tunnel vision; it blinded him to
all else. Then he thought, 'that's bollocks'. His thoughts
wandered aimlessly on, a stream of consciousness with no
particular goal in mind, idle thoughts drifting around his
head as he waited and sipped.

The fax chirruped.

It was so slow, regurgitating paper reluctantly.

He grabbed it before it was scarcely out of the scrimping
mouth of the fax machine.

He focused on the images printed on the paper. He
was aware of that tugging insistent idea at the back of his
mind that just wouldn't be retrieved. It was there in ghostly
form when he had bent to get his fallen mobile and spotted
the rivet; it was there, still ectoplasmic, when he had looked
down at his feet. And it was here now. It was beginning to
annoy him. He had to flesh it out.

The tyre tracks. Tris Harrier had supplied him with the
tyre tracks found at the Wingent cottage, or at least, those
visible at the lane entrance to the cottage, and he'd given them
the merest cursory glance at the time, as there was no knowing
when the tracks were made, or who made them. It was more
than likely that they were made by some innocent visitor
– a postman, a milkman, a neighbour - or Adam Wingent
himself, if not his brother. He'd sent Sandy to check with
Tris whether he also had a copy of Adam Wingent's car tyres
– or any other cars resident at the cottage.

Sandy had reported Tris as saying, with some acerbity,
that obviously he had - it was not something he would have
overlooked. The tracks of the garaged car, labelled, were
included in the fax.

Like fingerprints, tyre tracks were individual, and these seemed to belong to different vehicles. At the entrance to the lane, one of the tracks proved to match those taken from the car in the Wingent garage and registered to Adam Wingent, but, in addition, there were three which stood out crisply, and one of the three was very distinctive, with a break in the pattern. It was the faint engram of seeing this flaw in the repeated pattern of one of the tyre illustrations in Tristram's report which had been twanging his memory when he saw the rivet in the Corsa's tyre. A retrieval cue, Mark would have called it.

Which brand of tyres made these tracks, he had no idea, nor even if certain brands went with certain makes of car. That would be down to Tris.

Could he ask the Scenes of Crime Unit here to take a print of every car tyre along the street? That would be pushing it a bit far, and in spite of what he'd said to Jock, there was no way of telling if cars present now were present at the time of the robbery, and the ones he held in his hand proved nothing unless... He rubbed distractedly at his forehead, not finishing the chain of reasoning.

Anish Seth entered his office.

"Any luck? He asked.

"Not sure." He flapped the sheaf of faxes. "Copies of tyre tracks taken at the Wingent cottage. Apart from tracks from a Wingent car there's no way of knowing whose cars these belong to, or if one of these three other track sets belongs to the attackers' vehicle, and I guess it's way too late to check the street here to see if there's a match. But there is something...," he hesitated, reluctant, but leaving an unasked question dangling.

"I understand your hesitation, being on a strange patch, Paul, but if these two crimes are connected as you think, then we both have a responsibility to do all we can to clear them up. Forget niceties for the moment. What is it you want to do?"

Paul favoured him with a rare smile, and told him.

: ¤ :

They eventually snatched a parking spot, earning a blast from a BMW driver, in the busy Fulham Broadway, and found the address above a pub called the 'The Fentiman'. Inside, it was dominated by a giant TV screen tuned to a football match, and full of noisy Aussies and Kiwis.

Paul, followed by Anish, clattered up the outside black iron stairway to a blue-painted door.

Jock came to the door at once and seemed surprised to see them. Perhaps he'd been expecting someone else.

"What do you want now? I thought we were finished – for the time being, anyway." He had changed his clothes. Now, he was dressed in a khaki T-shirt which had seen better days, and an old pair of ripped and faded jeans. His hair was in the same untamed peaks that reminded Paul of Stan Laurel. There was a definite cooling in the atmosphere.

"Expecting someone else, Jock?" asked Paul, ignoring his comments.

Jock looked at him steadily, then silently, he stood aside to let them in. It had been decided earlier that Paul would do most of the talking, as he thought he'd established some sort of rapport on the first visit to FW. He wasn't so sure now – something seemed to have altered. Jock seemed to Paul to be unduly anxious and this translated into an immature assertiveness.

Anish was to sit there quietly enigmatic and brooding. He'd said he was quite good at that.

They were led up a narrow flight of stairs, threadbare carpet, which had once been royal blue Wilton, wood showing through on the worn treads, to a communal living room. The TV was on, showing BBC 24 Hour news, and newspapers were scattered about with abandoned mugs of coffee. One had scarlet lipstick smears. Perhaps Jock wasn't as chastely devoted to the cause as he seemed, or at least, not to the exclusion of other delights. That shade was familiar.

Jock gestured towards a sagging sofa, springs evidently exhausted, covered with a green throw, while he slumped into a slightly tilting armchair opposite.

Overall, the flat had the scruffy, down-at-heel appearance of a student pad, furnishings shabby and dog-eared and for Paul, who'd been in student digs himself, holding faint echoes of quarrels over whose turn it was to do the washing-up and hoovering.

"You share this flat?"

Jock glared at them, challengingly

"I would think that's fairly obvious. I'm the only one in at the moment. The other two are downstairs in the pub." He picked at a loose thread on the arm of the chair. "There's a match on," he added by way of explanation.

Paul nodded his understanding. Traitorously, after the Saints relegation, he'd decided he was going to follow cricket more closely from now on – his waning interest revitalised since the return of the Ashes in 2005.

"Not keen on footie yourself?"

"Prefer rugby any day."

"Share the flat with just the two blokes?"

"Yes." That sounded defensive. So the lipstick came from a visitor.

This was going to be difficult with Jock in terse mode. What could have changed his attitude so drastically since the last time they'd met?

"Jock, I'd like to ask you a few more questions." Without waiting for an answer, he continued. "Can I take you back to when we first met at the FW? You'd heard nothing from Colin Wingent, and you were sleeping over in case he contacted you."

"That's right."

"Were you the only one sleeping over?"

"Yes."

"How is it you never thought to check Colin's emails on his terminal?"

Jock looked up from picking at the loose thread, frowning.

"I had no reason to – if Col was going to email us, he would have used the general FW email address and it would have come to all of us."

Paul nodded, not fully convinced, and decided to change tack.

"Can you suggest why anyone would want to break into FW offices and steal files and hard drives?"

An exasperated look came over Jock's face.

"It's pretty obvious, isn't it?" he said again. "All this has been about illegal logging. You don't have to look very far to find the culprits in this case."

Paul raised his brows as a query. He wanted Jock to say it.

Jock sighed theatrically.

"OK. It's self-evident that Rouge-Bolles are the ones with most to lose right now, and you yourself came belting over from Hampshire to see if Col had left anything on his email."

"True. I did, and he had." Paul then, playing to the script, addressed himself to Anish. "We found the photo of the two suspects on Wingent's PC, and emailed it back to Cameroon, to a good friend of mine, Professor Rees - he'd already been the target of Rouge-Bolles' attentions – with a warning to avoid the pair at all costs, and to get the photo circulated asap. I thought once it was in the open he would be safer."

Anish, nodding his understanding as though he was hearing this for the first time whereas he already knew most, if not all, the details, but Paul was using him as a handy foil to open Jock up.

Jock had leant forward during this, and asked, "What happened to your friend?"

Maybe it was working.

"Well, that's the thing, Jock. He's perfectly alright as far as I know. But that's in no small measure down to the Cameroon police force."

Anish, too, appeared intrigued to know Mark's fate.

"How was that then?" he enquired, playing his part.

"They captured the illustrious pair during a botched kidnapping of one of Mark's – Professor Rees' – colleagues. They're both in jail, where I hope they rot."

Paul scrutinised Jock, trying to gauge his reaction.

"These are the two who murdered Col then?" asked Jock, his face pale.

Paul nodded, then paused, waiting to see if Jock had anything to add. He didn't, staring at the far wall with a strange intensity. Paul turned his head slightly to see where his gaze was fixed. Jock was apparently absorbed in a FW poster, showing a lush, verdant forest from above, with the line 'Your Heritage Destroyed!' in lurid red-dripping lettering slashed across the middle. Hideously prescient.

Paul wanted to bring him down to earth, to refocus his thoughts.

"Since these two geniuses had already been arrested in Cameroon, doesn't it make the break-in superfluous? What do you think, Jock?"

Jock was still distracted, and Paul realised that he'd had a real affection, even admiration, for Colin Wingent. Maybe, hearing a brief outline of what had gone on in Cameroon, the full horror of Colin's fate had hit home. He hoped so.

When he finally broke his mesmerised gaze from the poster and looked back at Paul, his eyes were still unfocused.

"Mmm? Well... *I* don't know. . .maybe they thought there was still some damning evidence in our offices. That file we photocopied for you, for instance, contained confidential information."

"Why *then*, though? You were in possession of that information for some time, no?"

Jock rubbed his eyes.

"Look, I can't second guess those bastards. Who knows what goes through their sick minds? I know only this – that they'll do anything to protect their own interests." His gaze returned to the poster. "Anything."

An expression of fear crept over his features.

Chapter 44

The next day, a red-eyed Jock Campbell was brought in for questioning. Paul and Anish let the impression blossom that this was an altogether more serious interview. They'd let him know yesterday that they'd need to question him again – and take that thought to bed with him, niggling and scraping away at his sleep.

Why had they picked on Jock? Paul's own sleep in the too-soft hotel bed, with the heating system set too high, was similarly racked, but he knew there was something Jock was holding back on. The spare environs of the Shoreditch Police Station just might press the right buttons.

They let him wait for forty minutes absorbing the odours of stale sweat and unfathomable sounds, guessing that this was a totally alien and deeply uncomfortable environment for the likes of Jock. Nothing to stare at, nothing to read, just your own flitting thoughts to tame.

When Anish accompanied by Paul entered the interview room, they had decided that this time Anish should lead.

They both sat silently, seriously.

"Am I under some sort of charge?" asked Jock, not quite carrying off an assertive tone.

"This is merely an interview to ascertain certain pieces of information. You're not under arrest. We're not recording. You have the right to leave whenever you wish." Anish rattled the spiel off.

Jock sat very still, apparently considering what Anish had said, then from somewhere, it seemed, he rallied a little courage. He gave a dismissive wave.

"I've nothing to fear, anyway. Particularly not from these cheap theatricals, leaving me stewing here for –," he looked at his watch " – forty minutes."

"Excellent," Anish said with what sounded like genuine approval, his tone excised of any irritation. "Now, how long have you worked for Forest Watch?"

The question evidently perplexed Jock.

"What do you want to know that for?"

Anish waited, without answering, his gaze fixed steadily, calmly, on Jock. Paul approved of his style, patient, giving nothing away.

"About two years. Why?"

Paul restrained himself from assuming the hackneyed 'we ask the questions' approach and manfully waited for Anish.

"I'm interested, nothing more. Does it pay well?"

Jock gave him the gimlet eye.

"What do you think? Not for a graduate, at least. But if you're thinking that my impecunious state might lead me into a life of crime, you're very much mistaken. I don't need much money. I live a simple life."

"Very commendable, Mr Campbell. Would that there were more like you we might be a less selfish, materialistic people." He paused. "But why would you mention a life of crime at all?"

Paul now wasn't sure where this was going, but guessed that Anish had his own strategy, was willing to play the long game.

Jock shrugged, and looked around.

"I'm here for some reason, aren't I?"

"Indeed you are. To help us with our enquiries, as I said."

Jock gave a faint smile.

"Fire away."

"Where were you between the hours of five pm and eight pm on Thursday last?" There was a subtle change in Anish's tone, and a detectable whiplash to the question.

The change of manner was designed to throw Jock. It caused him to pause, mouth slightly open, before stammering an answer.

"I – I – can't think. Not just off the top of my head." He clasped his hands together.

Paul, having read in an article that seventy-percent of all communication was non-verbal – although he maintained a healthy scepticism about the high figure - watched Jock's behaviour keenly.

Anish let the silence stretch until Jock was prompted to try an answer.

"Thursday last? Um – I must have been out." His eyes were wandering about. Not the whole truth. Possibly.

Anish waited again.

Paul observed the tiny droplets forming on Jock's upper lip and the knuckles of his clasped hands were white. Jock was oddly disturbed, more so than one might have expected given the straightforward question. Unless he had something to hide.

Anish allowed some impatience to leak into his voice.

"Come along. It's a simple question, and Thursday is not so long ago."

Jock's head dropped, and stayed bowed for a long beat. Then he raised his head, and Paul could see a resolution of sorts in his face

"All right. I was with someone, but I'd prefer they weren't brought into this."

"Can this person verify where you were between those hours?"

"Some of the time, yes. Well, from seven fifteen pm."

"Why so precise?"

Jock paused again, appearing to prepare his answer.

"Well, we had agreed to meet earlier, at seven, and I was checking my watch."

"Then I'm afraid we may have no choice but to interview this person to establish where you were, Mr Campbell."

Jock scratched at his forehead hard enough to leave a red mark on the pale skin.

"Why do you need to know this anyway? What am I supposed to have done?"

All apparent assertiveness gone. Almost an assumption that *he* – no one else - might be responsible, yet not knowing what for. Taking upon himself the burden of guilt. Paul recalled what he had read of Jock in a hastily complied file; Anish Seth had ordered files to be compiled on all the staff at FW. He was pleased he hadn't been too far out with his 'ecclesiastical whiff': Son of a retired Presbyterian minister; an only child; a late pregnancy. Could it have been a strict upbringing, instilling guilt, watchful of temptations, condemnatory of all the multifarious sins of this world?

Paul felt Anish tense slightly, about to give out the choice, telling bit of information. This was it.

"Between those hours I gave you, Adam Wingent was murdered by a person or persons unknown."

Jock's face whitened, the skin tightening under the eyes, pupils enlarging.

In fact while the pathologist, Charles Terman, had pinned down the time frame of the murder to between five and six pm, they wanted to know what had gone on within a wider window of time since Jock lived in Fulham and the murder was in Hampshire.

"Adam? Col's brother? What? How? " His voice was hoarse.

He half rose, and slumped back again, he eyes riveted on Anish.

"Adam?" he repeated. " No. You can't possibly think it was me, can you? Is this what this is all about? You suspect *me*? You can't suspect me!"

Now the words were tumbling out, tripping over themselves to emerge. Paul glanced over at Anish. Either the boy was a consummate actor, or he wasn't guilty. He was too scared, the responses unfeigned.

He was clearly in a state of ferment, which could only be damped by pulling his attention back to the question. Paul was beginning to feel sorry for him.

"You're not being accused of anything, Jock," Paul reassured him, leaning towards him, the 'nice' cop. "But we need you to be absolutely up front with us. You can see how serious this is. Just tell us where you were, who you were with, during those hours."

Jock stared at him blankly for a while. "I was working up to about – I think – a quarter to six. I was in the Uni library doing some research and ordering some inter-library loan books." His voice sounded exhausted.

"Is that the Senate House Library?" asked Anish.

"Yes. I'm sure you can check that out. After…," he hesitated for a long beat then turned back to Paul.

"OK, OK. I was with James Crombie. We – we met at a bar." He placed both hands flat along the table top. "I suppose you'd call it a gay bar. At seven fifteen pm."

Whew. I certainly got that wrong, thought Paul, diverted by the scarlet lipstick – not as astute as I like to think. Although it was clear that Jock was not properly reconciled to his homosexuality, probably hadn't come out – certainly not to his parents, Paul guessed. And I thought he had an unrequited lust for the enticing Sam Ball. Ah, the potent mix of a puritanical upbringing in which, on the one hand homosexuality was no doubt the most iniquitous of sins, and on the other the temptation of forbidden fruit.

"I would like your friend's address and telephone number, please," Anish asked, readying his notebook.

"I can't believe that Col's brother is dead, too. Murdered. It's horrible. What about their parent. I know Col had a mother." Jock's hands went up to his face.

"Never mind about that now. We'll deal with all that. That address?" Anish was all briskness.

He took his hands away. "I don't have it. Really. We met only recently, and always arranged to get together somewhere else - a bar, pub. Does anyone else have to know about this?"

"About what? Your relationship?"

Jock nodded quickly.

"It's not a crime these days, Jock. I don't really see the difficulty unless this Crombie is underage." Paul needled him deliberately hoping to elicit more about Jock's apparently conflicting emotions.

"Christ, no! What do you think I am? He's about my age, a bit older, maybe. No, it's more my – parents - I was concerned about." He scratched at the red mark on his forehead again.

"That's entirely between you and them. None of our business. But if I were you, I would tell them soon anyway. Best to have it out in the open."

Jock gave a mirthless bark. "You're not me – and I wouldn't expect you to understand."

Paul said, "I think I do understand, Jock. A Free Presbyterian ruling elder wouldn't look at all kindly on such 'deviance' – is that it?"

Jock turned away, his mouth unsteady, took a deep breath and seemed to steady himself.

"That's about it, yes. They'd reject me. There's no other child, just me. I can't do it. Not yet. I know they're narrow-minded, but it would kill my father and my mother follows whatever he says. They're getting on," he added in a soft voice, as though this explained everything.

"There's no need for us to say anything, Jock. Be reassured. Now, if you and James made arrangements to meet, you must have his phone number at least."

Jock sighed, and reached into his jeans back pocket. He pulled out of his wallet a scrap of paper which he handed over. Anish copied down the number.

"Are we finished now?" Jock asked.

"Sorry. Just one or two further questions." Anish, all business, was scribbling some more notes down.

"Well, in that case, can I have a cup of tea first? I could do with one."

Having unburdened himself of his great life's secret, Jock seemed to have relaxed a little.

Paul rose, accepting the phone number from Anish, and went towards the door.

"How do you like it?" That could have been better put.

"Milk and two sugars."

Paul went up the corridor, collaring another young PC for the tea with 'two' in Interview Room 2, and tried Crombie's number on his own mobile phone as he paced up and down.

It rang emptily. Then – a switch over to voicemail, first, the service provider, then, the usual 'get back to you'. An interesting voice, low pitched. Was there an accent? Too few words to tell.

Jock was going to have some difficulty establishing his alibi unless this Crombie could be traced.

Paul leaned against the corridor wall, one leg bent backwards, staring at the floor. The station seemed unnaturally quiet for a Saturday. It was neat and ordered, just like Anish, the vinyl floor polished to within an inch of its life.

Lost in his thoughts, head down, he only gradually became aware of another figure approaching. Anish.

Paul waggled the phone at him and made a wry face, shaking his head.

"Ah, I see. Let me take the number over to the IT people – see what they can extract."

Paul handed back the phone number.

Anish walked briskly off down the corridor, the scrap of paper in one hand. As the cup of tea was coming the other way, Paul asked the obliging PC to pass it to the guy inside and then place himself outside the door for a short spell while he took a breath of air. Really, he had a sudden craving for a fag, something he tried with mixed success to resist. He'd found it depended on the circumstances prevailing at the time – and these particular circs demanded succumbing to the craving.

He wandered around looking for a rear exit.

He needed to think. That something was odd here wasn't in doubt. It was all about timing.

He tracked back, mentally, to the dreadful discovery of Adam Wingent's body. There was roughly a two to three hour gap between his and George's discovery of that murder and his arrival late that same night at FW HQ. In all honesty, he'd half expected that he would have found the office already broken into when he'd arrived. Then, if he had the timing of events correct, the infamous pair featured in the mobile photo had already been caught in Cameroon – which, as far as he could figure it, made any attempted theft to recover said photo from FW terminals entirely pointless. That is, if the Rouge-Bolles villains had the sophisticated communication between the UK and Cameroon that he assumed would be essential to run a dirty cross-borders operation laundering timber.

He pushed against a fire door and went outside, wedging a piece of paper in the door jamb. He found he was in an alleyway, so he strolled down it towards the main road, digging out his ciggie packet.

Nonetheless, the Forest Watch Headquarters were broken into, and all the hard drives and papers removed. But – again, if George had the timing down right - the 'Mr Fixit' at the Cameroon end had been fingered *before* the break-in. And this canny individual, as well as having wodges of cash in mixed currencies, put by for a cosseted retirement, had the foresight to put aside papers on the whole filthy operation, naming places, naming names – again, this courtesy of Mark who seemed quite pally with the Commissaire in Yaounde. Said insurance policy with the right whispers in the right ears concerning its existence, would keep him safe from his own venal partners in crime, or if he was lifted, might earn him a reduced sentence for grassing up his erstwhile colleagues. So, given that, again - wouldn't the raiding of FW have been redundant? The information was already out there. But then the value of such insurance decreases – disappears? - if there are other sources. Maybe that was it.

Paul, in the clear air outside, took a deep drag on his cigarette, thus cancelling out any of the health benefits of Shoreditch's oxygen, and gazed up the road at the converted warehouse where FW was housed.

Was there something FW had that even the resourceful 'Mr Fixit' lacked? Unlikely, as he seemed to have been quite thorough, according to Mark via George. Or was it a ploy? A decoy to cover something else entirely. Something? Or someone?

And here we came back to Jock. His change of behaviour, of attitude starting at the cafe. Almost fearful, certainly apprehensive, with a dash of petulance born of insecurity. It had snagged Paul's interest. He felt more strongly that Jock was the key, or *a* key. They needed verification on his whereabouts at the crucial time. What about the boyfriend? To murder Wingent between five and six on Thursday, and get back to London to meet the boyfriend at a club at seven was tight, but could be done given a fair wind. But where *was* the boyfriend?

Then, there were the tyres…

Stubbing out his fag, he returned to the fire door to spot Anish peering up the corridor looking for him, evidently impatient to get on with the interview.

He walked rapidly down the corridor.

"Sorry, I needed to get my head straight on one or two points. His alibi, for one, on Thursday late afternoon. Then there's the night of the break-in. What do you think?"

"We should tackle that first. There are other questions, such as motive. That, I think, is the most problematical. I cannot see that this young man would murder someone and break into his own office, considering how he feels about the work, and how upset about the death of Colin Wingent – and his reaction to Adam Wingent's murder."

"And his upbringing. I'm not sure I'd pin that on him either, Anish, but something's not right here. His attitude towards me, the police, has changed. Something's troubling our Jock, and I'm not convinced it's just the fact of the break-in."

"Well, he had just been told that Colin Wingent's brother was also murdered."

"Yes, but the change predated that knowledge."

"Let's forget that then, for the time being, and, as they say, stick to facts – concentrate on the alibi for Thursday."

"Fair enough."

They entered the room to find Jock's anxious gaze flicking from one face to the other.

Anish began: "We can't raise James Crombie, Jock. Any idea where he might be? Any address? Common friends?"

Jock digested this for a while.

"Uh, no, no. We – uh – we hadn't known each other that long." He looked desolate.

Paul wasn't sure this was the truth, but didn't think directly challenging him on that would get anywhere.

"Well, then, we'll have to visit the bar where you met. It's possible that he's just turned his phone off, or lost it. Or he might be going to the bar regularly to try to contact you."

Jock shook his head, sadly.

"I gave him my mobile number. He could have rung it anytime." He fiddled with the spikes of his hair, and said, "Adonis."

"What?"

"Adonis. The club where we met."

"No mistaking the clientele there, then," Paul said, earning him a reproving look from Jock. "Sorry," he added. The lad could do without his snide remarks. It hadn't bothered him before; perhaps it was just because he'd misread the signs. He didn't like to be wrong.

: ✿ :

The usual gleaming, glossy designer-dictated interior. Brushed steel and pale woods, too-high bar stools, a bewildering variety of bottles containing luridly coloured fire-waters. Discrete frosty up-lighting, and a smooth-faced, slightly superior bar steward gracefully floating around checking bottles and glasses. Paul loathed the pretentiousness of such places, gay or straight.

He gazed around. Practically empty at this hour. Time to check the stocks, clean glasses before the Saturday night rush.

All they'd to go on was Jock's description of his friend. No photo. So they'd brought Jock along in the hopes of triggering the bar staff's memory.

Paul explained the situation.

The bar steward's face changed from bland disinterest to intrigued. After listening to Jock's description of James Crombie — tall, slender, very dark hair and eyes, smartly dressed, again, usually in dark-toned clothes — eyes wide, he declared himself interested.

"If I find him first, can I keep him?" Then waved away the remark with a light giggle. "Ignore that, but he does sound dishy. Now, what can he possibly have done that brings you all here?" He rested his elbows on the bar ready to hear all.

"We can't say, sir. But could you tell us if you have seen anyone matching such a description in the company of this young man?" Paul indicated Jock.

Seemingly for the first time, the steward concentrated on Jock, tilting his head and looking him up and down.

"Well, let me see. I may have seen you before. Recently, would it have been?"

Jock nodded, a hopeful expression on his face. "Thursday evening, about seven."

"Hmm. Hard to be certain."

"We were sitting over here." Jock moved to a table in the far corner, dimly lit.

"Oh well, not surprising I didn't spot you and your friend over there. You picked well — very discreet." The steward grinned slyly, then inclined his chin towards the ceiling. "There is that thing, though. It might tell you what you want to know."

They all looked up at the CCTV camera nestling in the corner of the ceiling.

"We'd like the tapes for Thursday evening, if we may, sir."

Faced with DCI Seth's meticulous politeness, the bar steward complied straightaway.

As they left the bar with the tapes, walking back to the police car, Paul said, "Disappointing for you, Jock – not unexpected though. But we'll go through these tapes thoroughly. Now, there's just one more thing I need from you before you get rid of us. As with all the FW staff, we need to eliminate certain tracks – tyre tracks, that is – from the scene of the Adam Wingent murder."

"What? What are you talking about? I've never even..." Jock stopped so suddenly that Anish clattered into the back of him. Jock was apparently frozen.

"What is it? What's the matter?" Paul asked.

"You want tyre tracks from my car?"

"That's the general idea, yes – from everyone at FW. We need your permission for that. Of course." Said in such a way that refusal wasn't really an option.

"Eliminate? Hah," Jock muttered. Evidently, he came to a conclusion and resignedly threw his car keys to Paul.

Paul noticed a slight tremor in his hands

"Do your worst."

: ¤ :

They stood around the black VW Golf. Paul, hands on hips, was exasperated.

"That's that, then."

Anish bent for a closer scrutiny.

"Clean as a whistle. Brand new, too. All four must have been changed very recently – see? There's virtually nothing in any of the treads, but we'll give it a go." The Scene of Crimes investigator, Jerry Isaacs, seemed perversely pleased, as some are when others are disappointed.

They were in the vehicle section of the forensic science laboratories, grouped round the black VW Golf. Isaacs turned and laid out on a bench the four tyre prints one of his team had taken from the VW. Paul added the faxes George had sent.

They all stared at the array and the prints from the Golf.

"Nothing like," stated Jerry, satisfied. He had a nasal tone of voice which Paul thought would grate if you had to listen to it all day.

The other two murmured agreement.

"You can see. These three sets of tyre prints, from your bunch, show various stages of wear."

"Pity. It was a promising idea. What would you like to do now?" Anish asked Paul.

"We need explanations at the very least. It gets my suspicious antennae twanging that the tyres on the Golf just happen to have been changed so very recently. And there is just one further thing."

He explained what he needed to Isaacs, who obliged immediately while managing to appear disgruntled about it, and placed the traces of the material obtained from under the wheel arches into an evidence bag.

"I'll need a sample for comparison from your lab people," Issacs said.

"Done. The results can be faxed. I'll get onto it."

: ¤ :

Anish Seth had assigned a young PC to scrutinise the video tapes from 'Adonis' – coincidentally enough, Paul noted, the same quiet one who'd brought in the tea. Your all-purpose PC.

He'd been provided with a photo of Jock and the description of Jamie Crombie, and he'd been at it for half an hour, but now he'd come to fetch the DCI.

Paul slumped in front of the video screen depicting a somewhat grainy black and white 'paused' picture. The VCR on 'pause' was distorting the picture, pulling it to one side.

He leaned forward and took out a pair of glasses that he was vainly trying to deny he needed because they symbolised the unstoppable onward march of time. Preening fool that he was, who was he kidding?

He ran the video. It was a crowded scene, full of movement, figures swirling around, some, more static, at tables and on the bar stools. He imagined the hubbub, the clink of glasses, sudden bursts of laughter. There - that was the shadowy area where Jock claimed to have sat with Crombie. A figure approached the table set in a corner, but from the back it was difficult to discern who it might be. This second figure was joining another already sitting at the table in the gloom. There was no hug, no kiss.

He watched, feeling the tension in his neck. He rolled the tape further back and saw the first figure arriving. He still couldn't say for sure if it was Jock.

Forward again. Ah, now. They were going to order something – the first figure turned around, half profile. Yes, could be Jock! Now, if only he could see the second figure. He ran the tape on. No luck – the second figure never glanced up. But if this was the elusive Jamie Crombie then…Paul glanced at the time given on the tape - 7.16 pm. Jock had an alibi for the murder of Adam Wingent.

No, scrub that. It was merely *unlikely* that he could have travelled to Hampshire, searched the house, murdered Adam between 5 and 6, returned to London and been here to meet someone by 7.16 pm. Unlikely, but not impossible. If his library alibi worked out, though, and he was in the University Library up to 5.45pm then he was in the clear.

But – he was there *before* the second figure, waiting. Again, he ran the tape back to when Jock entered the club. There – 6.53.

That didn't make it much clearer.

Curious, he peered closely at the other, mysterious figure which remained stubbornly elusive. All he could tell was that it was a 'he' and he was dark-haired. He remembered the voice on the mobile phone's voicemail. Paul wondered if he dare ask for image enhancement to work its devilish magic and clear up the dark image of the second person. He'd better not – even Anish had his limits, and his budget.

Then as he watched, musing – a hand slid over the table to touch Jock's. No – not to touch with affection. To pass something to him. Paul hitched himself closer to the screen, squinting. What the hell was that? Now if *this* could be image enhanced. Something caught the light and briefly sparkled.

He ran the tape backwards and forwards, concentrating, knowing this was important. Was this why they'd met? For this transaction?

It fitted easily into the hand, a roundish shape, reflecting the light in sharp shards. There was something else – metallic maybe – suspended from it. And, like suddenly recognising the answer to a crossword clue, he knew what it was. It was, at this moment, resting in his jacket pocket.

He snatched it out. The car key fob to Jock's car. It was a clear plastic sphere, cut into facets like a diamond. He held it up to the screen, rolled it in his palm; it caught the light and reflected it prismatically.

What the hell did this mean? Jock'd lent his car to Crombie…new tyres…why?

The young PC had been watching, forgotten, standing behind Paul, and now decided to contribute. His voice was as soft as his sudden appearances with the tea.

"We can get that image cleaned up, sir. It looks like it could be the car key you have there, but with a spot of twitching with the right software, you can be more certain."

"You read my mind. Do you think you can enhance the image of this person here?" He pointed to the second figure.

The PC bent closer to the screen. "That might be harder, but we can give it a go, sir."

Paul was grateful. He'd not even had to ask. He left the young PC to it - to trot over to the Video Enhancement Unit, get the picture cleaned up, and also to find, if he could, the time when the two men left, either separately or together.

He was glad to get up and stretch his neck vertebrae even after such a short period. Let's assume Jock lent Crombie his car for some reason, and then Crombie changed the tyres for new ones. Was it because it had a distinctive tread mark – a flaw? Trace evidence? So if anyone had travelled to Hampshire and back at the relevant time, it wasn't Jock – at least not in his own car.

He was relieved for Jock and thought that maybe there lay the explanation for Jock's changed behaviour: That he had begun to suspect that his car had been used for no good purposes, and when they'd asked to see the tyre treads, it clicked. That very evening when he got his car back, the tyres had been changed. No doubt at the time he'd been given some plausible explanation and was more than happy to have a free new set of tyres.

How had he come to suspect Jock in the first place? He'd begun to harbour suspicions that the ransacking of the FW HQ, designed to look like an outside job, was, in fact, an inside job; he had little concrete evidence for this in truth, except elimination. On the other hand there was scant reason that he could deduce for Rouge-Bolles to risk a break-in after the arrest of the two guys who had imprisoned Mark and Sue and the subsequent arrest of 'Mr Fixit' aka Wilkins. Even less point since the papers from Wilkins' safe, now in police hands, dished the dirt – and it was unlikely that FW here would have any more information than the 'bad guys' themselves. So why the burglary, that was still the puzzle? To hide something else, something that no one else must discover?

It was this reasoning, combined with Jock's altered behaviour that had Paul's thinking snaking towards him as a possible suspect.

But who was this Crombie?

They had to interview him again. Urgently. Meanwhile Paul looked up the number of the University Library.

Chapter
45

It was dark, the autumn rain slashing down as they stood once again in front of the blue front door, banging the knocker against the streaming wood.

No one. Paul knew it was empty. He was getting a feel for abandoned houses.

"Where the hell is he? I told him to keep himself available."

"Let's try downstairs in the pub." Anish was turning and descending the iron stairway.

As they went inside 'The Fentiman', the sheer volume of noise broke like a wave over them. The place was heaving with raucous Antipodeans. It must be like this every night.

Paul used his shoulders and fierce frown to get to the bar and eventually grab the attention of the harassed barman. He had to shout to be heard.

"Do you know where Jock is? Jock Campbell? Lives upstairs?" he yelled.

"Jock? Yeah, mate. He took off to see his parents, up north? Takin' a break, you know?" The upturned phrases said this was an Aussie. But one that seemed to know Jock quite well.

"Are you his flatmate?"

"Yeah, mate." By now, he was giving them suspicious glances while checking along the bar.

They struggled back through the throng, and stood at a loss on the pavement outside, oblivious of the hissing rain.

"Bugger." The rain was washing into Paul's eyes, blurring his vision. He fished out some Nicorette and began chewing vigorously.

"I'm not so sure he would go off just like that, Paul. Did you see his face when we left him? Outside the 'Adonis'?" Anish had had the sense to wear a flat cap, and he now turned his mac collar up.

"What do you mean?" Had Anish been speculating along the same lines as himself?

"He knew then. I saw his face. I think he guessed where his car had gone on the afternoon of the murder, and he will have been told about the new tyres when he got it back. Also, he finds he can't now contact this other fellow, Crombie. He's put two and two together."

"I'm beginning to believe in telepathy; I'd thought along similar lines myself. You think he spun his flatmate a yarn about high-tailing it back to Scotland but he's really gone to search for this Crombie character?" Paul considered this for awhile. "It hangs together – *if* Jock believes that he was set-up for the murder of Adam Wingent – and that it was all planned, premeditated, that he should be the fall guy."

"I would be extremely angry, if it were me, wouldn't you? I would demand to know what was going on."

"I wanted to be able to tell him face-to-face that he was in the clear, that his library alibi worked out."

Paul chewed, and thought, as they climbed back into the police car.

Anish' mobe rang. He read the caller ID.

"Isaacs, at the lab."

: ⌗ :

They were silent, lost in their thoughts as Anish drove through the slanting rain back to the Shoreditch Station.

Paul was the first to break the quiet.

"Where the hell could he have got to?"

"Who – Jock or Crombie?"

"Find one and we'll find the other. Little doubt now that Jock's car was at Wingent's place – and I'd bet good money that Crombie's responsible for Adam's death. Then he brought the car back to London, had new tyres fitted here because there'd be no trace evidence in them to match the substrate around the Wingent place, shoved it through the car wash – which, lucky for us, didn't wash out all the trace evidence under the wheel arches - and handed the keys back to Jock at that club."

"Why have the tyres changed if you wanted to drop poor Jock in it?"

"Another puzzle, another enigma. And why then forget about the muck under the wheel arches – Isaacs found they yielded a perfect match for the substrate recovered from the lane down to the Wingent cottage - mostly chalk, which you don't get in this part of the woods– when everything else at that cottage indicated professionalism?"

"A fickle mind. A mind that likes to play nasty games, perhaps? To enjoy confusing us plods? Or lay false trails." Anish chuckled quietly.

"Psychopathic tendencies," murmured Paul.

A long silence followed, broken only by the soporific swish of the window wipers.

"Oh, another thing I'd forgotten to tell you about the crime scene. There *was* more than one person there." Paul's voice was low as though reluctant to break the soothing rhythm.

Anish turned.

"How do you know that?"

"One to hold him down and the other to do the dirty deed. We have the DNA of the one who was over him and likely struck the fatal blow."

He stopped. Paul stared out the side window at the shimmering shop lights. Jock didn't have Crombie's address, but...something in Jock's sitting room...and a comforting gesture.

"Hang on a mo', where did I put it?" He rummaged in the pockets of his jacket, found and flipped open the notebook.

"Here we are – Chalcot Crescent. This is the address we want, Anish. This is where he goes when he's upset." Paul tapped the page.

Anish quickly glanced at the address Paul held up.

"Are you sure this is right?"

"Stake my reputation on it. May have to."

"Near to Primrose Hill. Some seriously wealthy properties over there. Shoreditch to Primrose Hill. Rags to riches."

: ✪ :

They'd parked the car some distance away around the corner on Erskine Road, now they stood staring at a beautifully proportioned three-story corner-of terrace house, of yellow London brick and white stucco.

"A king's ransom, this would cost," said Anish. "Listed, too, I'll be bound."

"Hmm," grunted Paul, determined not to be impressed.

They climbed the four rounded steps to the heavy double front door, and knocked.

To their surprise the door was swiftly snatched open, and a tall figure stood there staring, apparently taken aback. The light from behind in the hall haloed his face so it was difficult to make out the features, but the black hair was fashionably cut and gelled. He seemed to be dressed in leathers.

The image enhancement of the figure in the 'Adonis' hadn't given up much but it did show the hairstyle quite well. It could only be one person.

"James Crombie?" asked Paul, showing his warrant card and attempting to hide his surprise.

"Who are you?" The voice was well-modulated, but hostile. The mobile phone voice. He glanced over at Anish, also holding up his warrant card. "Police?"

Just then there was another voice, calling from the shadows at the end of the spacious chequerboard marbled hall.

"Who is that, darling?" A slim female form, also in leathers, and carrying a visored helmet, approached down the hall and halted suddenly, widened eyes fixated on Paul.

In the same instant the door was violently slammed shut.

"What the hell is going on here?" asked Anish.

Paul just stood there for a few seconds, stunned, then shook himself.

"They're working together," Paul grabbed his shoulders. "No time now. Where's the back door to this pile?"

Anish led the way round the corner, shouting back over his shoulder, "I don't know the lay-out, I'm only guessing. And who's working together?"

Round the corner was a narrow alley-way, backing onto the gardens and set with wooden doors spaced along its length. The end garden wall was high, too high to climb, and the door was locked.

Paul realised his basic error too late. One of them should have stayed at the front. What the hell was he thinking, ignoring basic procedure?

"Anish, stay here. I'm going round to the front again." He wasn't sure how fit Anish was, or what he'd be able to do if faced with the fleeing pair.

Paul trotted back round the corner, mind awhirl, and straight into a swinging helmet, landing on the pavement and slamming his head against the kerb.

His vision blurred and wavered, as he watched, detachedly, a black leather boot moving slowly, inexorably towards his head...

: ¤ :

The motion was lulling him, his head gently rolled. He made a snuffling sound, like an old man with catarrh.

"Paul? Paul! Wake up – now!" The voice came through layers of cloth.

His shoulder was shaken, at first gently, then roughly.

He murmured a protest at the rude awakening, and shrugged away from the annoyance. Lights were coming and going, flashing in a regular rhythm. His head began throbbing in time to the flashes.

"PAUL!"

"What?" His mouth felt full of cotton wool.

"Stay awake, please. You've had a blow to the temple, and I think you have the beginnings of a black eye. How do you feel?"

"What sort of stupid question is that?"

"Ah, thank God. Not too bad, I see." Anish swung the wheel hard right and squealed around a right-hand corner, flinging Paul against the car door.

"Christ, what the hell are you up to? Where are we?"

"You have a choice to make right now. We can go straight to the nearest hospital and get you sorted out." Another squeal, this time to the left. "Or we can continue to pursue that motorcycle." He indicated a speeding bike weaving ahead of them in the driving rain.

"Why? Who's that then? Aaah, my head's pounding."

"Glove compartment. Paracetamol."

As Paul leant slowly forward so that his head wouldn't fall off, his memory of the last few minutes – was it minutes? – came back in flashes.

"Is that them?"

"Hospital or pursuit?" Anish was insistent. "Now!"

Obviously it was them.

"No contest. Don't spare the horses."

Anish, perversely, seemed to be enjoying himself. He was a skilled driver, sticking like glue to the rear light of the bike.

Paul dry-swallowed two paracetamol, and took out a tissue to wipe the blood off his face and gingerly touch his temple, while hanging grimly on to the car-door handle with one hand. There was a growing egg on the side of his head and a pounding headache rip-tiding through his brain.

"Where?" he croaked, squinting through the side window.

"Shepherd's Bush. It's my guess he's headed for the M4. It's what I would do in his position."

A wave of nausea swept over Paul and he held the tissue to his mouth. When it receded, what Anish had said came back to him.

"You said 'he'. Just the one?"

"Just the one."

"The bastard decked me, I think." He screwed his eyes tight shut and groaned gently.

Anish gave Paul another quick glance, a frown furrowing his smooth brow.

When he looked back at the road, the motorbike had disappeared.

Paul thought he heard some mutterings, flowing eloquently, as Anish scanned the area, now driving slowly, the wipers flicking the rain aside.

Paul leaned carefully forward to pick up the car radio, asking Anish for the call sign. He then requested that someone get over to Chalcot Crescent, taking all due precautions, enter number 22, one way or another, and search it.

He was asked by a hesitant voice over the radio, what they were supposed to be looking for. He wasn't that sure but he knew what he dreaded them finding.

Anish grabbed the radio from Paul, briskly gave his rank, and demanded at least four officers get themselves over there immediately and search the place, and take into custody anyone they found there, plus search for any evidence of who lived there.

"We know who lived there." Paul's voice was thick. "Her. Sam Ball. Jock went to see her. But *he* was there – Crombie... that lipstick on the mug...Jock's flat...her hand over his."

"But he was gay."

"They were friends. He thought so, anyway. But he was used." He wasn't making much sense.

Anish was still crawling past the ends of streets, nearing the Hammersmith Flyover, window wound down so that any burbling engine sounds might be detected.

"Why?"

Just then, ahead of them a flash of orange hurled itself into the rain-drenched sky, and a whoomph rattled the open window.

"My God!"

"What the hell was that?"

Anish accelerated towards the source of the flames climbing into the sky, licking the underside of low bruised clouds.

As they neared the flyover, they could see below the source of the fire, the crumpled mass of metal glowing in the centre of the blaze.

Paul gazed up the ramp. Ahead, through the rain coursing down the windscreen he could see the wavering lines of Erskine's Ark, like a huge liner left marooned when flood waters receded. It seemed as though the motorbike had skidded on the ramp – an oily patch made lethal by the rain, probably - and somersaulted over the barricade to land down there, pulverized, on the road below. In the distance, they could hear the sirens Dopplering as a fire engine approached. Someone must have phoned straightaway. A small quiet crowd was gathering below, standing in the rain under a cluster of inappropriately brightly coloured umbrellas.

They made their way to the site of the crash, which by now was the province of the Fire Service

Giving out his cards and telling them where he'd be for the next couple of hours, Anish arranged with the local police and the Fire Service to be sent immediately any information about the crash and the body, while Paul stood swaying slightly, staring at the flames and the mangled wreckage.

: ⌺ :

After a hasty visit to the A & E at the Hammersmith Hospital in Du Cane street, during which Anish shamelessly queque jumped, demanding immediate attention, Paul, after an X-ray, was given the all-clear plus a couple more of the ubiquitous paracetamol. They returned to Chalcot Crescent.

What they found there staggered both of them. Two police cars and an ambulance were parked outside, and another officer was in the process of unwinding police tape, looping it round a nearby lamppost. A window in the front room had been broken and the voile curtains were flapping damply in the rain sucked out through the jagged opening; they could hear the rattle of the Venetian blinds.

They dashed in through the open front door. Officers were scattered throughout the spacious house, searching, but as they entered the front room, one stood there, gaping at the two figures lying on the Persian carpet – he was young enough to be both fascinated and repelled by the sight of two dead bodies.

The man known as James Crombie was lying prone, pallid but still darkly good-looking in his motorbike leathers. His head lay to one side, dark eyes wide open, arms flung wide, one over the body lying next to him. Dead as a dodo. His blood – was it his blood? - had soaked into the richly coloured Persian carpet. Next to him lay Jock Campbell, supine, eyes closed. Two paramedics crouched beside him; one fished an oxygen mask out of his bag and applied it to his ashen face.

"He's alive?" asked Paul going over quickly and crouching down.

The nearest paramedic looked up and nodded, adding, "No external injuries as far as we can tell, but he's flat out. Unconscious."

"What's wrong with him?"

The other paramedic stood up. "Can't say. We'll get him back to Hammersmith and sort him out."

"This one?" Paul indicated Crombie, knowing what he would say but needing to hear it confirmed.

"A job for the coroner." He loped off to get a stretcher.

Paul turned, looking for Anish. He was in a corner of the room, having just finished a phone call arranging for the police doctor and Scenes of Crime to attend, after having liaised with the local force.

"What the hell happened here, Anish?" He knew he sounded angry. "Her and him, Crombie — partners? *She* was on the motorbike? How did *he* die?" He swung round and addressed the remaining paramedic still kneeling beside the motionless Jock. "Any idea how he died?"

The paramedic looked at him as though he were stupid. "Stabbed, wasn't he." He pointed to a tear in the back of the black leather jacket which Paul hadn't noticed. "Right through the heart, looks like."

"Through the heart," he repeated, facing Anish. "Adam Wingent — similar MO. We'll need the type of knife. And why isn't Jock dead?" Was he making any sense at all?

Sam Ball. The luscious, lovely Sam Ball. I'm a moron not to have seen it before, blinded by that seductive siren-like sexuality.

Paul resumed glaring at Crombie as though he would eventually furnish the answers he wanted. He doubted that

Crombie had ever been gay since he and Sam seemed to be living together. He'd played a part in order to seduce Jock. Poor innocent, trusting Jock.

He looked back at Jock. Paul's guilt, having been so easily coshed by a helmet and kicked senseless, and consequently not having found Jock immediately, was alleviated a little when he saw the boy's eyelids flutter.

He was loaded on to the stretcher and taken out to the ambulance.

With Jock removed, Paul's thinking processes had slowed to a crawl. Just when he thought he'd figured it all out, the whole damned thing slithered away from him. So it was *her* on the bike, genius - he gingerly touched the lump on his right temple — and she who'd walloped him; but both had been in bike leathers, so they had planned to flee together, James Crombie and Sam Ball. Or maybe, she'd planned to leave him behind all along, tie up loose ends. She'd no compunction about ditching her partner when push came to shove.

He crouched besides Crombie's body. But why kill him? It must have been her; he stared closely at the tear in the jacket; it could be the type of knife used to kill Adam Wingent. He had no doubt that she was the senior partner in their enterprise — whatever it was. Hadn't done her any good, though — broken at the bottom of the Hammersmith flyover, her body lying charred and sodden in the rain. He felt affected in spite of himself.

Artless Jock had been their patsy, set up to take the fall for the murder of Adam Wingent, or at the very least, act as a red herring, which would divert and confuse the police investigation and permit time for a quick getaway should it be needed. At the end, Jock had deduced some or all of this when he realised his car had been borrowed by his new boy friend on the very day that Adam had been murdered, and he had a nice brand new set of tyres. He came here to confront the person who had introduced him to Crombie, Sam Ball.

The biggest question of all, though, remained unanswered – who the hell were Sam Ball and James Crombie? And what were they really up to here?

A young WPC entered the room holding some passports out to DCI Seth.

"Sir? Found in a bedroom." Paul peered over Anish's shoulder as he shuffled through a medley of 'his 'n hers' passports from UK, France, Algeria, Spain. Flicking them open, he showed Paul the many aliases the couple had used. She was given as thirty-one, he slightly younger, at twenty-nine, similar DOB's for all the passports. Whether these were their real ages was anyone's guess. They were variously described as botanist, horticulturalist, economist (her), and mechanic, IT consultant (him).

"Double bed?" Paul asked the WPC. It wasn't just prurient curiosity, was it?

She nodded.

" Right. Why's the window broken?"

"We couldn't break down the door, sir, and time was of the essence. We could see two bodies lying on the floor."

" Huh. OK." He turned towards Anish. "Doesn't get us any closer to knowing who they really were, though." Paul tried to swallow another paracetamol, but his throat was constricted. He sent the WPC out for a glass of water to get rid of the bitter taste.

"Undoubtedly, she had another one of those with her when she fled." He indicated the passports. "Another name, another occupation, another country. She would have got away with it but for the rain."

Anish scrutinised him. "I've called your DS - George Thynne? - to come and get you, and drive you back home. You're looking distinctly green around the gills."

Paul didn't feel like arguing, so merely nodded which was a mistake as it sent his vision spinning.

Anish took hold of his arm and guided him to another room, less busy and furnished with creamy leather sofas. Paul sat heavily on one, while Anish paced around, examining the room and its contents.

"They worked together as well as lived together, you reckon?" Paul asked.

"It's always less suspicious when you see a couple together. Clearly, they were both working for Rouge-Bolles, with the girl, Sam Ball, on the inside. That way she could keep an eye on all the goings on at FW."

"And she was placed there to prevent information damaging to R-B going any further than FW." Paul paused. "She must have been the one to warn the Cameroon operation that Colin Wingent was on his way looking for damning evidence on R-B's illegal activities."

"Forewarned is forearmed. She signed his death warrant."

"Then later, she must have been told to get hold of the Colin Wingent photo which, in turn, led to Adam Wingent's death."

"That was a big mistake. If it had just been a house-breaking, the police would never have devoted the same amount of time and energy to the investigation, but once it was murder – they triggered a far more intensive operation."

"Until the time came when the Rouge-Bolles linchpin at the Cameroon end was lifted. They must have recognised then that the game was up, for the time being at least – these companies never really die — and she decided to cut and run."

The WPC returned with the water, looking apprehensive.

"Sir," she addressed Anish. "A call has come through for you from the Fire Investigation Service on the land line."

Anish looked around, found a phone and took the call. Paul got up carefully, still experiencing waves of nausea if he moved too fast, to join him, watching his face closely.

"Are you sure? There can be no mistake?" His voice was tight, accusatory. "No, no, of course not. I appreciate you telling me so promptly." Then he adopted a more conciliatory tone. "Can you let me know the result of any further investigation?...Yes. You have my number...Thank you, again."

He replaced the receiver slowly, his forehead wrinkled.

"What?"

"No body there. Literally, no *body* there at the crash site." His voice held a sense of wonder and confusion.

"You're kidding." Paul felt a wave of goose bumps run over his body. "She's not there?" He wanted to be absolutely sure he knew what they were talking about.

"No. No sign of a body. Naturally, they searched around a larger area since the bike flew off the flyover — but nothing."

Silently, they both slumped onto the expensive pale cream leather sofas, while they waited for forensics and the police doctor.

: ☿ :

They stood either side of the bed looking down at Jock, his papery hands lying over the blanket. Paul pulled out a chair and sat down on one side of the bed. Anish dragged a chair over from the neighbouring bed and sat on the other side.

"Do you feel like talking, Jock?"

He closed his eyes briefly, with a quick jerk of his head.

"Yes, I'm OK, thank you. Just a bit tired."

Without being asked, Jock began to relate what had happened to him in a surprisingly clear, strong voice.

"I can't remember everything. It's hazy but it might come back in dribs and drabs. What I can recall is that I was angry. I'd been used by that bastard Crombie. He'd borrowed my car with the excuse that his was being serviced. When you questioned me, it came together – my car was taken to Adam's place, he'd killed him," – he swallowed hard, then resumed – " brought the car back and handed over the keys telling me that he'd given it a new set of tyres because he'd had a puncture on the way back and noticed the other tyres were well worn."

"Was this when you met him in the 'Adonis'?"

"Yes. At the time I was simply grateful for the new tyres – they're expensive. I never even asked him where he went. Bedazzled and stupid, I guess."

That last comment mirrored only too well how Paul had reacted to Sam Ball. They'd made a seductive pair, those two.

"What did you decide to do then, after you realised you'd been duped?"

"Decided to have it out with him – except I didn't have his address, like I told you, and there was still no answer on the mobile. But it was Sam who'd introduced us, so I went to see her."

That much I'd guessed, thought Paul.

He paused and asked for water. Paul got up and poured some water from the large plastic jug and passed it to him. He seemed drained, hollow-eyed, the blue veins visible at his temple contrasting with the white skin.

He sipped the water delicately.

"You knew her address? At Chalcot Crescent?" Anish asked.

"That's where she'd introduced me to Crombie. A mistake on her part." He gave a wry smile. "I do like Sam, really, but there was always something – I don't know. I don't really trust her. You saw that, didn't you, Inspector?" He was addressing Paul.

Paul nodded sadly, thinking that Jock was probably the ideal fallguy. Innocent of the ways of this wicked world – well, mostly. It must have been a shock to find them both there at Chalcot Crescent.

"Sam? Where is Sam?" Jock asked suddenly.

"Ah, she has disappeared, I'm afraid," answered Anish.

Jock looked blank for a moment.

"Disappeared?" His head flopped back on the pillow. After a pause he said in a low voice, "I know I resented her – petty really. Maybe I was jealous of her sophistication, her style. It was easy for her, came naturally, but there was always... oh, I don't know, a little worm of doubt. I felt awkward, gauche in her presence, even though she was really friendly, even warm, towards me. In the end, though, she used me as well." He turned his head aside, visibly upset.

It's humiliating to think you've been duped, especially by someone who, in spite of your own doubts, you aspired to be like. Was there a way to ameliorate the damage a little?

"I think she may have saved you, too," said Paul quietly.

"I don't see how." Jock was frowning. "Anyway, after I got there I can't remember much…sat down…had a drink, I think…we talked…I was angry…upset…funny…can't remember much." He massaged his temples.

Paul and Anish exchanged glances. They were both thinking the same thing – a drugged drink maybe, even though the medics hadn't found traces of rohypnol or GHB. There'd be no trace of metabolites in his urine after this interval of time but the length of Jock's blackout was about right for rohypnol.

Anish said, addressing Paul. "We'll have a good search in Chalcot Crescent – including the glasses. There may be something since she left in such a hurry."

"Wouldn't be at all surprised," Paul said, and turned to Jock

"No memory for anything that followed?"

"Sorry," Jock said. "It seems foggy."

"Any nausea when you came round?"

"Yes, some. Aah, you think I was drugged, don't you?"

"Looks that way." Paul nodded.

Then Paul outlined to Jock what they guessed had happened immediately after they had shown up at the door. The drug had already rendered Jock unconscious and he was lying on the floor. Crombie answered the door, saw it was the police and slammed the door on them. He and Sam were ready to flee on their motorbike, but then – to judge by his position lying next to Jock's now unconscious form - Crombie decided he had to deal with Jock permanently;

he was about to dispatch him when Sam intervened, knifing Crombie in the back, decking Paul with her helmet and then escaping on her motorbike.

Jock listened to this with wide eyes that filled with unspilled tears.

"She did save me then," he whispered.

"In her fashion, yes." said Paul. It seemed important to Jock that Sam hadn't seen him as little more than a useful tool, that, at the end at least, he had some worth, some value to her. "I think she was genuinely fond of you, Jock, and wasn't going to let Crombie just bump you off, but she had to kill him to do it. Her partner."

They would test Crombie's DNA with that found in the spittle - containing male DNA - on Adam Wingent's clothes; Paul had no doubt there would be a match. Whether he was the 'holder' or the 'stabber' they'd probably never know. Also, the stab wounds on the two bodies, he was sure, would point to the same sort of knife with a serrated blade. Even though she might have redeemed herself to some extent by protecting Jock, the two of them together had callously killed Adam Wingent just because he was there.

Another problem – the break-in.

"Jock, do you have any idea why the break-in took place at the time it did?"

At this, Jock looked surprised.

"I thought you knew. Didn't you read the file that Sam photocopied for you?" He raised round eyes to Paul and Anish.

They looked blankly back at him.

"Oh no," he muttered. "You didn't get it all, did you?"

Paul sat back. Good grief. That siren – confused by her striking looks or some batsqueak of desire, it hadn't occurred to him that she could so easily have omitted some pages from the photocopying. He felt again the warm photocopies pressed against his chest

Jock settled himself more comfortably, smoothing down the bedspread. There was even a slight smile. He had the right to enjoy centre stage for a change - only an audience of two, but these two were riveted, leaning forward on their chairs.

"Right then, I'd better put you in the picture. Retrospectively, I can see that the most sensitive material in that dossier concerned a letter from the Smithsonian Institute Landsat Analysis Systems - SILAS."

"Eh?" That was strange, very strange — he was sure he'd thought of Silas Marner only the other day.

"This was something brand new, a breakthrough, something we'd been hoping for but scarcely dared to think might happen, but it all depended upon Col's findings." Now, his eyes were alive, darting from one to the other.

"Can you explain please?" Anish pleaded.

"If Col had been able to get evidence of Rouge-Bolles and the other major players in the area breaching their concessions, extending beyond those boundaries and taking trees selectively from the Dja Reserve, then the Smithsonian Institute Landsat promised to take a look at that area, as others have for the Amazon Basin. A letter in that file confirmed it."

"Why's that so important?"

"Well, it would be a first for FW, a first for West Africa! This is a new analysis, potentially a very powerful weapon. The method allows each pixel of a satellite image to be searched for the amount of forest left and works out the overall ratio of forested to deforested land." He waited expectantly. His features were more animated now, a sparkle in the eyes. Either the effects of the drug were wearing off, or feeling so deeply about these matters was counteracting the influence of the drug. Or both.

"So?" asked Paul.

"It would give a whole new picture of the Congo Basin – and the extent and location of selective logging. Selective logging, taking out the most marketable trees, in an area like the Dja is devastating – it releases twenty-five percent more carbon dioxide into the atmosphere each year *above* that of deforestation - decomposition of plant material, a thinned canopy making the forest drier and prone to fire."

"So the upshot was that had Colin been able to get his evidence of selective logging in the Dja Reserve, you would be able to secure this Landsat System to get an overall picture of the damage being done to the Dja."

"Exactly." Jock pushed himself up against the pillows. Some colour was returning to his cheeks. "It would be able to cover a much larger area, it would be accurate; we'd be able to see the extent of the damage without having to send scarce experienced field operatives into extreme danger. We'd have incontrovertible evidence."

Paul sat back. It seemed as though Rouge-Bolles were desperate to prevent satellite surveillance of their patch. Such analysis would almost certainly put paid to their illegal operations.

"It seems to me that Sam Ball bided her time as a mole in FW," said Anish. "She knew Colin Wingent had to be stopped – without his evidence there was no chance of persuading the Smithsonian Institute to divert their very expensive equipment toWest Africa. Is that correct, Mr Campbell?"

Jock made a gesture of agreement, and took another sip of water. Now, having divested himself of this information he seemed to deflate once more. More likely though, it was the realisation that in a real sense they'd lost the battle with RB. No Colin, no proof, no satellite.

"And then there was the business of the photos. She and Crombie had to act to prevent the culprits in Cameroon being arrested as they could name RB as their employers – and they murdered Adam in the course of recovering the picture. This didn't work as the two killers in Cameroon were arrested anyway, but worse than that, so was the kingpin of their operations in Cameroon," Anish finished.

Paul took up the thread.

"Right. She effectively prevented me from seeing this letter about SILAS, removing it from the file during the photocopying but there was no guarantee that you wouldn't mention it sometime, Jock, so she staged a break-in removing all damning evidence, making it appear like an outside job to get the photos and files – a diversion, again ."

"By this time there was an obtrusive police presence thanks to murdering Adam – and meanwhile things were unravelling over the water in Cameroon. Things were hotting up. I think she decided to cut her losses and flee; to live to fight another day."

"And she is – ready to fight again. She got clean away," Jock said, nodding.

He was surprised to see a small smile appear on Jock's face.

Epilogue

Two months later, during which time there had been no indication of what had happened to Sam Ball, Paul zipped up his carryall and peeked out of the window, waiting, with that usual mixture of apprehension and excitement, for the taxi he'd ordered to take him to Southampton Airport. Only about one hour twenty flight time to Brussels – he could cope with that. He wasn't as bad as Mark, but he got very restless during flights.

This short trip he saw as remedial, a compensation for not having arrested the accursed woman. Some compensation, but, with a fair wind, it could prove to be much more. At least that was his fervent hope. If all went well, it could mean a great deal more than the arrest of Sam Ball.

One item had been recovered from the motorbike wreck – a large jade ring, the gold twisted with heat. A small part of him reluctantly admired her style. She had a touch of Raffles.

This afternoon he was due to meet up with Steve Frampton, Mark and Matthew Green, MP at the Brussels hotel. Pretty illustrious company for a lowly plod, but he, just as much as the others, deserved to be there.

: ¤ :

When the corridors of the European Parliament building were quieter, they'd come from the hotel to stand here, all four plus the Green MEP for the South-East, Sara McDonald, and gazed in some awe at the magnificent double doors that soared above them. Grandiose, fitting for some megalomaniac's delusions of grandeur, fitting the ascendant new European imperial style. This was the first time most of them had seen *sapele* wood fashioned into furniture. It glowed.

Earlier that afternoon, with the five grouped round a table in the corner of the bland hotel bar, Steve Frampton had briefed the others on his DNA research, patiently and clearly, then Paul had described the 'chain of custody' that had brought them here, to the very doorstep of the European Parliament.

Most of this, they'd heard before, but, on the eve before their plan was to be put into operation, they needed to go through it all again, check for snags and glitches.

Mark had described the illegal logging and the effects on the indigenous peoples and the wildlife. He had, he said, the scars to prove that these companies would not hesitate to take extreme action to protect their resources.

He'd praised the work of Commissaire Beti in capturing the killers of Colin Wingent, and, laughing, described how they'd entrapped Wee Willie Wilkins and his own futile schoolboy attempt to slug him. This had brought smiles to the other faces – such small triumphs of David against Goliath served to bolster any quailing nerves, and they were apprehensive. But more, much more, their plan might result in the dissolution of the largest company engaged in illegal logging, Rouge-Bolles. But it was going to be a protracted war.

Rapt, hopeful faces had then turned expectantly towards Paul. He was loath to destroy those looks of hope, but the bad news had to be given - that the senior espionage operative for R-B, Sam Ball, involved in spying on anti-logging organisations, had escaped, untraced so far, after murdering her spook colleague, Crombie. The callous killing of Adam Wingent, Paul saw, shocked the others, particularly as his brother had been murdered by the same organisation. Paul had sensed the heady tang of retaliation in the air, the desire to bring such mega-corporations to heel. And, discussing and arguing, they thought they had the means to stage a *coup de grace*.

If they could administer a killing blow, then the EU parliament might be stirred up enough to actually do something. That, at least, was the fervent wish.

The two politicians got their heads together to go over the details of the procedure that Sara was to follow.

Paul smiled over at his friend, and thought how nearly he'd been lost, how much he'd come to value his companionship. Mark grinned back, raising his glass of Belgian beer 'to us and the Baka', a naughty schoolboy anticipating mischief.

: ☌ :

None of them could possibly miss this. It would be something to relate in their dotage on long winter evenings. They sat bunched together in the nearby press room where the proceedings of the parliamentary plenary session were being relayed via audio/visual link

The Sara McDonald MEP, sitting in the Federation of Green Parties section, was objecting to the amount of illegal wood brought into the EU and where it went. She was formidable when she needed to be, would brook no brush-off by superannuated MEP's more interested in protecting their lavish expenses and pensions than in doing the jobs they were elected to do. Still, with assiduous lobbying beforehand, she knew she could rely on the support of most of the Labour MEP's as well as the Greens.

There was to be a debate on plans to further strengthen the EU legislation on the banning of illegally felled timber by proposing an amendment. Not that, to date, there had been any enforcement worthy of the name. It was time for the Commission to rectify this – she said – as the continuing felling of irreplaceable forests had consequences too numerous to cover in detail here, but included fuelling the bush meat trade, decimating the numbers of protected species, losing plants that may prove invaluable in fighting diseases, increasing the short-term likelihood of local flooding, releasing more carbon dioxide into the atmosphere and ruining the lives and health of indigenous peoples like the Baka of the Cameroon.

Taking a deep breath, she scanned the semi-circular auditorium, noticing that not too many of the royal blue seats were left unfilled, yet despairing that so few seemed to care so little. She could see several heads bent towards each other, chatting about their expenses, no doubt - but she had her secret weapon. Her hand fastened on the grip and she swung the device onto the lectern with a loud thump and waited. Gradually the hubbub subsided, as more and more heads turned towards her, expectant and slightly surprised that she had stopped talking.

She tucked a strand of ginger hair behind her ear and began.

"I want you – all of you - to observe very carefully what I am about to do. But first, I need to explain the function of this instrument." She tapped it, near enough to the microphone that the metallic sound rang out. It was a bright red hand-held lamp.

Translation was almost immediate, so she could see the changing facial expressions alter, with little delay, from boredom to mild alarm.

"This reads the bar codes of smart water." That would stump most of them who had as much idea of matters scientific as a gnat.

"It is normally used to protect items that might be stolen, such as computers and DVD's. Smart water is sprayed onto an object – and it is as individual as DNA or the barcodes you see on shop goods – which, if stolen, can be identified by their bar code. If an item has been sprayed, this machine will emit a UV light which shows up as a bright smear."

She seemed to have their attention now, principally because they didn't really know where this was going and they were intrigued to see if she'd fall flat on her face.

No way. Wait and watch.

"You may wonder what this has to do with protecting forests. Let me tell you all a story, précised for the sake of time and because much of the detail is sub judice." And because you'd nod off, otherwise.

"Professor Steve Frampton of Southampton University has developed a means of pinpointing the geographical origin of trees using DNA profiling, giving eighty percent certainty. This alone is a great breakthrough, but it was by combining this technique with some fragments of wood obtained from a British subject – an EU citizen – working for Forest Watch, who was monitoring the felling of illegal timber in Cameroon – that Professor Frampton's team was able to say that a certain tree, a *sapele*, supposedly banned for export, came from the Dja Reserve, a world heritage site. *A world heritage site!*"

She slapped her hand down on the surface of the lectern making a sharp sound and reviving some of the sleepier MEPs.

"This EU citizen was brutally murdered in the course of his work!"

That caught their attention. An audible intake of breath. Some of the more alert may have guessed now where this was going.

"The very tree against which he fell, dying, his throat slashed, and from which the traces of the wood were removed from his body and analysed, was traced to a warehouse in Southampton and sprayed with smart water. It has its own particular bar code."

"Some clever detective work followed the 'chain of custody' of the tree as it progressed from timber agent to joiner to builder to final installation as the finished product."

She paused and took a deep breath. This was it.

"We have all seen this wood today, walked through it into this very chamber."

She flicked the switch and dramatically swung the UV lamp round towards the magnificent blood red doors. All heads turned as one, gazes fixed on the doors as the violet-blue light played over the surface.

She knew just where to focus the light, but playing it round like this increased the theatrical potential – and in order to stir this lumpen crew into action, barring pyrotechnics, drama was what was needed.

The light slowed and moved to a spot near the middle-top of the left hand door. There in all its lurid glory, was a bright glowing smudge. She held the light there.

The murmuring grew in volume. There were one or two angry shouts, but she ignored these and kept the light fixed on the smudge.

"These beautiful doors that grace our chamber come from an endangered tree that an EU citizen tried to protect, and was brutally killed trying. The identical bar code. That is the price we pay for importing illegally felled wood – it is paid for in blood. Here, you have the proof of that. Is this what you want?"

Arms folded, she left the light focussed like an accusation, and waited for the furore to die down.

Some distance away, the press room was in an uproar – a listener would have been astounded by the raucous cheering.

Now, at last, they would have to do something. *Something.*

Printed in the United Kingdom
by Lightning Source UK Ltd.
135306UK00001B/7-27/P